SHATTERED PIECES

SHAYNA ASTOR

EDITED BY NICE GIRL NAUGHTY EDITS

COVER DESIGN COFFIN PRINT DESIGNS

FORMATTED BY GARNET CHRISTIE

Shattered Pieces

FROM THE AUTHOR

Shattered Pieces is a full-length, stand alone that features strong language, mature situations, explicit sexual scenes, implied underage intimacy, grief and loss, and physical abuse. Reader discretion is advised, and this book is intended for readers age 18 and up.

Many of these chapters are quite long in length. That is intended for how the story needs to be told.

Thank you so much for reading my novel! I hope you enjoy reading it, as much as I enjoyed writing it!

*Take risks, give second chances.
Sometimes they turn out to be the best choices of your
life.*

Part One
When it all falls apart

Age Nine

"Come on, Mackenzie! You have to keep pedaling or you'll fall." My sister's stern voice shouts back at me from up the road.

"I know, Shannon. I'm trying. It's too hard on this bike. I want my bike from home."

Shannon's back tire kicks up gravel as she comes to a sharp halt next to me after turning around.

"I know, I like mine too, but this is what we have while we're here. Daddy said maybe next year we'll bring our own bikes since we have the house now. But if we leave them here, other people can use them."

"I don't think I want to ride anymore."

With a roll of her eyes and heavy sigh, she shrugs and moves to get back onto her bike, but stops as two boys walk in our direction.

It's the week before school is set to start and our family is on our yearly vacation in the Outer Banks of North Carolina. Mom and Dad sent us outside to be "out of their hair" while they cook dinner tonight.

The neighborhood, if you can call it that, is relatively small, a row of houses right against the beach, with another row just behind them before the road in the development. Other houses line the sides, but are harder to see the ocean from, which Mom and Dad said was a necessity. They're all large, able to house up to fourteen people, with at least five bedrooms each. Details I learned while listening to Mom and Dad talk about which one to buy. The single lane, main road lies behind us, but I haven't seen many cars driving by today.

The boys stop right in front of us.

"Hi. I'm Scott Henshaw. This is my brother, Jake." The taller boy touches his chest before holding his hand toward his brother. "Our parents told us you bought this house. We wanted to say hi. We stay at the one over there." Turning, he points toward a blue house about three down from ours.

Aside from being the taller of the two, Scott seems more confident, doing all the talking. It makes me assume he's the older brother.

"Hi, I'm Shannon Allen, and this is my sister, Mackenzie." Much like Scott, Shannon is more sure of herself than I am.

When Shannon says my name, Scott looks over at me. His eyes are so dark, I squirm under their gaze. There's something about them that makes me take a step closer to my sister.

Shannon flips her long blonde hair over her shoulder. It falls in a straight sheet down her back. "How long have you guys had your own house? We just bought ours, but we've been coming here for four years."

"About five years now. How old are you?" Scott runs a hand through his jet-black hair, eyes darting my direction every so often. I wish he'd keep them trained on Shannon's warm green ones instead.

"I'm thirteen. Mackenzie's nine." As Shannon turns to jerk

her chin at me, I get an image of our father. She inherited all his features. "How about you two?"

"Fourteen," he says, pointing at himself. "Jake's eleven."

When Shannon and Scott start talking about other things, I tune them out, looking down at my feet as I work a pebble with the tip of my shoe.

"Hi." At the sound of a low voice, I glance up and find Jake's brilliant blue eyes trained on me. They're the same shade as the sky.

"Hi," I respond as I nervously start twisting one of my dark brown curls. I'm never really sure what to say around boys, and I avoid them at school when I can. Shannon swears I won't always feel this way. I'm not convinced.

That's all he and I say to each other before Shannon and I are called in for dinner, though we stand with our blue eyes locked on one another's for what feels like hours. Normally, I'd feel uncomfortable, staring at somebody I don't know. But for some reason, I'm filled with more curiosity than discomfort.

Going our separate ways, I'm not sure what to think. He seems nice enough, so maybe we could play sometime. It'd be fun to have somebody other than Shannon.

Two days later, we run into them at the beach. I'm in the middle of building a sandcastle when Jake carries over a bucket of water.

"I don't need your help. I can do it by myself," I tell him with the same attitude I often give Shannon.

Shrugging, he shakes some of his shaggy blond hair from his eyes. "I'm sure you can, but I want to help. I like sandcastles too, but Scott says they're for babies. This lets me make one, and it just looks like I'm helping."

"They're not for babies. Scott's stupid."

Jake laughs, and it makes me smile, though Jake's fades quickly. "Don't let him hear you say that. He doesn't like it."

We continue to build in silence for a little while, my eyes darting back to Jake every few minutes because I feel like I said something wrong.

"Thanks for helping me. Shannon doesn't like to do things with me." I dump a bucket of wet sand as I talk, not looking at Jake.

"Older brothers and sisters can be a big pain sometimes. Scott isn't nice to me a lot either."

"Must be something with the names that start with *S*."

Laughing, he stands and reaches a hand out to me. I've never held a boy's hand before, besides Daddy's, but he doesn't count.

Noticing my hesitation, he puts his hand back at his side. "Want to play in and out with me?"

"What's that?"

"We go down to the water and run in towards it, then run away when a wave comes and do it all over again. It's fun and nobody else plays with me."

"Yeah, that does sound fun." Standing up, I brush sand off my butt and start walking to water's edge. The few times the water catches us, we both burst into a round of laughter.

We see each other a few more times before the week ends, saying goodbye in the same place we met six days earlier, before getting into our own cars and driving home. I have to admit, playing with somebody besides my sister is fun, even if he is a boy.

TWELVE

"I'm so happy we were able to coordinate with the Henshaws again this summer. It's been so nice for you two to have somebody else to spend some time with the past three summers. And your father and I as well. Having another couple to go to dinner with has been so delightful." Mom turns around in her seat to give me a smile.

I return with one of my own, albeit a bit fake. It certainly has been nice, giving me a bit of a break from spending time with just Shannon, who seems to just barely tolerate my existence, but I'm still pretty unsure about boys, which means that I haven't been the nicest to Jake. Somehow, he's still always polite and friendly to me. He asks me to play games, like Kadima, while we're on the beach. When our families go out to do things together, like dinner, he makes sure to sit next to me.

Every summer, our conversations grow and change. It started with things we like to do, our favorite subjects in school, and other small things, like favorite colors and foods. As the summers have passed, we've told each other about our friends from home, like Anna, who I've known since I was three. In return, I know all about his group of boys in his neighborhood and how they've all been friends since they were in diapers.

The first day of each summer, we reconnect like no time has passed, just two old friends seeing one another once again.

"Hey, Mackenzie, want to take a walk with me?" I'm lying on a towel, reading a book when Jake's shadow stretches over me. It's our first full day here, having arrived late the night before.

"Where?"

"I found something cool. Come on."

As I follow him up the beach, he slips his hands in his pockets and turns to me.

"So, your best friend is Anna, right?"

"Yeah, we've been friends since we were really small, before we even made our own friends, really." When he turns to me with a quizzical look, I expand. "Our parents were friends, so we started spending time together because our parents wanted to. But as we got older, instead of drifting apart and finding different groups, we grew closer."

Silently, he nods. "What's your all-time favorite moment with Anna?"

"Hm." It takes me a minute and ten years of memories to sort through before I land on one. "Okay, we live near this old train station, and there's a bridge that has a road on it that used to be open for people to use to go to, like, some weird mental health place that's on the other side of the tracks, that's now closed. The road is too. So, one day, actually, only a few weeks ago, we rode our bikes to the bridge, stood at the edge, and threw rocks off." The smile that spans across my face makes my cheeks hurt.

Until I turn to look at Jake and find his brow furrowed and lips tight. My face drops immediately, my heart sliding to my feet.

"What?"

"That doesn't seem very safe, Mackenzie. For you two *or* the trains." Clear disappointment hangs off his words, making my chest deflate.

Narrowing my eyes, I huff. "Fine, tell me yours, then."

As though thinking intently, Jake taps his finger against his chin, smirking, and glancing over at me, clearly trying to get me to laugh. When it doesn't work, he lowers his hand.

"I guess I have to say the time we stole a statue from the garden of the really mean lady in the neighborhood. It had been raining for a few days and the yards were all muddy. My friend, Pete, slipped and fell when we were leaving." The lightness in his voice tells me he's trying not to laugh.

But when he looks at me, he has the same reaction I did.

"You don't approve?"

"It's mean, Jake."

"Trust me, if you knew her, you'd understand." With a roll of his eyes and a shake of his head, he puffs out a breath. "She told our parents that we're doing things we weren't, like breaking bottles on her driveway because she found broken glass once. It was a beer bottle...we're fourteen. Where would we even get that?" When he explains it like that, I can understand his irritation.

"Either way, it's not very nice to take something that's hers."

One brief glance in my direction is all it takes for his shoulders to slump. "You're right, it's not very nice. But what you did isn't very safe."

When he comes to an abrupt stop, I have to take a step back toward him. He's led me to a small tide pool. Crouching down in front of me, he points at the fish inside.

"They wash in with the high tide and get stuck," he explains. As he's looking down into the small circle of water,

I notice that his hair is a little shaggier than it was last summer.

Glancing over his form, I take in his sandy feet, tanned skin, and lean body. He has the vaguest outline of muscles in his chest, even at fourteen.

Looking up at me, he smiles, bringing a flutter to my chest, a strange and concerning feeling. Is something wrong with me? Am I getting sick?

The tiny fish dart around the small space, and I squat down next to him to watch them go back and forth. They seem scared, like they're trying to find their way home, but know they're trapped.

"Are they going to die here?" My heart drops as I look up at him and take in his down-turned lips.

"They might. I don't know how much longer until the tide comes up." The sincerity in his eyes helps, but I miss his smile.

When we get back to our families, I'm feeling confused about what happened. Why did my chest flutter? Shannon and I don't get along all that well these days, but she's my big sister and full of wisdom. Or at least, as much as a sixteen-year-old can have, which to me is a lot.

"Shannon, something weird happened." To make sure nobody else can hear me, I keep my voice low as I kneel next to her towel.

Sliding her sunglasses down her nose, she glares at me. I've interrupted her tanning time. The look very clearly says to go away, and I'm sure she'll say it if I don't beat her to the punch.

"I was with Jake, looking at a tide pool. He smiled at me, and my chest felt...weird." Rubbing my palm against my chest, I try to make the feeling go away.

A grin crosses her face. "Aw, Mackenzie. You have a crush."

"What? No, I don't." It's not possible. Boys aren't something I concern myself with.

"Yes, you do. It's a good thing. Trust me."

A crush? For the first time, I have a crush on a boy. Is it good or bad that he's my friend? Does that change things? I'd ask Shannon, but I'm not sure I want to admit it just yet. Not to mention, this is the first time Shannon has been somewhat kind to me in the past year, at least. Normally, she huffs, flips her hair over her shoulder, and tells me she has better things to do than talk to a twelve-year-old.

Now the real question is, what do I do about this suspected crush?

THIRTEEN

There's a jitteriness settling into my bones as we approach the beach this summer. Jake has been on my mind for months, and I'm looking forward to seeing him. The crush Shannon helped me figure out has not gone away over the course of the year.

Due to the fact that Scott is leaving for college, and not planning to return for future summers, our families have decided to spend two full weeks in the Banks. This makes excitement bubble in my stomach and adds to why my leg is bouncing.

In addition, my breasts started to develop over the last year. For some reason, I'm looking forward to Jake noticing them.

The first day I see Jake, he bumps his shoulder into mine, the smile I haven't stopped thinking about spanning his face. "Hey, Kenz. How's Anna?"

"Hey, Jake. She's good. How about the guys?"

"All good. Trying to stay out of trouble, you know."

Though I nod, I have to go through the hello again. "*Kenz?*"

Lifting one shoulder, he turns to me, his blue eyes twinkling. This summer, I have to tilt my head up more to look up at him. "Yeah, I mean, we're friends. I feel like you should have a nickname."

"You're the only one who hasn't gone to Mack."

"Well, then it's special between us. That okay with you?"

Unable to speak due to the racing of my heart, I nod furiously.

For the first few days, everything we do, we do together. Whether it's spending time on the beach, visiting one another's house, or going somewhere with the other's family, we're practically inseparable.

Five days into our trip, our parents are hovering a little further from us than when we first arrived.

"Hey, Kenz, want to take a walk with me again?" Eyebrows raised in question, Jake stands by the foot of my towel, his wet hair sticking to his forehead before he shakes the droplets from it.

"Yeah." Jumping up from my spot, I fall into step next to him. For a few feet, our hands brush with the closeness of our bodies, a tingling working through me every time. As his fingers link with mine, my breath stops for a moment before I turn to him and smile, my heart thudding as loud as the waves next to us. Though I've never held hands with a boy before, it doesn't give me the icky feeling I was afraid it might.

We walk for a few minutes before Jake pulls me to sit. There aren't many people in this area of the beach. Sitting right next to me and still holding my hand, he looks out at the ocean. The first morning we were here, he started taking surfing lessons, and I know he's thinking about the water since he talks about it all the time.

"I really want to do something, but I don't want you to feel like you have to." His voice is barely audible over the ocean in front of us.

"Okay." A slight tremble has taken over my body as I timidly respond to his seemingly nervous tone, not sure what he's talking about.

Jake turns to me, his blue eyes shining bright and making my stomach flip. Taking my chin in his free hand, he leans in slowly. For a second, my breath halts and I have no idea what's going to happen. But when his lips lightly connect with mine, my blood flows as warmly as the sun beating down on us.

Any hesitation or nerves I felt were unwarranted. Sure, I didn't know what to expect, but the moment Jake kissed me, I knew it was something I'd been desiring all year.

As the days go on, so do our adventures in kissing. We sneak away whenever we can, thinking our families would tell us we're too young if they knew what we were doing.

The last afternoon of our summer, we're in the downstairs room at his house, movie playing, mouths sealed together when he stops.

Leaving his hand on my cheek, he locks his eyes on mine. "I just wanted to tell you...I like you, Mackenzie. I like you a lot."

"I like you too, Jake."

The smile that breaks across his face has become one of my favorite things to see. Not just because I like knowing I make him happy, but because it causes such an uptick in my pulse.

Pressing his mouth to mine again, we sink deeper into the cushions we pulled to the floor. We kiss, mouths open, tongues meeting, until our lips are sore.

It's the perfect way to end my summer, and while sadness tries to creep in because we'll be apart, I'm already looking forward to seeing Jake again next year.

Fourteen

With the way things ended last summer, to say I'm eager to see Jake would be an understatement. And to make things even better, we're staying an entire month this time. It's Shannon's last year joining us because students are expected to be at college before our vacation is over.

While a discussion had happened about moving the trip either earlier, or ending it sooner, Shannon insisted she doesn't want us all to go with her and will fly out from Norfolk International on her own when the time comes. The only reason my parents agreed to let her, is because Jake and I are becoming good friends, to say the least.

Mom's exact words were, "You two seem pretty fond of each other." If only she knew exactly how *fond of each other*.

The first morning on the beach, I stop dead in my tracks, a cold wisp of shock weaving through my body. Scott's here again.

As Jake walks toward me, the chill melts away.

"Hey, Kenz." Leaning down, he wraps me in a tight hug.

He's filled out a bit, his muscles more defined than they have been.

"Hi, Jake." The airiness in my voice has to give away the flutters in my chest.

A twinkle skitters across his eyes as he releases me. Sliding his hand down my arm, he weaves our fingers together and starts walking.

"I'm surprised to see Scott again." There's a coldness to my tone, an uneasiness that I'm sure if Jake's paying attention, he'll pick up on.

"Yeah, my parents were kind of shocked he wanted to join us this year. He says he'll be leaving before the trip is over, but he'll still be here most of the month." It's impossible not to notice the change in Jake's posture and tone. His shoulders now slump, and disappointment coats his words.

We settle into what's become our spot, sitting shoulder to shoulder, our hands still linked in my lap. Turning to take in Jake's profile, I can't help but be awestruck by him. Each year he gets better looking, and while I denied it at first, my feelings for Jake have only grown.

There's a question that's been plaguing my mind, and I swallow harshly before daring to ask. "So, sixteen now. Do you have a girlfriend?"

Turning toward me, with his notable smile stretched across his face, he pushes against my side. "No, Kenz, no girl-friend. I've been looking forward to seeing you again. Just you."

A zing runs through my body. Before I can respond, he leans in and brushes his lips against mine, his hand cupping my jaw.

Pulling back slightly, our gazes meet for all of a second before our mouths are moving against one another's again.

When Jake and I are together, especially when we're kissing, it's like no time has passed. That we haven't spent months apart.

A week into our vacation, we're lying in my bed at my house, a heavy make-out session underway. Our parents started giving us more freedom since we're both a bit older. It may not have been their wisest decision, but who are we to argue.

Pulling away, Jake rests his hand on my hip and meets my eyes. "I want to try something. I don't want you to feel like you have to. I don't want to push you."

The last time he had said that, he kissed me.

Even though I'm only fourteen, I know a little about sex and the things leading up to it. Shannon had been all too excited to fill me in on every detail, not caring that I was only thirteen at the time.

Biting my lip, I take a few seconds to think it over. Am I ready for whatever it may be? What if he wants to have sex? I'm only fourteen. But I have real feelings for Jake. Whatever that means at my age. All I know is that I want to be around him all the time. I'm comfortable with him, and I feel safe in his presence. And he knows me better than anybody else, even though we only see each other a few weeks out of the year. I've always felt like I can tell him anything and everything.

So I nod, too nervous to use my voice.

When his mouth meets mine again, his hand slides up my side to rest on my breast, which has developed into a small A-cup. After a few minutes in that position, he breaks the kiss and his gaze darts around my face, trying to read me. "Is this okay? Do you...do you want me to stop?"

I shake my head. "No, no, it's okay." Pushing my mouth back against his, I part my lips for his tongue to slide over mine.

After that afternoon, we spend hours and hours alone together, making out, moving on to sliding up the inside of my shirt.

One night, with his hand on my breast, things get even more heated, and he kisses down to my neck, sucking and biting. When we separate, both panting heavily, I go to the bathroom to make sure I look the same as I did when I left my house, when I notice a round, red mark on my neck, right where his mouth had been moments earlier.

"You gave me a hickey! What am I going to do?" Despite trying to rearrange my collar and adjust my hair, nothing really hides it well.

"I'm sorry, I couldn't help myself." Appearing right behind me, hand on my waist, Jake stands a few inches taller. Looking at us in the mirror, I can't help but notice how well we fit together. While our hair is starkly different, our eyes are both a gentle blue, though different shades, and when we stand close, we look right together.

When I get home, I sneak into Shannon's room, pulling out her makeup and trying to hide the mark. Confusion swirls through my mind as I look at everything she has to work with. My very limited makeup knowledge is confined to eyeshadow.

I'm leaning toward the mirror, dabbing something skin-toned on the hickey when Shannon appears in the door, and I freeze, a chill running through my veins. She scowls, crossing her arms tight against her chest, as she takes in the situation.

While I expect her to yell at me for being in her room and touching her makeup, she doesn't, instead crossing the room and taking things from my hands, tilting my chin so she can get a better look.

Apprehension flows through me, and I barely breathe while she looks me over and says nothing as she starts to apply something to my neck.

"What are you thinking, Mackenzie? You're *fourteen*." Despite her tone and the reprimanding, I'm thankful it's her and not my parents.

"I love him."

"You think you love him." Anger boils my blood as she downplays my feelings for Jake.

"No, I really love him."

"You just need to be careful."

"We're not having sex. We're just kissing, I promise." His hand on my breast is still just kissing.

"Even still. I'll teach you how to do this"—she wiggles the concealer in my face— "the right way, so if it happens again, you can do it yourself." The gentleness in her voice causes my mouth to pop open. At least part of me was expecting her usual, nasty tone and indifferent attitude.

While my sister and I have never gotten along that well, at this moment, she is my favorite person.

At the end of the summer, Jake and I are standing in the road, so close together I can feel his breath, warm on my cheek.

"I got a cell phone a few months ago. Here's the number, and my email address. I want to talk to you this year." Unable to tear my eyes from his, he slips a piece of paper into my hand.

Looking both ways, he checks to see if anybody is watching. I'm not sure if nobody is, or if he just doesn't care, but he tilts my chin up and places a tender kiss on my lips.

"I love you, Mackenzie." My heart hammers against my breastbone. It's the first time he's told me he loves me, and all I can do is hope it's not the last, that I'll get to hear it again and again.

"I love you too, Jake." Nothing in my life has ever been truer.

The corners of his mouth reach up toward his eyes, making them sparkle. Leaning down, he gives me another quick kiss before walking toward his family and climbing into his car.

Clutching the piece of paper with his number and email

address against my chest, I keep it there the whole fourteen-hour drive back to New York.

Within minutes of getting home, I rush upstairs and send him an email, to which he responds almost immediately.

When my parents get me a cell phone for my birthday, he's the first person I text. He wishes me a happy birthday and tells me he loves me, which causes me to hug my phone, wishing I could jump through it to be with him.

We message every day, talking about school, friends, even other boys or girls we talk to.

One night, after a particularly rough day, I call him in tears.

"Kenz, what's wrong?" There's a tension clearly audible in his voice.

"I failed a math test today." The words come out between sniffles. But I hear Jake trying not to laugh on the other end of the line.

"That's it?"

"It's a big deal! I've never failed a test before."

"Really? Never?" Shock coats his questioning.

"Nope. Not one."

"Well, I can assure you that I've failed some here and there. Most people do. And I'm convinced that anybody who says they haven't failed at least one, is lying. So now you get to be honest."

The line is filled with silence for a moment as I try to regain steady breaths.

"Kenz, listen. It doesn't change a single thing. It doesn't change who you are or how smart you are or anything about you. It just means you didn't do so well when you took that one. Don't let it get you down." His tone has changed to one of calm and his voice is lower than before. "Plus, if you want, next time, I can always help you study over the phone."

My heart picks up tempo at the thought. Anna and her so-called-boyfriend study together all the time. I always want to be able to do those things with Jake, but clearly can't. Over the phone is better than not at all.

There's a night in May where I worry that Jake is getting sick of me.

"So, what did you do today?"

"Not much. You?" He's been quiet for the whole ten minutes of our call, barely giving me more than a one-or two-word response, and his voice is low and almost...sad. So I force myself to ask the one question swirling through my thoughts.

"Jake, what's going on? Is there somebody else?" My heart drops into my stomach at the very thought.

"What? No. Of course not, Kenz. There's nobody in the world that could ever compare to you."

"I feel the same way about you. So then tell me what's going on."

"I'm not sure what you're talking about." His voice lowers even more as he mumbles the words, a clear sign that he's not telling me the truth.

"Jake."

A huff comes through the speaker pressed to my ear.

"It's Scott. He's been a little...rougher than usual lately. The other night, he grabbed me by the collar and yanked me toward him, spitting in my face. He's gotten taller, and while I have too, it's not enough to close much distance, so when he pulled, I was basically standing on my toes." There's nothing but dejection in his confession.

Fear snakes through my mind and I can barely breathe. A hand flies to my chest, and I try to fill my lungs but can't.

"Kenz?"

"I'm...I'm here." With a sharp swallow, I close my eyes and take a long inhale. "I'm worried about you. It doesn't seem safe that you're living there with Scott."

"I'm alright, Kenz. I promise. He's not here a lot. He's been away at school for most of the year, and even now he's not around too much, so we're able to avoid each other. It was just a bad night."

There's no way to really argue with him because I don't know what the dynamic is like at his house. But I do know it's enough to have him shaken.

"Well, we'll be together soon enough. Right? You're still coming to the beach this year?" I don't know what I'd do if Jake didn't come.

"Of course. I'm counting down the days."

My lips pull into a smile, and after that, Jake's in a much better mood.

Throughout the year, we talk about everything and anything, but we never go a day without communicating.

Fifteen

"It was so delightful to be here for the whole month last year. Very relaxing. And oh, My Fire, I'm so glad you and Jake have become so close. He's a sweet boy. It's going to be wonderful spending another month this year." The fourteen-hour drive down to the Outer Banks never gets easier. The impatience crawling under my skin to see Jake makes it nearly impossible to do anything but watch the minutes tick by on the clock.

"Yeah, wonderful." Even though I've asked Mom to stop calling me by the nickname she gave me years ago, I let it slide this time. I just hope Dad doesn't pitch in with his *Firebird* nickname that he made in response to Mom's.

With Shannon not joining us, I'm subjected to having to talk to my mom any time I'm awake. Car rides tend to lull me to sleep, but with the pinpricks poking around my body, I can barely even close my eyes.

The first day we arrive is always my least favorite. It's usually after ten at night, and dark out, so my parents refuse to let me go see Jake.

Me: Hey. We're here but my parents won't let me out.

Jake: That's ok. I'll be surfing in the morning but up early. Can't wait to see you.

Me: I'll come find you first thing. I can wait if you're not done.

Jake: Good night beautiful.

Me: Night.

Picking up a book, I try to focus on the words in front of me, hoping that it will make me tired enough to fall asleep. When I can't concentrate, I decide a cup of tea may help settle my jitters.

I'm almost to the kitchen when I stop on the stairs, my parents' hushed voices just barely audible. Leaning against the wall, trying to stay out of sight, I stretch my ear toward them to listen.

"Ashley, I don't like that she spends all her time with that boy," my dad grumbles.

"Oh, Jim, it's fine. Jake's a nice boy. They have a strong connection. She says she loves him, and Nadine says that he talks the same way about Mackenzie. It's just puppy love, let it be."

"I think they're doing things she's too young to do." Pressing farther to the wall to try to remain hidden, I walk up a few steps.

"Let her decide that for herself. Mackenzie is responsible and level-headed. She's choosing to spend time with him, and she wouldn't be doing that if she wasn't comfortable. Besides, you've known Jake for years. You know he's kind and a good kid." The firmness in Mom's tone is something I recognize well as her holding her position.

"We only know them over the summer." There's a hesitation in Dad's words, which means he knows he's on a slippery slope with Mom.

"But you know his parents. You know how he was raised." My mother's tone doesn't change.

"Well, they also raised that Scott boy."

"He's a different story, and you know that. Jake's a good boy. He's sweet and caring with Mackenzie, protective. I've seen them together, and it's almost like he shields her, hovers around her. They make each other happy. Just, let it be. Trust that we raised her to know her limits and not do anything she isn't ready to do."

I've heard Mom talk to her friends about the teenage years, and I've also seen how bad it was with Shannon. I'm not like them. Things between Mom and me can be rocky at times, but in this moment, I'm very grateful for her. Because she's right, I do know my limits, and I know I love Jake.

My parents can think it's puppy love all they want, and they can say the same to Jake's parents, but we know it's so much more than that. Even at fifteen and seventeen, we know it's real. It lasts beyond summers; we're able to pick up right where we left off the year before.

The next morning, I'm on the beach early. Seeing him walking out of the water, still in his wetsuit, I run to him and jump into his arms, pressing my mouth to his and not caring who sees.

After a step back, he wraps his arms around me, one hand getting lost in my hair as his tongue swipes through my lips.

Setting me down, he rests his forehead against mine and slides his hand to my neck. "Hi."

"Hi." Tipping my feet to the side, I pull my lip between my teeth. My body is humming at his nearness.

Linking our fingers, he pulls me toward our houses, but my whole body freezes over when my eyes lock on Scott. He's gotten even bigger, in both height and bulk, making fear wrap around my ribs. There's something about him that makes my blood run cold.

While Jake has also filled out more, making my already racing hormones go haywire, it's impossible not to notice the flinch when he sees where my sights have landed. It's so imperceptible that I'm not sure anybody but I would notice it.

"I wasn't expecting to see Scott again." The hesitation in my voice is undeniable.

"Yeah, I wasn't expecting him to come either. Can't change it, though."

When we get close to our destination, we give Scott a wide berth.

It's the first morning of many spent in the same fashion. Meeting Jake on the beach is the highlight of my day, because his whole face lights up the second he sees me.

Falling into a pattern, our days become routine and filled with one another's company.

We spend our time together exploring each other's bodies, doing things with each other we've never done with anybody else and couldn't dream of doing with another person. Electricity courses through my veins when his fingers touch me, when he puts his mouth on me in places other than my lips.

One particular afternoon, we're at his house.

He stops. "Shh. You're going to get us caught."

"Nobody's here," I breathe, barely able to hold in the sounds escaping me.

"It doesn't matter. If they come back, they'll hear you."

"Fine, just don't stop." With a smirk, he continues what he was doing.

I'm thankful to Shannon for teaching me how to cover hickeys last year because I get many more, including in spots that would be difficult to explain to my parents, like on the tops of my breasts.

Four weeks go by way too fast for both of us. We want nothing more than every day, every week together. We tell each other we love each other every day and know we meant it.

Hatching a plan to spend Christmas together, we beg our parents to take us to the beach houses. Jake and I want to spend it together. He'll be turning eighteen in March and going to college the following September. Our parents have already planned to let us spend the whole summer together at the beach, knowing it's going to be hard for us to be apart, but we want Christmas too.

Our parents agree, taking us down to North Carolina. While we're with our families, he finds a way to make it special.

By some Christmas miracle, everybody ends up with other plans. Our parents have a dinner party they want to attend at the restaurant, while Shannon and Scott decide to head to a bar, "together but separate" as she so artfully described it. After making sure we didn't want to tag along to their dinner, our parents leave, an hour after our siblings have.

Jake asked me to meet him twenty minutes after the coast is clear, but anticipation draws me sooner. Over the past few months, we'd discussed what this night could mean to us, what we want to happen. Without knocking, I walk in on the bottom floor, making my way up to Jake's room, where I find him lighting dozens of tealight candles.

A hand flies to my chest as all the air leaves my body and Jake turns at the sound. His cheeks hue pink and he holds his hands out with a smile on his face and a small rise of his shoulders. Setting down the lighter, he walks over to me and wraps an arm around my waist, swooping some curls behind my ear.

"We don't have to do anything at all, Kenz, especially anything you're not ready for. I just wanted to make this special, even if it's just watching a movie." His voice is low and gentle, soothing, and I know he means every word.

That's the thing about Jake. Even though we're young, he makes me feel how a girl deserves to be treated by her boyfriend; safe, protected, and above all else, loved.

Sixteen

Getting to the beach, I'm filled with mixed emotions. Excitement courses through me, but there's an underlying sensation of nervousness settled deep in my bones. Jake's eighteen, and he's going to college in just a few weeks, leaving earlier than we usually do.

We arrive the weekend after classes end, a few days after Jake's graduation. Everybody's with us this summer, and even though we have extra time, it's not enough.

Over the year, Jake and I talked about all our plans for the summer. He wants to take me on real dates; dinners, milkshakes at John's, out to Jockey's Ridge, picnics on the beach, even to just drive around the island so we can be alone together. I'm looking forward to it all.

Per usual, we get in too late for me to do much more than drag myself up the stairs and collapse onto the bed.

In the morning, I know exactly where to find Jake and head straight to the beach.

It's been just shy of a year since I've last seen him gliding through the water, but I can pick him out in the waves like I've watched him every day. As he paddles in, my heart starts to flutter. The moment I've been waiting for, the one I've been building up in my head for the past several months, is finally here.

The warm sand slides under my feet as I run toward him at full speed. A huge smile spans his face as he drops his board and I jump into his arms. I don't care that he's still in his wetsuit and soaking wet.

Wrapping my legs around his waist, my arms around his head, I look down at him and peace washes over me. This, right here, is what I've been wanting for months.

"Hi." His voice is low and gruff. It's the voice that makes my heart soar, and while I've heard it almost daily, it's so different in person without the added tinniness from our phones.

"Hi."

Setting me down, he slides his arm down my back, hooking his thumb through my belt loop with one hand while the other grabs his board. Tugging me into his side, he kisses my temple. "I missed you, Kenz."

"I missed you too, Jake."

"Let me change, then we'll go to our spot to catch up."

"There's nothing I could want more." Except some alone time. But we have almost two full months to get to that.

About two weeks into our vacation, I meet Jake on the beach after his early surf. After that first day, I've been out here every morning. I watch from afar as he makes his way to shore, giving his shaggy hair a shake from his eyes. As he undoes his wetsuit, I notice a tattoo on his left pectoral. It's the first time I've actually been able to see him shirtless this summer, our alone time being far more limited than we anticipated, thanks to my parents wanting to spend time with me.

Squinting, I try to make it out. It's a Celtic symbol of some sort. It almost looks like two hearts in an infinity shape, with a diamond in the middle. All the lines are interlocked. And it almost looks like...fire behind it.

Biting my cheek, I wonder why he got it, what it stands for. A plan on how and what to ask starts assembling in my mind, when something else catches my attention.

My thoughts are completely distracted from the tattoo, and my stomach slides to my feet, when my gaze settles on a giant bruise residing on his ribs. The thrumming with excitement to see him that had been rattling my body, dissipates as a chill runs through me.

Usually, I wait for him to come to me, but this time I march across the beach.

"Hey, Kenz-"

"What happened?" I cut him off, reaching to touch the angry purple with my fingertips.

He recoils from me, shrugging. "I got a little knocked around today. That's all." His eyes are trained on the sand, so I know he's lying.

"Jake, tell me the truth. You did *not* get that from surfing. What happened?"

Sighing, he takes my hand. "Come with me." We walk up the beach and sit near a dune. Picking up sand and shaking it through his fingers, eyes out on the water, he takes a deep breath. "It was Scott."

My eyes grow into saucers and my breath catches in my lungs. "Scott? Scott did this to you?" There's a shrillness to my tone that I wish I didn't have. It screams panic, and I know that's not what Jake needs right now. What he needs is for me to be calm, peaceful. Taking care of me, calming me, is not something he should be thinking about.

Nodding, he refuses to look in my direction, instead tipping his head down. "Scott's been coming back drunk almost every night. I try to stay out of his way, but a few times I've been a little later getting back from seeing you, or I'm just not asleep yet. He gets in my face. This is the first time he's actually hit me."

Before it had been words, a shove, intimidation. This? This is different.

"Jake, I…" But I don't know what else to say. What is there to say?

Taking my hand in his, he turns it up and kisses my palm, resting it against his chest. "I'm okay, Kenz. I promise."

"No, you're not. I'm here, Jake, just…know that. For anything. I love you."

"I do, I know. I love you too." The tenderness that usually resides in his eyes when he tells me he loves me isn't there. I know he means it just as much as always, but I hate that Scott is having this effect on him.

Standing, Jake pulls me up too. "Come on, let's get changed. Lou's getting some people together later to hang out, and I said we'd go."

An hour later, we're sitting on the beach with a group of kids our age. Sitting between Jake's legs in the sand, leaning my back against his chest while his arms encircle me, everything feels right with the world.

Scott may be an asshole, and Jake may be leaving in a few weeks, but this moment, right here, is perfection. With Jake, I feel safe, I feel loved.

Tipping my head back, I kiss his jaw, earning one of my favorite smiles. Leaning down, he closes his mouth over mine, his fingers grazing along my neck and chin.

"I said go away, Loose Lips! I'm not interested." The stomping past us and screaming is nothing new, and we pull apart to watch as Susan stomps away and we laugh at their somewhat routine exchange.

"Come on, Stone Cold. Give me one chance, you won't regret it." Lou chases after her, arms outstretched.

"He's never going to learn his lesson, is he?" I watch the scene unfolding, both of them talking with big hand gestures, with Susan's hand on her hips while listening.

"Nope. He's head over heels for her. Kind of like I am with you." My pulse racing, I turn to find Jake's intense stare. His eyes still mesmerize me, the pure blueness still the same shade as the sky on a perfect summer day.

"Kenz, I know I'm leaving in a few weeks, but I need you to know that I mean it when I tell you I love you. Ending our summer early is going to suck, and if I had a choice, I wouldn't. But know that nothing has to change."

Trying to swallow with an arid mouth, I run my hand down his jaw, speckled with spots of stubble. "I love you too. I think I'm most worried about you finding somebody new and better when school starts."

"Impossible, Kenz."

"We met when I was nine, Jake. Of course, you could meet somebody better now that we're older."

"No. You're everything to me. You need to know that."

"I do. I just hope it's enough."

"I've never even thought about another girl. That won't change just because I'm in college." Moving his mouth next to my ear, he speaks low against it. "Come back to my place. Let me show you how much I love you. Scott went down to Nags Head for the day, and my parents were planning to go shopping in Kitty Hawk. They'll be gone for hours, and I want to spend time alone with you."

A shiver of anticipation runs through me at the thought of so much time alone with Jake. Biting my lip, I nod, and he quickly stands, pulling me to my feet. Wrapping an arm around my waist, he presses his chest against my back, and we start walking in the direction of his house.

"Hey, man, we're going to go. See you in the morning?" Clapping Lou on the shoulder, Jake prepares our out.

"Yeah, see ya. Hey, Mack, if you see Susan, try to get her to give me a chance."

"Wish I could, Lou, but you know Susan, there's no convincing her." Every so often, Susan and I end up on the beach together in the morning. She's often out running while I wait for Jake. Being a visitor instead of somebody who owns, her plans vary year to year, but we've gotten to know a few people. Lou surfs with Jake and is a local, always around when we are.

"Yeah, yeah. Thanks anyway. See ya around." Running back toward the others, Lou's off in typical Lou fashion.

Entering Jake's house, anticipation rolls through my body like the waves outside. What I've been waiting months for is finally here, and I can't wait for the alone time with Jake.

Four weeks into the summer, and Jake and I have spent as much time together as possible. Sneaking around isn't nearly as difficult as it had been in previous years. At the moment, Jake has me up against the wall in the shower, and his teeth dig into my shoulder, causing me to scream.

All of a sudden, he stills, putting his hand over my mouth. Ready to ask him what he's doing, I turn my face away, but he shushes me. Meeting my gaze, he mouths 'sorry' and jerks his head toward the door, ear tilted like he's listening.

When we hear a bang, our eyes widen. Quickly, he puts me down, climbing out of the shower and wrapping a towel around his waist. Reaching in to turn off the water, he holds a towel out to me.

I've just finished wrapping myself up when Scott bursts through the door. His eyes dart back and forth between us, clad in towels, and for a second, I'm sure his head is going to explode.

Beet red in the face, he starts screaming. "What the fuck is going on in here?"

"Nothing, Scott, just go." Jake's voice is low and calm.

"This doesn't look like nothing! Are you fucking her?" Jake has moved in front of me, one arm reaching behind him to hold me against his back, the other held out to his brother.

Scott keeps yelling, saying horrible things about how Jake better not be forcing me to do anything and not understanding what the hell I see in him. "She must be pretty fucking easy if she's sleeping with *you*." Scott's voice is dripping with disdain.

"Hey! You will *not* talk about her like that. Get the hell out of here, now." Jake's yelling. I've never heard Jake yell before, and the tone of his voice startles me, causing me to shrink against his back more. The arm he has around me tightens.

Scott doesn't say anything, but anger sears through his eyes as I peek over Jake's shoulder. Without a word, he turns and leaves.

The second he's out the door, Jake immediately spins around and wraps me in his embrace. Taking my face between his hands, he tilts it up to his. It's taken until this moment to realize how much taller he is than last year. "Are you okay?"

I nod. "Yeah. I'm fine. Are *you* okay?"

Glancing at the closed door behind him, his jaw ticks. "Yeah. I will be." His voice is low and tight.

"Do you think he'll say anything?" At sixteen, I'm not a crazy age for most girls to lose their virginity, but I still don't want my parents to know. I'm afraid they won't let us be around each other anymore, and that would kill me.

His eyes are back on mine. "No." Gritting his teeth, hands balling into fists, he looks at the floor. "It would take away his leverage." His tone sends a shiver down my spine.

Taking his chin in my hand, I tip it up. "Hey, don't listen to him."

"But did I?"

My brow furrows, confused. "Did you what?"

"Did I force you? I mean, fuck, Kenzie."

Wrapping my arms tightly around his neck and twisting my fingers into his hair, I make sure I have his attention. I need him to hear me. "No. Okay? No. You have never, *never* forced me into anything. I have never done anything with you that I haven't wanted to. Don't you remember how many times you've checked with me? You asked me, before and during, every single thing we've ever done if it was okay. I don't care how old I was, how old we are. We love each other. That's all that matters."

All he does is nod in response. Knowing he's not convinced, I push up on my toes to kiss him and rest my palms on his cheeks.

"Scott's an asshole. You know that more than anybody. But I love you." I keep my voice level, calm but firm. I can't let him blame himself for anything. I've given myself to him willingly.

When his eyes meet mine, they're missing the brightness I know and love. Instead, they're dimmer, sad. "I love you too. Let's get dressed before somebody else comes. I should probably take you home."

Going home is the last thing I want, but I don't argue. It would be futile.

Getting back to the house, it's mostly dark and quiet,

except for the lights my parents leave on, so we don't walk into pitch blackness.

"Mackenzie." A scream leaps from my throat as my hand clutches my chest at the sound of my name.

"Jesus Christ, Shannon. Why are you lurking in the shadows?"

"I'm not lurking, I was reading. And waiting for you."

My eyes narrow as I look at look her. Waiting for me? "Why?"

"I know what you're doing with Jake, that you two are being intimate." Breaths grow hard to come by as my heart races. She knows?

"I'm not about to give you a lecture, Mack. I wasn't much older than you when I lost my virginity, and it definitely wasn't to a guy that I had strong feelings for, like you do Jake. I may not understand it, because you two only see each other a few weeks out of the year, but I won't discredit it because I see you together. All I want to say is, be cautious."

"Careful, Shannon, you may actually sound like a sister who gives a shit." Since when does she care about what I do or who I do it with? For years, I tried to ask her questions, to talk to her about Jake, about anything, and over and over she pushed me away and shrugged me off. Only once did I get a single breadcrumb of sisterly love or advice.

Walking off toward my room, her hand around my arm stops me. "All I'm saying, Mack, is that you don't want to do something irreversible."

"And what would that be, Shannon?"

"Getting pregnant."

Rolling my eyes, I spin to face her and shake her hand off. "We're not stupid, Shannon. We use protection. It wasn't a spur-of-the-moment thing. We planned it, talked about it, and Jake made sure I was comfortable and okay with everything before it happened. He still checks, because he loves me and cares about me."

"Good. I'm glad. I know you haven't told Mom and Dad, and I won't either. It's not my business to tell, and I'm not going to rat you out. But I had to make sure you were being safe."

"Thanks for the sudden interest in my life. I'm going to my room now." Without giving her a chance to respond, I stomp off.

Could I have been nicer to her? Probably. But after years of getting the cold shoulder and her negativity, not to mention everything that just happened with Jake and Scott, I don't have it in me to be the kind, caring sister.

I don't see or hear from Jake for the rest of the day except when I text him that I'm going to bed. The responding message merely wishes me good night and says that he loves me.

Until my phone chimes at one in the morning.

Jake: I need to see you

That's all it says. With groggy eyes, I type out a quick response.

Me: Come right over.

Dashing down the stairs, I rip the door open just as he's walking up the front steps. The second he's in the light, my breath catches and my hand flies to my mouth.

There's purple and blue bruising all around his left eye.

Grabbing his hand, I pull him into the house. It's easy to immediately connect the dots based on the past few weeks and the events of earlier today.

Jake's gotten more bruises as the weeks have gone on, always hidden on his torso, always something he brushes off. But after finding us in the shower earlier today, and Scott yelling, Jake yelled back. Something he says he's never done before. When Scott left, I thought that was the end of it.

Clearly, I was wrong. This time, Scott didn't even try to hide it.

Pulling him up the stairs while he drags his feet, I find my parents in the kitchen. Mom's in her bathrobe and Dad has on his OBX shirt and flannel pants.

"You have to let Jake stay with us."

"Mackenzie, what is going on? Why are you up in the middle—" Mom stops talking as she looks behind me to see Jake, head down, but face clearly visible.

"It's not safe at his house, Mom. He can't stay there anymore. Please, let him stay with us."

"Kenz, it's fine. I can go back, I just wanted to see you."

Turning to face him, I close the gap between us and rest my hands on his chest. "No. I won't let you go back. Not at night at least."

"Jim." By the tone of Mom's voice, I know that she's not really asking, but mostly telling Dad to say it's alright.

"I suppose it's fine if Jake stays for a while. But he and I will be having a chat before that happens. Understand, son?"

"Yes, Mr. Allen."

"Mackenzie, go back to your room. Jake will be down in a few minutes."

Squeezing Jake's hand, I meet his eyes. They're pained, their usual twinkle nowhere to be found. With a tiny nod, I push up on my toes and kiss his cheek before looking back at the wall that is my parents. They agreed to let him stay, and that's enough for me.

Climbing into bed, I fight to keep my eyes open. It's late, and the day before was draining. But I need to wait for Jake, to know he's here, he's safe.

Just as I'm about to lose my battle to stay awake, the bed dips behind me and warmth envelops me. With a tug, I'm pressed against Jake's chest.

Jake's salty, sweet scent wraps around me and all the tension oozes out of me.

"Good night, Kenz. I love you."

"I love you too."

Dad must feel bad for Jake to let him sleep in my room. That or he set very strict guidelines. Probably both. Even still, I'm shocked at the turn of events. I'm not going to question it, not going to bring it up in case my parents change their mind or Jake's trying to sneak something past them.

At eighteen, Jake's not scrawny, but he's still no match for his big brother. The little bit he stood up to him today proved to be a bad idea. I'm sure the only reason Dad lets him stay with me is because Mom assured him it's okay. They know Jake takes care of me, that we love each other, and that we only have so much time left together.

I spend every night for the next four weeks sleeping with Jake pressed up against my back, his arm around me, telling me he loves me before falling asleep. It's the best feeling in the world.

And then, all too fast, the worst feeling consumes me. The day Jake leaves will be burned into my mind forever. We're standing in the road, his hands wrapped around mine against his chest, as I cry. His head is tipped down, his forehead touching the top of my head as his shaggy hair is spread over mine, mixing light and dark.

"I love you, Kenzie. Please know that. I really, truly love you. I promise I'll still call you and message you."

There's a steel vise around my heart, tightening with every second. "I love you too. Please don't forget about me at college."

Tilting my chin up, I take a long look into his sky-blue eyes, needing as much time as possible to brand them into my mind even more than they already are. "I could never." Leaning down, he places a gentle kiss on my lips. As he pulls away, he brushes the tears from my cheek with the pad of his thumb before pressing his lips to mine again. "I wish I didn't have to go, but I do. I'm sorry." Another kiss, and he backs away, his fingers holding mine until the last second.

I cry the whole way home that summer.

At first, Jake calls to tell me about college, about his classes. But then the messages and calls start coming farther and farther apart. He tells me he's having fun, going to parties, making friends. That he hasn't been interested in any girls, and that he's still in love with me. But then it's a whole week before I hear from him again.

And when I do, it isn't anything I ever wanted to hear.

The words I never could have planned for come out of his mouth; he thinks it'd be best if we stop talking so much. That he needs to focus on school, embrace the experience, and that means letting me go. Returning to the Outer Banks isn't something he plans on doing. Despite all this, he tells me that he truly loves me and will never forget me.

As his words cross the phone line and drift into my ear, dread settles into every corner of me it can.

In that one five-minute conversation, my heart shatters at the loss of my first love.

Everything inside me feels like it's been smashed with a hammer. The world has taken on a darker hue, sounds are dulled. There's an emptiness residing in my chest.

When I can't stop crying, Anna tells me he was just an imaginary boyfriend anyway, that she never really believed he exists, so why am I so upset. She changes her tune when I show her all the pictures of us together, pictures I've coveted to be mine and mine alone. Yes, Jake was my boyfriend, my first love, but it was private, just for us.

Taking all the pictures and memories from over the years, I

put them into a box and shove it in the back of my closet to rest and collect dust. Right now, I know the wounds are too fresh, but hopefully someday they'll be no more than scars and reminiscing about him won't hurt so much.

Closing Jake into a box is easy in theory, but hard in practice. My refusal to return to the Outer Banks doesn't shock my parents, though it does disappoint them. Instead, I busy myself with a job. Anna drags me out on double dates, tries to get me to meet new guys, but how can any of them compare?

Even with college looming, my heart still aches at the mere thought of Jake. If the sky is just the right shade of blue, a million memories of his eyes flash through my mind.

I have to move on, I have to let myself start over. And maybe the place to do that, is exactly the place Jake did.

Eighteen

Anna says the fact that I know it's been exactly two years to the day that Jake said goodbye to me in the road in North Carolina is a bad thing. She's probably right.

That also means it's been four weeks shy of two years that I heard the words that broke me into a million pieces, ones I still haven't completely put back together.

Now, I'm starting my own college experience, and while I should be excited, looking forward to the prospect of meeting new people and working toward my degree in education, I'm not. As hurt as I was, my heart is still holding on to Jake. I've spent far too much time wondering about what college might look like if we were still together. Daydreaming of what life would have been like if we were on the same campus.

I applied to his school. I got in. But I didn't want to be the desperate ex-girlfriend that followed after the boy that clearly isn't interested anymore. Even more so, I knew I wouldn't be able to handle seeing him on campus with another girl. It would have been inevitable. He's gorgeous and sweet, so I'm sure any girl who meets him wants him.

The decision to embrace my college experience isn't one I come to lightly, but one I know I have to make to heal my heart.

Deciding to start easy, I work on getting to know my roommate, Jessica. It's hard, being away from Anna, my sidekick for the past fifteen years, but Jessica's kind and funny. She manages to find ways to keep me laughing despite my darker disposition. One thing Anna said after the breakup is that I've adopted a pessimistic outlook on life. I had to explain that that's not all that difficult when the love of your life dumps you over the phone just a few weeks into college. Especially after promising not to forget about you.

"So, I know you have this weird thing about meeting new people, but I think it'd be a good idea to leave our door open the first few days. As much as you're comfortable with, of course. It could help us get to know some of our neighbors. We'll be living with these people for the next several months, at least. May not be the worst idea." We're about five hours into our third day of freshman year when Jessica broaches this subject. So far, she's the only person I've met or talked to outside of the RA who showed me my room.

"Sure, whatever you want." Shrugging, I keep my eyes on my book from where I sit curled up on my bed.

Opening the door, she takes a seat at her desk and starts typing furiously on her computer. I haven't given her much detail, just that I'm trying to overcome some serious heartache. A little understanding has gone a long way so far. Thankfully, she hasn't pushed for the story or more than just knowing I'm struggling.

Leaving our door ajar is how I meet our neighbor, Nick. His room is diagonally across the hall from ours, but he seems friendly enough and likes to chat, which I appreciate since it takes the pressure off me while Jessica's not around. I've started to not like talking about myself much, especially because it appears that talking about past relationships seems to be a pretty big part of the *getting to know you* experience, college edition. At least it has been for every other person I've met while leaving the door open.

About a week in, I'm sitting at my computer when I hear Nick's voice. There'd been a note on my door from him saying he had to ask me something, so I poke my head into the hallway. But Nick's not alone. The guy standing with him is only an inch or two taller than Nick, but that makes him at least four inches taller than my five- five frame.

"Hey, Nick," I say timidly.

As Nick's friend turns around, I'm met with the warmest forest green eyes I've ever seen. They contrast nicely with his dark brown hair.

"Hey, Mack. This is my friend, Gavin." Nick gestures his hand toward Gavin, who gives me a quick once over before a smile spreads across his face. "We met at an event last weekend and got to chatting. We have similar music interests." Is that supposed to mean something to me? I'm not quite sure why he shares that factoid.

"Hi, nice to meet you." Gavin holds his hand out toward me. This, right here, is what I had been hoping to avoid.

After a moment of hesitation, I extend my hand to grasp his. A shock runs straight from my fingers through my whole body at his touch. "You too."

"So what are you thinking of things so far?" The green of his irises shimmer with his question.

I was expecting to just ask Nick what his question is but feel it's rude not to answer Gavin. "It's good...I guess. Not too far in yet. Nick, what—"

"And your classes?"

"Um, they're decent." Narrowing my eyes, I tip my head as

I look at him. Interrupting doesn't impress me, and he seems persistent in knowing about my start.

"Sorry, I'm only asking because you look familiar. Are you in my English 105 class? The big lecture in Halfton on Tuesdays."

"Yeah, I am in that class." Interesting. I'd never noticed him, despite his undeniable good looks. Then again, I haven't really been looking.

Gavin continues talking as I listen intently, thankful he provides information instead of asking for it. In just five minutes, I learn that he's a sophomore, but in the same intro class because he pushed some prerequisite classes back a year, and he's majoring in photography. When I give him little more than a nod or an 'oh', he moves on to talk about the school itself and what I can expect as the year progresses.

"I know I just talked a lot, but is there any chance you'd like to get coffee with me sometime?"

Coffee. Two classmates, getting coffee. It could be innocent. Or it could be a date. Not being in a place to determine the difference, or be interested in the latter, I give him the only answer I can. "Sorry, but no." Turning to Nick, I jut my chin in his direction. "I'll find you later."

Without so much as a goodbye, I retreat to my room, closing the door behind me.

Gavin could be the perfect guy to move on with, but I'm not ready. Two years may feel like an eternity to some, but the hurt is still so fresh, so raw. At some point, I'll be ready, and maybe then I'll be able to give somebody like Gavin a chance.

As it turns out, Gavin is very patient. And persistent. The first Tuesday after we met, he's waiting for me outside my dorm, falling into step beside me. Not only that, but he takes the seat next to me in class, a seat that so far has been taken by a nameless, faceless girl.

This continues for a few weeks, and he even amps up his attempts, inviting me for coffee two more times and starting to pass me notes during the lecture. Most of them are funny, containing jokes or interesting anecdotes. Some are sweet, complimenting me in ways that often make me adjust in my seat. The first time he writes that he thinks I'm beautiful, I shift my body away from him and keep my eyes on my notebook for the rest of class. The last boy to call me beautiful was Jake.

Three weeks after our meeting in the hallway, the note is a little bit longer.

I know I usually keep these short and sweet, but I have more to say today. I know I've asked you out for coffee three times now, and three times you've turned me down. But I like walking to class with you. I like getting to know you on those walks. I like your anecdotes about your friend, Anna, and your sister, Shannon, (I'm using their names so you know I pay attention.) I know you drink coffee, a lot (again, paying attention). I can tell there's a reason you're holding back, and I respect that, but I want you to know that I'm a patient man. I'll continue to wait, and continue to ask, until you say yes.

A tiny flutter in my heart works its way through my body. Gavin really likes me. And when I allow myself to think about it, I realize that there's at least an interest in him that resides in me. Besides being sweet, he listens, and he's handsome, but very different from Jake, with his darker features. Wearing more fitted shirts, showing off a toned body underneath. There's definitely no denying that I'm *physically* attracted to him.

This is how I move on. This is how I finally let Jake go.

I pass a small piece of paper over to him with one simple word.

Yes.

The smile that breaks across his face is infectious, and I find myself truly smiling because of a boy for the first time since Jake left.

We go for coffee right after class.

"Don't you have another class right now? Isn't that why you usually don't walk me back?" I ask him as we pack up our books.

Shrugging, he flings his backpack over his shoulder. "I do, but it's worth missing for this. I wouldn't want you changing your mind on me." He winks at me, and a giggle pulls from my chest.

We walk to the campus center and Gavin insists on buying my coffee. "I asked you for coffee. That makes it a date. And since I asked, I pay."

I tuck some hair behind my ear, a nervous habit I've picked up in recent years. "Well, thank you. Do you want to sit or walk back?"

"It's a nice day, let's walk."

Walking back toward the dorms, we take our time going at a slow, leisurely pace. "So you like coffee a lot, huh?" It had come up during one of our conversations when walking to class. The biggest size cup available must have sold it for him.

I nod enthusiastically. "About as much as I like oxygen."

His laugh sends a tingle from my ears straight to my chest. "You know, you have a good sense of humor. I don't think you've ever made a joke before."

"Thank you. I needed something growing up with my

sister. She can be a bit much at times. Not the nicest. I had to be quick with the comebacks."

"Yeah, siblings can be tough. Or so I've been told. I don't know, being an only child." This is the first time he's shared that with me, even though I've told him about Shannon. Quickly tracking through our previous conversations, I realize I've shared more about myself than he has. How did that happen? Normally, I'm more guarded.

"They certainly can be." That's at least one way he's different from Jake. I shake my head. I need to get Jake off my brain. He's been popping up more than I like since Gavin and I started spending time together.

"Something wrong? You look distracted."

"Huh? Oh sorry, just something I'm trying to forget about." A whole romance and love-filled adolescence. Much easier said than done. So much of our time together still plays on repeat in my mind, especially in my dreams. The nightmares are when I relive the breakup. The one I never saw coming.

Pursing his lips, he nods as though he can read my mind. "So, I'd really like to take you out again. Maybe dinner?"

My whole body stops abruptly. Stopping a few steps ahead of me, he turns to face me.

"Look, Gavin, you're a really sweet guy. But I'm still a little hung up on somebody. It was...complicated. I'm not really sure I'm over him yet."

Walking right up to me, he catches my eye and takes my hand in his, which halts my breath. "Listen, I understand. But I like you, Mackenzie, and I'm not going anywhere. I can be patient. I can wait for you to feel ready. It took four tries to get you to say yes to coffee, so I can wait for dinner. Maybe by the tenth try, you'll feel ready." A full toothed smile spans his face, and if I didn't know better, I'd swear it was dripping with confidence. The fact that he wants to take me out, still, causes my pulse to skyrocket.

Despite me turning him down, Gavin continues to walk me to class, sometimes bringing a coffee with him when he picks me up.

Two weeks later, I say yes to dinner. Jake still pops into my dreams nightly, but I figure the best way to truly get over him, is to jump into something else feet first.

Gavin takes me to a nice dinner at a local Italian restaurant, Nona's. It's a quaint little place with round tables covered in crisp white linen tablecloths and white napkins. Every table has a small candle in the middle, allowing the room to flicker under the low light of the overhead fixtures. There's a soft din of the voices around us.

Our own conversation flows just as easily as it has on our walks. For some reason, I haven't realized until tonight how easy he is to talk to. Not so much that I over share, but more that I don't feel like I have to hold anything back. I can just say what's on my mind. Part of me thinks I've been looking at our chats across campus as convenience, something to fill the time as we walk together. Now, I'm realizing it's not like that at all.

Gavin makes me laugh a lot; he has a good sense of humor as well. It seems as though he and his friends have thoroughly enjoyed their college experience so far. He tells me more embarrassing stories about his friends than I'm sure they'd care for me to know.

"So I've heard a lot about the things your friends have done. What about you? No embarrassing stories involving you?" He's told exceptionally few about himself, by design, no doubt.

As I call him out, he turns a bright shade of red, causing me to giggle and glance down at the table before meeting his eyes again. "Well, I'm sure there are some, but I'm not sure we're at a point where I'm ready to tell you."

"Oh, really? But won't it be awkward when I meet your friends and know all of these embarrassing things about them?"

Shrugging, he runs a finger up his water glass. "Maybe. But I'm trying to impress you. They're not."

It's my turn to redden, as his eyes catch mine. "So you've been here a year and some weeks now. You haven't found anybody you wanted to date? No girlfriend?" I'm a little baffled by this. How could somebody so attractive and charming be single?

"I found one." Looking right at me, he makes my heart hammer against my ribcage. "What about you? Any high school boyfriend I need to know about? I don't want to get to a certain place here and have some guy show up and kick my ass for crushing on his girl."

I tuck a curl behind my ear as I look down at the table. I'd decided to push Jake as far from my mind as possible, but it's hard when something about him is directly brought up. "It's complicated."

Gavin sits up straighter, the smile disappearing from his face. "Oh. Um, I'm sorry. I didn't realize, I wouldn't have asked you if I knew you had somebo—"

Thinking I had already covered this before he asked me out, it's a little unnerving to have to go over it again.

"No! Sorry, it's not like that. We're...we're not together anymore. Haven't been for a while. But it was a big deal for me. It was hard to get over." To say the least.

His shoulders lower a little, and his muscles lose the tension they'd held, knowing that I am, in fact, single. "How long?"

As I take a deep breath, I prepare myself for even the simple rehash that will make my heart ache for the rest of the night. At least. "We knew each other for six years. We were in love for at least two. I don't know, like I said, it's complicated."

Nodding slowly, he takes my hand on top of the table. "I've said this before, but I'll say it again. I like you, Mackenzie. And I'm willing to wait for you to feel ready. I thought agreeing to dinner meant you were. If you're not ready now, though, I can understand that. You're worth waiting for."

Glancing up, I meet his eyes for the first time since he asked about my history, about Jake. They hold nothing but sincerity.

This moment is when my heart starts to open for Gavin. Not a lot, not enough to jump into a relationship, but enough to let him in a little more. Enough to see that there is a light at the end of the very dark tunnel I've been in.

Gavin may just be the one who can help me out.

NINETEEN

My nineteenth birthday is in February of my freshman year. Gavin and I have been officially dating for about two months. After our first date, he continued to walk me to class, adding hand-holding to the routine, and sat next to me every time like he had done before.

At the end of every week, he'd swing by my dorm room and ask me out on another date. For weeks, I turned him down, and for weeks, he kept his word about being patient, never showing an ounce of anger or frustration when I politely declined.

By the time November rolled around, we'd been on three dates, and I hadn't seen Nick for weeks. Apparently, he'd had a bit of a crush on Gavin, and when Gavin started hanging around me and asking me out, he realized his feelings would go unrequited.

At the end of the third date, at a local sandwich shop, we walked hand-in-hand to the car. Gavin has always been incredibly chivalrous and walks me to my side, opening the door and holding my hand while I get in. This time, before lowering me to my seat, he cupped my cheek and lightly brushed his lips against mine.

At the time, I was taken off-guard. I'm not sure why, we'd been talking for over two months, and it was our third date, if you don't include the times he walked me to class.

Hesitating for a minute, I ended up leaning into the kiss. His lips were soft and gentle. He timidly opened my mouth with his, not being forceful to push it open, but gently parting his against mine. It was the first kiss I'd had since Jake, my mind immediately filling with the first kiss I shared with him six years ago.

The thought rocked me to my core. I hadn't thought about Jake in months. I'd been happy getting to know Gavin. Yet there I was, kissing the boy I had grown to like, my stomach swooping like every good romantic comedy said it should, with thoughts of Jake running through my mind.

Breaking the kiss, a giant smile spread across his face. "I've wanted to do that for a while now."

I smiled back at him, trying to make it seem natural. If he picked up on anything, he didn't mention it. Two days after that kiss, he asked me to be his girlfriend.

For my birthday, he's gone all out.

Walking up the stairs from an extremely exhausting history lecture, I halt at my door and perk right up. The whole thing is covered in wrapping paper. Part of me isn't surprised; he's been doing cute things all week like bringing me coffee, buying me the new book I wanted, and even brought me a bouquet of brightly colored daisies on Wednesday.

"Happy Birthday, Mackenzie." Spinning around at the deep voice, Gavin stands, holding a cupcake on his outstretched palm. It's chocolate with pink frosting, my favorite flavor and color. My stomach grumbles at the sight, and I realize I haven't eaten since breakfast, even though it's four in the afternoon.

Taking a step closer, he kisses me on the cheek, taking my hand and putting the treat in it.

"I know you didn't get to eat much today, and I wanted to bring you a little something special." A smile pulls at my lips as my heart warms.

"Thank you. And my door?"

Shrugging, he reaches around me to twist the knob and push it open. "I may have had a little help."

Inside, Jessica is sitting at her desk, all smiles. "You like it?"

"I love it. Thank you, both of you."

"I was happy to help. It was super sweet of Gavin. He's been amazing all week. You have a good one, Mack."

Turning to Gavin, he winks at me, and I know I really do.

Looping hair behind my ear, I turn away from both of them, setting my cupcake and books on my desk.

"Get changed, I'm taking you to dinner."

Turning back to face him, there's a twinkle dancing through those forest greens I've come to love staring into. "Gavin, no, you've done too much already. You've been bringing me gifts all week! I don't also need dinner."

"Nonsense. It's your birthday."

"But I'm only nineteen, it's not a big birthday or anything."

Leaning in, he kisses me tenderly. "I think the day you were born is worth celebrating any year." The words are said quietly, right against my lips.

Heat rushes my face. Gavin always knows the right things to say and do; he's been okay taking things slow in our relationship, never pressuring me for more. Two months in, and we haven't had sex yet, even though neither of us are virgins and we spend almost all of our time outside of classes together.

"Okay, I'll get ready. What should I wear?"

"Whatever you want. It's your day." He spreads his arms wide, like the whole world is my oyster.

"Where are we going?" Narrowing my eyes, I arch an eyebrow, but have a feeling he won't share this information with me.

"I don't want to tell you, but you can wear anything you want. You don't need to be fancy." Hm. Mysterious. I kind of like the intrigue.

"Alright, then. How long do I have?"

"I can give you as long as you need."

"Give me twenty minutes?"

Pressing his lips to my temple, he turns to leave. "Sure. I'll be downstairs."

Quickly sorting through my clothes, I throw on a pair of jeans, a sweater, and some Converse. After a deep breath, I bounce down the stairs. It's the first birthday I've ever spent with a boy before, and I'm not quite sure what to expect. Previous years, it was only able to be acknowledged through a phone call.

When Gavin sees me, he smiles and stands from his chair by the entrance, linking his fingers with mine and pulling me out the door.

"Where are we going?"

His eyebrows dance up and down and a flutter starts in my stomach as I giggle. When he gets on the highway, I know we're heading to Pineville, the largest local town nearby, which is about a half hour away.

"Okay, well, it's clear we're leaving town. So we're obviously not going to Nona's or Valentina's."

"Very astute."

Glancing over at him, his lips are pressed tightly together but turned up at the corners and the hand not on the steering wheel is resting in front of his mouth.

"You're not going to give me anything, are you?"

"Nope." He pops the *P* and squeezes my leg, just above the knee, sending a zing through my body. Leaving his hand there, he looks comfortable, like this is the most natural thing in the world to him. On some level, I'm sure it is.

In so many ways, it just feels right with Gavin. My hesitance to give him a chance seems ludicrous at this point.

Pulling into the parking lot, my eyes grow wide, and I start bouncing in my seat.

"Bento?" The excitement in my voice makes it crack slightly.

"You get your favorite for your birthday." A few glances back and forth between me and the road, and a smile spreads across his face. "And I really wish I had my camera to take a picture of your excitement right now."

"But you hate sushi."

"I don't need to have sushi. They're fusion anyway, so they have a huge selection. Tonight's not about me, though. It's about you."

He leans across the armrests and takes my chin in his fingers, kissing my bottom lip.

Guiding me inside, he asks for a hibachi table and my excitement grows as I grab at his arm. The whole night is very Gavin, filled with laughs and fun. We both miss terribly when the chef tosses pieces of chicken in our direction, which only causes us to grab onto each other and laugh until tears well in my eyes.

When the waiters come over and gather around me with a bowl of ice cream, singing to me, heat rushes my face as a bead of sweat drips down my back. I try to hide in Gavin's shoulder, but his shining eyes mesmerize me, and I stop halfway, staring into them.

After we finish eating, we walk around town a bit, finding a small coffee shop to duck inside on the cold night.

"Can't not get coffee on your birthday, right?"

"Oh, of course not. That's sacrilege."

Sitting at the table, sipping our piping hot beverages, a layer of fog on the windows from the warmth inside and frigid winter air outside, Gavin places a small box on the table between us.

I tilt my head to the side, staring at him, mouth parted. "Gavin, no. You've already given me too much. I can't accept this." I make no move to take it, keeping my hands wrapped around my paper cup.

"No, no. I insist. You mean a lot to me, Mackenzie. I want to make your birthday special." There's a tenderness in his voice as he pushes the box to rest right in front of me.

Very carefully, I open the perfectly wrapped box. Inside rests a circular, diamond encrusted necklace. It's absolutely stunning. Taking it delicately in his hands, Gavin stands, leaning down as he puts it around my neck. Moving to stand in front of me, he runs a finger down the chain to rest against the heart, which falls just below the collar of my sweater.

"Want to head back?" There's a gravel in his tone and an intensity in his gaze that's undeniable. It sends a pulsation straight through my body, settling between my thighs.

Swallowing through an arid throat, all I can do is nod.

Before opening my car door, he presses me against it, my back flush against the side as he leans down and closes his mouth over mine. Wrapping my arms around his neck, I part my lips for his as his erection presses against my thigh and need stirs within me.

"Come back to my room. I have one more present I want to give you," he breathes against my mouth.

He doesn't give me time to do more than nod, connecting

his mouth to mine again as our tongues war and one hand cups my face while the other squeezes my hip.

There's a battle setting root inside me. My feelings for Gavin have grown exponentially in the few months we've been together. His presence calms me, and he makes me happy. But the scorch marks from the last time I was burned are still smoldering, and I want to keep my wits about me this time.

Wanting Gavin isn't a problem, but there's a wall that's been put up that tells me to pace myself. While that wall is coming down in large chunks, there's still a little left. The problem is that as much as my mind and heart tell me to pace myself, my body is racing to feel his. Once you know what it feels like to have somebody surrounding you, over you, inside you, it's something you crave when you've developed strong feelings for someone, like I have for Gavin.

Before we even make it into Gavin's room, his lips are on mine again and we start peeling off each other's clothes. I back away before he gets to my pants. "Leo?"

His response is a smile against my mouth. "I asked him to disappear for twenty-four hours."

I'm not entirely sure how I feel about the fact that he clearly planned this ahead of time. But the need building inside me is too strong to focus on that.

Crashing against his mouth again, I pull myself against him. Putting his hands on my waist, he lifts me onto the bed, climbing up after me.

He leans me back slowly and starts kissing down my neck, across my collarbone, down my chest, and all the way to my navel. Once he gets to the hem of my jeans, he pulls them and my panties off in one fluid movement. Anticipation and nerves mix and bubble in my stomach, settling a slight jitter in my extremities.

Trailing his lips along my hipbone, he keeps going until

he's settled between my thighs. Looking up at me with a smirk on his face, a flame flickers in his forest irises before he lowers his head. "Happy Birthday, Mackenzie."

My lungs halt the second he puts his tongue on me. When he starts flicking his tongue against my heavy clit, I reach down, twisting my fingers into his hair to pull him closer. It's been so long since anybody has touched me there. I've almost forgotten how good it can feel to be with somebody else and not just myself.

Twirling and swirling his tongue around me, I lose any sense of hesitation toward sex with Gavin. If he asked, I'd let him fuck me, right here, right now.

As I begin to rock against him, he starts moving his tongue faster, with more urgency and pressure. Just as I'm sure it can't get any better, he slips two fingers inside me. Arching right off the bed, my hands grip fistfuls of his sheets as the pressure peaks and I sigh his name.

Starting at my inner thigh, Gavin kisses all the way up my body until he's lying next to me, elbow against the bed, propping his cheek on his hand.

"Good present?" Roping his arm around me, he pulls me into his chest.

"Great present. The best one in a string of very excellent gifts this week."

"Good. I just wanted to make your birthday special."

"Well, you certainly did. And I'm very thankful. But you should be careful. I may come to expect this level of spoiling every year."

"I'd be happy to spoil you, for years to come, if you'll let me." My heart hammers in my chest as my finger falters against his muscles.

"I suppose you are kind of growing on me," I tease, as I snuggle into him. His ever-present woodsy scent wafts into my nose and my muscles loosen. As soon as I'm settled, he runs his hand down the back of my head, pulling my curls out straight before letting go.

After a few moments of lying in silence, Gavin takes my chin in his hand and tilts my face to his. "Mackenzie, I love you."

My entire body freezes, even the blood in my veins, as I look at him. While things have been going well, I wasn't quite expecting this. But his eyes are locked on mine, full of sincerity that restarts my pulse with new vigor. "I love you too."

His smile is so wide it sets free butterflies in my chest. "Will you stay here tonight?"

"I'd be happy to."

Rolling over, I press my back into his chest. I *do* love Gavin. The realization hit me a few days ago, but I couldn't be the first one to say it.

But if I know I love Gavin, why does a single tear roll down my cheek before I fall asleep?

Needing some expert advice, I call Anna the next morning. "I don't know, Anna. I know I love Gavin. I haven't even thought about Jake in months. What was that about?" Pacing my room, I have the phone pressed to my ear, fingers working the necklace Gavin gave me last night.

"He's the first guy who's told you he loves you since Jake. Which makes total sense. It doesn't mean you don't love Gavin or that you're not over Jake. It just means that hearing it for the first time since then brought up some emotions."

"I guess," I mumble, but I'm not so convinced.

"Listen, you have a right to feel that way. Jake was a *major* part of your life. He was hard for you to get over. You're having a strong connection again, so it makes sense for those past feelings to come up. But it by no means detracts from what you and Gavin have."

"You're right."

"But, Mackenzie?" My steps, which had slowed, now falter. I don't like the tone in her voice, the hesitation and questioning.

"Yeah."

"You do love him. Right?"

"Yeah, I do." There's zero waver in my voice, because it's a fact.

"And you are over Jake. Right?"

"Right." There's no doubt I'm over Jake either. It may have taken me a few years, but I know it's happened. I don't think about him. I don't miss him. And while my heart still stings at the thought of him, I know it's because he hurt me, and being in love again just brought everything with Jake rushing to the surface; it reminded me of the heartache.

I'm sure that's all it is. Like Anna said. "Thanks, Anna. You're always good when I need advice."

"Anytime, love. I hope things are going well otherwise. I miss you!"

"I miss you too!"

I keep what Anna said in mind any time strange thoughts arise. But every day I spend with Gavin, my feelings for him grow stronger and any residual oddness I feel regarding Jake melts away.

This helps more so when I finally talk to him about my initial hesitance.

Taking his hand, I pull him to my bed. We have the whole afternoon together, alone, since Jessica has class until seven on Tuesdays.

"You've been incredibly patient, and I know you've never

asked, but that you can tell there was something holding me back at first. It's time I told you about it."

"Mack, you don't have to."

"I know. But I want to. You have a right to know my history." Swallowing, I steel myself, preparing for the conversation I hate to have, and hope it's the last time I'll ever have to share it.

"I fell in love with a boy I met on vacation when I was nine years old. Every summer, we'd each go to our beach houses in the Outer Banks of North Carolina for a week or two at a time. For years, he and I spent our time together. He's two years older than me, and we just got along well. At some point, that friendship turned into love."

A tight squeeze on my hand causes me to look up from my lap to find forest eyes on mine with a softness I don't deserve. No words are needed for me to know he's encouraging me to continue.

"The summer I was sixteen, he left for college. We planned to stay in touch, stay together, but he broke up with me a few weeks in. I was absolutely crushed." Despite my best efforts, my eyes flutter closed, but I'm able to stop the tears from spilling over. I don't want Gavin to think I'm crying because I'm still in love with Jake; it just hurts to bring it all up again.

"It's why I was unsure at first, why I've been hesitant to have sex. I needed extra time, to make sure I was healed and could give you that part of me."

"I can understand that, Mackenzie. I can't say I've been in the same position, but I can understand it. You needed to protect yourself from being hurt like that again. But, Mack, I love you so much. I could never imagine doing anything that would mean not being with you. I'm okay that we've taken things slow, gotten to know each other. I think it's important for a strong relationship."

Gavin's understanding in this whole situation is something

I appreciate more than I can ever truly vocalize. I'm not sure most guys would be as understanding. It was a long time ago, and I've been told by many that I just need to get over it. But not by Gavin.

"My only question is, why now? Have I done or said something that made you think you needed to share this with me now?"

"No, not at all. It's just, we're coming up on six months, and I realized that's a really long time to be with somebody without them knowing your dating history and the reasons you've been holding back on a few things."

"I appreciate that, but it wasn't necessary. I don't need to know, Mack. Whatever happened, it's made you who you are, and I love that person." While his words speak confidence, there's an unsurety coating them.

Slapping his knees, Gavin stands. "I should go, I have a paper to finish before tomorrow."

"Oh." Shock weaves through my body like an icy wind.

"I'll see you tomorrow?"

"Sure."

Leaning in to kiss me, he cups my cheek, running his thumb under my eye. "Hey, everything's good. I just want to get the paper done."

"Okay." The corner of his lip tips down, and I know that I'm not convincing enough.

Pressing his lips to my forehead for an extended minute, he leaves, and I'm alone with my thoughts and worries.

Did I share too much? Is he now worried about where my heart lies? Maybe I didn't make it clear that I'm over Jake, and that I'm in love with him. Our six-month anniversary is this weekend, so maybe I should plan something special.

I'm still mulling over the ideas of what I can do for Gavin on Wednesday. Zoning out in class helped make it zip right by.

Meeting me outside class, Gavin immediately weaves his fingers with mine. We don't have any classes together this semester, but instead, he has one in a nearby building that ends a half hour before mine on Mondays, Wednesdays, and Fridays. Despite my protests, he's insisted that he's happy to wait for me so we can have the extra ten minutes together while he walks me back to my dorm.

With having such varying schedules, it doesn't give us the ability to spend much time together outside of dinner and weekends. Every so many nights, we'll stay together, but it comes at the comfort, or lack thereof, of our roommates. I don't want to impose on Jessica, and while she says she's okay with it, I feel bad having Gavin in our room too often. Likewise, I feel bad taking up space in Gavin's and making Leo have to adjust for my presence.

"I want to do something special to celebrate our six-month anniversary. I was hoping we could go to Lakeside for the night. What do you think?" One eyebrow is quirked up in question, a smirk on his face, a glint in his eyes. I've come to know that glint as excitement.

The Lakeside hotel is a local area attraction. With the frigid and snowy winters, it was built as sort of an all-inclusive hotel. Aside from being enormous, it has so much in the building. Everything from bowling to a half dozen restaurants, a small movie theater, to an indoor pool. There's even a dance club.

"I think that'd be amazing!" A night away with just Gavin and not having to worry about roommates? Fantastic.

"Okay, I'm glad you said that. Because I already booked a hotel."

Smiling up at him, I pull my lip between my teeth and push him gently. "You knew I'd say yes, didn't you?"

"I had a pretty good feeling."

"Well, I'm glad your feeling was right. And it sounds really great." I'm glad that he knows me well enough to know how I'd respond. With things being set, we won't have to worry about not having a room.

"I was thinking we'd leave Saturday, around noon. We can check in around one-thirty, but it takes at least an hour and a half to get there if there's no traffic."

"Sounds good to me. Have you ever been?"

"I haven't, but I've heard the food is really good. Plus, lots to do."

"Either way, I'm excited. It's going to be nice to be alone." A burn starts in my chest and works its way outward as I think of all the time we'll have.

"My thoughts exactly." He hesitates before looking sideways at me, face solemn and serious. "I just want you to know, though, I have no expectations or anything. I don't want you to think I do."

Stopping in my tracks, I lean in to kiss him. "I know. You've been so patient with me, and I appreciate it. I really do." We finish our trek at a slower pace as my dorm is only a few feet away.

"It's worth it. Besides, the other things are pretty fun too." He flinches as I smack his arm.

I look up at the four-story building in front of us, with purple curtains, courtesy of Jessica, visible in my window. "Okay, this is where I leave you."

"I still think you're crazy for walking me back to my dorm to just walk back across campus for class. I mean, I love the time with you, but it's way more than necessary."

"Nonsense. We barely got to see each other this semester outside of this walk, dinner, and weekends. I'm just glad it's almost over."

Pushing up on my toes, I hold on to his arm and press my lips to his cheek. "Well, I appreciate it. Now go, so you're not late. I'll see you later." Standing outside in the warm May sun, I watch him walk away, turning around to blow me a kiss that pulls my mouth into a smile before I head upstairs.

Saturday, Gavin picks me up outside my dorm at noon. My overnight bag is packed with a few different things since I'm not really sure what I want to happen, if anything, but I do want to be prepared. Lingerie is not part of my wardrobe, but I figure I can sleep in just a t-shirt if I want to be a little sexier. That or naked.

The drive is pretty smooth, a straight shot down the highway. But the closer we get, the more the butterflies start to flutter in my stomach and my knee starts to bounce. Walking up to the desk, I'm practically shaking. I have a feeling the concierge knows exactly what is going on when a young couple walks up to check in.

We're shrouded in silence as we go up to our room. Gavin seems unsure of himself, running a hand through his hair, down his pant leg, into his pocket. It brings me a sense of comfort to know he's nervous too. The way we're acting is strange and confusing. Sure, we're nervous; this weekend holds some lofty possibilities. But right now, we're acting like we barely know each other.

Opening the door, we walk into a stunning hotel room. It's far fancier than any hotel I've ever stayed in, with a wall of floor-to-ceiling windows, a tiled bathroom, and a mosaic carpet. The lights are more like chandeliers than fluorescent lighting.

And sticking into the middle of the room, is a king-sized bed.

"Wow."

"Uh, why don't we go check out the place. It's huge. I'm sure there are a few things to look at." I'm thankful Gavin is able to put together a coherent sentence, because I'm pretty certain I can't at this moment.

"Yeah, yeah, that sounds good." More awkward silence follows us in the elevator down.

The hotel is enormous, much more so than I ever could have imagined, to a point that I'm afraid we'll get lost. To make sure we don't separate, Gavin keeps his hand tight around mine the whole time.

Following his lead, we take a pathway leading us away from the main floor. We stumble upon a small gift shop, filled with all the things that you'd expect in a tourist store. "Oh, I love these stores! Let's go in!" My voice is so high-pitched, I'm surprised it doesn't crack.

I practically drag him through the doors. Standing right behind me as I look around, he has a smile on his face. "What's so funny?"

One shoulder tips up as one side of his mouth curls higher. "You're cute. You're all excited about these little things."

"I've always loved these shops. Though I can never find my name on anything." A brief flash of the shops in the Outer Banks infiltrates my mind, but I quickly shake it away. It's the last touristy spot I've been to.

We look around a bit, trying on some of the fun hats and scarves they have hanging up. Gavin finds a small section that contains all the name merchandise. Even looking through every single one, he doesn't find my name on any of them.

"I told you!"

"Well, if it makes you feel better, I don't see my name on anything either."

"I guess it does help a little." At least I'm not alone anymore. My whole life, everybody else has always been able to find their names everywhere.

"How about this, let's buy those mugs over there. A way to

remember our time here. And a testament to your coffee intake."

My giggle brings a lightness to my chest. "Okay. I guess they'll work, even though they don't have our names on them."

Pulling out my wallet, Gavin puts his hand on my arm. "No, no. My treat."

"But, Gav, you're paying for the room."

"I insist."

Knowing arguing with him won't get me anywhere, I acquiesce, waving my hand toward the checkout.

We keep wandering through the hotel, hand-in-hand, while Gavin carries our mugs in a big plastic bag that has the hotel name sprawled across it.

As we walk back into the main part of the hotel, the smells wafting from the restaurants mingle in the air, causing my stomach to grumble. "I'm actually a little hungry."

"Ya know, I am too. Why don't we bring these upstairs and figure out where we want to eat and then have an early dinner."

"That sounds great."

Even though there are at least five restaurants that we can find, we opt for the buffet, figuring there are so many choices, they'll definitely have something we want to eat.

What Gavin had heard is right. The food is *really* good. There's so much variety, we keep going back and getting more, something new each round. Most times we're so indecisive, we each fill a plate and then share.

"So, the sushi is really good. The wings are okay. The sliders are awesome." I start taking stock.

"What was that one thing we both really liked? I can't remember what it's called." He looks around the plates piled around us before mumbling under his breath, "Maybe we ate a little too much."

A small laugh pulls from my chest as I think through the

many things we've tried tonight, a list I'm sure is incomplete. "I don't remember either, but I know what you mean. It was all really good, though."

"Want to get dessert?"

"Are you serious? How do you have any room left to eat anything?" He's either crazy or has five stomachs because I am completely stuffed.

He raises his shoulders and slides his finger through the condensation on his water glass. "I don't necessarily, but come on, look at the dessert table!"

"Ugh, I don't think I can eat anything else." Folding my hands over my stomach, I lean back in my chair.

"What if we go upstairs for a little bit to rest and then come back later?"

"Now that sounds like a good idea." A little time to rest sounds perfect.

But when we get there, we aren't quite sure what to do with ourselves.

"Um, how about some TV?" There's an unusual timidness to his voice.

"Sure, yeah." The nerves I thought we both lost appear to be back in force. Though I'm still not really sure why. We're together all the time. But somehow, this feels different.

Probably because it *is* different, and on some level, we both know exactly how and why.

Turning on the TV, we lie down in bed, as Gavin spoons me, running his fingers up and down my arm.

Finding a show we like to watch together, we're about halfway through an episode when I feel him, hard at my back.

The thought makes wetness start to pool between my legs. I've been wondering for weeks what it would feel like to have Gavin inside me, but I haven't been ready to find out.

Until tonight.

I roll over in his arms, putting my lips on his, forceful and determined. His hesitation lasts no more than a second, and he tugs me against him, his mouth parting mine as his tongue seeks my own. One hand slides up my shirt, pushing under my bra immediately. Rolling me slightly so I'm on my back, he hovers over me.

He kisses down to my neck while his knuckles rub over my hardened nipples, the sensation causing a sigh to release from my chest. Straddling my legs, he loops an arm behind my back, pulling me up partially and tugging my shirt off with one hand. Some quick work of his fingers unhooks my bra. Kissing from my shoulder, down my arm, he slowly slides it off before lowering me to the bed and reaching behind his head to rip off his shirt.

I've never taken the time to truly appreciate Gavin's body, but right now, as I pull my lip between my teeth, I take an extra minute to take him in. His chest is toned and lean, muscles showing in all their glory. From this vantage point, every curve and angle are clearly visible.

Gliding his hand down the side of my body, he stops at the waistband of my pants. The reason for his hesitation is clear, so I cup the back of his head and pull his mouth down onto mine. His lips press harder against mine as he deftly undoes the button on my jeans, taking my direction to keep going. Moving off me once again, he removes my pants and panties.

His strong hands cup my breasts, and he gently massages them, swiping his fingers over my nipples. Starting at his shoulders, I trail my hands down his chest, sliding them over every ridge until I hit his jeans, which I quickly undo and push down as far as I can while trapped under him.

With a groan, he climbs off the bed and kicks his pants off, then boxers too. My breath halts at the sight of his full naked form and eagerness sprawls through me, especially when he looks at me like he can't wait a second longer to have me.

As he gets back on the bed, he runs his palms up my legs with a hiss easing from his lips. Kissing along my hipbone, he continues to move his mouth up until he closes it around my nipple while his hand moves to rest between my legs, slowly sliding two fingers inside me.

Moving his fingers and tongue in tandem, I squirm beneath him, gripping at his arm and back as I whine.

"Gavin." His name comes out a sigh as I can barely fill my lungs through the heavy breathing that comes with reaching orgasm.

Making his face level with mine, there's pure desire swirling through his eyes.

"I want you." His voice is low with a gruffness to it that has my core clenching.

I take his face between my hands and pull his lips to mine, pushing my tongue into his mouth, hoping it's enough confirmation for him that I want him too. Badly.

Kissing down my neck, he finally presses himself into me, my back arching as my chest meets his. Slowly, he starts moving.

Clamping my mouth together, I pull my lips in between my teeth. We've fooled around plenty, done everything short of sex, and while I wasn't ready until tonight, I've always imagined what sex with Gavin would actually feel like. My imagination has failed me tremendously.

It's not just the fullness of having him inside me, though it's amazing. It's the connection we've built, the way he's looking at me like I'm the only woman in the world and holding me like I'm the most precious gift.

As he picks up momentum with his hips, I move mine to meet his, craving every ounce of the pleasure he's giving me.

My head tilts back and my eyes roll in my head. The only sound around us is labored breathing and bodies meeting. He's always been a more quiet lover, but I thought he'd give me a little more the first time we had sex.

Squeaks start to ease from my lips as he pumps faster and harder. Every so many thrusts, his chest brushes over my hardened nipples, sending a trill through my body at every pass. The pressure builds in my lower belly again, begging for release.

Digging my nails into his shoulders, I moan loudly, the only audible sound as I succumb to my orgasm, and his thrusts pick up as he gets closer. Dipping his head to my neck, he groans into my flushed skin before collapsing against me.

We're both still catching our breath when he rolls to his side, looking at me intently. "Are you okay? Was that, was it okay?"

Turning my body, I look at him in his beautiful green eyes, which are begging for gratification that makes me smile. "It was better than okay. And I'm fine. I wanted to. I was ready."

Smiling, he pulls me against him and rolls to his back.

As I lay in his arms, his fingers tracing circles on my lower back, I'm happy and content. But the moment is quickly over. His finger hesitates, and I know he wants to ask me something, but isn't sure he should. Not wanting to press, I let him decide.

"So, we never really talked about it. I know you lost your virginity to Jake. But when?"

My breath halts, and my blood runs cold. This can be uncomfortable to talk about. It doesn't bother me, though. I have zero regrets and would do it the same way if I was given the option. But I know others can be shocked by it. And choosing this moment is questionable, but I tell him anyway.

Gavin's fingers stop moving, and he completely stills beneath me, every inch of his body tensing up. "Are you serious?" There's something in his voice I've never heard before, but I know isn't good.

Leaning up on my elbow, I look down at him. "I am. Why?"

"Because that's too young."

I jerk backwards and knit my brows together. "Excuse me?" Anger laces my words.

"I said that's too young. I mean, are you serious, Mackenzie? You were basically a child. And he was what, two years older than you? Did he force you or something?"

Pushing away from him, I sit cross-legged and cover myself in the sheet, suddenly not feeling comfortable with him seeing me naked. "No, he didn't *force* me to do anything. I did it all willingly."

"I don't understand how you could do that. How could you be so stupid?"

"*Excuse* me?" Now I'm raging. But so is Gavin.

"You barely knew him! What, some guy you saw for a week or two for a few summers? You think that means you knew him enough to sleep with him? He was probably sleeping with other girls all year long and just had his nice piece of summer ass waiting for him at the beach."

"It was more than a few weeks or a few summers. It may seem meaningless to you, but it wasn't to me." This judgmental side of Gavin has come out of left field, and while I understand the thought process behind it—we *were* young—I don't appreciate the words he's saying or the tone he's using. Or the fact that he's diminishing what was clearly important to me.

"Barely, it was barely more than that. If you add up all the time you spent with each other, it's less than what we've spent together. I feel like I've practically had to beg you for sex, to take our relationship to that point after six months of dating.

And yet you were with him for a few broken up weeks and slept with him that young."

"How dare you." My voice is low and even. "How dare you say that to me. You don't understand it, you couldn't possibly. But I knew him, I knew him better than anybody, and he knew me better than anybody, probably still does. I trusted him completely when he told me he wasn't sleeping with anybody else. And he never pushed me. He never had to try to convince me to do anything. We learned together; it was new for both of us. I loved him and he loved me, whether you can understand that or not." My voice drips with anger and disdain. I know the jabs I threw in might make things worse, but I'm seeing red.

How could he say he had to *beg* me to have sex with him? Yes, I've been hesitant, but he's been nothing but patient and understanding, never seeming frustrated or even really asking to do more. He even made it clear there were no expectations for tonight. How is that begging me?

Gavin shakes his head. "You were too young to realize what was going on. There's no way you could make good choices at that age."

"I want to go back to school."

"What?" His brows furrow together like I've said the most absurd thing.

"I want to leave. Right now." I'm already off the bed and pulling my clothes back on. "I'm not willing to stay here with you tonight, so if you won't take me, I'll get a cab."

Throwing off the covers, he hops off the bed and angrily rips his clothes on. "Fine."

We don't speak the whole way back. I can feel anger rolling off of him as I'm sure he can from me. When we got back to the dorm, he walks me to the front door.

"Mackenzie, listen, I'm—" His voice has softened, but I'm not having it and hold up a hand to stop him. He tried to belittle what I had with Jake. And that's not okay. Either he accepts all of me, or he doesn't. And while my time with Jake may be confusing to him, it's part of me and my history. It's helped shape who I am today.

"No, Gavin. I don't want to hear it. I'm going to bed, alone. I don't want to talk to you. I don't want to hear from you. Goodbye." Turning on my heel, I walk into the building, leaving Gavin on the sidewalk looking sad and confused after me.

I'm sad and confused myself. I'm not really sure what just happened. We had a great day, took a big step in our relationship. And yet it ends like this.

The future for me and Gavin is suddenly murky. All I know is that if he can't come to terms with my past, all of my past, then there's no room for him in my life.

I don't talk to Gavin the rest of the weekend. He tries to call me and message me all day Sunday, and I ignore every single one of his attempts.

On Monday, he doesn't meet me to walk me back from class, but there's a note on my door. He basically just apologizes over and over, says he's sorry and doesn't know what he was thinking, what had come over him. That he's sorry he ruined what otherwise had been a wonderful day. That he hopes I can forgive him, or at least listen to him so he can apologize in person.

Angrily folding the note, I shove it in a drawer and slam it shut.

"Everything okay?" Jessica looks over at me with wide eyes.

Pushing a hard breath from my lungs, I smooth my hand over the top of my head. "Honestly, I don't know. Gavin and I got into a fight Saturday night, and I'm still not sure how I feel about it. Besides angry."

"I figured something was up when you didn't see him yesterday. And were completely miserable."

When I got back on Saturday, Jessica was already asleep. Despite her numerous questions and inquiries about what was wrong and how things went and why I was back early, I gave her nothing. By noon, she stopped asking.

On Wednesday, I come back to a coffee on my desk.

Eyeing it with a raised eyebrow, I turn to Jessica, who's at her desk.

"Gavin brought it over not even minutes ago."

"He's been walking me back from class three days a week, so I guess he knows what time I get back." He also timed it so I wouldn't have to see him but so that the coffee would still be hot.

I walk out the door, then dump it right into the bathroom sink.

Getting back in my room, her eyebrows are at her hairline and her lips are pulled into her mouth. She still hasn't asked for details, and I haven't offered any.

On Friday, he's waiting for me outside my dorm when I get back. "You have a class to get to." Pushing right past him, I open the door to get into my dorm.

Before I make it through, he grabs my bicep and turns me toward him. "Mackenzie, wait, please."

I rip my arm from his grasp. "Get your hands off me." My voice is low and cold. You'd never know that a week ago I was happily in love with this man. Right now, I'm *still* in love with him, but I'm also hurt and angry, which not only makes the situation harder, but makes it more difficult to see things clearly. My thoughts and judgements are clouded.

There's so much sadness and regret filling his eyes.

"Mackenzie, I'm sorry. I'm so sorry. I never should have said anything. I...I was curious. I don't know why, I just was. It was none of my business. And even knowing, I should have just accepted it." At least he can admit to that. It's a big step in the right direction. Sighing, he looks up at the sky. "I feel like I'm competing with Jake."

The chill that runs through my body stops my heart and freezes the blood in my veins. "How?"

"I watched you when you talked about your relationship with him. The way you lit up when you talked about him and the good times, the way your whole body dropped when you got to the part about him leaving and how heartbroken you were. He was your first...everything. How could you not compare the two of us?"

"I told you I was over him."

"Yeah, but you also weren't when we started hanging out. You told me as much. And I pushed. Maybe I should have left you alone."

Softening at his thought process, I take a deep breath. "I had told you it was complicated, and it was. But I didn't say I was still in love with him, that I hadn't gotten over him. He hurt me, badly. It had been two years, and while I was over him, had prepared to move on, it's hard when you've been burned before. I was hesitant to open up and risk feeling that pain again. But I did. Because I *liked* you. And our relationship progressed, and now I love you." Resting my hand over my heart, I pat my chest twice.

His eyes swim with remorse, and he opens his mouth to respond, but I hold up a hand to stop him.

"Gavin, here's the thing. I know you don't understand it. I know it makes no sense to you that I could fall in love with somebody I only saw over the summers. But you don't have to understand it. It doesn't have to make sense to you. You just need to accept it."

"I know, it's just—"

"No, no, see, that's the thing. There is no 'it's just' or 'I just' or 'but what about' here. It just is. That was my past, and I have moved on. I'm here, with you, and I'm happy. Maybe not at this very moment, but overall, I'm happy. I've let him go. You're the one who brings it up, not me. He's my past, I can't change that. And even if I could, I'm not sure that I would. Because once upon a time, he really meant a lot to me; he will always mean something to me because he was my first love. I'm sure there are people in your past who hold a special place in your heart, and I don't fault you for that or hold it against you. It's part of you."

Taking a deep breath, I steel and prepare myself for the next part, which I know can go a different way than I want it to. "You need to decide if it's something that you can live with or not. And if not, I'd rather you tell me sooner than later, because if you can't, I'd like to move on before I get more invested."

Gavin stands quietly for a few minutes, staring at his shoes. "I've been doing all of these things to show you how I feel about you, to show you that I want to be with you."

"But you still have questions. You still have concerns. You still wonder if I'm holding on to him. Even though I never, not once, have given you any reason to think that I am. I have only even uttered his name because you asked. And even though I don't want to think about those memories, because in some ways, yes, it is still hard, I do it for you. Because you are curious, you want to know. And I can understand that, which is why I tell you. But I've moved on. I've gotten over my past. Now you need to decide if you can too, and if you can trust me."

His eyes flick up to mine. "I trust you."

"No, no, you don't. Maybe you trust me in certain aspects, but you don't wholly trust me. If you did, this wouldn't be an issue. You don't trust that I'm over him. I'm never going to say he doesn't mean anything to me. He always will. But there's a difference between being over somebody who once meant a lot to you and still being in love with them. I am not still in love with him. If you truly trusted me, you'd see that, and believe it."

He nods an understanding, but doesn't say anything.

"I think we need to take the weekend. You need to decide if this is something you can live with. You need to decide if you can be with me, knowing all that you know. I've never hidden anything from you, and I won't hide things from you. I was fifteen, I know that seems young. But I really and truly *loved* him. I have not even liked or felt anything for another guy until you. You have to understand what that means and that you're special and important."

Gritting my teeth, I ball my hands into fists, refocusing the hurt this next part is going to cause me because it needs to be said. "We shouldn't talk this weekend. You need to think about what you want, really, truly want. If you can't be with me, knowing all these things, or thinking that I'm still in love with Jake, then we can't be together. I don't want you thinking about being without me. I want you thinking about being with me, all of me, even the things you don't agree with, because they're part of who I am. If you're not going to be able to look at me the same way, well, then you need to decide that now."

"If you don't want to talk, then how will you know what I decide?"

"If you decide you can be with me, that you still want to be with me, meet me after class Monday. If not, well, then I'm sorry it came to this."

With a small nod and what appears to be tight lips, he keeps his face down as he spins on his heels and starts to walk away.

"Gavin!" I call after him before he's even two feet away. With a straight, thin mouth, he turns to look at me. "I love you."

"I love you too." He smiles, but the corners of his lips only tick up slightly, not his usual full-face grin. With slumped shoulders, his whole posture looks defeated.

The weekend goes by in a combination of a speedy, yet crawling, blur. The anxiety gripping my insides makes it hard to breathe, hard to concentrate, and causes my body to shake involuntarily.

My mind has absolutely already decided that he doesn't want to be with me, that he's very clear on how he feels about all of this. Yes, he says he wants to be with me, but I don't think he can accept everything and leave it alone.

Heartbreak is surely on the horizon for me, though I try to hold out hope that I'm not the only one who wants to continue this relationship.

At a certain point, Jessica realizes something's wrong. While the conversation has melted into the background of my mind, I gave her a complete history, and she was in tears by the time I finished telling her about Jake.

Agreeing with Gavin, she did feel that fifteen was on the young side, but that I clearly had been so deeply in love with him that she completely understands and would have done the same thing.

Calling Anna seems like a good idea when I decide it's my next step. She was with me through my relationship with Jake, the one there trying to heal my broken heart. Her firm belief that Gavin is being stupid and will come to realize such is less than helpful. As is her comment that if he thinks he can do better than me, he's sorely mistaken. When she says he should keep me despite any of my past he doesn't agree with, or any fears he has, I know calling her was a mistake.

I don't want him to stay with me just because he thinks he can't do better. I want him to stay with me because he wants *me,* good and bad.

Waking up Monday, my body is tight all over and there's a steady tremor residing in my hands. There's also an ache in my chest. I haven't talked to Gavin all weekend, and I miss him. The bed was cold and lonely without him, since we usually spend weekend nights together. I haven't seen those dazzling green eyes in days. Throughout the day, he'd always send me cute texts to let me know he was thinking about me.

While in class, I stare at the clock and will the minutes to tick by faster. There's a chance Gavin won't be waiting for me, but at this point, I just need to know.

When the professor dismisses us two minutes later, I practically fly out of class looking for Gavin. But when I get outside, he's nowhere to be found.

Deflated and defeated, I start the walk back to my dorm, my feet shuffling and shoulders curled inward. Gritting my teeth, I will the tears not to spring from my eyes until I'm at least safe behind my closed door.

Noticing a presence on my left, I turn to find Gavin in step beside me. "Sorry, I'm a little late, I had to get this." Extending his hand, he holds a paper coffee cup.

I don't even think as I throw against him, accidentally knocking the coffee to the ground. His lips are on mine immediately, his hand cupping my face. Our lips move against each other's like we're stealing their oxygen, but when we pull apart, I can barely breathe.

"You're here." The words hardly come out around the lump in my throat.

"Of course I am." Using the pad of his thumb, he brushes away the tears that have sprung loose. Pulling me into his chest, he kisses the top of my head. "I'm so sorry, Mack. I never should have brought it up, or judged you like that. It was wrong and unfair, and I'm sorry. I love you."

With the lump still in my throat, and not wanting more tears to come, all I can do is nod in response. Gavin holds me against him for a few more minutes while I take a few deep breaths to steady myself.

When I'm ready, I straighten up with a quick swipe under my eyes. Taking a slight step back, I rest my hand against his chest. "Okay. I'm okay. You're probably running late now, so you should get to class. I can get back by myself. I'm alright, I promise."

Before I've even finished talking, he's shaking his head. "No. Class doesn't matter right now. You do. I want to be with you." Wrapping his arm around my waist, he pulls me against his side and starts walking back toward the dorms.

"Is Jessica up there?" With narrowed eyes, he looks up at my room.

I give a quick shake of my head. "She has class until five."

"Your room it is."

When we get upstairs, Gavin climbs up on the bed and slides under the covers, opening them for me. Crawling up and curling into his chest, the tears return.

He holds me tightly against him as over a week's worth of emotions pour out of me. The anger, the fear of losing Gavin, the uncertainty of our relationship, the happiness that he wants me, it all flows out until I fall asleep, wrapped up in the man I love.

TWENTY

Gavin decides to throw me a party at his new apartment for my twentieth birthday. At the end of the previous year, he and his friend Nate decided to get an apartment off campus to start their junior year, while Jessica and I chose to room together again.

The better part of the fall semester was spent at Gavin's place after class and many nights a week. Leading into the year, we arranged our schedules as well as we could to have as much of the same free time as possible. With a little luck, it also turned out to be very opposite of both Nate and Jessica's schedules, giving us a lot of alone time.

The party comes after another week full of presents and fun. Aside from the party itself, he surprises me by walking out with an ice cream cake and has everybody sing me *Happy Birthday* while he holds my shoulders so I can't run away.

"I can't believe you did all this for me!" I gush as we lie on the couch after everybody leaves. The apartment is a disaster; balloons, streamers, and red cups scattered all over the place. Parts of the floor have a strange stickiness to them. Instead of cleaning, like I desperately want to do, I'm leaning against his chest, feeling warm and fuzzy, the room spinning slightly.

He has an arm thrown over my shoulder, hand resting on my bicep. "Of course I did! I had to make your birthday special."

"You made my birthday special *last* year."

"And I was pretty sure last year I told you I'd do it for you every year."

Every year. My heart races as the room spins a little more.

Snuggling into him, I take a deep breath as my nose fills with his woodsy scent. "I love you."

"I love you too." Kissing the top of my head, he slides his hand from my arm to my chest, the warmth from his fingers heating my chilled skin. Slowly, he slips his hand under the collar of my shirt, fingertips running over my nipples as they harden against his touch.

My breath catches in my throat, which earns a sigh from Gavin. His free hand tilts my chin up as his mouth closes on mine. "Ya know, I think there's something else I owe you." The words tickle against my lips.

Scooping me up off the couch, he carries me to his room, stumbling a bit as I giggle. Nate had been kind enough to vacate with the rest of the guests from the party, giving us the apartment to ourselves.

As he puts me down on the bed, he drops me slightly. Not wasting a second, he tears off my pants, quickly pulling off his clothes as I strip off my shirt. I reach for him as he climbs on top of me and starts kissing sloppily all over my body.

Resting between my thighs, I gasp when his tongue touches me.

He starts gently, moving slowly up and down as my breathing rate increases. At the first sound, he uses more pressure and moves his tongue faster. I squirm as rippling sensations work through me. Sliding his hand around my thigh, he pulls me closer.

Fingers slipping into his hair, I tug gently as I buck against him. One of his hands presses over my abdomen to keep me still, but I fight against it, tugging and bucking until I'm screaming out his name.

Running his tongue along the inside of my thigh, he glides his body up over mine. And a whine pulls from my lips as he eases into me.

"Happy Birthday, Mackenzie," he whispers against my ear, electricity coursing through me. I scrape my nails against his taut shoulders as he moves inside me, faster and faster. It's hurried and uncoordinated thanks to the alcohol, but even still, I tighten around him, screaming his name again while he sighs mine. Collapsing against me, he breathes heavily.

With a quick kiss on the tip of my nose, he flops onto his side and looks at me. "Good birthday?"

"*Great* birthday. Again. Thank you for making my last two birthdays so special."

"It's the least I could do. You make every day special." He always knows the right things to say to make my heart skip a beat.

I roll onto my side to face him. "Like I said last year, I'm going to get used to this level of spoiling on my birthday."

"And as *I* said last year, I will gladly spoil you for your birthday every single year."

"So, how far in advance do you start planning these things? Are you already planning for next year since this year's over?"

"Oh, absolutely. I'm thinking maybe something bigger next year. So far, I've been able to up it a little bit each year, so I'll have to do something really big next year."

"Like a parade?" My tongue pokes through my teeth as I tease him.

Bringing one hand to his mouth while looking at the ceiling and scrunching his eyes, he puts on the perfect thinking face. "Hm, maybe." Moving his hand to rest on my hip, he lifts a shoulder. "I guess you'll just have to wait and see."

"That's not fair."

"Well, it's my secret. I like to surprise you every year."

"You've done an amazing job so far. I just feel bad that I'm not as creative for your birthday."

"I don't need anything special. Having you is enough." Taking my hand in his, he brings it to his lips, kissing the back of it. "Listen, Mackenzie, I know we've only been dating a little over a year, but I love you. Like, really love you. I'd happily spend every single birthday, for years and years to come, with you."

A smile pulls up my lips, and I want to melt into the comforter. "I'd like that too."

His eyebrows raise to his hairline. "Really?"

"Yeah, really. I don't know why you're surprised. I love you too. A lot."

He smiles so wide, I think his face might break in half. Sliding his arm under my neck, he pulls me against him, kissing the side of my head. The room is still spinning slightly, but Gavin's steady breathing and his tight hold on me helps me stay grounded. The swirling of his fingers on my back relaxes me enough to fall asleep.

Late in the spring, Gavin brings up the idea of us getting an apartment together.

"You're basically at my place all the time anyway. You'll be a junior next year, so you can move off campus. Come on, what do you say?"

While I'm a little nervous, the idea is quite intriguing. "Yeah. Yeah, let's do it."

The next morning, we go to the local supermarket and pick up a few newspapers and some college housing specific flyers. It takes us only three different apartments to find one that we like. It's ready for move-in starting in June.

Sitting at what's become our table at a local café, we talk with a pad of paper and go over the possibility of getting the apartment.

"Can we afford it? I mean *really* afford it?" My hands are wrapped probably a bit too tightly around my paper cup, eyebrows raised as I look down at the pad.

When we'd brought the idea up with our parents, they both said they wouldn't help financially because if we were old enough to get an apartment, we were old enough to be responsible for the expenses that go along with it. Up until now, they've supported not just our college expenses, but any additional spending money we've both needed, including what Gavin has spent on me, though he hasn't told his parents that after the one time he mentioned a necklace and his mom basically said I only want him for his money. Sorry wait, *their* money.

"Well, looking at what we would have leftover, so to speak, from room and board...it would be tight. We'd have to get jobs. But ultimately, yes, we can afford it."

"So now I guess the question is, do we really want to?"

"I do."

"Living together is a big deal, Gavin. It's not the same as just staying over for the night. We have nowhere else to go if we need a break. Not to mention, it's ready way earlier than we need it to be."

"We can spend the whole summer here. Get it ready, buy what we need, start making it homey."

While some part of me isn't quite sure about rushing into this apartment, I'm excited to live with Gavin, and I think taking the summer to work will be a smart choice. Plus, it means we don't have to work out who will visit when like we had to do last year.

"Okay. Let's go for it."

With one phone call, a deposit—thanks to our parents—and some signed paperwork, the apartment is ours. When school ends in May, I move what things I want to keep with me into Gavin's apartment, bringing the rest home. With some help from our friends, we're moved in on June first.

Though the day and time of life is filled with excitement, apprehension wraps my ribs like a ribbon. It's the first summer I'll be away from my parents. I've never lived with a boy before. Sure, I've stayed at Gavin's place plenty, but what is it like to actually *live* with a boy?

With some financial assistance from our parents, we're able to go to Target to pick out necessities, like towels, sheets, dishes, and cutlery. Though they've given us help, both our families make it abundantly clear that it's a onetime thing to get us started and we need to find jobs as soon as possible, especially since it's summer and school's out.

Gavin's parents are less than thrilled about us living together. They haven't really taken a liking to me, though Gavin refuses to see it, swearing he can't possibly understand why they wouldn't adore me. When he called them, they tried to convince him that it was a terrible idea, but he made it clear he'd do it with or without their help. Since he'd have no money otherwise, they decided to help him out.

Since most of the college kids go home once classes end, we're both able to find jobs almost immediately. One of the local clothing stores is hiring, with incredibly flexible hours, which is helpful. It means I can work as much as I want over the summer and then keep the job once school starts. Gavin's able to find work with a local photographer. To start, he'll mostly be answering phones and getting photos printed, but he's excited to learn his craft from a well-known local.

By the end of June, we're both working as much as we can to save money to buy things. When we moved into the apartment, we hadn't had enough money for a couch and tables, so we've been saving for that and some other furniture.

It's busy, and we don't see each other as much as we want to, but the times we do have together, we try to make fun.

Come August, we've worked enough to go to a local discount furniture store in town. The prices are low enough that we're able to buy a couch, a living room table, and some dressers, as well as the cheapest bed we can find at the mattress store.

Despite the less expensive furniture, that doesn't really match at all, our apartment starts to feel homey. Though the TV is still on the floor, and we eat in the living room instead of at a kitchen table, we're getting by.

Our meals are often the cheapest thing we can find. Neither one of us had really learned to cook before we left home, so living on our own and having to feed ourselves is quite the experience, but going through it together makes it special. There's been a handful of laughs, a few fights...and a lot of tears, all of which were mine.

By the time school starts up again, we've been able to save up a little to help us get by while our hours shorten. But with classes and needing to work, our time together plummets. If we weren't living together, I'm confident we wouldn't see each other at all.

One night, in the wee hours of morning, I can't sleep. Sitting in bed, my knees pulled into my chest, tears stream down my cheeks, and I try to keep the sobs at bay while Gavin dozes next to me.

"Baby, what's wrong?" Gavin's voice is slow and sleepy.

"It's just, we never see each other. What if this was a mistake?"

"What if what was a mistake?" Rubbing his eyes, he props himself up.

"This!" Frantically, I wave my arms around the room. "All of this, moving in together. What if it was a mistake?"

"Why do you think that?"

"Because we never see each other!" I know I sound hysterical. But I don't know how to calm down. I'd barely seen Gavin for more than an hour before we went to sleep tonight, and most nights I'm falling asleep on the couch within minutes of sitting down together.

My class schedule is busy, and to make sure I still have money coming in, I work most evenings. The store doesn't close until nine on weeknights, ten on the weekends.

Gavin is sitting straight up now, his head hanging a bit, clearly still working out of sleep to catch up with my breakdown. "It's temporary."

"How long can we do this? How can we keep a relationship going when we don't see each other? And we're still broke!"

With a heavy sigh, he opens his arms. "Come here." When I make no movement, he pulls me against him. He strokes my hair while I blubber against his chest. "Listen, this is all temporary. I know it's really hard right now, but we'll get through."

An even, or full, breath is hard to come by. "How?"

"Because we will. Because we want to be together. We wanted this. We knew it would be hard, we knew there would be challenges. No, we don't see each other much anymore, but my schedule will be a lot less next semester."

"You think we can make it the rest of the semester like this? We're only a month and a half in!"

"You think we're not going to make it? Like our relationship?"

"What do you think I mean? We barely see each other. We haven't even had sex in three weeks. THREE WEEKS! We're not some old married couple, Gavin. We've only been together for two years." All the tension, the unsurety, the yelling, sets a tremble rolling through my body.

Putting his hands on my shoulders, he pushes me backward, lowering his head to meet my eye. "Mackenzie, look at me." His voice is calm, but firm. "We will get through this. I know it's hard right now. I know we don't see each other, and I miss you. But I like the time we do have. Most nights, you fall asleep in my lap, but that's become one of my favorite things. These are times we're not going to get back. These are the hardships people talk about when a couple first starts out. I know we will get through it. And trust me, I'm acutely aware of *exactly* how long it's been since we've had sex."

All I can do is look up at him as my lip starts to quiver again, not feeling any reassurance from his words.

Sighing, he pulls me back to him as a new set of tears breaks free. Leaning back against the pillows, he keeps me tightly against him. The steady movement of his hand sliding down my head, to my lower back and up again, makes the tears slow. As the hitching of my breath starts to level out to smooth, even breaths, I drift off to sleep.

By some miracle, Gavin and I make it through the semester, though it's hard on our relationship. After that night, Gavin and I had a chat, where he revealed that he felt frustrated that I had such little faith in our love for each other and the strength of our relationship to be able to withstand a difficult situation. Somehow, I was able to convince him that it was actually the opposite, that I was worried we were losing that connection, that fire, that had brought us together and made our love so strong.

The winter break is upon us, and it's six weeks long. We've decided to devote it to reigniting our relationship. Working only as much as we have to, with no classes, we have extra time to dedicate to one another. Friday afternoons we set aside as time for each other, clearing it from work. Since we still don't have a lot of extra money, we do a lot of at home dates. A few of which involve cooking together and trying to become better at it.

I have a tendency to get frustrated in the kitchen. A lot of things come easily to me, but cooking isn't one of them, and I don't like that fact. The only solace I find is that Gavin isn't much better.

"Well, I'm okay with peanut butter and jelly sandwiches for dinner every night," he says while wiping his hands after another failed dinner attempt.

Huffing through my nose, I glare at him. "It's not funny! We can't survive on that. We need to eat real food. I hate that I can't figure this out." Anger rises in my chest that my mother never taught me cooking basics. After the catastrophe that was teaching Shannon to cook, which lead to the fire department coming, she didn't want to even attempt it. Not that I complained as a teenager. But now? I wish I knew at least some easy meals.

"It's not an equation you can solve; there's no answer at the end of the riddle. It takes practice."

"Yeah, well, the practice just frustrates me."

"Oh. Then maybe we should make it fun." There's a hint

of something in his voice that I'm too frustrated to try to decipher.

"And how exactly do you plan to do that?" I ask with a stubborn huff.

Before I know what's happening, a handful of potatoes hits me in the side of the face. There's been some discussion as to how they turned out to be both crunchy and mushy at the same time.

My whole body freezes, icing over my veins. For a second, anger surges through me. I'm not in the mood for this. But then again...

Grabbing a handful of very overcooked carrots, I throw them in his general direction. Some of them mush into his cheek, causing me to burst into a round of laughter.

With a firm swipe of his hand, he wipes the carrots off his face and onto the floor. "Oh, you think that's funny, do you?" His voice is low and steely, but there's playfulness dancing through his eyes. Before I can react, or get away, he grabs my wrist and yanks me against him. Holding me tightly with one arm, the other reaches back for more potatoes. "I'm going to enjoy this," he says with a devilish smirk, as he wipes potatoes across my face and into my hair.

Leaning up, I wipe my face against him, smearing potato onto his face too. "I like sharing."

Lunging for the counter where the carrots are, he grabs a handful and mashes them in his hand, dripping it onto my head and pulling out the front of my shirt as he wipes his hands along my chest.

"Nice and mushy," he murmurs with a smirk. Instead of pulling his hand out of my shirt, he leaves it there, lingering. Standing in place, we look at each other for a moment before his mouth crashes down on mine, his hand sliding under my bra, fingers grazing against my nipples as they harden at his touch. A tiny moan pulls from my chest as his mouth forces mine open, tongue sliding along mine. His mouth tastes like potatoes, that in addition to being both mushy and crunchy, are way too salty.

Separating from him, I link my fingers through his. "Let's go take a shower." My voice is low and sultry, filled with need.

Backing up a step, he furrows his brow at me. "A shower?"

"Yeah, a shower, together. It'll be fun."

"What? No."

And just like that, the moment is over, the fire in me doused. "No?"

"Showers aren't for sex." Realizing then that he still has his hand in my shirt, he removes it.

"Says who?"

"Says me."

"So all those people who have sex in the shower, what about them?"

"It's not something I'm comfortable with."

"Um, okay. Can you explain why?" Color me all sorts of confused. The fact that we've only had sex in a bed is something I thought is just out of convenience, or time. Not some sort of moral objection to anywhere else.

"I'm just not."

"Okay. Well, what about the floor, then?" Maybe I can salvage this still. If he puts his hands on me again, I know we can save it.

But he looks appalled. "The floor? Really?"

"What's wrong with the floor?"

"Can you remember the last time we *cleaned* the floor? Because I can't."

"So let's put a blanket down."

He looks at me, stunned. "Who are you? Where is this coming from?"

I jerk back. "What, are you serious? This is coming from the girl who wants to have sex with her boyfriend. I don't understand the big deal of the shower or the floor. It's fun. It's exciting."

Shaking his head, he plants his hands on his hips. "It's degrading."

"Degrading? Are you being serious right now? How is it degrading?"

"I just don't think it's right."

"So okay, no shower, no floor. Where is it acceptable?"

"The bed."

"And?"

"That's it. The bed."

My eyes grow wide. "How has this never come up before?"

"That's a good question. I thought we were on the same page."

"Well, I guess not. I'm sorry if I think it's fun and sexy to have sex somewhere besides the bed."

"Are you speaking from experience?"

My jaw drops as a breath puffs out, and I stare at him, absolutely dumbfounded. "I'm not answering that question. We've been over this. We agreed, no more talking about my past. If you haven't had sex anywhere besides a bed, and you want to share that information, fine. But I'm not asking, so don't ask me. You've already proven you can't handle it if you don't like the answer you receive."

"So that means yes."

"No, that means I'm not fucking telling you. Maybe we had sex a hundred times in a hundred different places. Maybe we had sex five times, all in the bed. It's not something I'm going to talk about with you." Growling, I spin around, hand gripping the counter. I'm vaguely aware that I'm still covered in food.

I turn back to face him, keeping my voice level. "My past is just that, the past. It doesn't matter right here, right now. I want to have sex with my boyfriend. I thought it might be fun. If that's not something you're interested in, fine. But don't drag my sexual history into this. You agreed. You agreed that you could and would get over it. It's been a year and a half since then. There wasn't an expiration date on that agreement."

His eyes sear into mine. He looks mad, hateful even. I hadn't even noticed his body was tense until he visibly relaxes. But his eyes don't. "You should go shower. I'll wait."

"Don't you think we should-"

"I don't...want to talk about it right now. I need to decompress a little."

Nodding, I run my tongue across my teeth. "Okay." Heading off to shower, I stop before walking through the door, turning on my heel. "Gavin? I love you. I'm here, loving you, wanting to be with you, despite not having money, or knowing how to cook real food. Isn't that enough? Doesn't that say enough?"

His eyes soften slightly. "I love you too."

When I get out of the shower, Gavin has already cleaned up the mess and thrown away what we tried to cook. "I splurged and ordered a pizza. It should be here in a half hour. I'm going to go shower." Walking past me, he touches my arm and gives me a quick peck on the cheek.

Sitting on the couch, hands between my knees, I bite my lip, waiting for Gavin to come out of the bathroom. I'm not sure where his head is at, but I desperately need to know. During our last conversation, he had assured me that he could handle my background, that he could get over it, let it go. He agreed not to bring it up again. What if this is just another thing about that time that he dwells on? What if he decides that it is, in fact, too much for him to deal with?

I spend so much time spinning in my head, worrying over all the facets of what could happen and what he could say that I don't hear him turn off the shower or come into the living room, jumping when he says my name.

"Sorry, didn't think I'd startle you. Do you want to get drinks and napkins? I'll load up the show we've been watching."

Staring at him for an extra second, I'm not sure if I should mention what happened or just move on. If he's moving on, then maybe so should I.

"Sure." Jumping up from the couch, I busy myself getting napkins and sodas. I've just shut the fridge when the doorbell rings. Perfect timing to help us avoid getting back into our conversation while having nothing else to do when waiting for the food.

While we don't order food often, saving all the money we can for when school starts again in January, after the fiasco over dinner and the argument, I know it was easiest, and I'm thankful Gavin ordered as my stomach growls.

Sitting on the couch, we eat in silence, watching some show about space that we'd started watching. I can barely focus, still thinking about what Gavin is going to say.

When he finishes eating, he leans back against the couch. Elbows on my knees, I lean forward, not quite sure what to do with myself. After a minute, realizing I'm not going to move back, Gavin takes my shoulders and pulls me against him, wrapping an arm around me and drawing lazy circles on my upper arm.

Snuggling against his chest, feeling the steady rhythm of his heart, a sense of peace washes over me. Maybe we didn't sort through our argument...maybe there are leftover emotions to work out, but right now, this is what we both need.

The heavenly scent of coffee draws me from sleep. Sitting up, I find myself in bed. With a stretch and a run of my fingers through my mess of hair, I get out of bed and follow the smell of coffee like there's a cartoon line in the sky. Gavin's standing at the stove, attempting to cook something. He must have carried me into our room at some point during the night.

Though I try to be quiet, he must have heard me coming since he turns around as I enter the kitchen. "Pancakes." Tipping the spatula to the pan, he smiles at me.

With syrup, the pancakes aren't *terrible*. While we want to learn how to make them from scratch, figuring it will save us money in the long run, right now, it just means they aren't very good.

"Thanks for the pancakes." Silence shrouded us while we ate, the only sounds were of forks hitting the plate. This is the first I've really spoken to him since sitting down at the table.

Frowning, he puts his hands in his pockets and leans against the counter near where I'm cleaning up. "Sorry they weren't very good."

Shrugging, I run a sponge over a plate. "They weren't so bad."

"I wanted to make you something special. I know how much you like pancakes. I just wish I could make them better."

"Well, it was nice of you to make something for me. We'll get there. I hope." I'm not so sure myself. Part of me is afraid we'll be eating terrible food for years to come.

"What do you want to do today?" He had insisted we both take the day off from work, wanting us to have one Saturday together because we haven't in months. As much as I'm worried about us having the money to handle it, I miss him, so

I had agreed. That was before our disagreement last night, which I'm still not sure where we stand on the matter.

"Oh. I don't care, I'm flexible."

"I want to do something you want today. So you think about it. Why don't you start with a nice relaxing shower. I won't even bother you."

My eyebrows knit together. "What are you up to?"

"I have no idea what you're talking about. You work hard, go to classes. We're having a day together, so I want you to have a good day, to relax."

Keeping the heat low, to keep costs equally low, I'm almost always cold, and a hot shower sounds nice on this especially chilly morning. "Okay." Giving him a quick kiss, I slip away and into the bathroom. There are tiny tea candles all over the sink and toilet. My heart flutters. When did he even have a chance to do this?

Taking a long shower, standing under the hot water for a little extra time, the tension slips out of my body and down the drain with the soapy water.

After I finish doing my hair, I walk out to find Gavin sitting on the couch, reading the newspaper.

"How was your shower?" Folding the paper into his lap, he looks up at me. His face is completely solid, no hint of a smile or that he had done anything.

"When did you do that? It was so sweet of you."

His brow furrows together. "Do what? What are you talking about?"

Tilting my head at him, I walk over to the couch and straddle his lap as he puts the paper to the side. His hands glide down to my lower back as I lean forward to him. "Thank you for making my shower special," I say against his lips.

His lips lock on mine as one hand slides up to hold the back of my head, pulling it against him as his tongue seeks mine. Tilting my hips forward, I lift slightly before easing back down onto his lap. He hardens against my thigh, and I smile against his lips. Before I can even ask him if he wants to take this to the bedroom, he stands, holding me tight against him, his lips never leaving mine.

When he lays me down on the bed, he kisses along my jaw to my neck, hand gliding up my shirt, and he presses his hips into me. The need to have his skin on mine sears through me, and I pull at the hem of his shirt.

Reaching over his shoulders, he tugs it over his head, his hands flying down to unsnap my pants and send my shirt sailing across the room. A smile spans his face as he notices I chose to forego a bra. His tongue wraps around my nipple as I gasp, parting my legs for him to fall against me, his erection pressing into my pelvis.

The roughness of his jeans rubs against my palm as I slide it along his erection, grasping him firmly and causing his breath to catch. Quickly, he hops off me, shoving his pants to the ground and tearing mine off in one quick movement. Chills rush down my spine as he climbs back on the bed, his mouth grazing my skin as he slowly slides himself over me.

Gently, I trace my fingers up his arms and over his shoulders, feeling his taut muscles. I lean up so I can graze my lips against his, falling back onto the bed as he tries to close his mouth around mine. A smirk spreads across his face as his mouth crashes down with an urgency, immediately pushing it open with his tongue.

Sliding his hand down to rest on my hip, he eases into me.

My head tilts back as my body arches up to meet his. He trails one finger gently down the side of my face, grazing it across my lower lip. "I love you, Mackenzie."

Before I can answer, he starts thrusting hard and fast inside me. I grip his shoulders, his muscles shifting beneath my fingers.

There's something frenzied in his movements, a desperation in the way he wraps his hands around my shoulders and grunts in my ear.

His movements are lacking their normal fluidity and gracefulness. The connection between us is almost nonexistent. Normally, it's potent, tangible, almost something you can feel in the air around us.

Today? It's nowhere to be found.

With that link between us missing, I'm having a hard time getting into it, and thus having a hard time enjoying myself. The sex isn't bad, but I'm not sure I'll get where I need to be to orgasm.

Gavin seems to have no idea, completely lost in the act. So, for his sake, I fake it. I'm not sure if it's the right move, the right answer, but he seems to need this right now.

"Fuck, Gavin." Was that whiney enough? Will he even notice if it wasn't? To add to the charade, I arch my back and drag my nails down his back, moaning loudly.

When he buries his face in my neck and grunts before slowing, I know my show was convincing. That, or he just doesn't care.

Have we drifted this far apart?

Later on in the evening, we're snuggled on the couch watching a movie when big, fat, heavy snowflakes start drifting slowly from the sky. It hasn't snowed yet this winter, which is surprising for our part of upstate New York.

The first snow of the season is always my favorite.

"Let's go outside!" Gavin's already thrown off the blanket, pulling me to stand next to him.

"What?"

"Yeah, come on, it's snowing. You love the first snow."

"I do, but you don't. You don't like any snow, really."

He shrugs, holding out a hand to pull me up from the couch.

"Well, okay. You don't have to ask me twice!"

We loop on scarves, pull on coats and hats and head out into the winter wonderland. It's already started to accumulate a tiny bit. It's the perfectly peaceful snow, where the world around you is silent and all you can hear is the gentle puff of sound the snowflakes make as they fall to the ground.

Arms wide at my side, face tipped up to the sky, I twirl around as a smile spreads across my face. The icy cold of tiny little flakes peppers my skin, melting immediately.

When I look back down, Gavin is down on one knee. My hands fly to my mouth. "Gavin, what are you—"

"I love you, Mackenzie. I love you so much. I know we've only been together for two years. I know we're still in school. But I don't care. I cannot picture my life without you. I don't want to. I know times are tough for us right now, and I know we don't know what the future holds for us after graduation. But I know that I cannot possibly live without you. Please, make me the happiest man in the world and marry me?"

I'm completely struck. My brain can't even think of a coherent word, let alone phrase. *Marry me*? He wants to marry me? But we're so young! We've only been together two years. We're still in school. It's all the things he said and more.

There's a tiny sliver of doubt working its way into my mind. Can we make it? Is this some sort of act of desperation? It's been an incredibly hard year, and we're only part way through it.

But I love him. I love him so much. Imagining a day without him seems impossible.

"Yes." It comes out barely a whisper.

But Gavin hears me, and his face breaks into the biggest smile I've ever seen. He slips the ring on my finger and stands up to pull me against him, kissing the side of my head, just above my ear.

Staying in Gavin's embrace, I push my hand out in front of me, trying to get a look at the ring. It's not much, a simple, small, solitaire on a white gold band, but I have no idea how he could have afforded it. We have no money. Unless he's been saving it for months.

"How'd you afford this?" It pours out before I can stop it.

Immediately his cheeks pinken, and not from the cold. "Um, about that." Taking a deep breath, he holds it for a beat before it leaves smokey tendrils drifting up into the air. "My parents helped me out. They gave me the money." My eyes narrow at the admission.

"What? Why would they do that? They hate me."

"They don't ha—never mind. It doesn't matter. They did it because I told them it was what I wanted."

"And they just willingly gave you money for an engagement ring to somebody they don't even like?"

The look that flashes through his eyes tells me it wasn't quite that easy. "They said they weren't going to be involved anymore. That if I was going to insist on proposing to you, they weren't going to help out financially again. That they weren't going to be part of my life anymore."

My eyes widen, and I push away from him. "What? You gave up a relationship with your parents? Why would you do that?" My voice is raised and anger bubbles in my chest, but I'm not quite sure why. Yes, what Gavin's parents are doing is ridiculous and wrong, but why am I mad at Gavin?

His brow furrows as he takes a step toward me with outstretched arms. "Because I love you."

"But why? Why now? Why not wait?"

Now he looks hurt. "You sound like you're on their side. They said exactly the same thing."

"I'm not on their side, Gavin, but I don't understand! What, do you think you're not going to love me in two years or something? When I'm not in school anymore?" I take a step toward him.

"Of course I will."

"Then why now? Why right now?"

"Because I wanted to now. It's been a hard few months for us, and we've made it through."

"Barely."

His eyes shoot to mine, anger raging through his irises. "Well, I'm sorry that things haven't been perfect for you, princess. But this is life. Things get tough."

"Oh, come on, don't give me that bullshit. What would you know about things being tough? You grew up with plenty of money and plenty of things that you wanted and everything you needed. You and I both know that we've *both* had every-thing paid for until we got this apartment." I open my arms wide to show the space, even though we're outside.

"That's besides the point. It's part of life, part of growing up. Coming out of your parents' shadow, your parents' care."

"Yeah, but not out of their lives! Gavin, they're your *parents*. I know you love me, and I love you too, but I am not worth sacrificing a relationship with your parents for."

"I guess we feel differently about our relationship, then." Without looking at me, he walks straight into the apartment, slamming the door shut.

With a drop of my head and a heavy sigh, I follow him inside. Some proposal this has turned out to be. What should be an extremely exciting and memorable moment has turned into an argument. Memorable for sure, but for the wrong reasons.

I find him already in bed. Changing into my pajamas, I climb in with him, not sure what else to do. He's far on his side, so I opt to go more toward the middle, hoping at some point maybe he'll want to be closer to me than the feet of space he clearly wants now.

"Is this because of our fight the other day? Is this because of my past?" My voice is calm, quiet.

"So what if it is?"

My eyes widen and shock winds through me as I turn to face him, though I'm met with his tense back. "Gavin, that is *not* a reason to get engaged! Getting engaged, or even married, isn't going to fix your issues and concerns with my history."

"Well, at least then I'll feel comfortable and know that you'll always be mine!" I flinch as he yells, barely glancing over his shoulder to look at me.

I don't know what to say. Or really, I don't know what *more* to say. Because I've said it all. If he doesn't know that I love him, that I'm over Jake by now, then I'm not sure he'll ever really know.

Aside from this one Jake hang up, even being broke, our relationship is great. I said yes because, overall, despite the hardships, I'm happy and I love him.

But with this? This apparent inability to move beyond my first love, giving up his parents for me, proposing because he doesn't trust that he has me...

With it all swirling through my head, I lie here and wonder if maybe I made a mistake.

TWENTY-ONE

My twenty-first birthday is six weeks after Gavin's and my...disagreement. In that time frame, things have been strained, to say the least. We had opted to stay home, just with each other, for both Christmas and New Years. It allowed us to work the days before and after, which we desperately needed and still do. After the argument, we both picked up extra hours, claiming to make up for the lost time, but I really think it was just an avoidance tactic. We also happened to pick up opposing schedules.

Gavin doesn't go as big for my birthday as he has in previous years. Despite the extra work, money is still tight, so he wasn't able to get six days' worth of little gifts, possibly didn't even want to. Instead, he leaves notes for me to find each day.

Since we're both finally old enough to go to the bars legally, we set aside some cash for a night out. We invite Jessica and Nate, who had started seeing each other after my party last year, and a few other friends from school and work to join us.

"What time are we meeting everybody?" Even though I

know the answer, I have to break the hours' worth of silence we've been sitting in. Gavin's standing in the kitchen, leaning against the counter, reading the paper while I sit on the couch, twiddling my thumbs.

"Nine." He doesn't even look up at me to respond.

"Where?"

"The Tavern. They give out the birthday glasses, remember?" There is a bite to his tone that makes me cringe.

"Okay, I get you're still mad, but it *is* my birthday. Any chance you could be, I don't know, nice?"

Dropping his head, he sighs heavily. "I'm sorry. It's just hard right now. I asked you to marry me, to fucking *marry* me. And it became a fight. A *fight*. On what should have been one of the happiest days. And sure, you said yes. But do you even mean it? Do you want to marry me?"

"Of course I do! How could you even think that?" Jumping to my feet, I spin to face him, my heart dropping at both his words and the look of absolute defeat etched into his features.

"I don't know, Mack, how about because you weren't happy and giddy and excited. You asked about affording it, and then talked about how young we are and how I shouldn't have even considered choosing you, the love of my life, over my parents." He practically spits the words out at me as he throws the paper onto the counter and walks over to the table, closing the space between us by a few feet.

To me, those were all legitimate questions and fears. His frustration, while understandable, is stressful and confusing. "I said yes, didn't I?"

"Yeah, yeah, ya did. But do you still wish you had?"

I don't know what to say. In the past few weeks, I *have* questioned things. A lot. At one point, I had thought that maybe it's a bad idea. And like most other major life crossroads, I had spoken with Anna about it. For the first time, she wasn't filled with sage advice, not quite knowing what to say. I think she was just shrouded in shock. She brought up the same concerns, but ultimately doesn't know what the right course of action is. She asked if I love him, which she knows I do. But I know that she meant do I love him enough. And I knew what she was getting at.

Do I love him as much as I had once loved Jake.

But that's not a fair comparison to make. Because I was with Jake when I was a kid in high school. And while I am still young, I've grown more into an adult over the past year than I had in all of my years at home combined. I wanted to marry Jake back then. But I want to marry Gavin, and only Gavin, now.

The problem isn't so much whether or not I *want* to marry him. It's if now is the right time, and the reasoning behind the urgency, the rush, makes me question it even more.

"Your hesitation says it all." His voice drips with irritation.

"Gavin, that's not fair. You laid a lot on me here. Don't you get that?" While I'm trying to be patient with him, it's starting to wear thin.

"I think it's pretty simple, Mackenzie. You either want to marry me or you don't."

"It is *not* that simple. Not even a little bit."

"How? How is it not?"

I stare blankly at him. Does he really not understand? Does he not see the problems in getting engaged under the circumstances we did?

"How is it that simple when your parents basically said they won't speak to you again? How is it that simple when your reasoning is some fear or insecurity that I'm still hung up on my high school boyfriend, who I haven't spoken to in four years? Somebody who I don't even think about, but you seem to spend enough time thinking about for both of us."

"My parents will get over it. And how do I know you don't think about him? How do I know that you aren't—" With a tick of his jaw, he turns away from me.

"Aren't what? What are you not saying?" I take a few tentative steps in his direction, trying desperately to get to the bottom of this.

He grips the back of a chair, his muscles taut, head hung low. An eerie quiet has overtaken him, and he won't look at me.

I jump when he shoves the chair against the table.

Still refusing to even glance in my direction, he sighs. "How do I know you're not just waiting until you can find a way back to him?" It's so quiet, I'm not even sure I heard him correctly. But when he turns slightly to look back at me, I know that I had. And everything inside my body crystalizes.

Carefully, almost timidly, I complete the walk over to him. I know he'd never hurt me, but I don't want him to leave. When he won't meet my eyes, I wrap my arms around his neck.

How can he really think that I'd leave him for Jake? And how can I convince him I won't?

Before I have a chance to explain, he pulls away, taking my arms from around his neck and putting them at my sides. With a frown, he stalks away, slamming the door to the bathroom before turning on the shower.

All I can do is collapse onto the couch, staring blankly at the wall.

Is this the end? Am I losing everything?

We make it to the bar a little after nine, after having barely spoken another word to each other the rest of the day. How

I'm going to pretend to be happy when all I want to do is fall apart, I have no idea.

Jessica immediately senses the tension, but she also immediately hones in on my ring. I haven't taken it off; I don't want to, because I *want* to marry Gavin.

Right now, I'm not really in the mood for celebrating, my birthday or an engagement.

She pulls me aside within ten minutes. "Okay, tell me what's going on."

"I don't know what you're talking about."

"Oh, bullshit, Mack. Tell me. You know I'll get it out of you one way or another, but if you tell me now, I can help you tonight. Run interference if I need to."

Knowing there's no use arguing with her, I sigh. "Gavin proposed." I hold up the ring and put on a fake excitement act. "And then we got into a huge fight. His parents basically cut him off. And we're young, we're so young. I still have two years of school left. It seems rushed. And he still has a hang-up on Jake. He said something about wondering if I'm just waiting for a way to get back to Jake." Dropping my chin to my chest, I shake my head.

I expect Jessica to respond immediately. For her to say he's crazy, and that I'm right. But she remains quiet and chews on the inside of her cheek for a second, looking for something in my eyes. "Are you sure you're not?"

"That I'm not what?" My face scrunches in confusion.

With down-turned lips, she tilts her head at me, and my brows shoot sky high as my heart thuds.

"Are you serious? Why do I have to convince everybody that I'm over my ex-boyfriend, the man who left me broken-hearted and shattered? Who I haven't spoken to in over four years. Can somebody please explain this to me?"

"I think it's just the story. I know he broke your heart, I do, but, Mackenzie, *I* was in *tears* over it. The love you had for each other..." Her hands fly to her chest. "It was something amazing and deep. I could tell from the way you talked about it how much it meant to you, how much he meant to you. I'm sure Gavin could too the first time. And don't forget, you didn't want to go out with him at first, even after two years of not talking to Jake."

"It wasn't that I was still hung up on Jake, though, it was just the idea of being hurt again. And I know you heard the love story, but you *watched* me fall in love with Gavin. I mean, does it seem like I'm faking or something? I'm so confused about how anybody could think I don't love him." All of my blood is coursing through my body at lightning speed as my breaths become shallow.

"Oh, Mack, it's not that you don't love him. It's that you don't love him as much."

Raising a hand, I shake my head vehemently. "It's not a comparison. I'm not choosing between two guys here. I'm not even choosing between a possibility and what I have. I have chosen. And I've chosen Gavin. I'm happy with my decision. I'm happy with Gavin. I'm not waiting for something to happen, for something to change, for a random phone call from Jake that he made a mistake. I closed off those feelings and that part of my heart from Jake a long time ago. And it's sealed shut."

With narrowed eyes, she looks me over for a minute. "Are you sure?"

"God, I need a fucking drink." Rolling my eyes, I back away as my stomach starts to churn.

Clearly getting the message, Jessica insists that everybody gather around the bar while I order my first legal drink. She stands next to me, taking a picture. Gavin stands a few people away, but I catch his eye as everybody else cheers and screams around me. His face is solemn, sad. Holding up his drink to me, he tips his head down before taking a sip.

Everything about this feels so strange. I'm surrounded by my closest friends and my boyfriend, fiancé, is the farthest one from me. He's the only person I truly care to celebrate with, and he's the one out of reach.

As the night wears on, I get increasingly hammered. So much so that I'm having trouble standing by the time the night is over. It seems Gavin had anticipated as much and stopped drinking early on. Jessica helps me walk over to him when she decides I've had enough and unceremoniously tosses me into his arms.

Seamlessly looping an arm around my waist, Gavin pulls me against him. Jessica already helped me into my coat, so we leave, with Gavin thanking everybody for coming to wish me a happy twenty-first birthday. It's a good thing he takes over as I'm slumped in his hold and barely able to put words together.

We start walking slowly back to our apartment, which thankfully is only a few blocks away.

"It's cold," I whine as I snuggle in closer.

"I know. We're almost there, though." His voice is calm, even, but there's a loss of caring.

"Why are you helping me? I thought you hated me?" I tend to get childish when I drink. Obviously, I know he doesn't hate me, but he also hasn't been nice to me all day.

"I'm helping you because you're my girlfriend, and I love you." With an adjustment of his arm around me, he pulls me into his side. His warmth helps ward off some of the biting cold.

"Fiancée," I correct him.

He looks down at me. "Are you?"

"Am I what?" With a hiccup, I lean against him a little

more. Now he's supporting almost all my body weight and acting like it's nothing.

"My fiancée."

I hold up the ring. "Well, yeah."

"Wearing a diamond ring doesn't make you my fiancée."

"I said yes, didn't I?" Are we really about to get into this here, on the sidewalk as we walk home in the freezing cold, on an early February night, while I'm drunk?

"You did. But did you mean it?"

"Of course I meant it."

"Well, I like to think I'm usually pretty respectful of you when you're drunk, but I'm going to take a little advantage of you tonight and go for your inability to lie. Are you using me to kill time until you can get back to Jake? Or until he comes to find you?"

"No." I hiccup again. Right now, I'm not entirely sure that I'm not going to be sick.

"Are you over him? Completely and truly over him?"

"I'm in love with you."

He nods and chews his lip. "That doesn't really answer the question, though." I have to hold in my huff at his incessance.

"I have been over him for a long time. But he will always mean something to me. I can't say he won't, because he will, because once upon a time, he meant something to me." I'm not really sure I'm making any sense, but I've said this all before.

"Do you love me more than him?"

"I don't know how to explain that. It's different. You're different people, so the love is different."

"The love can be different, but still more or less."

"Haven't you ever loved somebody?"

"I have, but none of them compared to what I feel for you. None. Not even close. Which is why I'm struggling. You can't just say it's more. It's different, you're happy with me, you aren't waiting for him. But that doesn't mean that this is your truest love. I'm not sure if I can live with that."

"I wanted to marry him when I was with him. But I'm with you now, and I want to marry you." Oops, that didn't come out right.

"So if we break up, will you want to marry the new guy because you're with him?"

"That's not what I meant. I'm not able to make very clear thoughts at the moment." I shake my head, trying to backtrack and come up with a way out of this hole I've dug myself.

"See, I'm worried that you *were* clear."

I let out a huff through my nose and tilt my face up to watch the white tendrils float to the sky. We're finally back at our apartment and Gavin keeps an arm around my waist as he opens the door. As I walk through the threshold, I trip.

Strong hands on my waist prevent me from face planting into the floor. Gavin pulls me to standing and I sway in his grasp. With a sigh, he scoops me into his arms, kicking the door shut behind him. He carries me into our room and lays me on the bed, brushing some hair out of my eyes.

Gently, he takes off my shoes, tossing them on the floor with loud thuds. Taking my hand, he pulls me to sitting and takes off my coat. Then he walks over to the dresser and pulls out a t-shirt, coming back and carefully taking off my clothes. I want to tell him I can do it myself, that I'm not *that* far gone, but I like that he's helping me, being nice to me, being close to me. Touching me. It makes a warm sensation crawl through my body, and I'm pretty sure it's love and not alcohol.

Once my clothes are off, he slips the t-shirt over my head. It takes me until my arms are through it to realize it's one of his. He pulls back the covers and adjusts my legs, slipping me in, and giving me a tiny kiss on the head before he walks out, not saying a word.

A few minutes later, he returns with a glass of water and a garbage pail. "Just in case," he says quietly as he points to it.

With his head down, he sits on the edge of the bed and sighs, hands between his legs. "I just don't know, Mackenzie. I love you. I know you love me. But I wonder if it's enough. I wonder if that part of your life is really over, or if it's just on pause. If he showed up tomorrow, begged you to come back to him, to be with him again, if you would."

I know he's not looking for an answer, that he's talking out loud. And I'm thankful he doesn't want one, because thanks to my inability to lie, I wouldn't be able to hide my answer.

That I'm not sure.

The worst part is that I didn't even know I had even a sliver of doubt until this very moment. A cool tendril of guilt weaves its way through my body, causing me to shiver. I'd closed my eyes when Gavin started talking, and I'm glad I did, because I can't see his face right now. I don't know what to say, so I decide to say nothing at all.

It's the first birthday Gavin and I have shared together that we aren't intimate. Not only that, but we're barely on speaking terms.

My head is spinning, and for more reasons than just the copious amounts of alcohol in my system.

In April, Gavin decides to take a trip with some friends. Though better because we're talking, spending more time together, and officially engaged, there's still a tension between us.

When he brought the trip up a week and a half after my birthday, he hadn't planned to go. But things being what they are, he feels he needs to. It's one last trip before graduation, before jobs start. And he needs time. Time away from me. Time to think. Time to just relax and have fun. They'll be camping and hiking, with no cell reception, which means no communication between us.

Over the course of the week that he's gone, I work, a lot. And Jess comes over whenever she can. I'm a nervous wreck, so sure he's going to come back and break up with me, take back his engagement ring, and leave me brokenhearted. All because of somebody I had once loved, but had gotten over long ago.

But when Gavin gets home, he's a completely different person. He walks in with a broad smile on his face as soon as he sees me.

Quickly putting down the book I'm reading, I stand to greet him, a bit startled at his arrival. Anxiety creeps through my body as I pull at my shirt sleeves.

"Oh, hi. I wasn't expecting you for a few hours still. Sorry, I meant to clea—"

In five strides, he crosses the room, one hand cupping my face while the other wraps around my waist and pulls me into a deep kiss.

I hesitate at first, since this was not at all the greeting I was expecting. I'd prepared myself to go through another verbal sparring match, going round for round until we were both too tired to keep going. But my body catches up, and I throw my arms around his neck, pushing up onto my toes as my mouth parts for his, and his tongue curls along mine.

His hands slide down under my thighs and lift me up as I loop my legs around his waist. Speed walking, he takes me to the bedroom and sets me down on the bed. He quickly strips off his clothes, then pulls my shirt over my head, hand flying around my back to unhook my bra before throwing it to the floor. Tugging me to stand, he pushes himself right against me as he runs his fingertips down my chest and stomach to the button of my pants, tearing them open and dropping them to the floor. With his hands on my back, he presses himself against me as he slowly lowers me to the bed.

He wastes no time closing his mouth over my nipple as his hand drifts down between my legs. His fingers dive inside me and move in tandem with his tongue as I squirm under him.

For weeks, this has been all I've wanted, all I've dreamed about. Our sex life has been almost nonexistent since our fight, and certainly nothing this full of need and desire.

I'm vaguely aware of his scratchy face, not having shaved in the week he was gone. But at the moment, I don't care. His whole body could be covered in the scratchy stubble, and I wouldn't care.

With one giant intake of air, I dig my nails into his biceps as my breathy whimper fills the room.

Gavin releases my nipple, kissing hungrily up my chest to claim my mouth with his as he slides into me without hesitation. A weak moan dies against his lips.

Keeping his mouth on mine, tongue curling around mine, he moves inside me at the perfect pace. The telling sensation starts to build in my pelvis again as I pull away from his mouth, sighing, letting out tiny sounds with each exhale. His lips find my throat as I tighten around him and moan out my release that flows through my body.

He groans against my neck as he finishes, then drops his head to my shoulder. Kissing along my collarbone, he rolls off of me.

With one hand on his chest and the other flung across his eyes, he lies on his back for a moment, panting heavily.

I'm suddenly aware that he hasn't said a word to me since he walked in the door. Which means he hasn't said anything to me since before he left, a week ago. Was this happy sex? Or was this goodbye sex?

Rolling to face me, he leans in and rests his lips against mine, smiling as he pulls away and brushes some hair from my face. "I missed you." His first words to me in a week, and they make my heart flutter.

"You did?"

His brows pull together and his forehead crinkles in confusion. "Of course I did." He takes my hand in his, running his thumb along the back. "Mackenzie, I have never, ever doubted my feelings for you. Hell, I haven't even really doubted your feelings for me. I've just wondered if they're enough. But I came home early because I missed you, so much. I needed to be with you again. I needed to be here. To talk to you about everything."

With a deep breath, I steal my emotions and try to steady my heart as it tries to beat out of my chest. "Okay. Should we get dressed and go in the living room for this?"

"Absolutely not, no way." Giving a solid tug, he pulls me against him, tracing circles on my arm.

"You seem like you're in a better mood."

I feel his lips spread into a smile against my head. "I really am. It's kind of amazing what a week in the woods can do for you. And it was nice to just chill with the guys, ya know? No distractions. Just drinking and shooting the shit around the fire."

He's quiet for a minute, his fingers stilling for a second, before they resume their round path on my arm. "We found a few hiking spots that were really nice, and I got a few awesome pictures. Really, I just had time to clear my head. To be alone with my thoughts, work it over without a distraction. I was away from you, and I think that helped."

All my breath sticks in my lungs. Being away from me helped? Instead of asking, I let him continue.

"Seeing you made it harder somehow. Being away, it made

me realize the little things you do and say every single day that show me how much you truly love me. And I was able to think, really think back to our time together. And you're right. Never once have you brought up Jake or compared anything to that relationship. Not since we first started talking and you told me you were working through the emotions of something that was complicated and then told me about it. It was me. It was all me."

Wow, it must have been some trip. "You realized a lot on your own up there."

"Well, Ben's a good listener." I shake with his chuckle. "I actually think he and Anna would get along great. We should try to hook them up at our wedding."

Popping up, I lean on my elbow so I can look at him. "Our wedding?" It comes out on a puff of air as I can barely breathe.

His eyes meet mine. "Yeah. Assuming you'll still have me after all the nonsense I've put you through over the past few months."

"I will. Of course I will. I just want to be sure, you're sure."

Matching my stance, he leans on his elbow, trailing his thumb down my cheek and against my lower lip. "Mackenzie, I have never been more sure of anything in my life." He brushes away the tears that spring from my eyes. "I think we should wait, though. There's no reason to rush. Let's wait until you're done with school. It's only another year or so."

"I'll have grad classes too, though."

He lifts one shoulder to his ear as his gaze trails down my body and back up. "We can find a way to make it work. I want to marry you. I'm sorry about everything. I'm ready to let go of the past, I promise. Ben made me realize how incredibly stupid I was being. He even said if I didn't come back and let it all go and marry you, that he would."

My eyes grow wide.

"Don't worry, I didn't give him intimate details or anything. Just that you had a pretty significant relationship and love that ended in a way that was difficult. That you had a hard time after it ended. But he asked good questions. He asked if you'd ever made mention of Jake—I didn't tell him his name.. Which I realized, no you hadn't, not unless I had. He just helped me realize it was my issue. Not yours. It was really easy to let it go after that."

"Well, I'm thankful to Ben. We should send him some alcohol or something."

Placing a hand on my hip, he tilts his face to the ceiling and lets out one loud laugh. "Oh, trust me, that's already been taken care of. I basically just gave him what I had left. I think it's going to be a while before he wants to drink that much again."

Scooching closer, I snuggle against him. His familiar woodsy scent washes over me and envelops me in a cloud of Gavin. He takes my left hand in his and brings it to his lips before holding it out and turning my hand in the light, looking at the ring. "Everything got so chaotic, I didn't get a chance to ask you. Do you like it?"

I'd spent a lot of time going over this in the last few months, especially while he was gone. It isn't the sort of ring I'd imagined for myself. It isn't the sort of ring I'd have selected. But Gavin picked it, which is enough for me. "Of course I do. I love it."

A megawatt smile graces his face, and he kisses the top of my head. "Good. I spent a while looking for the right one. I know some people like to pick their own, but I wanted it to be a surprise." He hesitates for a moment. "Actually, I called Shannon."

I bolt upright, not caring that I'm stark naked. "You called my sister?"

Shoulders lifting, he shrinks slightly, looking sheepish. "Yeah. I wanted her input. But she wasn't very helpful."

"Why does that not surprise me. I don't know why you'd call her, of all people."

"I don't know...I guess I figured she's your sister? I know you guys have your issues or whatever, but I figured for this, maybe things would be different."

"And?" I lift a knowing brow.

He sighs heavily. "And they weren't."

"Wait, so does this mean my parents already knew?" When I had called to tell them after my birthday, they seemed shocked. Genuinely shocked. They also felt it was early, but I told them we'd already discussed that, and a wedding wasn't coming any time soon, even though we hadn't gotten far enough to think about a time frame. After we had some discussion on the matter, they were happy for us, even if we weren't quite there yet ourselves.

"She promised not to say anything. Now, I don't know if she did or didn't, obviously. What did she say when you told her?"

Now it's my turn to shrink a little.

"Mackenzie. You haven't told her yet?"

"No. I haven't."

"She's your sister!"

"I know...I know, she is. But it's so strained. And you and I weren't exactly in the best place. I didn't need any of her negativity. I didn't need her making things worse. I'll tell her soon. I promise." Without another word, Gavin tucks me into his chest and lies back, running his hand down my hair.

Somehow, he's able to convince me to call Shannon later in the day. She doesn't answer, which I'm thankful for.

"Hey, Shannon, it's Mackenzie." We've always been formal with names, never *sis* or *Shan*, or *Mack*, as our friends called us.

"I'm calling because I have some exciting news. Gavin and I are engaged! I just wanted to let you know, because you're my sister. Okay, well, hope you're good!"

A text pings in a few hours later.

Congrats.

That's all it says. One word. I know I should feel bad, that I should be upset that this is the way my sister reacts to this news, especially exciting news for me. But I'm not surprised. So I'm not upset. It's just another perfect example of the relationship I have with Shannon.

Strained.

In May, I sit in the crowd with families all around me as Gavin walks across the stage. His parents refused to come. As it turns out, they meant what they said about not coming if we got engaged so young. That's the reason they gave, but I know it's more if he got engaged to *me* over our age.

Though he denies it, I know he's upset far more than he'll let on that they aren't coming. He really believed they'd change their minds, that they wouldn't really miss seeing their only child graduate. While he acts like it's fine, says it's fine, I know deep down, he's hurting. He keeps telling me it doesn't matter, that he chose me, and he'd choose me again. Anger seems to be the dominating feeling. That they did this in the first place, that they're trying to make him choose between them and me.

Though I know he's in a hard place, I don't know what I can do to make his parents like me. They're convinced I've somehow pulled him in and thrown his life off course. Yet nothing has changed from when I met him. He just graduated with a photography degree, with a 3.8 GPA at that, and he's still the same person he started school as.

I come from a family with money too, so they have to know I'm not after his. The only difference is that he's happy and in love. And yes, he proposed early, but I had nothing to do with that. Jessica and Anna both agree it's probably because he's an only child, his mom's only son. But I have a hard time understanding that.

After the ceremony, he tracks me down, a giant smile on his face. Grabbing me tight around the waist, he lifts me off the ground, spinning me around as I squeal and grip his shoulders. "It's over. I did it."

Taking his face between my hands, I kiss him as he sets me down. "You did, baby. I'm proud of you."

"So, Nate and Jess are having a party at their place later. I said we'd go. Sound good?"

"Yeah, that sounds fun. Anything else you want to do today? It is your graduation day, after all."

He leans in and kisses my ear. "You."

The low register and grit of his voice send chills racing down my spine and heat creeping up my neck, the warring sensation causing me to giggle.

Gavin slides his arm down my back and grabs my ass quickly. With a flick of my wrist, I smack his chest, causing him to burst out laughing. A smile pulls at my lips, and I'm happy to see him in such high spirits.

The crowd starts to thin, but we stick around as Gavin says goodbye to friends and classmates, keeping me nearby at all times and not letting me be more than a foot away from him. My heart swells; it feels good to be so close again, to have him want to be around me all the time. I'd missed it, I'd missed him. There hasn't been another mention of Jake or my past or anything regarding it.

I'm happy. *We* are happy. Now that he's graduated, Gavin is moving up with the photographer he's been working for.

Wally is going to start taking him out on assignments as an assistant, which involves a pay raise. We've started talking, a little bit, about our wedding, wanting to get married next year, after I graduate. It may be soon, but we don't see a reason to wait any longer than that. I may still have grad school, but it shouldn't be an issue.

The party at Nate and Jess's is fun, but an overtone of sadness hangs in the air. It's a small group of people we've become friends with over the years, most of whom are leaving within the next few days. With nothing keeping them in the area, they're heading off for grad school or jobs. Some are going home with no other prospects. Nate and Jess are staying for the same reason we are, since Jess is still in school for another year.

They've really turned into a strong couple, which always makes me smile.

It's a somber goodbye at the end of the party, knowing it's one of the last times we'll ever see some of our friends.

But for us, summer is starting, and our time is mostly our own again, outside of work. Jess is excited to help with some wedding planning ideas, as she loves the whole wedding scene, which freaks Nate out to no end because he's nowhere near ready. Jess admits she isn't either, but likes the way it makes Nate panic, so she brings it up around him as much as she can.

If I'm being honest with myself, sometimes I think I understand how Nate feels more than how Jess feels.

Twenty-two

Summer and fall slip by without much going on. Wally keeps Gavin busy with shoots and events, giving him a little extra most of the time, and I'm caught up with work and classes. Heading into my senior year, I'm ready to be done.

By the time my birthday rolls around, I'm in need of some rest and relaxation. Instead of little gifts, Gavin plans a whole week of wedding planning, including a cake tasting. Our wedding is set for May, a week after my graduation.

On my actual birthday, we sit on the couch talking about some of the finer details, like things we want to have and do during the ceremony, and we both agree we want it to be quick and nonreligious.

"I'd really like to do some sort of fire thing. I don't know, maybe like we both light a candle and then together light a single candle?" A quick internet search helped me come up with examples, but nothing that I was dead set on. I think I'm just too worn out to really choose on my own.

"Fire? Why?"

With a scrunched brow, I turn to him, confused that he doesn't know what I'm talking about. "My name."

"What about your name?"

"Do you really not know? I'm sure I told you."

His mouth is parted slightly, forehead creased, and he looks genuinely confused. "I assure you, I have no clue what you're talking about."

I'm completely thrown. Have I really never told him? "My name. It means 'of fire.' My dad calls me *Firebird*. And my mom has always called me her *Little Fire* or *My Fire*, I'm surprised you've never heard either of them use those names for me. Mom always used to joke that the red tint my hair has in the sun is from the fire burning through me. She's always said I don't have an attitude, I'm just fiery, living up to my name."

"Oh. I had no idea." That's all he has to say about it...?

"Well, I'd really like to do something fire related. If you're okay with it."

He leans in and kisses my cheek. "Whatever you want, my love." There's a puzzled look on his face. "Your hair has a red tint in the sun?"

I'm really not sure if he's joking. While my hair has lost some of its luster, having not seen the sun all summer long from working so much, it's still pretty evident and stands out against the darkness of my hair otherwise. When I don't fight my hair, the copper coils through my curls. And it shines in streaks when I decide to straighten it, something that happens less and less frequently these days. I'm complimented on the highlights all the time, often being asked where I got it done. "Yup."

"Oh, hmm. I guess I never noticed." Has he really never noticed?

Aside from that one hang up, much of the planning has been fairly easy. We agree on most things, or Gavin just lets me have what I want, stating that he just wants me to be happy and doesn't really care about colors or favors or table set up. All he wants is to marry me, whatever package that may be wrapped in.

While many aspects are fun, something is still eating away at me. Gavin hasn't spoken to or heard from his parents since he proposed. Though he swears he doesn't care, that it doesn't bother him and that he's happy with his decision, and with me, I know deep down, it does. There's no way it couldn't.

Gavin is an only child. He didn't have a sibling to grow up with, to count on, rely on. As strained and alienated as things have been with Shannon, we'd at least always had each other growing up. We had a playmate, a confidant. If something were to happen to our parents, we would have each other. And as much as I hated to admit it, she'd helped me out in some tough spots when I was younger.

But Gavin had nobody else.

So when we mail out our invitations in March, I decide to write them a letter and include it in their invitation. I don't tell Gavin I'm doing this, but I hope they'll read it and maybe change their minds about me, about *us*, and come to the wedding. It would mean a lot to Gavin to have them there.

Dear Mr. and Mrs. Walker,
I need to take a moment to write to you. I understand that you were not pleased with Gavin wanting to propose to me. I'm aware that you have never been very fond of your son's choice in me, though I am not entirely sure why.

Gavin informed me you had concerns when he mentioned proposing. I want to let you know that I had the same concerns.

When he told me he was willing to cut off contact with you, I was angry. In fact, Gavin and I had a rather large fight over the whole situation. I didn't find it the right course of action.

Now, while I don't think your reaction or ultimatum was right either, I don't think he should have progressed as he did. I did want to let you know that we waited to get married. We will be tying the knot this May, after my graduation.

For a little life update, Gavin graduated with his degree in photography in May of last year. He's doing quite well as an assistant to a local photographer, the same one he started working for when we moved into our own apartment. We're still in the same one for now, as we haven't seen a reason to move, since once I'm done with school, we may leave the area. I will be graduating with my degree in education in two months.

Honestly, I'm not really sure why I'm writing this. I'm not even sure if you'll read it or just throw the whole invitation in the trash. But I know it would mean a lot to Gavin if you were at our wedding. You're his parents, his only family. I know that you don't accept me, that you may never accept me, and I'm okay with that. Because I love your son, so incredibly much. I know things have been tough for us, but we've struggled together. And we've grown together. Neither of us comes from a family that struggled, but I think it's been a good learning experience for us to have gone through.

Please, at least consider attending. For your son. Your only son.
-Mackenzie

With a heavy sigh and a racing heart, I fold it and put it in the envelope, sealing it shut before I can change my mind. I'm not sure they'll read it. I'm not even sure if they'll open the invitation. But I have to try. I have to try for Gavin. He won't try for himself; he's given up, *made his peace with it*, whatever that really means.

Despite my relationship with my sister, I want her at my wedding. I've even asked her to be a bridesmaid and was one in hers six months ago. She is my sister, after all.

Gavin has done a lot to make me happy through this whole planning process, so I just want to do something to make him equally as happy. And I think having his parents there would do just that.

The second weekend in May, Gavin and I pack up our wedding favors, cake topper, and our wedding clothes and leave for our trip. Our wedding will be in Rhinebeck, New York, a few hours south of our apartment. We found a beautiful spot that's nestled in the woods. It's quaint and perfect. The actual building where the reception will be has a cozy log cabin look and feel to it.

Gavin's parents had RSVPed that they will be attending. The box checked 'yes' had rendered me speechless and breathless for a moment as I sorted through the mail that day. My heart had literally stopped for a beat, mouth hanging open.

Though I wasn't surprised, there had been nothing else in the envelope, no response to me, nothing.

But I decided to take it as a good sign. Even if they still want nothing to do with me, I want them here for their son. I haven't told him, wanting it to be a surprise. I just hope it's one that makes him happy. The thought that it may not be makes fear and apprehension twist through my body, adding to the wedding jitters I've had for weeks.

After dropping off everything at the venue, we make our way through town. It's a cute little place with tons of shops and places to eat, a nice location for our friends and family to have a good weekend.

As we turn toward the hotel, Gavin takes my hand in his, lacing our fingers. He must sense my nerves. I'm staying alone in our room tonight while Gavin stays with Ben.

Before we get too far from the desk, I'm bombarded.

"Mackenzie!" Anna literally crashes into me with the force of her hug, almost knocking me to the ground. I wrap my arms around her and squeeze tight. I've missed my best friend.

To get far away from home, she'd gone to college in Texas. I haven't seen her since the first holiday break during our freshman year, and I had spent a lot of time with Gavin during that break when we visited each other. While she and I talk constantly, it isn't the same. She broke the news a few weeks ago that she'll be staying in Texas.

"I missed you," I murmur into her hair.

With a squeeze, she pulls away, but loops her arm through mine. "I can't believe you're getting *married!*"

"I know. It's a little crazy. Seems surreal." My pulse skyrockets and my eyes widen at the thought.

"I feel like just yesterday we were riding our bikes down the street saying how we thought boys were yucky."

"Well, back then, they *were* yucky."

She laughs, and it's a comforting sound, one I've known most of my life. "Good point."

Arm in arm, we walk over to Gavin, who is waiting patiently by the elevators. "Hi, Anna. It's nice to see you again," he says as he gives her a quick hug.

"You too, Gavin. Though I must say, I'm none too pleased you're stealing my Mackenzie from me."

I look at her sideways. "Um, excuse me, but I think Texas stole *you* from *me.*"

She lifts one shoulder. "I only decided to stay because I knew you were in good hands here with Gavin. You don't need me anymore."

"I always need you."

"Gavin, do you mind if I grab her for a little bit?"

With a kiss on my temple, he slides his arm around my waist and pulls me into his side. "Of course not! Babe, I'll see you later?"

"Will you be okay?" I ask, biting my lip, hoping he'll send me on my way so I don't feel guilty.

"Of course! I'll bring this stuff upstairs and go find Ben and the other guys."

"Okay." Relief makes my shoulders sag and a smile span my face. I point my finger at him. "No peeking." There's been some mention of him wondering what my dress looks like, what style it is.

He holds his hands up in innocence. "I wouldn't dream of it."

After a final fitting with my mom last week, I picked up my wedding dress. She offered to keep it for me, but I wanted to have it. Gavin had tried to see it once, at the same time saying he wants to be surprised. While I think he's okay waiting, given the alone time, I don't want him to try to get sneaky.

Anna guides me outside. Part of what we liked about this

hotel is that it has a nice patio area outside for sitting to chat. They also have a fire pit, which we figured might be nice for our friends and family staying here.

Our wedding isn't going to be big. We invited a little over one hundred people, with only about eighty attending. Our hundred people were hard to come by. We each have good friends from home and school, but both of us come from small families. Wally is doing our photos for us, for free, as our wedding present. That's in addition to the time off he's giving Gavin this weekend and all of next week for our honeymoon. We can't afford to go anywhere, so we're taking a staycation and ordering all sorts of things, trying restaurants we've been wanting to try but haven't had time for.

"So how are you doing?" Anna always gets right to the point.

"I'm okay, nervous." My voice has a hesitation I don't intend.

"Yeah? I thought you wanted to marry Gavin?"

"Well, of course I do! That's why we're here. That doesn't mean I'm not nervous, though."

Though she nods, her face says something different. "No second thoughts?" She chews her lip as she looks at me out of the corner of her eye.

Adjusting my stance to face her head on, I look her dead in the eye. I know what she's really asking. "No, not a single one."

Her face stays solid for a minute, looking at me intently, trying to read me. She's known me the longest, longer than anybody, aside from my parents and Shannon. But she doesn't know me best. That role has gone to somebody else.

Deciding she accepts my response, she shakes her head and moves on. "Okay, so, tonight. You're alone, Gavin's alone. What time am I coming over?"

"Oh, you don't have to do that. I'll be alright."

"Nonsense. What time is dinner? Six, right? So, figure we're done somewhere around eight?"

"We were thinking of having a fire before we finished the night and just making sure we're each in our own room by midnight."

"Oh, that sounds fun! And hair and makeup are at nine tomorrow morning?"

"Yup. And it's just a few of us, so it shouldn't be too long."

"It's going to be so fun!"

"It is." We sit and catch up for a long time. Others come and go, including Jess.

Thankfully, Jess and Anna had gotten along great when they met at my combo bridal shower and bachelorette party we did one weekend, so Anna only had to fly out once before the wedding. My bachelorette party was very low-key. I didn't want anything crazy, it's just not my style.

As we're walking into the hotel to get ready for dinner, I spot Gavin's parents at the desk. My whole body freezes, including my heart. Anna does too. "Are those?" She can tell they're his parents because Gavin is the spitting image of his father.

I nod, mouth wide open. "Uh huh."

"Wow."

"Uh huh." I shake my head, clearing the sudden haze. "I invited them...they said they were coming. It's just weird to actually see them here."

We run into the elevator before they can see us, giggling at our childish escape. I'm not ready to see them, especially without Gavin.

After parting ways at the elevator, I slip through my door.

"Hey, beautiful." Gavin's voice floats through the room.

I jump, hands flying to my chest as I fall against the door. "You scared me. I didn't think you'd be in here."

Walking over to me, he wraps his arm around my waist, brushing my hair behind my shoulder as he leans down and kisses below my ear. "I'm sorry. I wanted to be here when you got back to get ready for dinner," he murmurs against my neck.

A sigh escapes me as he keeps kissing along my neck and collarbone. One hand gently slides my shirt off my shoulder, the other gliding down my back and tucking into my butt pocket, pulling my hips tight against his.

He's certainly excited to see me.

As he keeps kissing me, I groan, the tingling between my legs getting harder to deny. "We have to get ready." The words come out on a breath that I hardly mean.

"We have time."

"Not enough."

He smirks against my neck. "I don't need long." Moving his hand from my back pocket, he slips it under the front of my jeans. "Come on, it'll be your last time as Mackenzie Allen."

"Okay, maybe just real quick."

Without hesitation, he grabs under my thighs and lifts me off the ground, his mouth finding mine. He sets me down by the bed and strips his clothes off before reaching for mine and pushing me onto the mattress.

His tongue wraps around my nipple and his fingers dip inside me, moving immediately. My head tips back and my fingers grip his shoulders. It takes no more than a dozen strokes before I'm writhing beneath him and digging my nails into his back.

Quickly, he replaces his fingers with his erection and presses inside me.

"Fuck, Mack."

For a second, I'm thrown. Gavin's usually fairly quiet in the bedroom. But then he starts thrusting, and I forget about everything but this moment.

We're late to our own rehearsal. "Stop looking at me like that," I whisper as we rush into the room with our small group of family and friends waiting for us.

"Like what?"

"Like you've just seen me naked and are thinking about the things we just did."

"Oh, there's no way that's going anywhere." I playfully smack his chest, and he just barely holds in a laugh.

"Everybody's going to know."

"So what? We're getting married tomorrow. Let them know." He shrugs with a wink, clearly having not a care in the world. I can't help but smile.

Anna falls seamlessly into step beside me. "I know why you're late," she singsongs under her breath, further enforcing my point. Heat rushes to my face as Gavin chuckles next to me, squeezing my hand.

"Well, now that the happy couple is here, we can begin." Tammy, our planner from the venue, is sure to enunciate despite the tight smile on her face. It screams that she's frustrated she had to wait for us. While she's been wonderful, going through the whole process with us slowly and step by step, she was very clear we needed to be on time today.

After our brief rehearsal, we go to dinner at a small Italian restaurant in town. The room is filled with laughter and fun as the wine flows, most glasses never empty for long. Though we aren't really spending time together, I notice my sister doesn't have a drink all night, which is somewhat unusual for her because every other time we eat together, she has at least one glass of wine. I have an inkling as to what's going on, but I'm thankful she doesn't try to steal my day by announcing her pregnancy to everybody.

When dinner is finished and the group starts to disperse, we head back to the hotel. Our friends from our small bridal party, which consists of Anna, Jessica, Ben, Nate, and Luke, sit around the fire outside on the patio. I sit in Gavin's lap, my head against his shoulder as he runs his fingers along my thigh. Everybody is telling embarrassing stories about us.

Around ten, one of the hotel personnel comes out and asks us to quiet down because we're disturbing some of the other guests. We agree we will, and then burst out laughing even louder once he's back inside.

After that, we keep it down, not wanting to be asked to go inside. By Anna's lead, everybody starts sharing their favorite stories of Gavin and me. She starts with a speech about how much she loves me, how long we've known each other, and how she knows I'm truly happy with Gavin.

"Shouldn't you be saving this for tomorrow?" I tease her from my spot on Gavin.

"Oh, don't worry, I have way better material for tomorrow." Internally, I cringe, knowing there will be at least one truly embarrassing story for all to hear.

Everybody shares a sweet story, and some share funny ones. Jess talks about a fight we got into, but that she knew we were going to be together forever because of how we still took care of each other and how we were able to talk it out and resolve it. Everybody quiets down after a while, and we just sit comfortably around the fire, enjoying each others presence as the flames lick the charred wood, getting lower and lower.

When an alarm sounds, I jump, practically falling off Gavin's lap. He reaches into his pocket to silence his phone, gently sliding me off. "Okay, babe, this is the end of the road. When I see you tomorrow, it will be time to become Mrs. Walker."

Flutters start in my chest, but I smile as he leans down to cup my chin and kiss me. "Good night. I love you."

"I love you too." He points at Anna. "You better take good care of her tonight, and make sure she gets down that aisle on time."

"Aye aye, captain!"

With one more kiss, Gavin is off, with the guys not far behind. Jessica gives me a quick hug before going up with Nate, leaving just me and Anna.

She throws her arm over my shoulder. "Come on, let's go to bed. It's your last night as a single lady!"

It's been a long day, so I fall asleep quickly. Excitement and nerves fight within me, causing a tremble in my bones. When I wake up, I'll be getting ready to become Mrs. Walker. And I can't wait.

The next morning, Anna wakes me, relatively unceremoniously by ripping off the blanket and jumping on the bed. "It's your wedding day, it's your wedding day! Wake up, wake up!"

All I can do is groan at her. I've never been a morning person.

Instead of getting any understanding, she throws a pillow at me. "Come on, rise and shine. It's the big day! We need to go get our hair all done up and make you look like you *didn't* go to sleep at one in the morning."

I throw the pillow back at her. "Five more minutes."

"No, now." Faster than I can protect against, she smacks my ass. Hard.

That gets me whipping up to sitting. "Ow! What the fuck, Anna!"

All she does is shrug. "At least you're up."

There's not much for us to do to get ready. We need clean faces for makeup and the hair ladies will be dealing with the rat's nest that's residing on my head. Anna drives me and Jess over, meeting my mom and Shannon there. I had picked a place that has a Starbucks next door, knowing I'd need the caffeine boost.

My mom and sister stand outside waiting for us, my mom with two coffees in hand, and she promptly hands me one with a big smile on her face. "Here, honey, I knew you'd need this."

"Oh, thanks, mom, that's really sweet." Darting my eyes over to Shannon, I notice she doesn't have a beverage.

As we get our hair and makeup done, we talk about other weddings, other couples. Jessica fantasizes about hers, hoping Nate isn't too far from proposing. While he'd freaked out in our planning stages, he seems calmer now that Jess has graduated. Maybe watching Gavin and I go through the planning helped. Maybe he just realized he doesn't want to be without Jess, and with her having now graduated, he knows that life and a career may take her elsewhere.

Shannon is in the chair next to me while we get our hair done. Glancing around, I find the other girls on the other side of the shop getting their makeup done while my mom looks at products up front. It seems like everybody is distracted.

"Congratulations?"

She looks at me, eyes wide. "How'd you know?"

I shrug and try to contain the sting that she didn't tell me. It shouldn't matter if we're close or not, we're still family, still blood. "I didn't officially. I noticed you weren't drinking last night, and no coffee this morning. It was a guess."

"Well, it was a good one. Nobody knows, except mom and dad."

"I promise I won't tell anybody. I appreciate you not sharing the happy news this weekend."

"It's your big day, I'm not here to steal the spotlight." Though I roll my eyes, she either doesn't see or ignores me. She'd stolen the spotlight from me constantly growing up.

When my hairdresser spins me around, hair finished, makeup done, and veil placed at the back of my head, I can't help the gasp and tears welling in my eyes. Nor can I help the stutter in my chest that turns into a tremble of my hands.

It's really happening. Mom reaches for a tissue behind me, dabbing at her eyes. Even Shannon, of all people, is teary. Though for her it's probably just the hormones.

When we get back to the hotel, everybody is really cautious, trying to make sure Gavin doesn't see me. The way they're sneaking in and peering around corners is giving me such a giddy feeling, causing me to contain a laugh, that I don't bother to tell them the guys are out playing golf.

While I was hesitant to agree, he promised he would not be even one second late for pictures. It's times like this that I realize how much easier guys have it than girls in terms of getting ready for things.

With some extra time on our hands, we hang out in my room for a while, trying to keep our hair from mussing. I keep fussing with my veil, twirling it in my fingers, picking at the seam along the edge, reaching to adjust it before somebody smacks my hand away.

After what feels like an eternity, it's finally time to get dressed. Mom and Shannon had gone back to their rooms to change over an hour ago. My sister was looking a little green before she left. I assume she wasn't feeling well. Wally arrives at my room at one to take some getting ready pictures. Everybody is back and in their dresses, everybody except me.

Wally gets a few shots of me standing by my dress, which is

hanging from the curtain rod. Then he gives me privacy to change. Anna comes in to help me as my veil is somewhat long and I don't want to step on it. Holding the dress against me, partially buttoned, we open the door. Wally wants a few pictures of Anna and Mom finishing the buttoning.

It's not until the limo ride to the venue that my nerves come back full force. Anxiety bubbles in my stomach and the tremble returns to my extremities.

Gavin and I decided to take pictures together before the actual ceremony. We were given the choice of before or during cocktail hour, but we want to be able to spend the time with our friends and possibly eat something.

With a deep breath to steel my nerves, I walk to the back of the venue, a small, wooded area with a clearing. The grass is so vibrantly green, I'm not entirely sure they don't have it spray-painted to look like that. Wally is in place, ready to see Gavin's reaction when he sees me for the first time.

I hear him take a deep breath and watch his knees shake as I approach. I'm unsure if he's just feeling the anticipation or can sense me getting closer. Stopping about a foot away from him, with a waggle of my fingers, I reach out and tap his shoulder.

Everything inside me freezes as he slowly turns around. But it warms like the sun shining on me when a smile so wide I can see his wisdom teeth spreads across his face. He wraps an arm around my waist and pulls me against him, cupping my cheek and parting my lips with his. When he lets go, he holds my hand and twirls me around.

"Wow. Baby, you look absolutely stunning." I had found an A-line dress, covered in an intricate bead design that I just fell in love with. It forms to my chest and waist, accentuating my shape in a way that makes me feel incredible.

Pulling up the bottom of my dress up a bit, I show him my

shoes. "Even in these?" My feet are donned in blue Converse. I'm not much of a heels girl, but I live in Chucks.

"Especially in those."

"You don't look so bad yourself." The black tux he's wearing is fitted almost as though it was tailor made for him. His white shirt is crisp and bright, a lavender bow tie and pocket square accenting the ensemble. The whole look makes my heart race and panties grow wet.

After we take a few posed photos together, Gavin leans in to whisper against my ear. "So, I saw my parents are here?"

Pulling my lip between my teeth, I look up at him nervously. "Yeah, I know. I invited them without telling you. I knew they were coming, since they RSVP'd. I thought it'd be a happy surprise? I hope you're not ma—"

He cuts me off with a kiss. Then he leans his forehead against mine. "Thank you."

We stay in that intimate embrace for a few moments, forehead to forehead, his hands on my waist, mine wrapped around his neck. I already know these will become some of my favorite pictures.

For the next hour and a half, we do a whole collection of photos with our friends and family.

"Do you want to call your parents? Have them join us for a few pictures?" At the moment, I'm leaning my head back against Gavin's shoulder, watching Jessica and Nate do their pictures together.

"No, that's okay. I saw them, but didn't talk to them. I'm not sure inviting them to do this too is the best choice. It may be a bit much." His arms are looped around my waist, as they have been any time we're not in the shot. Every so often, Wally turns around to snap a quick, candid one of us.

Wally normally does the bridal party photos for an hour, but he gives us two. He says it's because he wants to make sure he gets the perfect pictures, but I've never seen a bad picture from Wally. I'm confident it's because he wants to give us as many pictures and as many different angles as he can.

When we finish at three, we're brought back into the bridal suite of the venue. Our wedding is set to start at four. They give us the hour to get something to eat or drink if needed and to give our guests time to mingle and sit as many arrive at least a half hour before the wedding.

Tingles sprawl through my body, increasing in intensity as we get closer to four o'clock.

At three forty-five, we're separated, Gavin and his boys going one way, myself and my girls going the other.

Before we part ways, Gavin gives me a quick kiss. "The next time I kiss you will be when you're Mrs. Walker." It eases the butterflies momentarily.

On pins and needles, I wait patiently and watch as each of the girls who are here to stand with me, walk toward the front of the aisle.

When Dad takes my arm, I inhale a deep, steadying breath. "You ready, Firebird?" Sometimes I became frustrated that my parents still hadn't dropped my childhood nicknames. But today wasn't one of those days.

"I am. Let's go." I pause for a second. "Hey, Dad?"

"Yeah, sweetheart?"

"Don't let me fall." Though I'm not even wearing heels, I'm so nervous and shaky, I'm afraid I might fall over.

He gives my arm a squeeze. "I promise. I've got you." As I take another deep breath, he opens his eyes wide, and we start our walk to Gavin.

As we turn the corner, and I see Gavin up at the arbor smiling, an overwhelming sense of calm washes over me. Right now, he's all I can see, everything else around me falling away.

When my dad hands me off to Gavin, he immediately laces his fingers through mine.

I barely hear the ceremony, focusing only on the warmth of Gavin's hand in mine. We slide the rings onto each other's fingers with giant smiles on our faces. When our officiant finally announces us husband and wife and says we can kiss, Gavin pulls me against him and tips me backward as he kisses me deeply.

Our reception follows immediately after, and I'm forever grateful I wore sneakers instead of heels. The five hours go by in a blur of pictures, dancing, kissing, hugging and precious time with friends and family. So much so that we barely have time to eat.

Gavin talks to his parents, taking some time to bring them outside, away from the noise of the DJ. I give them the privacy to talk without me, hoping it's the easiest way to mend fences. All isn't forgiven on his end, but it's a step in the right direction.

As soon as they come back in, his mother pulls me aside.

"I wanted to take a moment to thank you for your note. It meant a great deal to me and made the difference for us to come today. We haven't been the most welcoming to you, and for that, I apologize. It's clear to me now that what I thought about you at the beginning, isn't true, and I'm sorry I spent this time being wrong and closing you off. I'm hoping, with some time, we can all reconnect and work to build a relationship."

Out of respect, I listen carefully, avoiding eye contact with those in the background trying to get my attention and not shaking off the hand she has on my forearm.

"I'm open to that, Mrs. Walker, but I'll be honest and tell you that it's entirely up to Gavin. He's who I did this for in the first place."

With a solemn nod and tight lips, she walks off without another word, and I breathe a heavy sigh of relief.

We close out our wedding, being some of the last to linger. When we get back to the hotel, our friends are all down at the bar, urging us to join them. Without more than a quick glance exchanged to agree, we join them for a few minutes before Gavin starts running his lips over my shoulder.

He clearly has other plans in mind.

We say good night to a room full of friends with knowing looks on their faces and go upstairs to our room, to make love for the first time as husband and wife.

Twenty-three

My first birthday as husband and wife has much less fanfare than any before. We moved into our first house in August after I got a job a few hours away from our college town.

We're insanely busy. Gavin is trying to jumpstart his photography business, which is struggling a bit in this new area. I'm working during the day and going to grad school at night.

"I just feel bad that I couldn't do more for you, baby." There's a sadness in his tone that feels like needles in my heart. He doesn't need to do anything special for me.

"It's because we're married now, isn't it? You don't have to try as much." To lighten his mood, I tease him with a hand on my hip.

"Yup, you caught me. I already won my prize, I don't need to keep trying anymore." With a laugh, he wraps his arms around my waist. "Whatever you want to do today, we'll do it."

"Anything?"

"Anything."

I raise my eyebrows, and he groans in response.

"You want to watch that stupid sappy love movie again, don't you?"

"I just love it so much. Please?" My body folds in on itself as my hands clasp at my chest.

Defeated, he sighs, dropping his chin to his chest. "Okay. I'll make the popcorn."

Squealing, I run and jump onto the couch. I've already made him watch this movie with me about ten times. Though he's constantly poking at plot holes, it's a cute love story, so I adore it.

I'm curled up with my knees facing Gavin as he sits with one arm draped over them. Every so many scenes, he'll groan and drag his hand down his face. Anytime he gets mad at the movie and starts to rant about something, which is frequently, I promptly shush him.

As soon as it's over, he drops his head against the back of the couch and stares at the ceiling for a few minutes. It's become a routine, and I know what to expect every time. Which means a long-winded rant is coming next. Gavin's a ranter, he always has been. In college, I found it a little annoying. Now, I find it endearing.

"I don't understand how you can like this movie."

I shrug. "It's a sweet love story. I like sweet love stories."

He scoots closer and wraps his arms around my waist. "Well, you've lived a sweet love story."

"I have, but it's still nice to watch another one. All those feelings of falling in love bubble up all over again."

"Oh, yeah? You falling out of love with me already?"

"Of course not. It's just not new and fresh anymore. We don't try to win each other over anymore, and there are no new first times, no surprises to learn about each other." I lift a shoulder slightly, heat creeping up my neck at the silliness of my feelings. While things may not be new, we have an established love, which is amazing in its own way. "It's just a movie. I know you hate it oh so much, but I just can't get enough."

He's quiet for a minute before pulling away. "It just makes no sense! The whole story line!"

A smile sprawls my face, and I laugh lightly. Standing quickly, he starts pacing the living room, ranting for another twenty minutes about everything he thinks is wrong with the movie. Jess once asked me how it doesn't make me crazy that he's talking so badly about my current favorite movie, but it really doesn't bother me. Especially because he'll watch it with me over and over if I asked.

"Okay, so now that that insufferable movie's over, and I promise I'm done complaining, what else would you like to do today?"

"Hm, I'm not sure!" Rising to my feet, I arch my back and stretch my arms above my head, making my shirt ride up a little.

With dark eyes, he takes a few steps to close the gap between us and brushes some hair over my shoulder, leaning down to kiss my neck. "May I make a suggestion?" His mouth claims mine before I have a chance to answer.

I part my mouth for his, his tongue seeking mine. His hand wraps around the back of my neck as he tips my head back, deepening the kiss.

Slowly, he walks me backward to the bedroom. As we fall to the bed, he slides his hand up my shirt, gliding along my side and stomach before reaching around to unhook my bra. Leaning up on his knees, he raises the hem of my shirt, kissing gently along my stomach, his palms rubbing up my sides and slipping under my bra to cup my breasts. A gasp leaves my lips as he runs his fingers over my hardened nipples. Expertly, he flicks open the button on my jeans. With one last pinch of my nipple, he pulls off my pants, panties included.

He kisses up my leg, running his open mouth along the inside of my thighs, before settling between them. The air catches in my throat when he puts his tongue on my clit. Wrapping his arms around my thighs, fingers digging into my skin, he pulls me closer. I wind my fingers into his dark hair as my back arches and my body begins to tremble. The more I moan, the faster he moves his tongue.

Backing away far too soon, he yanks his shirt over his head, dropping his pants before climbing over me and easing into me without hesitation, hissing in my ear. As he glides in and out, his chest touches mine every so often, grazing against my nipples and sending a zing dashing through me. My fingers dig into his shoulders as the pressure builds.

When his mouth finds my neck, I tangle my fingers in his hair and tug as I cry out his name. A few more thrusts, and he groans against my shoulder, resting his forehead on the pillow.

Propping up on his elbows, he leans in to give me a quick kiss on the tip of my nose. "Happy Birthday." He grazes his open mouth over my stomach as he rolls to his side.

Taking my hand in his, he kisses each of my fingertips. "What do you say to Japanese for dinner? From that place you really like?"

"That would be amazing! But I don't really want to go anywhere."

"I figured I'd go pick it up. And if you *really* want, we can watch that stupid movie again."

With a kiss on his chest, I giggle as my heart soars. "I'll only make you suffer through it once today."

"Are you sure? Because I can guarantee today is the *only* day that I will offer to watch it twice."

"I'm sure. We can find something a little more your speed. Wasn't there some sci-fi thing you wanted to watch?"

"I'm pretty sure there's always some sci-fi thing I'd watch, but today is your day, so I won't make you suffer through that either."

"I don't mind them. Much."

Kissing my palm, he chuckles lightly. "I appreciate when you're a good sport about it, but I'm sure we can find something that we'd both enjoy. Or maybe you a little more than me since it is your day." Sitting up, he looks at the clock on the nightstand. "Okay, it's two. Why don't we plan to order around five? That gives three hours. What would my queen like to do until then?"

I bite my lip, shoulders rising slightly.

But Gavin gives me a knowing smirk, resting his hand on my hip and tipping it toward him. "You want to read, don't you." It's not really a question.

"Kind of? I don't have to. I don't want to like, ignore you or anything. I just, I was really excited to read this...it's part of a character series, and I really loved this character in the first book, and—"

"Mackenzie. It's fine. If you want to read, you read. Only rule is, you can't put pants on."

A smile spans my face, and a tingle snakes up my spine. "I guess I can agree to that."

After throwing on a long shirt, I get my book and Gavin grabs one off the shelf that I've been trying to get him to read for months. I climb on the couch, resting my back against the arm, knees up, close to my chest. Gavin sits near me, pulling my feet into his lap.

Lazily, he grazes his fingers up and down my calves. Every so often, he'll glide all the way up my leg, sliding his hand up my thigh and over my hips, doing a quick pass over my panties.

Any time he does this, my heart races, my breath catches, and I notice a tiny smirk on his face, though his eyes stay fixed on his book.

Being so enthralled in my book, I don't notice how much time passes until Gavin closes his book and stands up. With his hand on the back of the couch, he leans down and kisses my cheek. "I'm going to order now."

"Okay." My brain is trying to catch up, having to leave the world I've been wrapped up in and re-enter into the real one I'm living in. Gavin knows what I like, so I don't have to worry about the order, but I rest my arms across the back of the couch and watch him make the call anyway.

I track him as he walks through our kitchen, phone to his ear, the muscles in his arms taut and pressing against the hem of the sleeves. He's taken to going to the gym after work a few days a week, and it shows, with his chest and arms now more defined. Somehow, I haven't noticed how much sexier I find him until this very moment, as fire rips through me, settling between my thighs.

Quickly, I drop my book to the floor and jump up from the couch, walking over to where he stands, bent over the counter as he writes down the total.

"Good news," he says as he turns to face me.

But I cut him off, taking his face between my hands and pushing up onto my toes to kiss him. He hesitates for a moment, confused, but his body quickly catches up, and he wraps one arm around my waist, his hand sliding to my ass as he pulls me against him. His mouth pushes mine open, tongue slipping against mine, and he hardens against my thigh.

I lower myself to flat feet while I take short, quick breaths.

"What was that for?" He's equally breathless.

Pinching my lip between my teeth, I shrug and look him

over again. "I don't know. I was just appreciating how sexy you looked over here and wanted to let you know."

One of his eyebrows arches sharply. "Sexy, huh?"

"Oh, incredibly." I emphasize the word and glide my hands up his chest, wrapping my arms around his shoulders. A hum vibrates through him and goes straight to my core as he leans in and kisses up and down my neck. "How long until dinner needs to be picked up?"

He glances over at the clock on the microwave. "I have to leave in twenty minutes."

A smile tugs at my lips. "Perfect." Taking his hand, I drag him off to the bedroom.

In May, Gavin and I celebrate our one-year wedding anniversary. I take Friday off so we can have an extra day together. It's been a long, hard year for us. Money has been tight, which feels like a perpetual problem. Gavin has struggled to get his business off the ground in this new town. I'm beyond busy and stressed with school and grad classes.

This weekend is meant for us to spend time together and enjoy one another's company, with no distractions.

Part of that involves the tradition of eating the top layer of our wedding cake. We'd spent time looking up the best way to thaw it, finding mixed reviews on it being good or terrible.

On Saturday, we take it out, sitting down with a fresh pot of coffee. With a clink of our forks, we dive in at the same time and take a bite.

Then our eyes meet. It's terrible.

Gavin jumps up and spits his in the sink, rinsing his mouth with the faucet. He spins around to face me, leaning against the sink, wiping his hands on the hand towel. "That, is disgusting. How on earth can this be a tradition? Who in their right mind saved a cake for a year and ate it, then said 'yup, that's damn delicious, everybody should be doing this?'"

And just like that, Gavin is off on one of his rants. Turning in my seat, I prop my arms on the back of the chair and smile as he keeps talking, his irritation building. I know he's really getting into it when he starts pacing and using his hands. "I mean, really, a year-old cake? We should have known it was going to be bad."

When he comes back to sit down next to me, he has two coffees in hand. He can get a lot done when he's on a rant. It's like his body needs to be busy while his brain and mouth are. There was one time he cleaned the whole kitchen while ranting about social media.

"You get it out of your system?" I pull the mug to my lips and take a small sip.

Slouching in his seat and sighing, he throws an arm over my legs. "Yeah, I think so." He leans over and kisses my temple. "Thanks for putting up with me."

Keeping my mug between my hands, I shrug. "I think it's cute. You're just so mad about such silly things."

Pink graces his cheeks as he chuckles and runs his hand up my thigh. "I mean, it was good at one point, right? Like, we enjoyed this cake, right?"

"It was. We liked it when we picked it. I don't remember from our wedding, though. Do you?"

"No, not at all. I don't remember anything we ate that day." His eyes dart around for a minute as his brow knits together. "Did we eat that day?"

"I know we did a little bit, but for the life of me I wouldn't be able to tell you what or how it was. Including the cake. But I do know that it was so good we ate the whole sample."

"That's right, we did. Remember that lemon one?" His nose wrinkles in disgust.

"Oh, yeah. It was *so* sweet." My mouth puckers and my stomach rolls at the thought. I swore I was going to get a cavity from just that cake alone.

There's still a distant look in his eyes as he picks up his cup and sips his coffee, his hand still on my thigh. "So sweet. Like it made my jaw hurt."

I turn to face him and rest my head against the back of the chair as adoration spreads through my body like wildfire.

He looks at me and chuckles. "What?"

"I'm just, I'm really happy. I love you." I run a hand down his cheek, his stubble prickling against my palm.

Putting his cup down, he faces me, pulling my feet onto his seat, between his legs as he holds my ankles. "I love you too," he says against my knees before he kisses them. Leaning forward, he rests his chin on their peak, tucking some hair behind my ear. "You're so beautiful."

I lean into his palm.

We sit still for a moment, staring into each other's eyes. The emerald color of his still catches me off guard at times, even five years later.

When Gavin's phone starts ringing, I jump, thrown by the outside interference. "Ignore it."

He groans, looking at it on the other side of the table. "I can't. What if it's for a shoot?"

"It's our day."

"Mack, you know I need to answer."

Anger boils under my skin and I let some steam out with a sigh and move my legs from his chair. "Fine."

When he gets up, I turn back to my coffee, now cold. Then I get up to get more as Gavin jots down some information on the notepad we keep near the fridge. Albeit a little unnecessary,

I put the coffee pot back quite unceremoniously, causing Gavin to turn and look at me, lips tight, eyes pleading.

He knows I'm pissed.

"Okay, you too, bye." Putting the phone on the counter, he takes a breath before flipping around to face me. "Mack, baby, I'm *sorry,* but you know I had to take that call."

I cross my arms across my chest. "We said we were taking the weekend off from work. I took yesterday off to spend the whole weekend, the *whole* weekend, with you. You didn't let me check my email, call the sub, nothing. But it's okay for you to answer the damn phone?"

Sighing, he runs a hand through his dark hair, tugging at the roots. "What do you want me to say? I said I'm sorry."

"But you're not! You're not sorry. You'd take the call again, will take another one, and you know it." This was the last thing I wanted today, and my shoulders slump as my stomach slides to my feet, knowing that this isn't where it ends.

"I'm trying to build a business!"

"I understand that. Trust me, I completely understand it. And I keep my mouth shut when you take calls during dinner, or miss things like my sister's baby shower for a shoot. I support you and your devotion to your craft because you're incredibly talented. But we had an agreement. It was one call, *one call.* It's why you set your voicemail to be business instead of personal." Leaning back on my hands, I grip the counter and try to keep the rage from boiling over.

"If you don't answer when they call, they move on."

"Or they don't. Maybe they actually, I don't know, leave a message and then wait for you to call back. Most people compare prices before deciding."

"I'm not going to apologize for trying to further my business. I'm doing this for us."

"Oh. For us. I thought this whole weekend was supposed

to be about us, and spending time together, which has been hard this whole year." A lump starts to build in my throat.

"And why has it been hard all year, Mackenzie? Huh? Are you not working *and* going to grad school? How much time do you make for us? For me?"

A sting starts in my chest and settles behind my eyes as I point at him. "That's not fair. That's not fair, and you know it. One of the stipulations for me getting my job was to work while I got my graduate degree. You knew that when I was offered the job. We agreed it was worth it, knowing it would be hard and that it would take all of my time."

He shrugs before crossing his arms and leaning his back against the fridge. "That doesn't mean I like it. That doesn't mean I'm not lonely most of the time. It was like we're back in our first year at the apartment again with how little we saw each other. And look how well that year went for us."

I'm stunned silent as an icicle drives in my heart, sending a chill through my veins. Is he trying to say that we've come close to breaking this year? "Have you thought about ending things?"

It's not until his shoulders drop and he visibly relaxes that I realize how tense he was. "What? No, of course not."

"That first year almost broke us." It comes out as barely a whisper as I can barely catch my breath, and he completely softens his tone when he speaks again.

"I know. We're stronger than we were then, of course we are. But it's been hard. It's been that hard again. I never once thought about ending things. But it's been really difficult not seeing you." He closes the gap between us, placing a hand on my hip while the other loops hair behind my ear. "Not to feel you." His mouth claims mine before I can respond.

Any residual anger dissipates as I melt into him, my arms roping around his neck as he hooks his thumbs through my belt loops, tugging me against him. His heart hammers so strongly that I can feel it in my own.

Sliding his hands from my hips to under my thighs, he lifts me as I wrap my legs around his waist. With quick steps, he carries me to the bedroom, laying me on the bed and ripping my jeans off before reaching back for his shirt.

Warm breath caresses my panty line as he runs his mouth across my skin, trailing his hands up my shirt to cup my breasts. Running his thumbs over my nipples makes them pebble, and I arch against him as need settles between my thighs.

One hand slips under my panties, his thumb rubbing circles on my heavy clit as he kisses along my stomach.

He's about to dip his fingers inside me when his phone sounds from the kitchen. Freezing, he turns toward it. The breath halts in my chest when he gets up.

Instead of going to answer it, he shuts the door, so if it rings again, we won't hear it.

"Where were we?" The grit in his voice sends a pulsation ricocheting through my body.

His mouth covers mine as he slides his fingers inside me. Arching against him, he traps my nipple between his lips.

Eagerly, he replaces his fingers with his erection, easing into me while his head tips down, and he chokes out a breath.

He's pulled out and pushed back in three times before we hear the distant ringing of his phone. Without even glancing in the direction, he picks up momentum, until we're starting to slick with a light sheen of sweat.

Sliding one hand between us, he rubs my heavy clit with one finger, which sends me spiraling. Dragging my nails down his back, I tighten around him, unable to make so much as a sound.

With a low grunt, he stutters his movements and falls

against me. Our chests heave and breath mingles while our hearts try to stabilize.

By the time we get up, Gavin has three missed calls, and three voice messages, all requesting him for family photo shoots.

TWENTY-FOUR

My twenty-fourth birthday is nothing special. I have to work, and don't think it's necessary to take a day off, though Gavin tries to convince me it is. When I explain to him that we're adults and birthdays don't need to be big shows anymore, his face crinkles with disagreement.

After some argument, he finally concedes. His business picked up a lot over the summer, which is wonderful for both him and us, but it keeps him busy. He's made the promise that he'll be finished by the time I get home from work today. After how much I loved it last year, we're ordering from my favorite Japanese restaurant again.

Assuming those two things are it, him being free to spend time with me and dinner, shock coils through me when a giant bouquet of flowers in a crystal vase arrives for me at school. It's so big that I struggle to carry it down the hall to my room, and then back again to get it in my car. Thankfully, Gavin sees me wrestling it while trying to get it out of the car and comes to my rescue.

"Happy birthday, beautiful." He leans in and kisses my cheek as he takes the vase from me and starts walking inside with them.

"Thank you for the gorgeous flowers! Everybody was jealous." My voice raises as he walks away from me and into the kitchen as I take off my winter coat, boots, and scarf, depositing them in the entryway closet.

"Including the bitch in third grade?"

"Especially her." Walking into the kitchen, I rest my forearms on the counter.

"Oh, good. My plan was successful, then." A wicked smile spans Gavin's face.

"Well, I love them, but they were entirely unnecessary. I told you, I'm totally fine to take this one slow and easy. I was happy with the plans of just your uninterrupted time and dinner from my favorite restaurant."

"I know you said that, but *I* like to celebrate big on your birthday. You know this. Let me do my thing."

With a few small steps, I close the gap between us and lift up on my toes to kiss him on the cheek. "Okay, I'm going to go wash up." I work in a germ factory and my birthday happens to fall during flu season. Washing up and changing my clothes are a must.

When I come out of the bedroom, Gavin hands me a cup of freshly brewed coffee. "A man after my own heart," I tease as I take the mug and gulp down a huge sip. Hot or not, I need the caffeine more.

Leaning his butt against the counter, he brings his cup to his lips. "So, tell me about your day." It's become somewhat of a tradition if we both get home at the same time. Freshly brewed coffee and Gavin asks me about my day. He always pays attention, asking about my students and remembering struggles or worries I've mentioned previously. He especially remembers the problems I've had with other teachers, since he doesn't like other people not being nice to me.

While I talk about my day, he watches me intently, asking questions and chuckling when I tell him that the kids sang me happy birthday. Twenty first graders singing is both adorable and torturous.

"And, babe, I'm telling you, you should have seen her face when I carried the flowers past her room. Twice." With my hands wrapped around my cup, I smile at my amazing husband. He's all too keen to listen to all the drama.

"Was it good?"

"Oh, it was amazing. You would have loved it."

Laughing, he shakes his head. "Take that, Rene!"

I love his solidarity against the one teacher who is overtly mean to me. She hadn't wanted to hire me, preferring a friend of hers who she had helped get an interview. But the interview team liked me better and went with me. Halfway through my second year of teaching, and she still holds it against me, even though I had nothing to do with the final decision.

Raising my eyebrows, I jut my chin toward Gavin. "How was your day? Did you get the Jameson gallery edited?"

"I did and I was able to start on the next one. I just got myself in the zone, determined to finish and be home in time for you. I was really into it because I finished much faster than I thought I would."

"Wow, impressive."

"Eh, I have my moments." He raises a shoulder and chuckles. "What would you like to do until dinner?"

I stretch my arms over my head. I hadn't really planned on doing much of anything. School is exhausting, and a nap sounds wonderful. Really, all I really want to do is relax and spend time with Gavin.

Stepping behind me, he puts his hands on my shoulders,

gently rubbing with his thumbs. "I have an idea. How about you go take a nice bath and read your book for a little bit." He places a kiss behind my ear.

"Mmm...that sounds nice." My eyes are already shut, and I sway on my feet.

As he steadies me, tightening his grip on me, he laughs lightly. "Why don't I get your bath ready for you while you pick what you're going to read. I noticed you finished something last night."

A few minutes later, I walk into the bathroom where Gavin has drawn me a nicely scented bubble bath, complete with tea candles. My heart swells at the sweetness that this man never ceases to show me. I slip off my clothes and slide into the tub, relaxation hitting me the second my toes touch the bubbles.

Sinking down, my chin rests on the foam, and my eyes drift closed. The warmth wraps around my aching muscles, loosening them and bringing relief. Standing all day takes a toll you don't realize until you have a chance to sit down. It's exhausting, mentally and physically, but I love every second of it. That's a big reason I wanted to work on my birthday. I love the smiling faces, the sheer joy that it's my birthday and how truly excited all twenty of them were for me. When you're six and seven, birthdays are huge, even if it's not yours.

I sit with my head back against the little towel Gavin folded up for me to use as a pillow for a few minutes before drying my hands and pulling my book off the floor. The book I finished last night is thankfully part of a series, so I don't have to say goodbye to the characters I've grown to love just yet.

So engrossed in the book, I jump when Gavin knocks. Dropping his head, he smirks at my reaction. "Good so far?"

"Huh? Oh, yeah."

"I just figured I'd order now. Unless you want to go out?"

"No, no. Here is perfect."

"How's the water?"

I hadn't even noticed that it's turned lukewarm. "It's cooled down a bit. I'll get out in a minute."

"Okay. I'll call and order. Shout if you need anything."

When I finish the chapter, I realize the water has quickly changed to cold. A cold bath in February is not so much fun. Shivers rack my body as I get out and wrap my towel around me. Gavin comes in to check on me at just the right time.

He takes one big step into the tiny bathroom and takes me in his arms. "You're shivering." His voice is low next to my ear, concern lacing through his words.

"It got cold a little quick." It comes through chattering teeth.

Sliding his arm under my legs, he scoops me up, and carries me into the bedroom. Setting me down on the bed, he wraps the blanket around me and takes out clothes.

I put my arms up as he slides one of his sweatshirts over my head. Taking my hands, he places them on his shoulders as he helps me step into panties and sweatpants, putting fuzzy socks on my feet. He pulls me against him, lying down on the bed, as he tosses the towel to the floor.

The heat radiating from Gavin's body starts to warm me immediately. "Do you have to leave?" I'm able to ask evenly once the shivering stops.

He squeezes me tightly. "I have a few more minutes."

I shift closer, closing any tiny fragment of space that exists between us. While I don't need his warmth anymore, I do need him close to me.

With a kiss on the back of my neck, Gavin starts to pull away. "I'm sorry, babe, but I gotta go to get the food. You okay now?"

I nod as I turn my head to look at him. "I am. Thank you for taking care of me."

Tenderly, he kisses me as his hand runs down my side. "Of course. That's my job." With two light fingers, he brushes some hair from my face. "One that I am happy to have." Sliding off the bed to leave, his hand tracks down my body, lingering until the last second and squeezing my toes as he lets go.

From my perch in bed, I watch him gather his things. It's nice and warm here, and my eyelids are leaden.

"Babe. Hey, Mackenzie. Wake up." A fingertip trails down my cheek. As my eyes flutter open, I take in Gavin's smile, the one that still makes my heart flutter. "Well, hi there."

I shoot straight up and frantically look around. "What time is it? I can't believe I fell asleep."

To steady me, and likely calm me, he puts his hands on my shoulders. "It's only been twenty minutes. I just got back with dinner and saw you weren't in the living room. You didn't answer when I called you, so I came to check on you."

My head falls into my hands, still hazy from sleep. It was one of those naps where you feel like you've been asleep for hours, yet wake up more tired than you had been.

"Do you want to just go back to sleep?"

I throw my head up to look at him. "No! No, not at all. I'm okay, let's go eat."

Extending his hand, he takes mine to help me off the bed. I shuffle into the kitchen behind him. He's already set the food out on the table, my birthday flowers prominently displayed.

I flop into my chair as Gavin raises his glass. "To my beautiful *wife* on her birthday. I'm so lucky to have you in my life." He leans across the table to lay a tender kiss on my lips. "I love you, baby."

"I love you too. And thank you."

"I wish I could have done more for you today."

"No, I like the low-key. Those things were fun when we

were younger, but now that we're older, I like that it's just you and me."

"I know. I just, I don't know, I like to show you that you're special, how much you mean to me." Disappointment coats his words.

"But you do that every day." To try to alleviate any ill feelings he has, I take his hand. "This, all of this here"—I point around the room for emphasis—"is perfect. I promise. If we just order from this restaurant every year for my birthday, it will be enough."

The down-turned lips and narrowed eyes tell me he isn't thrilled with that, but he acquiesces.

We spend the rest of the night doing whatever I want. I've found another romantic comedy that he doesn't hate quite as much. My head is in his lap as we lay on the couch, and he twirls my curls around his fingers. I lose my fight with sleep before the movie is even half over.

Sometime later, I wake up as Gavin lays me in bed. As he straightens, I twist my fingers into his shirt. He smirks as I pull him down.

"I didn't get my birthday present," I murmur against his lips.

Mouth crashing on mine, his tongue forces my lips apart to curl against mine. His hands slide up my shirt, cupping my breasts, thumbs rubbing over hardened nipples. I release my grip on his shirt and rope my hands around his neck, bringing him closer.

When his erection presses into my thigh, a moan escapes me, anticipating what comes next. He slips a hand under the waistband of my pants and panties, groaning as he feels how ready I am for him.

Both of our pants are off in seconds, Gavin climbing back over me as he pushes into me without a second of hesitation.

My back arches, my chest meeting his as a tiny moan escapes my throat, fingers digging into his shoulders.

The pressure starts to build as he moves steadily inside me. As my breathing increases, Gavin takes my chin in his hand and holds it, his eyes on mine. "I want to watch you." It comes out gravely, strained. He keeps his hand there as the sensation builds and I can't hold it anymore, eyes closing as I cry out, tightening around him.

Gavin lets go of my face and his hands grip at the blankets next to my head as he groans, collapsing against me. His breath comes in short, quick bursts, warm against my neck. With a kiss to my ear, he rolls to his side.

I turn over and snuggle against his heaving chest, feeling his heart hammering under my cheek. His arm curls around me, hugging me close. He slips his hand under the hem of the sweatshirt, tracing tiny circles on my hip. As I drift off to sleep, Gavin kisses the top of my head and wishes me a happy birthday.

The last weekend in September, Gavin wants to go to his friend's house. Sam just moved not too far away.

"Come on, Mack, we're staying home. I won't be gone long, I promise," he pleads. While he doesn't need my permission, he doesn't want me to be mad.

But I'm not thrilled with the idea. "I'm not saying no. I'm not your mother, you don't need my permission to go hang out with your friend."

"No, but you're not happy. And you're my wife, so I need you to not be mad at me."

"I'm not mad." My voice betrays me as it raises an octave.

Dejected, he sighs. "I don't have to go. I won't go."

Taking a few steps toward him, I wrap my arms around his waist and squeeze into his side. "Is it so wrong of me to want you all to myself? We still don't get a lot of time together. You've been shooting most weekends lately."

"It's the busy season; everybody's preparing for their Christmas cards, and it's the last of the outdoor weddings before it gets too cold."

"I know, but I miss you."

He put his hands together, pleading with me. "Just a few hours. I'll be back by ten, eleven at the latest."

"Fine." The idea of him being gone isn't my favorite. I get nervous being alone at night, but I want him to be able to have fun with his friend.

Bending down, he kisses my cheek. "I'll make it up to you tomorrow. I promise."

At eight, he leaves after making me dinner. While we've both gotten better at cooking, Gavin's skills have come to far exceed mine. He promises he'll only be a few hours and will keep me up to date on when he's leaving, knowing that I worry when he's out at night.

I busy myself with reality TV. When that gets boring, I pull out my book. I'm so engrossed in it that I jump when my phone pings. Vaguely, I notice that it's ten o'clock.

Gavin: *We're done. I'm leaving in a few minutes. See you soon.*

Me: *Ok. Drive safe.*

Gavin: *XOXO*

Putting my phone down next to me, I get back to my book. Gavin will be home within the next twenty minutes. It only takes fifteen to get back from Sam's house.

A car horn outside has me jumping up. Taking a quick peek at my phone, I notice it's been thirty minutes. I walk over to the window and look outside, but Gavin's car isn't there, and the horn wasn't him.

I send him a quick text. *Hey, everything ok? I expected you back by now.*

Looking back out the window, I wait for my phone to ding.

It doesn't.

Not after two minutes, not after five, not after fifteen.

At twenty, I call him, getting voicemail. "Hey, baby, it's me. Um, I'm wondering where you are. You said you were leaving forty-five minutes ago. Hope you guys are just chatting and are trying to leave. I know Sam can go on and on sometimes. Uh, call me back."

I pace the room for a few minutes, frantically looking down the street at every pass of the window, trying to see the headlights of Gavin's car. It's only been another five minutes, but I call again.

"Hey, um, I'm getting kind of panicked. This isn't okay, Gavin. You can't leave and not answer me when I'm trying to find you. I'm worried about you." My voice cracks as tears threaten to spring free. "Call me. Now."

My fingers are redialing before the screen has gone dark, tears streaming freely. It goes straight to voicemail this time. "Baby, I'm sorry. I'm worried about you. This isn't like you. And now I'm worried your phone died and you won't be able to call me. Please, just come home. Please."

Shaking, I walk over to the couch and lower myself down, resting my head on the pillow. My line of sight is straight out the window, so I'll see when Gavin comes home.

But I can't fight it when my eyes drift shut.

Headlights flashing across my face draws me from sleep. I jump up ready to stomp outside to let Gavin have it for scaring me and being so late.

But when I throw open the door, it isn't Gavin walking toward me. It's two police officers.

"Mrs. Walker? I'm afraid we have some bad new—"

Everything darkens and my knees give out as the world around me shatters.

PART TWO
GRIEF

Twenty-four

At some point, there's a funeral. All the days just mix together into a combination of endless tears, people trying to console you, and an indescribable ache in your chest. Eventually, my body stops being able to produce tears, probably because I haven't had anything to eat or drink in days. Maybe weeks. It's hard to say.

Gavin's parents were around at some point. I think. Some part of my brain seems to remember them being present, but I don't remember talking to them, and haven't heard from them since.

It's the little things you miss. The sound of their heart beating as you lay together. Hearing the shower kick on at the same time every morning. For the first few months after Gavin dies, I wake up every morning at seven, wondering why I don't hear the shower yet before reality smacks me across the face. Some mornings I wake up and turn the shower on, just to hear it. A few times I get in, sitting down as the water pours over me, crying until it runs cold.

There are days I drive to Gavin's gravesite and lie on the

ground above where he rests, just to be close to him. I talk to him, I cry. Sometimes I even get mad and yell at him for leaving me, for going to his friend's in the first place. With my hands in tight fists, I pound the ground and scream until the tears start flowing and I collapse, apologizing and telling him I love him, begging him to come back.

I pay ahead on the phone bill for two phones for six months so I can call his cell phone, just to be able to hear a little bit of his voice. Every now and then, I leave him messages, things I'd normally tell him after he came home from work, or things I saw that I think he'd be interested in. Every day I tell him how much I miss him, how much I love him. How much I wish he could come back to me.

On the really bad days, I wish I'd died along with him. At least then we could be together. Those days scare me the most.

Unless I'm going to the gravesite, I don't leave my house for months. I'd left my job because I can't bear the thought of being called Mrs. Walker. There are so many frozen casseroles in my fridge, I don't need to go to the store or cook. Somebody routinely drops off things like milk and produce. Sometimes it's Mom coming to check on me, sometimes it's a friend who hasn't left me yet, sometimes a neighbor who feels bad.

It doesn't matter, I don't eat much anyway.

My sister comes to stay with me for two weeks in November when my mom notices the casseroles are going uneaten. The doorbell doesn't stop ringing until I open the door, shock freezing me in place as I open it to Shannon with a suitcase standing on my doorstep.

"Hi, Mack. Mind if I come in?"

Without a word, I move out of the way, shuffling back over to the couch as she comes in and closes the door.

"I'm going to stay with you for a little while to help you out."

"I'm fine."

"Okay. Well, I'd like to stay anyway if that's alright with you."

"Whatever." There's no fight in me, there's *nothing* in me except a hollow ache. Curling in on myself, I lie down on the couch and zone out to the TV, nothing on the screen really registering.

Somewhere in the recesses of my mind, I acknowledge that Shannon is making phone calls, checking in on things. My parents had hired a lawn service to mow for the time being, and a shoveling service for once it started to snow. The call that I perk my ears up to is when she calls the cemetery, using the stern voice I'd always heard when I was caught in her room. She's making sure that Gavin's gravesite is being properly cared for, that any flowers are routinely removed, that it's maintained and free of debris. At the end of the call, she makes a promise that she'll be checking it herself multiple times.

One afternoon, I'm lying in bed, staring at the wall, numb to everything, when there's a dip in the bed behind me. My heart leaps, wanting it to be Gavin, wishing that I'd fallen asleep, and this was all just a horrible dream I was waking from, but my head knows that's not the truth. As time goes on, it becomes harder to lie to yourself about the reality of the situation. Shannon curls around, pulling my hair behind my shoulder and twisting it through her fingers.

Maybe at one point in time, we'd been almost that close. Sure, we played together, had fun. But over the years, something changed. Shannon changed. She pulled away even more, and left me.

"Why are you here?" There's no emotion behind it. No anger, no awe, no appreciation. Just four simple words.

"Mackenzie, your husband died. Of *course* I'm here." Her voice is soft, light, caring.

"But you don't like me."

My hair ruffles with her sigh. "Of course I do. I love you. We've just had our differences over the years."

"Differences. Sure." Nothing she says is really registering. None of it matters anyway. Gavin's gone; nothing matters anymore.

Shannon stays in bed with me for a few hours. At night, she sleeps beside me. Over the course of her stay, she makes sure I eat three meals a day, that I drink enough water to stay hydrated. She helps me shower, actually shower, not just stand under the water. Despite the chilly fall weather, she makes me get outside to get some fresh air and sunshine, insisting it will help.

While the sun feels warm on my skin, nothing can help this pain. Nothing except Gavin coming back.

Any time I ask, she drives me to the cemetery, giving me privacy to be alone with Gavin. I'm both thankful and lucky there isn't snow on the ground yet, as it allows me to sit with him. Shannon waits hours if it's what I need, staying in the car and not saying a single word about how long it took me or how cold I must be. Every time she puts the heat on full blast and points the vents in my direction.

I know I should feel something about how caring she's being, how concerned she is for my wellbeing, but I just can't. Not yet.

Yet each day, little by little, I do feel the tiniest bit better. More like myself, more human, less of a hollow shell. It may be just one second where I'm able to see something clearly instead of through the haze I've been living in since that night. It may be doing something more akin to my normal life.

And she's right, getting fresh air, sunshine, a shower, and real food *do* help me feel better. It makes me feel human, alive.

Which in turn, makes me feel worse, because it's a reminder that Gavin is not.

Two days before she's set to leave, we're sitting at the table, eating a dinner that Shannon made. She's become a very good cook. "Thank you." I say it so quietly, I'm not sure she heard me.

"For what?"

"For helping me these two weeks. I know it's not easy, that I'm not easy. I know it couldn't have been easy for you to come here with our relationship being what it is."

"Mackenzie, you're my sister. Of course, I'm going to be here for you. And I know that if the tables were turned, you'd be there for me too."

I nod, knowing I would be. "I always thought you hated me."

She scoffs like it's the craziest thing I could say, even though I brought it up the other night. There must be a noticeable shift in me for her to entertain a real discussion. "Hated you? No. I didn't hate you. I was *jealous* of you. And that made me distance you and do not so nice things, which made our relationship strained. Maybe beyond repair. But I've never hated you."

My brow knits together. "Jealous? Of me? Why?" Shannon's stunning and the perfect first child. She made our parents proud in more ways than one and was basically the golden child. It's not that I wasn't, but I lived in her perfect shadow.

She puts her head down. "I'm not sure now is the right time to bring it up."

"I'd like to know. I've spent most of my life thinking you hated me, when really, you were jealous. I'd like to know the reason."

With a heavy sigh, she lifts her head to mine. "Okay here it goes. I've always been jealous of your easy beauty. Your gorgeous curls, that you'd fought for years and years instead of appreciating, the ones people would pay good money for. The way that copper red coloring shoots through it is stunning. And I hate that you're thin without trying." She looks down quickly at our plates before pushing hers away and continuing.

"You've always known what you wanted to do with your life, and school came easy to you. But mostly? I was jealous of your relationship with Jake. Your epic love story. I mean, it was just so romantic, you two meeting as kids on the beach and then falling in love. I hate to admit this, and I hate myself for even thinking it or feeling it, but I was happy when it ended. I know you were brokenhearted, but part of me thought 'good, she doesn't get everything.'"

With a sharp intake, she shakes her head, eyes dropping back to the table. I'm not sure she meant to say that last part. "What a horrible sister, huh? But all of this? This is something truly tragic and terrible and not something I'd wish on my worst enemy, and especially not my sister."

Still trying to process her words, I stare at her for a minute. She was jealous of me and Jake? How could that have been? She's had plenty of boyfriends in her time, and now she's happily married and has started a family.

Before I even realize it's happening, I burst into giggles. I'm not sure where it comes from, but I'm laughing. Truly laughing. Shannon looks at me like I've finally broken. And maybe I have. "You were jealous of me? Because of my high school boyfriend? And that's why we have such a shitty relationship?"

She's stoic for a minute before she too doubles over with giggles. "It sounds so crazy when you say it like that."

We laugh for a few more minutes before settling back into silence, but it's less uncomfortable now.

A thought worms its way into my mind. "But, what about before that? We weren't super close before that."

"I'd been an only child for three years and suddenly you were there, following me, stealing my toys, my things. I mean, sure, we got along okay then. Even when we met the Henshaws at the beach that summer, we got along well. But I would have killed for a guy to look at me the way Jake looked at you all those years."

All I can do is nod. I don't understand it, but at least I know the reason now.

After dinner, we watch a movie and talk about the characters and how fake they are. Then we watch another. Shannon's careful not to pick anything that involves too sappy of a love story or marriage. It only leaves comedy. Part of me feels like she's intentionally choosing awful movies because it makes them even funnier.

Two days later, she leaves. But not before she makes a handful of new casseroles, instructing me to make sure I eat every single day, that it's important. Most importantly, that Gavin would want me to take care of myself.

But what does she know about Gavin? She'd only met him three times, one of which was at our wedding.

And then she's gone, and I'm alone again.

Twenty-five

Mom comes to stay with me for my first wedding anniversary without Gavin. Knowing it's going to be hard on me, she brings me to the gravesite early in the morning so I can spend the day with him. She packs a picnic and brings some books to keep herself busy while I stay with Gavin as long as I want.

I'd been doing a little bit better. Until I noticed it became May.

I run my hand over the curve of the tombstone as I get to his grave. Thankfully, it's a beautiful spring day. Relatively temperate weather, not too hot or cold, and it hasn't rained in a few days, so the grass isn't wet.

"Hey, baby." The tears are already pouring down my cheeks. "Happy Anniversary. I've spent the last day trying to figure out what silly thing you'd have planned for us today. Or what special thing you'd suggest we do to make me happy. But I gotta tell ya, if you came back to me, I'd never, ever want anything else ever again."

I can barely see through the tears. The sound of my knees thunking to the ground echoes through my emptiness. I collapse, chest to legs, my head against my knees. The car door slams, but nobody approaches.

My mom is watching as I fall apart.

"I just miss you so much. Why'd you have to leave me? Why did you go that day?" Salty water plunks onto my thighs and the ground, my hair getting stuck to my cheeks as I shake my head. "Today's supposed to be the happiest day; it's our anniversary. We always had such good days, even before we got married. Remember the year you took me down to the water, wanting it to be all romantic, but it was cold and wet, and you slipped on the rocks? Or how about when we tried the top of our wedding cake? Wasn't it terrible? I don't understand why that's a tradition. You were so mad about it, you went on for days. I'd give anything for one of your rants right now." My eyes flutter shut, and pins drive deeper into my heart. At this point, it feels like a pincushion.

"It's hardest at night. I've been doing a little better; surprisingly Shannon helped with that, but nights, nights are still so hard. I miss feeling you next to me. I miss hearing your steady breathing. I even miss your snoring. Okay, maybe not." Pausing and resting my hand on the stone, I try to collect myself.

"I keep hearing that I need to move on. That it's been months. But how do I do that? How am I supposed to go on without you? You've been my rock for so many years. And suddenly...you're just gone. How does one continue after that? I don't think I can. I don't think I'll ever be able to. But it hurts. It hurts all the time. It's like I have a gaping wound from where you ripped away from me. I don't know how to make it heal. Shannon said to eat, get fresh air, shower. And those things help, but it's like putting on a Band-Aid when you really need stitches."

Wrapping my arms around my middle, I try to bring relief to the sting. Amputees can have something called phantom limb syndrome, where they almost feel the pain of their missing appendage. That's what this is like. It's as though we had been fused together for years, our bodies connected, and when he died, he was ripped from my side, leaving me broken and bleeding out, a slow and painful way to live, forever missing that other part of me.

"This last birthday was really hard without you. You'd always done so much to make it special. This year it felt like just another day. I mostly refused to acknowledge it."

My rings glint in the sun, drawing my attention. I haven't taken them off. They hang loosely on my finger, almost slipping off from the weight I've lost from not eating. My hand reaches up to touch his ring. I'd strung it on a chain after the funeral home gave it to me. It hangs around my neck at all times.

I keep getting questions about them. People ask why I wear them if he's gone, or they ask if I'm married and I have to explain what happened, getting that awful sympathy look from them. The one I've grown to hate. I barely go out, but anytime I see somebody, neighbors, people at the grocery store, coworkers, it somehow always comes up.

The accident had been in the paper, so people knew about it because we live in a small town. They know who I am. It's like I have the word 'widow' tattooed on my forehead. The look of absolute defeat I've adopted probably doesn't help.

"I hate to even mention this, but I think I'm going to take my rings off. It's just, it's too painful any time somebody acknowledges them. Looking at them and remembering our wedding day...it kills me. It's like they're adding salt to the wound, a reminder that you're gone, even though I'm so acutely aware that you're not with me and the constant pain I feel. I know it's hard to hear, and I'm so sorry to even think it. But I just don't know what else to do.

"Anna mentioned changing my name back. I don't know the right answer. Hearing or seeing Mrs. Walker, it hurts. Am I still Mrs. Walker? I don't even know. Does that end just because you died? I don't feel like Mrs. Walker anymore because my other half isn't here anymore. I just, I don't know how to move forward. I don't know how to put one foot in front of the other without you guiding me."

For the first time since I got here, I look up and through the cemetery, checking on Mom. She's back in the car, book in hand. As my gaze turns back to the headstone, I see a cardinal sitting on a low branch.

I'd heard the saying about cardinals growing up. That when you see a cardinal, it means a loved one who's passed on is with you or visiting you. Even though it's folklore, I have to believe it's true at this very moment. I have to believe it's Gavin. That he's here with me. I stare at the bird, willing it to talk to me, to come closer, to turn into Gavin. But it sits there on the branch, looking around, before flying off again. I reach after it as it flies away, wanting nothing more than to be able to fly away with it. My heart pulls in its direction, as though it really is Gavin taking off with what's left of the worthless organ beating in my chest.

Lying down on the ground, resting on my side, my hand runs over the grass. "I miss you. I miss you so much. I got your message; I saw the cardinal. I remember the first time we saw one together, and you said that old saying. It made me fall in love with you a little more because I'd grown up knowing it, thinking it every time I saw one. But if it's okay with you, I'll keep the rings on a little longer, and keep Walker, at least for now."

I stay here, lying on the ground with Gavin, talking to him, until it starts to get dark.

Twenty-six

As my second wedding anniversary without Gavin approaches, my parents are worried about me. It's been almost two years, and I haven't moved on. I'm still cooped up at home most of the time, still too depressed to do anything. While I eat three meals a day, it's just enough to not starve. I go grocery shopping only when necessary.

I'd taken my rings off and changed my name shortly after that day at the cemetery. All it took was one bad run-in with a neighbor that sent me rushing into my house in tears.

Mom comes to see me a few weeks before the anniversary and is shocked to see I'm still doing so poorly. While we talk on the phone almost daily, she thought I was doing better.

I'm not.

She wants me to see a psychologist, to talk to somebody, but I can't bring myself to do it. She's scheduled several appointments since the week Gavin died, but I've never gone to a single one.

"Please, Mackenzie. Please. I'm losing you. You're not yourself anymore." Her face, voice, eyes, they're all pleading with me. She's scared. And I can't blame her.

"I don't know who I am without Gavin."

"Well, I think you need to find out. You need to remember who you are. You need to find clarity, to find a way back to yourself."

After she leaves, I spend some time thinking about it. I may be lost in the darkest depths, but I know she's right. In fact, I'm so lost, I don't recognize myself in the mirror. There's a dullness to my hair, which is usually piled on my head instead of cascading in spirals over my shoulders. My clothes barely fit, clearly from weight I don't know that I've lost. The deep circles under my eyes seem set in. I haven't picked up a book in over a year and a half. I used to always have one with me.

That night, I call my parents. "Hey, Mom. Can I borrow the beach house for a few weeks?"

PART THREE

PICKING UP THE PIECES

Twenty-six July

"Mackenzie? Mackenzie!" Faintly, I realize somebody is calling my name. I shake away the fog I frequently reside in and tear my eyes from the waves I've been staring at to look up. Somebody is smiling down at me.

Recognition slowly sprawls through my mind. Tilting my head to the side, I try to find the name that matches as my eyes finally focus.

"Jake." His name crosses my lips like it's a breath of fresh air.

He smiles widely, showing off dazzling white teeth. "I thought that was you. Man, I haven't seen you in what, ten years?"

"At least." I can't do math right now. The only thing that comes to mind with time passing, is how long it's been since I last saw Gavin, last heard his voice, last felt him.

Intent on distracting myself from the pain in my chest, I start to drink in Jake. When he walked up, I hadn't noticed that he's in a wetsuit, surfboard under his arm. He's taller, broader-shouldered, and far more handsome. A man now, when I had least seen him as a teenager. His dirty blond hair is only a little longer than it had been when we were teenagers, wet and plastered to his forehead. His jaw is more angular, sharper, and covered with stubble. There are small creases in the corners of his eyes as he smiles down at me.

But he's still Jake. My Jake.

What is this feeling I have? I haven't recognized any emotion aside from grief and pain in two years. Yet, I recognize this somehow. It's subtle, this ever so slight sensation of fluttering in my chest.

Those sky-blue eyes lock on mine and make my breath falter as he kneels in front of me. "What are you doing here? Why are you out on the beach so early?"

"I'm just taking in the waves. Enjoying the sounds, the smell of salty sea air." I haven't moved from my position, butt planted in the cool sand with my knees pulled into my chest, toes in the tiny granules. I'm afraid if I move, I'll fall apart, that my knees are the only thing holding me together.

He nods like I'm not a crazy person, who's sitting on the beach bent so tightly in half my stomach hurts, wearing a sweater in July. "What are you doing *here*? In North Carolina? Don't you live up north?" One of his eyebrows cocks up at the end of his questions. I used to love that look.

How do you answer a question like that? Tell him my husband died two years ago and ever since I've been lost? That I've been trying to find some tiny fragment of myself amongst all the shattered pieces of my heart, of my life? I decided to come to my parents' beach house to have some time alone, some time to reflect in a place that holds no memories of my late husband?

"I do, New York still. I just needed some time away, to clear my head. In a peaceful place."

Knowing what I mean, his head bobs up and down with tight lips. Nowhere is more peaceful than our stretch of beach here in the Outer Banks of North Carolina. It was my favorite place to be at one point. When I asked my parents for some time alone, they gladly canceled all rentals.

"Well, it was good to see you. I'm still at my parents' house. They don't come anymore, so they gave it to me. Maybe I'll see you around again." His words are calm and soothing, a delicate tone that warms me from the inside out.

I try to force a smile, but I'm afraid it looks odd and that it might break me. "You too, Jake."

Confusion settles into his irises, ones I had once known well. Jake and I have a past, a history, so I'm sure he's wondering why I'm being so cold toward him. Maybe he just thinks I've turned into a bitch. Maybe he thinks I'm still mad ten years later.

He turns and walks away, up toward the house his parents own; *he* owns. Lost in my own world, I hadn't even noticed if a car was there when I arrived. Nothing had really registered with me that day.

With a sharp exhalation out of my nose, I stand and brush sand from my butt before I go back to my parents' house, giving in to the darkness.

The next morning, I find myself at the beach again. I haven't been able to sleep later than seven in two years. In the same position as yesterday, knees to chest, I sit here, wearing Gavin's shirt that smells less and less like him each and every day, watching the waves. A familiar figure steps out of the water, giving his head a flick to clear the hair from his face.

It's Jake. I should have known. He was here surfing yesterday. It makes sense for him to be here again.

That same fluttering I had yesterday returns, but I still can't quite place it yet. It's a nice feeling, so much better than the pain and hurt I've had around the clock for two years.

A tight smile resides on his face as he waves at me, with a small dip of his head. My hand acts on its own and waves back. Hesitating for a second, clear indecision on his face, he says goodbye to another surfer and jogs his way over to me.

"You're here again." A touch of excitement flows with his words and spans his face.

"It would appear so." There's a tiny twitch at the corner of my mouth that indicates a smile is trying to poke out, all from the look on Jake's face.

He kneels in front of me again, picking up some sand to sift through his fingers. "You staying long?"

Tightening my hold on my legs, I raise my shoulders. "I don't really have a time frame. I just needed to get away, to—"

"Clear your head. Yeah, you mentioned that." Worry is etched into his features. "Listen, I know it's been a long time, but I'm here, if you need to talk." With a quick glance at the ground, he runs his hand through his sandy locks. It's something he used to do when he was nervous.

A smile stretches my lips. A genuine smile. "I appreciate that."

When Jake smiles in return, my heart flips, something I haven't felt in years. "You know where to find me."

"Yeah, I guess I do." I give a small nod to reiterate my words.

"I hope to see you around, whether you want to talk or not." Wait, he wants to see me?

"You too, Jake." Shock slithers through my mind and body, stealing my breath as I realize I mean it.

The next morning, I find myself on the beach for the third day in a row.

As soon as Jake steps out of the water, he sees me and comes running over, smiling. "Good morning."

"Morning." Saying that it's *good* may actually be impossible. But thanks to that lingering feeling when Jake's around, I can't exactly say it's bad anymore. The emotion is still unplaceable. Part of me thinks it's happiness. But I can't possibly be happy; I haven't been happy in two years. And this is the man who shattered my heart a decade ago. How could he be the one to bring me any sense of joy?

Glancing down the beach, he bites his lip before turning his gaze back to me. "Hey, will you take a walk with me?"

"Sure." I answer before my brain even has a chance to process the question and its implication. When I get back to my parents', I'll need to work on making sure my mouth doesn't speak without my brain's permission. But I can't help but smile in response to the one that spreads across Jake's face.

Standing, he reaches out a hand to help me up. Wiggling my fingers, I hesitate for a moment. I'm still not sure I won't break if I get up right now, but I take a deep breath and place my hand in his anyway. And I immediately determine the feeling I've been having.

It's comfort. Being in Jake's presence again feels comfortable, like an old favorite sweatshirt.

Thankfully, he doesn't try to hold my hand as we walk, which we do in silence for a few minutes. I'm not sure that's something I'd be ready to do. I've barely touched another person aside from a quick hug here and there to my parents or Shannon.

He speaks first. "I can tell something's going on in your head, something heavy. I know, I know our history is...complicated. But I want you to know I'm here. I haven't seen your family or anybody else, so I'm assuming you're alone. If you need anything, even just an ear, I'm here. Okay?" With a hand on my arm to stop me, his intense gaze greets me when I turn toward him. "I mean it. I'm here."

I'm not sure if I've forgotten how tall Jake is or if he's gotten taller since the last time we saw each other, but I have to tilt my head a little to look up at him. His eyes, I had fallen for those eyes, spent hours and hours staring into them. At one point, I could read him just by looking into those sparkling blues. I'd known them so well, almost as much as my own. They're just as brilliantly blue as when I last saw them. My heart races and my fingers tremble. Despite the time we've been apart, I can read the sincerity there.

"I appreciate that."

We walk back toward our houses in silence. The thing I find strange is that it's not weird or uncomfortable. It just is.

Over the next few days, I find myself on the beach every morning. I also find myself looking forward to seeing Jake, to the comfort he brings me. It's nice to feel something other than pain, something warm and soothing.

Each day after he steps out of the water, he comes over to say hi and we take a short walk, chatting about whatever comes up. Jake talks a little about himself, how college went and how he likes living here. To keep things light and carefree, he asks innocent questions but never pushes me to talk about anything I don't want to. If I hesitate, stutter, or just seem generally put off by the question, he immediately asks another instead. He still knows me well enough to know that I'll talk when I'm ready, if I ever am.

A week after my arrival, I'm sitting on the beach, looking forward to seeing Jake and our walk. I realize now that what I'm feeling is more than just comfort, but something more akin to longing. It's been ten years, I'd moved on, but seeing him again has made me miss him, miss our past.

Jake doesn't see me right away when he walks ashore. He undoes the top of his wet suit, revealing a toned chest and arms. My heart speeds up, and I choke on air just looking at him. Two more tattoos now decorate his skin. Adding to the entwined hearts on his chest, he now also has a Celtic knot on his upper right bicep, and something sprawled across his upper back, from shoulder to shoulder.

When he notices me, his face lights up and he jogs over. "Hi," he says with a smile.

"Hi." My voice is low and delicate, our old routine exchange resurfacing not just in our lives, but bringing with it an increase in this longing tugging at my heart.

"Want to take another walk?"

"Yeah, I'd like that."

Jake walks closer to me than previous days, so close that every so often our arms or fingers brush. A few times, I catch myself stretching out my fingers slightly, trying to touch his.

We go a little farther than previous days. When we stop, a sense of familiarity washes over me. Jake leans on his board, looking at me as I puzzle out where we are.

"Is this?" I ask, looking up at him, my eyebrows high on my forehead.

"The spot where I first kissed you? Yeah. Yeah, it is." A shy smile pulls his lips up as he pulls his gaze from mine, glancing down at the sand and shuffling his feet.

A rush of emotions floods my body. Happy and sad, but mostly...love. I'm struck with how much I had loved Jake. Overwhelmed, I fall to sit, pulling my knees up and looping my arms around them, the coping mechanism I've acquired to hold the feelings in. They may be different feelings, but it will work just the same.

Jake sits next to me and does the same. "Mackenzie, listen. I need to tell you something." He takes a deep breath, steadying himself, making a nervousness overtake my body. I straighten my spine, trying to stay calm.

"I never, not for one second, forgot the time that we shared together. But after that summer, I couldn't be around Scott anymore." With a quick drop and shake of his head, I know that hurt is still near the surface.

"I went away to college and didn't go back home if I knew he was going to be there. I hadn't expected him to be here the last few years he was, and I didn't think it'd be safe to come back again." The way he stops and glances at me briefly before looking at the row of houses behind us makes me feel like there's more he's not telling me. But one thing we both know is that we'll tell each other what we need to when we're ready.

"I haven't seen him since I left for school. That's what this is for." He taps the tattoo on his bicep.

"It means strength. I got it a few days after I said I couldn't talk to you anymore. I needed strength to keep going because that was the hardest thing I had ever done. Scott dealt me his bullshit for so many years and I just took it; I didn't break. But that day I called you and ended things...I almost didn't come back from that. I just...I didn't know what else to do." Turning towards the ocean spread in front of us, he takes a deep breath before looking back at me.

Curiosity plants and grows like a weed in my mind. What does he mean he almost didn't come back from it? And what else to do about what?

"When I graduated college, I stayed in Pennsylvania for a little while. I'd gotten a job at a place local to UPenn right after graduation. But I didn't want to stay there. My parents stopped coming here years ago and started renting it out to tourists. I told them I wanted to move here, because it reminded me of our time together. I've thought about you every day." For a second, at that last admission, I'm pretty sure my heart stops beating, and my lungs have forgotten how to take in air.

His chin drops to his chest. "Letting you go was the biggest mistake of my life. I'm surrounded by memories of you every day, and I'm okay with that because I want to be. Those were my best years." He sighs heavily. "I know this is a lot, really soon after reuniting, but I still have feelings for you. I don't think I ever really stopped."

We're stuck in a staring contest, unable to tear our eyes from one another's, the sounds around us blending together into nothing more than white noise. His gaze drops momentarily to my lips and a tingle spreads through them.

Hesitating, he leans in to kiss me. At first, I lean into the kiss, but then my brain snaps back, and I pull away, slightly shaking my head. His brow knits together and his eyes grow darker with concern. "I'm sorry, do you want me to stop?"

"Yes, no. I don't know. It's complicated." There's a war raging in my body. Some force deep within me is pulling toward Jake, begging and pleading to be set free. But the rest of me, my brain and possibly my heart, are still too broken and drowning in grief to let that force take over.

He nods resolutely. "It's okay, I understand. I hurt you, how can you trust me again?" The look on his face is nothing short of defeat.

To bring him relief, I put my hand on his arm. "No, it's not that. I mean, you did, badly. But it was a long time ago. The thing is—" I'm not sure I'm ready to tell him, but at the same time, how can I not? "The thing is. I'm a widow."

His head jerks back a bit and his eyebrows pull, eyes wide. He's clearly surprised, maybe even a little hurt.

"My husband died two years ago. I've been lost ever since. I came here to try to clear my head. It's a place not tainted with his memories. A place I always felt happy and comfortable and safe, relaxed. I came to find myself again. To find some sense of happiness again." As if it holds the answers to all my problems, I look out at the water.

"I've been so lost in my own world that the memories of you hadn't even come to my mind." I turn back to look at him. "Until two days ago. Seeing you, here, has made me feel something besides hurt and grief. And with that, I've been able to sense and remember things other than just how broken I am."

I'm sure he doesn't know what to say. How could he? What do you say to your first love, who you just admitted you still have feelings for, when she tells you her husband died?

"Will you tell me about him?" Not at all what I expected to come out of his mouth. Part of me had prepared for him to get up and leave me here, alone in the sand.

Instead, I spend the next hour and a half talking about Gavin. I tell him how we'd met. How he had asked me out, but I was still in a weird place about Jake, missing him and longing for him. Upon hearing that, Jake drops his head and apologizes. I glaze over it. He's just told me he still has feelings for me, but I'm not really sure how to respond, so I keep going with my story.

I tell him about when we started dating, when he proposed, our wedding. Mostly, I tell him about the type of man Gavin was and how he treated me.

"And then one night, he went to a friend's house. He didn't plan to be gone long, was just going over to play some video games. Around ten, he texted me saying he was coming home. It should have taken him fifteen minutes. When thirty minutes passed and he wasn't home, I got worried. When more than forty passed, I called him, but it went straight to voicemail. When an hour passed, I left a yelling message on his phone. Two minutes later, I called and apologized, in tears. I fell asleep on the couch after that."

My eyes start to fill, and I take a shaky breath to try to keep them at bay, knowing it won't work. This is the first time I've told anybody the whole story. "I was woken up by headlights flashing into the living room and over me. I went to the front door, ready to let him have it; for being late, for scaring me, for not charging his phone before leaving. But when I flung the door open, there were two police officers standing there instead." The tears are now pouring down my face. "Gavin had been hit by a drunk driver. He was dead before the cops even got there. It had been two hours since the text that he was leaving. Two hours and my world had shattered."

Jake doesn't hesitate to pull me against him, where I crumble into his chest. Warmth against my cheek permeates through my body, and a gentle tightness wraps around me as he holds me in his arms. There's a feeling that joins comfort. Safety.

I don't know how long we sit, how long he holds me for. When the tears stop flowing, I don't want to move from the cocoon I've found myself in, and Jake makes no movement to loosen his grip around me, so I stay there, pressed into his chest, hearing the heartbeat I used to know so well.

As I slowly pull my head away and meet Jake's gaze, he doesn't have the look of pity others have when I tell them about Gavin. Our faces are just a few inches apart. I'm vaguely aware of his hand on my waist. In this moment, all I can feel is longing. For Jake.

Before I know what I'm doing, my mouth is on his. He's still for a second before twisting his hand into my hair and pulling me closer. Now that I'm paying attention, his lips feel better than I remember, soft but forceful. My mouth parts for his as his tongue reaches out to meet mine. In the back of mind, alarms are going off, ones that say I shouldn't be doing this. But everything about it feels so right.

We sit here kissing until my tears are dry and my lips are sore. Eventually, I pull away and lean my temple on my knees, staring into Jake's eyes. He's looking back at me the way he did ten years ago, eyes full of love, as if nothing has changed and this is the way it's always been. My pulse flutters so strongly, I can feel the tremble at my neck.

And then I laugh.

"What's so funny?" he asks with a smirk.

"I was not expecting that. I'm sorry, you must think I'm crazy. I'm sitting here, telling you about my late husband, crying, and then kissing you."

"Don't be sorry."

Suddenly feeling self-conscious, I shake my head. Jake knows me well, really well. Maybe better than Gavin had. But this is a little too weird for me at this very moment. "I'm sorry, I should go."

I get up and walk away before he can stop me, leaving Jake sitting there looking nothing short of confused.

Despite feeling strange about what happened the day before, I go to meet Jake on the beach again in the morning. My want to see him outweighs any awkwardness about yesterday. I have so many emotions running through me, but grief and sadness are less and less day by day, especially when I'm with Jake. In fact, when I'm with him, I don't feel sadness or grief at all. It's very confusing and dizzying.

We go for our usual walk down the beach, reminiscing on some of our happier memories, Jake acting casual like yesterday hadn't happened. I keep reaching my fingers out again, trying to touch his. At one point, they intertwine a bit as I realize he's doing the same thing.

We look at each other and smile. It feels silly. I've had sex with this man. I've let him see every single inch of me. But that was ten years ago, and we're different people now.

A few steps later, he goes for it. Jake's always been that way, going for what he wants. He links his fingers in mine, fully, completely. I don't pull away. In fact, I lean in closer to him.

When we get back to where we've been meeting up, we slow, but don't stop.

"Let me walk you home," he says quietly. He doesn't want this to end, and if I'm being honest with myself, neither do I.

When we get to the slider on the bottom floor, we both freeze. Chewing my lip, I look down before meeting his intent gaze. "Want to come in?" I try to sound innocent and not nervous as hell. I'm not sure I'm successful.

"Sure." There seems to be a touch of nervousness in his voice as well.

He follows me into the house, looking around as we climb the stairs to the top floor. Our houses are set up the same as most houses in the Outer Banks. The bottom floor has a bedroom, bathroom, laundry room and slider to the beach access. The middle floor has bedrooms and bathrooms and a central living room, and the top floor has the master suite, kitchen, living room, and dining area. Every floor has a wrap around deck.

"Wow. Everything's exactly how I remember it. Like, everything."

Having Jake here, with me in the living room, a million memories come rushing back. Ones I've been keeping at bay for years, and have been fighting to lock away over the past few days. Looking over at him, I know they're flying through his head too.

Not sure what to say, I connect my fingers in front of my legs and turn my foot on its side. "Want some coffee?"

"Uh, I do, but I'm pretty wet under here." A thoughtful look passes over his features. "Tell ya what. That coffee offer still good if I run home and shower quick and then come back?"

My heart flutters. In the brief moment he mentioned he was wet and going home, disappointment had filled my chest. With the add-on that he wants to come back, it pops with joy, and I feel a lightness I haven't known for a long time. "Absolutely. Let yourself in when you come back. I'll be here or on the deck."

After he leaves, I busy myself making coffee and looking to see if I have anything to eat with it. There are some biscotti in the cabinet with a perfectly respectable best by date.

Hoping to distract my mind, I take a book out onto the deck while I wait for Jake to return.

"How did I know I'd find you here? Book in hand, no doubt." I turn around at the sound of Jake's deep voice. He has on tan shorts and a heather grey t-shirt, the tattoo on his arm peeking out from under the sleeve, the one on his back snaking out over the collar. A brilliant smile graces his face.

"Well, some things never change." The lie feels awkward and settles unsteadily in my stomach. How do I tell him that it's actually been quite a while since I've gotten absorbed in a book, let alone read one? That it's been years, but somehow, today is different?

Instead of saying anything of the sort, I stand and start to the slider. "Coffee's ready."

Before I can get to the door, he wraps an arm around my waist and pulls me against him, leaning down and brushing his lips against mine. I relax into him, my mouth parting for his.

After a few minutes, I'm completely lost in Jake, he stops

the kiss, teeth pulling against his lower lip. "Sorry. I just had to do that again."

I shake my head to regain the ability to think again. "It was nice." Nice? What is wrong with me? "Let's get coffee."

Linking our fingers, I pull him inside. It feels natural to have his hand in mine, like no time has passed, even though a lifetime has.

I pour our drinks as he slides onto a barstool at the counter. Putting the coffee down in front of him, I lean my elbows on the island. His eyes shift down as I do so, and I immediately realize he's getting an excellent view of my cleavage. Clearing my throat, I quickly straighten up, heat running up the back of my neck.

He chuckles. "It's not like it's anything I haven't seen before."

"Yeah, well, you haven't seen it in ten years."

We're quiet for a minute. It came out more like a jab than I wanted it to. We haven't really tackled the giant pink elephant in the room yet. Those years were hurtful and difficult in different ways, but we haven't hashed out what it meant, what it means now, or we're even doing here.

"So you haven't told me, do you have a girlfriend? A wife?" I try to act like I don't care, putting the porcelain rim to my lips. My heart races and I hope beyond all hopes that he's unattached. Especially because of all the kissing we've been doing. I probably should have asked earlier than now.

"Nope. Single. Just me." His eyes meet mine, a glimmer in them. They say what we're both thinking. Here we are, after a decade, both single. Our circumstances may be extremely different, but we're available.

Turning my back to him to try to contain myself and the blood rushing through my veins, I pour myself another cup of coffee as Jake laughs. "Still drink a lot of coffee, huh?"

"Oh, probably way more than before." With one slight exhale through my mouth, I drop my shoulders and face him again.

He shakes his head. "I always told you it was too much. I don't know how you're not just a giant jittering ball."

"Who says I'm not by the afternoon?" Raising one eyebrow at him, it brings pink to his face.

"Fair point." He lifts his hands in peace before cupping his mug again. "I was surprised your parents let you drink that much coffee."

"I think they let me do a lot of things I probably shouldn't have been doing." My eyes lock on his and a strange current passes through the air between us. It's so thick and forceful, I can almost see it.

With the slightest open and shut of his mouth, I know Jake wants to say more, but is wondering if he should. Though a battle occurs inside me every time I see him, I'm sure there's one going on inside him as well. "I'd like to see you again, for more than just our morning walk and this. I want to take you on a date. Please, let me take you on a date."

My heart both races and stutters, a warring of sensations. Part of me wants to go. But I also feel awful for even thinking about it. I came here to get over my husband, to find myself again. What I didn't expect was to come here and have feelings for another man, especially one who broke my heart terribly, and the one man my late husband felt so insecure about.

"Um, can I think about it?" I throw myself forward on the counter and bury my face in my arms. "I'm sorry, that sounds so dumb. But it's complicated."

"Sure. Yeah, I understand."

"I'm sorry." My words are muffled by my arms and granite underneath them.

"Don't be. I can see how it's a lot to process. It's just that seeing you again has brought back a lot of emotions for me."

Popping my head back up, I rest my chin on the heels of my hands, elbows propped on the counter. "Me too. That's part of why it's complicated."

His eyes, which had been staring into his cup, lock on mine. I just admitted that I have feelings for him, that maybe we're in the same boat.

"Come here." There's a gruffness to his voice.

My feet move of their own volition. Turning sideways in the chair, he makes room for me to stand between his legs. He leans forward a bit, so his head is level with mine. His hands are on my hips without hesitation, like they've always been his to hold and he does it every day, making my breath hitch, remembering when they were.

"I'm not going to push you, or try to convince you to do anything you don't want to do. Know that I'm here and I'm not going anywhere. I want to spend time with you. I *need* to. But if you're not ready, I understand that. And I'll wait until you are."

The words he says are so familiar, yet last time they were said by a different man under very different circumstances.

Something comes over me and I lunge at him, my mouth colliding with his, forcing it open with my tongue as it slips into his mouth. His grip on my hips tightens as he pulls me closer, straightening his spine as he closes the gap between us. He slides a hand under the hem of my shirt, slowly gliding up higher and higher. If he's waiting for me to stop him, he'll be waiting for something that isn't going to happen.

His hand cups my breast, bigger than when he last felt them, but still fitting perfectly in his palm. He pushes down the cup of my bra, taking my nipple between his fingers. My head tips back as I moan, his mouth finding my throat. As he kisses back up to my mouth, he removes his hand from my shirt and winds it into my hair. With the tiniest nip on my lower lip, he pulls away, hands finding my waist again.

"What if we take this slow for now? Until you're sure you're ready." He's a little breathless.

"I'm confused. I kissed *you*. I didn't stop you." I'm *very* breathless.

"I want you to be sure. We've done all of this before. It's going to be easy to fall right back into everything, since we're clearly still comfortable with each other. I want to make sure you're ready. I don't want you to have regrets or second thoughts."

Unable to speak, I nod. While I understand what he's expressing, I know what my body is saying. And it's screaming it wants more Jake.

Mid-July

About two weeks into my stay, I'm awoken by a phone ringing, the day after Jake asked me on a date. I'm so confused by the sound that I almost don't get up. It's the house phone, not my cell phone, which is what throws me off.

Who would be calling the house? And then I realize only a few people have the number; my parents, the rental agency, and the cleaners. Scrambling out of bed, I almost trip as the sheet wraps around my ankles, and I run to answer the phone.

"Hello?" A harsh swallow comes around my parched throat.

"Hi, sweetheart. How are you?"

"Oh, hi, mom. I'm doing alright."

"Did I wake you? I'm sorry. I thought it'd be safe to call at ten. I figured you'd have been up for hours."

Ten? Is that why I feel somewhat rested and not weary? "It's okay, I should get up anyway."

"Are you keeping busy at all? I know you wanted to go and just relax a bit, but I hope you're not just sitting around the house all day." Plopping onto a barstool at the island, I sit for what appears to be a long conversation waiting to happen.

"I am, mom, I promise. Actually..." I hesitate and pinch my lip between my teeth. Mom and I have always been close, but should I tell her? "I ran into Jake."

There's a silence on the phone for a few moments that causes anxiety to stir in my stomach. "Jake? Jake Henshaw?"

"Yeah."

"Wow. I haven't thought of the Henshaws in years." A wistfulness takes over her tone, and I can imagine the faraway look in her eyes. "Jake. You saw Jake?"

"I did." I know Mom well enough to know her mouth is pressed into a line and she's trying to figure out what to say. "What are you thinking, mom?"

"I'm thinking you haven't seen Jake in about a decade and the two of you have a strong history. How are *you* feeling about it?"

"Honestly? I have no idea. I was so shocked the first time I saw him. It was like I'd seen a ghost or something. I closed that box a long time ago, and I never expected to see him again. I hadn't thought about him in years. And now?" I stop, not sure how to finish the sentence.

"And now what, sweetie?"

As though Mom were here with me, I shake my head. "I don't know, mom. I mean, it's *Jake*."

"I know." Silence fills the line for an extended beat. "Wait. You said 'the first time' you saw him. Have you seen him more than once?"

Biting my lip, I look at the ground as the back of my neck prickles. "Yeah. The first time was just by chance. I was up early. I couldn't sleep, so I headed to the beach and watched the waves, lost in my grief and loneliness. Ya know, like I have been for the past two years. And he walked up to me. He had to get my attention, since I didn't even notice he was standing right in front of me. But I've seen him every day since then. Accidentally, at first."

"At first?"

"Um, yeah. I went to the beach a few more times early in the morning, not knowing he'd be there and running into him again. And then I started going, *knowing* he'd be there. He told me the third day he's there almost every morning." I take a deep breath and hold it, not sure what she'll say.

"How do you feel about that?"

Of course, she has a hard question. "I don't know. I want to see him again. I look forward to it. But I'm worried it's too soon."

"Can I give you some motherly advice? Something you may not want to hear?"

Switching the phone to the other hand, I swallow hard and prepare myself. "Sure."

"Honey, it's been *two years*. I know you loved Gavin, and all your hopes and dreams for a future were shattered in an instant. But you went down there to get away, to grieve, to move on. To find yourself again. Now I'm not saying that Jake is any sort of future or anything like that. But he knows you, My Fire. He may help you find yourself again, because he'll help you remember your past."

"I haven't forgotten my past, mom. I lost my husband. Tragically and suddenly."

"And you lost yourself in the process. You've lost yourself in the last two years. Gavin was your love, your husband. But he did *not* define you. I'm not trying to diminish what you had, not at all. I know how much you loved him. But you've been grieving for two years. This is the first I've heard you sound even somewhat happy."

"I just, it feels wrong. Like I shouldn't be happy, especially because of another man." Just mentioning this makes guilt twist its way through my body, wrapping around my lungs and squeezing.

"Mackenzie, you listen to me. Gavin loved you, he loved you so much." The kitchen starts to blur around me. "He'd want you to be happy. He wouldn't want you sitting around torturing yourself. He wouldn't want you spending your life grieving for him."

"I know. I know." I let out a growl of frustration. "But how do I not feel guilty? How do I not feel like I'm replacing him if I move on with somebody else?" That's not even necessarily what's going on here, but it's impossible to deny that *something* is.

"Who's talking about moving on? You're talking to an old friend."

"An old love, Mom, come on. You know Jake was so much more than a friend."

"He was. But that doesn't mean he has to be again."

"He asked me out on a date."

"And?" She doesn't have to say more for me to know what she means.

"I'm thinking I shouldn't go, that it's wrong. But I'm *feeling* that I want to. Being around him feels...natural, almost."

"You two were so inseparable. For years. Over the school year, you'd beg for us to go down at the same time they would be there. I remember that Christmas we all spent down there together. We almost never saw the two of you without the other. And that necklace, it was beautiful."

I suck in a quick breath, my hand flying to my neck. I had forgotten all about it. The Christmas I had convinced my parents to go to the beach house after talking with Jake about having more time together...the Christmas I lost my virginity.

We had a big double family dinner. After we finished eating, Jake took me out onto one of the decks, with a big, warm blanket in tow. We sat on the porch swing and looked out at the ocean as I leaned against him, the blanket keeping us warm. He pulled out a heart necklace with small diamonds in it.

I wore it for years after that. When the chain broke just before I left for college, I was heartbroken. Jake and I had long stopped talking by then. It was the last part of him I had. Mom had said we could get a new chain, but I took it as a sign that it was time to completely close that part of my life, my heart, and go to college with a clean slate.

I met Gavin about a month later.

"I forgot about that. How could I forget about that?" I told Gavin about losing my virginity over Christmas. Somehow, I'd forgotten, or more likely, blocked out, the rest, especially the necklace.

"It was a long time ago, sweetie. You've lived a whole life since then."

"I don't know, mom. What do I do? Should I go?" The push and pull is strong. My body is at odds with itself over every single decision, every thought.

"Only you can make that decision. But personally? I think you should. I think a night to remind yourself of who you used to be, whether that be before Gavin or just something that brings back part of who you were before you lost him, is a good thing."

Deciding she's right, I nod, even though she can't see me. I'm going to go. At the very least, I'll be in the company of another person I enjoy spending time with. "Okay. I'm going to let him know I want to go."

"I think that's a good idea. You'll have to let me know how it goes. Oh, I always liked Jake so much. I was so sad when you lost touch, when we lost touch with the Henshaws." That wist-fulness is back in her voice.

"Well, you didn't have to lose touch with them just because Jake and I stopped talking."

"It just happened, sweetie, it wasn't you two. We stopped going down to the shore when you stopped wanting to. We kept going after Shannon went to school because of you. And honestly, had you not had Jake and so desperately wanted to see him, we probably wouldn't have bothered since you didn't even go into the ocean."

"There's a lot more to enjoy down here than just going in the ocean, mom, you know that."

"I do. Just be careful, My Fire. Jake loved you way back when, but it's been a long while. I don't want you to open up and be crushed again."

"I will be, mom. I promise." How can I tell her I'm afraid I already am?

"Okay. I'll let you go. Call me in a few days and let me know how the date goes!"

"I will, I promise."

"I love you, My Fire." The nickname used to make me roll my eyes, but now I find it endearing.

"I love you too, mom."

After I hang up, I start a pot of coffee and take a shower while it brews. I eat a quick breakfast and brush my teeth, putting on a touch of make-up before I walk over to Jake's.

With a deep breath and a shake of my extremities to get out some jitters, I knock on the door. I wait for a few seconds with no answer, taking a peek out back. His surfboard is here, as is his car.

Maybe he has somebody inside. Just because he doesn't have a wife or girlfriend, doesn't mean he doesn't entertain other women. The thought makes my stomach roll, though it has absolutely no right to.

I'm about to turn and leave when he comes bounding to the door, buttoning a shirt.

When he yanks open the door, his lips tip up at the corners, and he ends his mission with the buttons, leaving it half done. My body reacts to seeing his perfect chest, sending a trill straight between my thighs.

"Hi," he breathes the word out.

"Hi. Sorry, I hope I'm not interrupting...anything. I don't have your number, and I wanted to talk to you."

"No, not at all. Please, come in." He steps aside as I cross the threshold and wait to follow him upstairs.

Once we reach the top floor, my feet freeze as I look around the living room, the kitchen. "Wow. It's so different. Yet so familiar." Even more memories come flooding back, only this time, the ones from Jake's house.

"Yeah, I changed a few things when I moved in. Made it a little more my style." His gaze looks around the room, now a shade of grey compared to the beige it had once been.

"It looks good."

"Can I get you anything? I don't have coffee brewed, but I can make some."

"Um, sure. That'd be great."

There's a nervousness in his movements as he sets to making coffee and his back is to me. "I'm sorry, did I interrupt something?" I ask tentatively, ready to run if I hear another voice.

"Huh? Oh, no. I had just gotten out of the shower when I heard you knocking. I was just going to get started with work."

"Oh."

Apparently, there's something very interesting about the coffee pot since he still hasn't turned around. "You weren't at the beach today. I was worried I upset you." His voice is low and strained.

I walk over to him and slide between him and the counter, holding his face between my hands as I push up on my toes to kiss him. "You didn't."

He rests his forehead against mine. "I've missed you."

"I've missed you too." It's the truth. While I had moved on and gotten married, being here with him has made me realize how much I truly missed him. It's as if I had compartmentalized my feelings for him when I started having feelings for Gavin. And now that Gavin is gone and I'm here, with Jake, free to have those emotions again, they came back to right where they had left off.

I move to the side to let Jake finish with the coffee.

"So, you wanted to talk?" he asks nonchalantly as he flips the lid closed, hits the button, and leans his hip against the counter.

"Yeah. I wanted to tell you that I'd like to go on a date with you."

His smile is so wide it reaches his eyes. "Yeah?"

"Yeah." My own smile graces my face, and my heart flutters.

"Are you sure?"

"I am. I talked to my mom this morning. She thinks it's a good idea. It's been two years. And you know me. You really know me. At the very least, maybe you can help me find myself again."

"At the very least?"

I shrug. "I'm not really sure what to say. There's clearly more than just two old friends connecting going on here. I'm a horrible person for even thinking it, but I'm feeling real things for you, ones I haven't felt in years."

His irises shine. "You are?"

I nod, eyes narrowing. "Aren't you?"

"Yeah. You know I am." He hesitates for a minute. "Why weren't you at the beach this morning?"

My lips pull into a smile. It's become so natural and easy in Jake's presence. "Because for the first time in two years, I was able to sleep later than seven." His brows knit together as he looks at me. "Gavin used to get in the shower at seven every day. It woke me up most mornings. After he died...well, I've been up at seven every day since then. Except today."

"Why do you think that is?"

"I think for the first time there's something other than grief and pain in my life."

Taking a step so he stands in front of me, he wraps his arm around my waist. It's carefree, simple, effortlessly natural. "And what's that?"

"Comfort."

His arm tightens but he doesn't kiss me like I wish he would. "So dinner? How about tonight?"

"Tonight?" My eyebrows shoot up. It's very sudden.

"Do you need more time?"

"No. No, I don't. Tonight sounds great."

Jake chuckles and shakes his head as he pours me coffee. I'm sure he knows I've already had the liquid elixir this morning and that he's just encouraging the habit I'm clearly intent on keeping.

With freshly filled mugs, mine to the brim, we sit on the couch, close enough that the sides of our bodies are pressed against one another. Over the next few hours, we talk about our pending dinner and reacquaint ourselves with one another, sharing parts of our lives and what happened over the past ten years.

On top of sitting so close, I shake with his laughter, and he keeps his hand on me in some way. Sometimes it's caressing my shoulder with his arm flung over the back of the couch, sometimes it's resting on my knee. No matter where it lands, I don't shy away, but instead, I lean into it, into him.

I don't want him to stop touching me. Every moment I'm with Jake, my sense of self starts to return more and more. I'm thinking less about Gavin, less about losing him. It's a strange feeling, but a good one.

When two o'clock rolls around, I leave to let Jake get some work done and give us time to get ready for dinner. He's going to be picking me up around six. That means I have four hours to kill and I'm willing them to fly by so I can see Jake again, so I can feel his hands on me.

Realizing that I want Jake's hands on me when we're not together rocks me to my core. I have to get some guidance. I need to talk to Anna. Flopping down on the couch, I pull open her contact.

Me: *Hey. Need some sage advice.*

Anna: *You've come to the right place. What's going on?*

Me: *I'm down in North Carolina, at my parents' beach house. I came to get some clarity, to be in a place I could relax and not be surrounded by memories of Gavin.*

Anna: *Sounds like a good thought. I gather there's more than just that.*

Me: *I ran into Jake.*

A little bubble that indicates Anna is typing pops up and disappears several times before I get her responding text.

Anna: *Imaginary boyfriend Jake?*

Me: *The very same.*

Anna: *Wow.*

Me: *Yeah.*

Anna: *And you're asking me if you should marry him?*

My eyes widen and my heart races as I jump up from my seat and start pacing the living room.

Me: *What? No! I'm going on a date with him, and I feel nervous. I feel like I'm doing something wrong.*

Anna: *First of all, you're not. Gavin's been gone a long time Mack. Do you think he'd never want you to be happy again? Do you think he'd never want you to find a love again?*

Me: *Who's talking about love? It's just a date.*

Except that I know, and she knows, that it's not that simple. I'm sure Jake is acutely aware of the same thing.

Anna: *It's just a date with your first love. Who it took you years to get over. And if I'm being perfectly honest with you, I'm not sure you ever really did. Mackenzie I'm pretty sure Jake was, maybe still is, the love of your life.*

The tears are welling, making it hard to accurately see the letters.

Me: *But I married Gavin. I was happy and in love with Gavin.*

Anna: *We don't always end up with the love of our life.*

I sigh, wondering if I should tell her how I really feel.

Me: *I'm having strong feelings for Jake. It's almost like no time has passed between us. I'm just as comfortable around him as I was the day he left. It feels wrong, like I'm betraying Gavin.*

Anna: *Listen to me. You are NOT betraying Gavin by moving on. You loved him, you grieved him, for YEARS. This isn't you moving on in a few days or weeks or even months. It's been TWO YEARS Mackenzie. Would you have wanted him to wait for over two years if he found somebody that made him feel happiness again? Would you want him to turn that away?*

From the speed with which this response comes through, I can imagine the way she'd be yelling at me if we were on the phone instead of typing. Her words make me pause on my trek around the living room and stare out at the vast ocean right out my window. Deep down, I know Gavin wouldn't want that,

that I wouldn't want that for him if the situation had been reversed.

But on the surface, I can't help the sting of betrayal crawling across my skin every time I think about falling in love with Jake.

Me: *No. I guess not.*

Anna: *Then be happy. If that's with Jake, then it's with Jake. You have such a strong history with him. And maybe that's all it is, maybe that's all you'll find here, is happiness and comfort in remembering the past, but that will be all it is, the past. But maybe...*

Staring at the phone, I wait for her response. But it doesn't come.

Me: *But maybe what?*

Anna: *But maybe you'll really pick up where you left off. Maybe you'll fall in love with him all over again. Or realize you always were in love with him. It's ok to love two people at once. No two loves are the same. What you had with Gavin is different than what you had with Jake. And if you have something with Jake again, or even still, it's still different than what you had with Gavin. But it's time to move on, and it's time you don't feel guilty for not being miserable and depressed all the time. Gavin would want that for you, and I think deep down you know that.*

My eyes have poured over while reading her message. She always knows how to make me cry.

But she's right. Even early in my relationship with Gavin, I'd compared it to what I had with Jake, as much as I felt horrible doing it. And it wasn't the same; there wasn't even a single second that it was. The feeling of love, the overwhelming feelings of happiness and comfort were there, but even they felt different than how they had felt with Jake. I had chalked it up to age. Maybe Anna's right, maybe it was just different loves with different people.

Me: *Thanks Anna.*
Anna: *You're welcome Mack. I love you.*
Me: *I love you too.*
Anna: *Go have FUN. And be open to falling in love.*

Setting my phone on the counter, I take a deep breath and go sit on the deck. I need to absorb everything Anna said. I know she's right. I know my mom's right.

Leaning against the railing, I stare out at the ocean and think about Gavin. After he first died, I used to talk to him, like he could answer me. Back then, I used to hope he would.

"How do I know if I'm ready?" I ask nobody, really, but it feels good, so I say more.

"Am I ready? Do you think I'm ready? I've missed you so much, Gavin." For a moment, I let all the air seep out of my lungs as my chest aches.

"But you always wanted me to be happy. We talked about this. I remember one car trip from New Hampshire, you took my hand and kissed it and said that if anything were to ever happen to you that you'd want me to move on, to be happy. I refused to talk about it, because I refused to accept that anything could ever happen to you. That was three years before you died. I'd forgotten about that conversation until I saw Jake again." My voice trails off at the end with a lightness of memory.

"Maybe part of me feels extra guilty because of how worried you were about my past with him, how much you felt like you lived in its shadow, at least at first. But he makes me happy. I'm feeling happiness again. I'm laughing. I haven't laughed in a really long time. And I still miss you. There are times I wake up in the morning, and for the briefest moment, I forget where I am and forget what happened, forget you're gone. But those moments are coming less and less." The sharp pain in my throat is hard to swallow around, the sting behind my eyes making them burn.

"Your shirt doesn't smell like you anymore. I'm pretty sure it was some miracle it still did after two years. Or maybe I just imagined it that way for a while, and my brain is having a harder time conjuring that scent."

Not sure what else to say, I hesitate. There's more, so much more, but I don't know how to put words to it. Not to mention, Gavin obviously isn't really here; he isn't listening, and he can't hear me or respond. This is for me more than anything else. But I have to get it all out. I swallow around the lump in my throat, ignoring the tears leaving salt stains on my cheeks.

"I think I can see myself falling in love with Jake again." It's barely a whisper. "And I'm so sorry for that. I guess, I just...I need to know that it's okay to fall in love again. That it's okay to fall in love with *Jake* again."

I wait. I'm not sure what for. Maybe I'm waiting for myself to feel better, to accept it.

But suddenly, I hear distant music, a car on the road driving by. I immediately recognize the song and the band. It's the same obscure band Gavin and my friend had connected over all those years ago, a band I can never remember the name of.

It's Gavin's favorite song. Even though all I can hear is the beat, I could sing all the lyrics from where I stand. I look up at the sky and smile. "Thanks, Gav."

I know it's a coincidence and nothing more, but I take it as a sign from Gavin. I need to.

And just like that, my nerves jump up and my hands start shaking. What does one wear on a first date with their first love?

It's as though Jake heard my question. My phone dings and

his name pops up on my screen with a message. I had told him a little fib early, as I could never bring myself to delete his number. At first, I had held out hope that maybe, just maybe, he'd reach out again. After that, I'd just forgotten it was still there. And at this point, I wasn't even sure it was still the same.

Jake: Hey, it's Jake. I'm taking a chance that your phone number hasn't changed in ten years. Do you happen to have a dress? Nothing too fancy needed.

With a very slow inhalation through my nose, I try to calm myself and quell the shakiness bouncing through me. I'm nervous. Around Jake. It's such a silly notion.

Me: Hey, you were right, it hasn't. As a matter of fact, I do have a dress.

Jake: Ok good. Would you be so kind as to wear it tonight?
Me: Absolutely.
Jake: Great. Looking forward to it.
Me: Me too.

Mom had been the one who convinced me to pack a dress. She said it was good to have just in case I wanted to go somewhere or on a hot day. That sometimes just putting one on can make you feel better.

So I picked a casual dress that's tight at the top and loose and flowy at the bottom. It's the sort of material that blows in the breeze and wraps around your legs. I remember when I bought it, my first thought being it was the perfect beach dress, which was silly because I hadn't been to the beach in years. At that time, I had figured it would be nice for Gavin and me to take a vacation together. We'd discussed Cape Cod or Maine.

Twirling it on the hanger, a range of emotions flows through me. I'm nervous and excited and eager. It's hard to pinpoint just one.

But I do know that grief is not in the forefront, if at all.

I'm pacing in front of the door at five forty-five when I see Jake pull up. With a deep breath, I smooth my dress, trying to settle my nerves, and open the door as Jake is about to step onto the first step. He freezes, eyes on me, glinting as he takes me in.

"Wow," is all he says. Heat creeps up my neck as I tuck some curls behind my ear. "You look incredible."

My lips pull apart in a wide smile. "You don't look so bad yourself." The blue button-up shirt he has on does nothing but accentuate his eyes. The cuffed sleeves show off corded forearms, and a stirring begins between my legs.

He holds a hand out to me. "Shall we?"

With a small nod, I take it, electricity zinging from my fingertips through my body. I hadn't brought any heels with me, not planning to actually wear the dress, but I had brought some strappy sandals, so they'll have to do. Jake opens my car door for me and holds my hand as I slide in. As he moves to his side, I glance around and note it's a nice car, somewhat new.

As he sits, he looks over at me, smiling. "You really do look gorgeous."

"Thank you."

We drive in a slightly awkward silence for a few minutes. Jake takes my hand in his, lacing his fingers through mine and glancing over at me to gauge my reaction. I give him a small smile and squeeze his hand in response.

With a grin, he turns back to the road. I'm vaguely aware of where we're going. It's been a long time since I've been here and I haven't done much in the past few weeks besides go to the grocery store, which is only a five-minute drive. When he pulls into the parking lot, he hesitates, looking at me with raised eyebrows, as though he's expecting some sort of realization from me.

"Wait, is this?" I ask as I catch up, unable to complete the sentence.

"Where I took you on our first date? Yeah."

The memory from when we came here floods back. We were dressed similarly to now, me in a dress and him in a button-up shirt and slacks. But we were so much younger, and didn't look nearly as put together as we do now. A hesitance had taken over me, sure it was too expensive since we were so young. But Jake had assured me he worked over the year, saving up to buy the necklace that hung around my neck and to be able to do things, like take me on dates to fancy restaurants.

"We don't have to eat here if it's weird or too much." His voice pulls me from my reverie and my hand flutters up to my collarbone, feeling for a necklace that no longer resides there.

"No! I'd love to."

Once seated, we look over the menu shrouded in silence. It seems silly. We have such history, we've been together every morning for two weeks, walking, talking, getting to know each other again. He had his hand up my shirt yesterday. And yet, here we are.

"Are you as nervous as I am?" Jake breaks the silence.

"Maybe more?"

He chuckles, a sound I didn't realize I missed until my heart pulls toward him. "I don't know why. This isn't our first date; we've been talking again for over two weeks. And it's just natural. But this feels..."

"Different."

"Yeah. Different, somehow." Some hair flies in his face as he shakes his head. "We're being ridiculous. We're just two old friends, catching up."

"Yeah." That almost makes me laugh. Sure, two old friends who have made out twice in the past week and have seen each other naked more than a few dozen times. And who have feelings for each other.

Jake orders some wine, and we place our dinner orders before we start talking. Once we get going, it flows easily. I find myself laughing, really laughing, as we remember some of the fun times and Jake tells me some embarrassing stories from college, usually involving alcohol.

Jake's smile is infectious. It's big and wide, touching his eyes in a way that makes them glimmer. I'd forgotten how his smile makes my heart flutter, or maybe that's a new reaction, I can't be sure.

We're still chatting, nursing our wine, after we've finished eating. Neither of us wants the night to end, and it's not something that needs to be voiced to know it's true. "So I can't believe I haven't asked, what do you do for a living? I mean, it's a Friday, and you were with me until two in the afternoon and then picked me up at six."

"I actually work for myself."

"Doing?"

"I'm a graphic designer. I work by contract for projects making designs for games, businesses, various virtual platforms. I code a little too, so I make websites sometimes."

My eyes grow wide. "Oh my God. You're a total computer nerd!"

He shrugs and smiles. "I guess maybe I am."

"A sexy computer nerd." My hand flies to my mouth. I did not mean to say that. To ease my discomfort, I start fiddling with the tablecloth and I can't meet Jake's eyes. Maybe wine hadn't been the best idea. Jake laces his fingers through mine to stop the fidgeting.

Looking up at him, his eyes are kind and sweet. "Let's take a walk." He cants his head toward the exit, seamlessly glazing over my comment and incredible awkwardness. Who knew it would be so hard to date again?

Jake pays the bill, and we leave, heading straight down to the beach. The nice thing about most places here is that you can go to the beach after eating, most having direct or nearby access.

Jake's hand connects with mine again the second we're out the door. I walk close to him, our arms grazing every couple of steps. When we hit the beach, we pause so we can both slip off our shoes. Wrapping his arm around my waist, he supports me while I rest my hand on his shoulder and remove my sandals, leaving them near the access.

The waves crash gently to our left, the stars and moon reflecting on the water. My hair flutters in my face, the hem of my dress linking between my legs in the gentle breeze swirling around us. I've always loved this time of year here. Nights are calm and peaceful. There isn't a lot of ground light, so you can really see the sky and stars sprawled out far and wide.

He tells me a little bit about his job, what he does and what kind of time it requires. Living here has been great for him, and he loves being able to surf every morning. It's good exercise and it gives him a nice way to clear his head and set up for the day. We laugh remembering his first lessons, and how hard he crashed.

"You were so hard on yourself, so sure you'd never be able to do it. Now look at you." Pride swells in my chest. I was his biggest supporter once upon a time.

"I'm no professional, but it's fun."

"That's all you need. Some fun."

A mischievous grin splays across his face as he twirls me away from him, my dress fluttering around me and between my legs, before twirling me back to him, pulling me flush against his chest. He holds me there, my palms cool against his shirt, looking down at me. His heart hammers below my fingers as he leans down to kiss me. Sliding my hands up, I wrap them around his neck as he lowers his to grip my waist, closing the tiny gap between us by tugging me closer.

My body relaxes into his as my lips part. His mouth becomes more forceful, pressing firmer against mine, like he's trying to make sure there isn't even a breath of space between us.

He hardens against my thigh, and my body reacts in kind. It wants to feel Jake again. It wants to feel his hands, his mouth, his tongue, anywhere and everywhere on my body. Things it hasn't felt in ten years.

"Take me back to your place," I whisper against his lips before I step back slightly, resting my forehead against his but keeping my hands around his neck.

He searches my eyes. "Are you sure?"

I nod, pressing my mouth to his again as I slide my tongue along his bottom lip, causing his breath to hitch. "I'm sure."

With a brilliant smile that I can see in the dark, he takes my hand, pulling me at a quick pace back toward the beach access. I'm not sure what to expect for the future, but one thing is sure.

I'm falling in love with Jake Henshaw again.

One hour later

Somehow, I had forgotten how amazing Jake feels inside me. How could I possibly have forgotten? The last time we'd been together, we were young and still learning, still figuring things out and exploring the newness, but it was good, really good.

Now? It's *incredible*. I thought sex with Gavin was great.

This is better, and I hate myself for thinking it. The feel of his strong chest grazing mine as he moves over me, the warmth encasing me, the way his strong hands grip my body. Every single aspect is just beyond anything I've experienced.

"Jake," I sigh in his ear as he reaches so deeply inside me, and he groans at the sound of it.

For a moment, I feel really strange. I haven't said another mans name during sex in seven years.

"Oh, Kenz. You feel so good," he sighs against my neck as his arm wraps around my head. Any feelings of strangeness are gone as soon as my name leaves his lips. This feels so right in so many ways.

His tongue slips inside my mouth again and he explores in rhythm with his thrusts.

My nails scrape against the back of his sculpted shoulders as his fingers tighten in my hair, a final moan escaping both of us as our mouths separate. Jake stops moving and leans his head against my shoulder, kissing just below my clavicle, his teeth grazing along the bone. He rolls off me to lie on his back, both of us breathing heavily, a thin layer of sweat coating our bodies. Smile spreading wide across his face, he turns to look at me and brushes some hair off my face.

"That was like riding a bike. A much better bike," he says breathlessly.

"A *much* better bike." I'm slightly breathless myself.

Moving to his side, he props his head up on his hand. Turning to look at him, I do the same. With his other hand, he gently traces down my arm.

"How is it possible that after more than ten years, we're still so good together?" His gaze follows the path of his palm.

"I don't know about you, but I'd definitely say that was way better than anything we did ten years ago."

His eyes grow wide, smiling from ear to ear. "Oh, I wholeheartedly agree. *Way* better. But there was no awkwardness. No figuring each other out. It was just..."

"Mind blowing?" With a raise of an eyebrow, I fill in for him.

"Mind blowing." His gaze scans down my body again, lingering at my lips before continuing the path to take in what isn't covered by the sheet. Biting his lip, his eyes slowly work back up toward my face. "Think it'll be mind blowing every time? Or was it just the first time after ten years?"

A twinge pangs between my legs. I want to find out, I *need* to. "I guess there's only one way to know for sure."

In three seconds flat, he's on top of me again, holding my

hands above my head with just one of his. Using his other one, he softly traces his fingers down my chest and over to my hip, before he leans in to give me a peck on the lips, then kisses me from jaw to my collarbone to my breast, closing his mouth around my hardened nipple.

As his tongue moves expertly, I gasp and arch, my wrists clamped in his strong grasp above my head, increasing my need for him even more. His other hand slides between my legs. When he feels how wet I am, he smiles against my nipple, sliding in one finger, then another.

With his fingers and tongue moving together, I writhe beneath him, my chest heaving with each breath, though they're getting harder to come by. I'm about to lose myself to the sensation, when he abruptly stops.

Opening my mouth to ask him what the hell he's doing and why stopped, instead a squeak releases as he pushes into me, picking up exactly where he left off with his fingers. When I try to pull my hands free, his grip on them tightens, his free hand flying to my waist as he looks at me with a playful smile spread across his lips.

"Uh, uh, uh," he murmurs, eyes locking on mine.

So that's how he wants to play it. Raising my shoulders from the bed as far as I can, I press my lips to his, running my tongue along his bottom lip before resting my head back on the pillows. He follows, pressing his mouth to mine and parting it with his.

A steep inhale pulls from me as he brings me closer to ecstasy. Turning back to him, I gently bite his lower lip as I wrap my legs around his waist. If he isn't going to let me use my hands, I have to find another way to show him I like it. Besides the noises I'm making.

He presses his forehead into mine as he runs his free hand down the length of my leg to hold my ankle, never stopping moving inside me. Our breath is mingling in the small space between us, the rate increasing as we both get closer and closer. It's like he's playing a game to see which one of us will finish first, yet refusing to be the one who caves.

Pushing my hands farther into the pillows, his lips find my throat, where he starts sucking, biting, slipping his tongue along my skin to ease the sting of his nips, and I cry out my release as his teeth sink into my skin. Jake smiles against my neck for the briefest moment before he lets out a low groan and slows his movements to a stop.

Leisurely, he runs his hand back up my leg, kissing from my collarbone to my shoulder as I unwind from his waist. Releasing my hands slowly, giving me a tiny nip on my earlobe, he rolls to his side, saying what I know. "Yeah, definitely still mind blowing."

Right now, I can't even think. I feel so light and airy, like I'm floating. My arms are still over my head, and I can't even turn to look at him, eyes pinned to the ceiling, breathing heavy.

The bed shakes as he chuckles. "You okay over there?"

All I can do is nod, which makes him laugh harder as he falls to his back, moving his hands to cradle his head, clearly pleased with himself.

I shake my head to regain my composure and bring myself back down. "Well, *that* was certainly like nothing we'd ever done when we were younger." Pinning my hands down is a new move for me. I like it.

With an eyebrow cocked up high on his forehead, he turns to look at me. "I think we've both learned a thing or two since then. You certainly didn't seem to mind."

"Not one bit."

Removing an arm out from under his head, he pushes it under my neck and around my back, pulling me into him. I rest against his chest as he draws small circles on my hip.

"It's incredible to be with you now. I was so sure I'd never see you again," he says, his eyes on the ceiling. His fingers hesitate for a second and I can tell he isn't sure he wants to say what he's thinking. "I know I already told you that I never stopped thinking about you. For all those years. I need you to know that I wasn't holding out hope or anything, but I feel like I compared every girl to you."

I snuggle into him even more. It seems crazy, that I could miss such a thing considering we only had our summers together, a few weeks at most. But I spent my school years longing for him, for this very moment. Then he left, and shattered my heart, leaving me to pick up the pieces and move on. Somehow, despite the heartache, the time apart, we've found a way back to each other. The very thing I'd longed for as a kid, the person I spent most of my time missing, is here right now.

But my cruel mistress of guilt reappears and digs her claws into my soul. Had I missed him while I was with Gavin? Had I thought about him more than I realized? And how could I turn my back on Gavin so quickly? Dating is one thing, but falling into bed is completely different. I had loved Gavin so much, enough to agree to spend my life with him. Is it okay for me to be here? To feel this way?

I loved Jake before I loved Gavin. But it was so long ago, it was a first love, not a forever love. Or so I had thought.

Taking my chin between his thumb and forefinger, he tilts it up to look at him. He's always known me so well, read me so well, so I'm sure he can tell I'm spiraling. "Hey. I don't expect you to feel the same way. You had a whole life, a whole romance, a marriage. I had girlfriends, sure, but marriage is different. I understand if it's different for you."

I push up on my elbows and kiss him. "Actually, I was considering that maybe I do...feel the same way, that is. As awful as I feel saying it and thinking it. I don't feel like I compared Gavin to you, or that I didn't love him, but I think I let you go because I had to. I did love Gavin, a lot. But this feels right in so many ways."

A devilish smile spreads across his face as he flips me to my stomach. His hands run down my back, squeezing my ass before coming to rest on either side of my head. I crane my head back to look back at him. "Again?"

"I've waited ten years to feel you again. I'm not ready to be done yet," he says against my ear.

He licks down my spine, stopping to bite my ass before sliding into me from behind, his hand fisting in the pillows. My eyes roll back into my head, face pressing into the bed at the amazing feeling this new angle brings me. I push up on my hands to meet him, wrapping my arm around his neck and twisting to pull him into a deep kiss. When he reaches around me to rub my clit in smooth circles, I collapse into the pillows. It's just too much at once, and I have to grip the sheets.

Every thrust has me whining. Just as the wave is peaking, Jake reaches down and pulls the pillow out from under me and bends down to nibble my neck.

"No, baby, I want to hear you," he growls in my ear. With that, I can't hold it in any longer. As I tighten around him, my moans fill the room, dropping off to sigh his name. His hands ball into fists on either side of my head as he says my name in a low, tight voice.

Leaning over me, he pushes my hair aside, kisses the nape of my neck and over to my shoulder, before rolling to his side to face me.

The corners of my lips pull up. He's gone from a sexy teenager, to an even sexier man. Even when we were younger, he knew how to make me scream. But now? It's a whole new ball game. It's like Jake knows the exact tempo, the exact places, and ways to touch me, to feel me. He does things before I even know I want them. He knows how to read my body and anticipate its needs.

The familiar pang of guilt resounds in my body as I think about something being new and different from my life with Gavin. Sex with Gavin had always seemed great, but this? This is earth-shattering. Jake makes me feel a freeness I didn't know existed.

With Jake, it's almost like it boils down to a biological level. He's ingrained in me, wound into every fiber of my being.

For a minute, I lay still, staring at the ceiling as I catch my breath. When the bed rattles as he shakes next to me, I turn to look at him. "What is it?"

"It's just...it's like our bodies just fit together. It's like we were made for each other."

Rolling over, I curl into his chest as he wraps his arm around me again, fingers grazing along my hip. I trace along the lines of the tattoo on his chest. The hearts and the diamond are one solid line; there are no breaks, no places to start or stop. I trace it over and over again, every so often going up to the flames.

"I remember when you got this. I was so surprised to see it. I didn't even know you thought about getting a tattoo." There's a lightness to my voice, reminiscence overtaking me.

"Did I ever tell you why?" I shake my head, and he takes a deep breath. "I got it for you. It's the Celtic love knot. And the fire around it is for—"

"My name." My breath stalls in my chest, making it come out as a whisper.

"Yeah." He pauses. "I loved you so much back then, Kenz. So much that I wanted something to remind me of you permanently on my body." For a moment, every necessary function of life stops, and then suddenly starts up again with newfound vigor, my blood rushing through my ears, creating a whirring sound focused solely on him.

"The day that I ended things, I was a mess. It was never my plan, never my intention. If it had been, I would have done it right. I considered driving to you. UPenn isn't that far from New York. But I knew if I was standing in front of you, I wouldn't be able to do it. But I *had* to."

There's an audible swallow that echoes through his chest and that tingling inkling that there's more I don't know nibbles at my mind again.

"I'd be lying if I said some part of me didn't hope to see you again when I moved here. I knew the chances were so, so slim. My parents said your family stopped coming after I left. But I had hope. And I held onto that. I'm not sorry I got the tattoo. It was a reminder of you, a constant reminder of my first love, the one I compared all others to." His fingers move quicker on my hip. I can tell he's lost in thought. "I don't know, I just, I need you to know that."

I tilt my head and kiss his chest, my fingers never stopping their path tracing around the love knot. "I'm glad you told me. I wondered all summer why you got it, what it represented, but I was afraid to ask."

"Well, you know now."

"So you have one for me, and one for strength, which also has a little representation of me. What's the one on your back for? Also something to do with me?" I'm teasing, but my head rises with his deep inhale.

"Actually? A little bit, yeah. I had moved back here, and it was harder than I thought. A lot of memories of you I tried to lock away came back. I still missed you. The other two have true symbolism, but this just gave me a distraction, something else to focus on. As far as the actual meaning, I have no idea; I just kind of thought it looked cool." Another one, partially for me. My heart hammers, and I'd be worried about him feeling it, if his wasn't doing the same. If his words don't say he missed me, his actions certainly do.

"I like them. They suit you." I glide my hand up his warm, hard chest to trace along the little tails of the tattoo that peek over his shoulders, the ones I can see near the collar of his shirt.

"Well, I'm glad you think so." He takes my hand in his before continuing, linking his fingers with mine. "I want you to know, I don't want this to be where things end. I don't want one more night together and that's it. I want more. I want more nights with you, more days with you. I thought I'd be okay if I never saw you again, then when I did, I thought I'd be okay with just getting to talk to you again, kissing you again.

"Now? Now I know no amount of time will be enough. I don't expect you to feel the same way. I know it's going to be harder for you than it is for me. But I don't want to waste time. We've lost too much already. And if this is too much, if being with me is too much for you, I'll understand that. But please tell me sooner as opposed to later."

"I don't want to make any promises, Jake. If there's one thing I've learned, it's that you never know what the future holds. But I don't want to go anywhere." It's scary. Jake had hurt me. And up until two weeks ago, I had been in mourning. But I can't deny the one truth I've found. That I want to be with him.

"Stay with me tonight," he whispers, bringing his hand up to cup my face.

"There's nowhere I'd rather be."

Putting his hands on my waist, he turns me to my other side and presses his chest to my back. Fire meets ice when his scorching skin touches mine, and it's never felt more perfect. Wrapping his arm around me, he squeezes me tightly, and I fall asleep in his arms, hearing his heart beating, a sound I've missed for ten years.

At some point in the middle of the night, with the moon shining in through the gauzy curtains hung over the slider, I awake to Jake kissing along my shoulder and down my arm, sliding his hand up to cup my breast, fingers running across my nipple. Opening my eyes, I find his intently on mine as he brushes hair off my face.

In the silver light of the moon, he looks younger somehow. More like the boy I loved and less like the man I'm falling in love with. When he trails his fingers down my spine, chills descend from head to toe. His mouth closes on mine gently as he rolls me onto my back. Anticipating my head tilt, his lips find my neck as he slips into me easily. I rope one hand around his neck, tugging at the ends of his hair as he slides in and out of me.

Teeth graze my collarbone, as he glides up to nip my shoulder. He moves languidly, but it doesn't matter. Despite the slow, steady movements, it feels incredible. Jake has always felt incredible, even the first time; where some say it hurts or is awkward, it wasn't.

Jake pushes up and locks his eyes on mine as my breathing picks up, whimpers and squeaks mixing in with each exhale. As I feel the pressure building, my head tilts back and my eyes flutter closed. Jake's hand cups my face, tilting my head forward as my eyes open to look at him.

Leaning down, he whispers in my ear with strained words. "I want you to look at me. I want to watch you come." He nips my earlobe before pushing back up to have his eyes on mine.

With a few more gentle pumps and the intensity of his

stare, I tighten around him, digging my fingers into his shoulder and tugging at his hair, a low moan rising from my throat.

I keep my eyes on Jake as he keeps pumping, a quick tick of his lip as his breath hitches, before he leans down, his mouth finding mine.

My body follows his as he rolls to his side and trails his knuckles down my cheek, his eyes looking lovingly at me. He kisses the tip of my nose, and I snuggle into his chest, his chin resting on my head, an arm wrapped around me.

His scent of salty seawater mixed with sweetness, the one I had come to know as Jake all those years ago, wafts into my nose. Completely surrounded by him as he invades all my senses, I fall asleep while he traces tiny circles on my lower back.

Jake wakes me in the morning by gently brushing his fingers down my cheek. My eyes slide open to see him standing, hand on the bed, supporting his weight.

"Good morning," he says with a smile that makes my heart soar. "I'm going to go for a surf." A sting ricochets throughout my body as I start to move to get up; he's asking me to leave. "No, no. Don't get up. Go back to sleep. I just wanted to let you know, so you didn't wake up to an empty house, but I *want* you here when I get back. And if you find yourself awake at seven, you know where to find me." Leaning down, he kisses my forehead.

He says the last part to show me he's listening. That he's taking it all in when I speak. My fingers graze his chest as he pulls away. I'm asleep before he's even out the door.

The nutty aroma of coffee brewing pulls me from sleep. Taking Jake's shirt from the night before, I pull it around myself and button it most of the way before I pad into the kitchen to find him standing by the stove, hair still wet. I'm not sure if it's wet from the ocean or a shower.

"Good morning," I say, running a hand through my own hair, taming what I can.

Turning around, he gives me a quick once over, a smile spreading across his face. "Good morning indeed. Breakfast will be done in a few minutes. That shirt looks good on you."

"Dinner, a sleepover, and breakfast? I'm certainly a lucky lady." I ease onto one of the barstools as he slides a cup of coffee across the island to me. His fingers graze mine as I reach for the cup, bringing a tingle to my fingers and a grin to my face. When he winks at me, I almost melt off my seat.

Two plates in hand, Jake comes to sit next to me. Before he starts eating, he skims his hand down my leg. He's made eggs, bacon, and toast with peanut butter instead of butter. "I hope this is okay. I need some protein after surfing."

"I'm not picky. And it's good." I manage to mess up eggs a lot.

"Well, thank you. I actually enjoy cooking."

"You'll have to cook for me sometime, something other than eggs."

"How about tonight?" My heart hammers and my pupils dilate. He takes a few bites of eggs and looks at me with one corner of his mouth upturned, the one he has when his mind is filled with dirty thoughts. "I had a nice time last night."

"I did too. More than once."

He almost chokes on his coffee as he laughs. I had never been shy around him, whether it be physically, or saying what I was thinking or feeling. I've certainly gotten bolder over the years and talking to him is just so comfortable, I know I can tell him anything.

After he eats his whole breakfast, far faster than I've eaten, he grabs my legs and turns me in my seat as he pulls them into his lap.

"So, I should probably go back to my house." The words come out cautiously. It feels like I'm trying not to slip and fall through thin ice. I have no idea what happens now and what the rules are.

As he turns to face me, his brows draw together, eyes narrowed. "What? Why?"

"Well, I don't exactly have any clothes."

"Oh, you don't need those." He smirks, running his fingertips from my knee to under the hem of my shirt, making me giggle.

"I have things at my parents. I'm staying there."

"Well...what if you stayed here?" Though his shoulders tip up the tiniest bit in a sign of nonchalance, I can see the seriousness of his question in his eyes.

"Here?" My eyes widen and I lean forward the tiniest bit.

"Yeah."

"Like, live together?" The thought isn't totally crazy. Even though it's been a very short period of time that we've been back together, those feelings are present and strong.

"Well, I live here. You live in New York. Right?" There's something in his tone that I can't place. It's almost like a challenge.

Where do I live? At the moment, I don't really live anywhere. I'd had my parents sell my house, and my stuff is at theirs or in storage, but it's not home. The beach house had been a temporary solution. I feel like a nomad. But the thought of staying with Jake makes my heart race, my chest flutter, and my mind wander. It's like I'm living out my childhood wishes.

"Okay. I mean, if I'm going to be staying for a while, and you don't mind having me, I can let my parents see if they can save a few of their reservations."

"I certainly don't mind having you." A ghost of a smile appears on his face, but it's gone just as quickly and he falls quiet for a minute, not looking at me. "Are you?" His gaze remains glued to his plate.

"Am I what?" My head tilts to the side and I purse my lips at the change in his demeanor and his question.

"Staying for a while?" There's uncertainty in his voice. Fear. I hate that I've put that there.

"At first, I wasn't sure. But now? Yeah, yeah, I'm pretty sure I'm staying." I intentionally leave off the 'for a while' part.

"Pretty sure?" His voice is tight, and I know he's feeling vulnerable. He's told me how he feels, and asked me to stay with him. It makes sense for him to want to know that if he opens his heart and lets me all the way in, that I won't turn around and leave him like he left me.

I lean in and kiss him next to his ear. "I'm staying."

His body relaxes beside me, shoulders lowering, and a puff of air pushes out.

"I'll go over after breakfast. Get my stuff. I'm sure you have work to do?"

He lifts one shoulder. "Working for myself has a lot of perks, including that I get to make my own schedule, as long as I hit my deadlines. I'll help you."

"I don't have a lot of stuff, but okay." While I can definitely do it on my own, since I moved down myself, I don't want to be away from Jake if I don't need to be. The speed with which the feelings have come rushing back continually amazes me.

We have all my stuff back at Jake's within two hours. I'd called my mom to tell her she can let the rental agency know they can reopen it for rentals.

"Are you sure, sweetie?" There was hesitance in her tone.

"I'm sure."

She's excited for me, but cautious. Part of me feels like she's expected this all along. But I know if something goes wrong with Jake, I won't be able to stay in the Outer Banks anyway.

Though I put my hair things in the bathroom, I feel it's a bit too presumptuous to put my clothes in drawers. I hadn't even really unpacked at my parents' house. As much as I want to be with Jake, around Jake, here with Jake, I'm timid, needing to protect my heart. It's only been about two weeks since we reunited. While it's natural and easy, we're still getting to know the people we've become. What if we realize we don't like those people?

Jake makes a tasty pasta dish for dinner, complete with wine. It's easy, flowing, like we've been doing this for years instead of a few days.

That night while lying in bed, after another earth-shattering round of sex, I can tell he's lost in thought. There's nothing specific I can put my finger on; it's just how well I know him.

"What are you thinking about?"

Taking a deep breath, he holds it for a beat. My sign that he's deciding if he should say anything or not. "It's not any of my business. I know it's not. But, have you ever, ya know. Have you ever faked it?"

Shock coils through me, and I sit up to look at him, my hand resting on his chest, finding a rapid pulse beneath my palm. "Are you serious?"

His lips have a slight downward curve. "I'm just, I don't know, feeling self-conscious, I guess. Things are great when we're together, and you seem to really enjoy yourself. But I'm not sure if it's me or if that's maybe just, how you are."

He won't meet my eyes. That's how I know he's being serious.

"Okay, for one, no, it's not any of your business. For two, not that I want to even *think* about it, but I can't imagine *anybody* faking it with you. For three..." Taking a deep breath, I mentally prepare myself. I don't love what I'm about to say. "Yes. There were times that I did with Gavin. But with you? Never. I have never, not once, in all of the times we've been together, faked *anything*." His eyes glance up to mine, uncertainty painted through his irises. "Never."

He puffs out a breath. "I'm sorry. I shouldn't have asked. It's none of my business."

"No, it's not. But I've never shied away from telling you to go to hell if I didn't want to tell you something. Ten years hasn't changed that. I don't feel like you should have asked, but I also wouldn't have told you if I didn't want to. But know this, it is *not* just how I am." I hesitate. He asked me, so I figure I can ask him. "Did something happen to make you feel self-conscious? Did I do something?"

His eyes widen and he wraps an arm around my waist, pulling me closer. "No, no, not at all. I love being with you, it's like a completely different experience than it's ever been with anybody else." Bile churns in my stomach, and I flinch at the thought. It's not fair; we both led other lives, but it's the reaction I have.

"I just, I don't know if I'm solo in feeling that or not. It hasn't been that way with everybody. I know it shouldn't matter, but I just want us to be open and honest with each other, so if something's off, not right, or even if it just doesn't happen, I'd rather you be honest." Chills wrack my body as he trails his fingertips up and down my arm.

"Well, you're certainly not solo in that feeling. And I'd never lie to you." Sliding out from under the covers, I kiss his chest, starting at the love tattoo and working over to the other side, then down. I work my way back up to the tattoo on his shoulder, tracing my tongue along it gently. Then I breathe gently in his ear.

"I'll happily show you again how much I'm *not* faking anything." With a nip to his earlobe, I fling my leg over his hips, pushing up to straddle him.

The look on his face tells me he's still not convinced. Taking his hand in mine, I slide it between my legs. His breath catches as his eyes lock on mine. "*This* is how much I want you. Just the anticipation of feeling you gets me..." I can't finish, biting my lip and throwing my head back with a slight moan.

His erection pokes me in the thigh, and I wrap my hand around it. He sucks in sharply as I start moving my hand up and down, his head tilting back slightly and his hands sliding to my lower back, thumbs on my hips.

A gasp tears from my mouth as I guide him inside me, he just fills me so perfectly. How can he not realize how truly amazing he makes me feel each and every time? There's no possible way anybody could ever make me feel the way he does, always has.

As his fingers dig into my hipbones, I start rocking. Bending forward, I rest my lips against his, not stopping my motion. "Only you can make me feel this good."

That wakes him up. Grabbing the back of my head, fingers tangling in my hair, he pulls me down, my lips crashing onto his, as he wraps his arm around me and flips me onto my back in one smooth motion.

His mouth locks on my neck, sucking and biting as he picks up momentum. I claw at his shoulders as he thrusts into me, bringing me closer and closer to the edge until I can't hold it in anymore, crying out.

Using his shoulders as support, I pull myself up to kiss him as he keeps moving above me, sliding my tongue over his, sighing against his mouth, a moan rising in my throat as he groans, pressing his forehead to mine.

I wrap my hand around his neck and tug him down with me as I fall back to the mattress. We lie there for a minute, foreheads pressed together, chests heaving, before I let him go.

Rolling to my side, propped up on my elbow, I run my fingers along the tattoo on his bicep.

"Listen, I don't like thinking about you with anybody else, and I *know* you don't like thinking about me with Gavin. But for me? This is different. Very different. And it always has been. We've never had to figure things out. It's like from day one, you've always just known what I want, even before I do. It's like you can read me."

"I could, I still can. Sorry, I guess I just got lost in my head. I think I was expecting it to take time or something. I don't know."

"Listen, if there are girls you have been with who faked it or just didn't get there, I'm good with that. I don't care about your ego, because it just makes me think this is because of our connection."

Taking my hand in his, he kisses my knuckles. "I like how you think about it."

There's something else I want to tell him, but feel like I'll be betraying Gavin if I do. Yet I want him to know, I *need* him to know, right now, while he's questioning things. Glancing down at the sheet covering my hips, an inability to look at him overtakes me before I share.

"I feel wrong saying this, but so you know how much I mean it, Gavin was jealous of you, for a while."

"He was? Why?" Sinking his head into the pillow, his brows knit together.

Still unable to meet his eyes, I shrug and twirl my fingers

along his chest. "He could see that you still had a hold on me. Even two years later, even after you broke my heart, and I spent that time trying to move on, I couldn't. I still thought about you daily. It hurt, for a long time. On some level, I'm not sure it ever *stopped* hurting."

I lift with Jake's heavy sigh. "I know how you feel, because I felt it too. And I can never apologize enough or tell you how huge of a mistake it was. Just know that every day I regretted my actions."

"Gavin could see the hold was still there. And as much as I hated myself for it, every first between Gavin and I, some part of me compared them to you. Even though I'd closed that part of my life and was happy with Gavin, some small part of me still compared."

There's a weight in my stomach, leaden and thick, and I feel like a horrible person. I've just betrayed my late husband's memory by divulging one of his vulnerabilities. It's like I can't help it, I want Jake to know all of me. I want him to know that I moved on but never forgot him.

He pulls me against him, running a hand down my hair over and over, as his salty sweetness wraps around me. It brings me such comfort just to have that scent wafting through my nose. It allows me to relax, to forget about all other things.

AUGUST

As sleep starts to dissipate, I roll over and reach my arm out. The bed is cold. Opening my eyes, I sit up and look around. There's a note folded on Jake's pillow.

Good morning beautiful. I went for a quick surf. I should be back by ten. I love you.
-J

A surf? Is he crazy? Throwing off the blankets, I hop out of bed and yank back the curtains to look out the sliding glass doors that overlook the ocean. Dark, choppy waves that are anything but inviting stretch for miles out to sea. The ominous sky of the incoming hurricane looms out over the water, already gray overhead. Glancing both directions down the beach, all I see are red flags on every post and every access.

I turn around to look at the clock. It's ten-thirty. Speed walking into the kitchen, I expect to see Jake reading the newspaper. But he's not here. "Jake?"

Nothing but silence. I check my phone, nothing. Since he's

sometimes late returning, I decide to give him a little more time to come back, busying myself making coffee and something to eat. But I have an uneasy feeling growing in my chest.

Though I sit at the counter with a plate of food in front of me, I can't bring myself to take a bite. Every time I check the clock, it's been at most five minutes. To distract myself, I pick up a book, but find myself rereading the same paragraph over and over.

Maybe using my hands will be a better distraction. I dive into laundry and cleaning the bathroom, sure it will take at least a half an hour, but it ends up only taking me fifteen minutes.

Unable to quell the uneasiness which has now turned into a tremble and borderline panic, I pick up my phone to call him. Maybe he's run into a friend or neighbor.

It goes straight to voicemail. "Jake? Where are you? I'm worried. Please call me." I try not to let the anxiety show in my voice, but I'm pretty sure I fail. He's now over an hour and a half later than he said he'd be. Panic is starting to bubble over.

Looking out at the beach again, thinking maybe I'll see him, my chest deflates as I lose the tiny shred of hope I was holding. It's empty. The waves are so choppy, I can't make out much more than the ocean, but I'm pretty sure I don't see anybody on the water either.

A shower, that has to be the answer. I can relax under the warm water.

It doesn't help. Instead, I find myself standing under the stream, lost in my head as steam fills the room and my skin begins to pink.

It's all too familiar. Waiting on somebody who never came home. What if Jake never comes home? My stomach churns at the possibility. I can't even think about it. Tears mix with the water from the faucet, and I can't tell which wetness is which.

Taking a deep, shaky breath, I wipe the tears and get out of the shower. As I'm drying off, I hear the cabinets in the kitchen closing. I throw on one of Jake's long-sleeve shirts and practically run into the kitchen.

There he is, in jeans and a white t-shirt that fits to show his muscles, the bottom of his tattoo peaking out from the right sleeve. He turns and smiles at me as I get closer.

As soon as I'm right in front of him, I smack him, hard, against his chest. He flinches back, arms coming up. "Ow, Kenz, what the hell?"

"Where were you?" My voice is low and shaky.

His brows furrow as confusion encompasses his features. "I went to go surf, but the waves were rougher than I felt comfortable with, so then I went to Food Lion to stock up before the storm. It was nuts. I'm glad I went, but, man, was it—"

"Why didn't you call me?"

"My phone died. You're always telling me I need a car charger. I guess you're right." That's when he looks at me. *Really* looks at me. All of the color drains from his face as he reads how upset I am. "Kenz? Kenzie, what's wrong?" He reaches out to me but I back away.

"I was fucking worried about you, you asshole!"

His brows furrow even deeper, causing crease lines in his forehead. "I left you a note."

"And then you were unreachable!"

With a tight jaw, he walks over and grabs the back of the couch. His muscles ripple as they cord. I don't know why *he's* angry. I'm the one who's freaking out because I had no idea where he was.

"I told you my phone died. I'm sorry you worried." He tries to keep his tone level, calm, since it's clear I'm hysterical.

"You said you'd be back *two hours ago*!"

"I'm sorry!"

"Don't you get it? I thought you *died*! I thought you were whisked out into the ocean or something. There's a hurricane coming, red flag warnings up and down the beach, and you decide to go *surfing?* Are you serious? Do you care about me at all?"

"Of course I do! You know I do. I was only two hours later than I said I'd be. It's not the first time I've been late."

"Two hours is all it takes." My tone is low, solemn.

With those six words, his whole demeanor changes. His body relaxes and his face drops as he stands up straight. He knows what can happen in two hours. "Kenz...Oh, baby, I'm so sorry. I didn't...I didn't think. I just—"

There's a burn behind my eyes and a pain in my throat, but I press on. "No, you didn't. You didn't think about me at all. You didn't think about what it would do to me. How it would make me feel. How I'd worry. Don't you get it? I thought I *lost* you! I can't lose another man I love!"

My hand flies to my mouth. Even though Jake told me a few weeks ago, I haven't said it yet. He understands that I may need more time. But I realize now that I've felt it all along. Maybe I never even stopped.

His hands twitch, and there's a slight shift in his stance. Clearly, he wants to come toward me, but he doesn't, respecting my anger. Part of me wants to run into his arms, but another, a bigger part, is still really angry. That part keeps my feet planted. We stare at each other for a few minutes, neither sure how to break the silence.

"I don't know how we can do this if you can't consider me and what your actions may do to me," I say quietly, my heart cracking at the thought.

His lips downturn and his eyes look at me, pleading. "Kenz, no, don't say that."

"We don't even know each other, Jake!"

"Of course we do. We've known each other half our lives."

"But you don't know me now. You don't know who I've become."

"Yes, I do." The statement is too simple to be true.

I shake my head in protest.

"I do, Kenz. You're still the girl who loves the beach but hates the ocean, afraid of sharks. You read so much, your eyes should probably be crossed by now, but they're perfect and beautiful, the softest shade of blue." My heart flutters when he utters the word *perfect*.

"You drink way more coffee than probably any one person should in a day. You like to turn the music way up and rock out to the perfect song with your windows down while driving, especially on the highway.

"Despite fighting your curls when we were teenagers, you embrace them now, and they're beautiful, that stunning red streak running throughout, making your hair almost look like it's on fire when the sun hits it just right." A twinkle skitters through his eyes, looking wistful. "You have a deep passion for teaching. I can see it when you talk about your students and how much teaching meant to you. I can tell you miss it even though you'll say you don't."

The storm had blown in more while we were fighting, and I jump as a big flash and rumble tear through the room. Jake chuckles softly. "You're still scared of lightning. You're strong, stronger than you realize. You've been through something horrible and traumatic and yet you've come out the other side. You've been able to find a way to laugh again, to have fun again, to love again."

His voice lilts up with the word *love*. Looking up from the floor, I catch his eye. Uncertainty resides there. I said it, he heard me say it, but he's not sure if I fully mean it.

Without hesitation, I cross the room and fall into his arms, leaning my head into his chest as the tears erupt. There are so many emotions. Leftover fear and anxiety from him being gone, joy to just feel him again after I'd convinced myself I'd lost him, and an emotion I can't quite place for realizing I love him. It seems a bit like betrayal to Gavin. Or maybe, it's more that I *don't* feel that betrayal anymore, and think I should. With one arm tight around my shoulders, the other holding my head against him while he rests his chin on top, he holds me tightly against him.

He doesn't try to shush me or calm me. Instead, he holds me and lets me cry. Slowly, and while keeping his hold on me, he walks us over to the couch. As he sits, he pulls me down with him, where I curl up in his lap, and he wraps his arm around my legs.

Every so often, he'll kiss the top of my head and apologize into my hair. We sit for a while, with him holding me and running his hand down my head to my back, leaving small kisses where he can reach. At some point, I doze off.

The sound of wind howling outside and rain pounding the windows jolts me awake. I sit up with a start and notice Jake lying next to me, head propped up on his hand. Without asking, I know he's been watching me sleep, as his eyes are full of concern.

"How'd you sleep?"

"Good. I think. I didn't even realize I'd dozed off." My mind is still a little hazy, my body sore from the tension of worry.

"How are you?"

It's a good question. How am I? "I'm alright." It's the best I can do. Very middle of the road.

His mouth presses into a line. "I was worried about you."

"Good," I snap, then instantly wince. I know he's sorry. I don't need to make him feel worse.

His eyes flash apologetically. Moving closer and sitting up next to me, he takes my hand in both of his. "Baby, I'm so sorry. I never, ever meant to scare you. I wasn't thinking." Exhaling heavily, he looks out the window.

"I went to go surf because sometimes when the storms are far enough out, you get some of the best waves. But it was worse than I thought it'd be, worse than they said it would be on the news. My only thought was you. What would you do if something happened to me? I couldn't put you through that again. I went to leave and ran into Tom; he was going to give it a shot but had the same thought.

"We ended up chatting for a bit, about storm prep and what we did and if we need any help after, to call. Then I headed over to the Food Lion to get some last-minute essentials and it was crazy. My phone died or I would have called to let you know where I was. I didn't think I'd be that late. I didn't think about what my lateness could mean to you. I'm so sorry."

Sliding his hand up my arm, he pulls me against him. I consider fighting it, some anger still bubbling under the surface, but I don't want to. Instead, I melt into him. "Please forgive me," he murmurs against my shoulder.

I pull back to look at him. "I will, I do. I may be angry for a little while. But you need to understand, you can't ever do anything like that again. I need to know where you are. I need to know when you're going to be back, and if you're going to be late, you need to tell me. You can't let your phone die."

He's already nodding. "I understand. Trust me, this will never happen again." While I can see and hear how much he means it, the only thing I can really do is wait and see how it goes, hoping for the best.

Gently touching my hair, he runs his finger down a lock

and pulls the curl until it straightens before letting it bounce up. "I really love your curls, by the way. Have I told you that?"

Looking down, I shake my head, letting them pour forward. I spent so many years fighting them when I was younger.

His deep chuckle makes my chest flutter and causes me to look up. There's a far off, wistful look in his features and swirling through his eyes. It's the most sky-blue I'll see for a day or two, but it's my favorite kind to look at.

"I remember the last summer we were together, you had perfected how to make your hair straight and it would hold in the humidity. I grabbed you around your waist and pulled you into the pool. You were so mad at me. You kept yelling that I messed up your hair, your perfect hair. But you didn't go fix it, you let it dry. And it was so beautiful even then."

The memory brings a smile to my face and a lightness to my chest. "My awful frizzy mess?" I think for a moment, my hands reaching up to touch my head. "Probably not too different than what I have going on now, huh?" It reminds me that I hadn't put any product in after my shower. I'm sure it's an absolute disaster.

"You're beautiful." With a gentle touch, he tucks some curls behind my ear. "I love it so much, I'm okay with you having about a million products all over the counter in the bathroom."

I can't help but laugh. It's one of the biggest parts of having curly hair. It takes a lot of product to keep it looking nice. They all serve a different purpose, even though I don't use them all at the same time. From day of wash to a refresh a day or two in, to even just something to help protect against the salt and chlorine while here.

"Did you mean what you said?" His voice is low, and I'm

pretty sure I'm the only one who would notice the hint of uncertainty in it.

"Yeah. Yeah I did. I do." I run my hand down his cheek as I stare into his perfect blues.

His brilliant smile spreads across his face, his eyes twinkling. With a quick glance down at his lap, then back up at me, bottom lip between his teeth, my heart dances and my clit throbs. "I don't know how I got so damn lucky."

My own smile spreads across my face as I look at him. I know what he means. Gavin had been a great husband, a great love. But Jake is who I'm meant to be with. Somehow, some way, we ended up here together again. We've grown and changed, but it's like we grew and changed together. Or at the very least, we grew into a person that the other can still love.

"I'm lucky too. I loved you when we were kids. And saying goodbye was so hard. I cried the whole way home that summer. But I never once regretted anything about you or our summers together. I missed them. But I locked them away, put them in the past. I would tell people I'd had a great young love, because that's what it was, a young love.

"I met Gavin, and he was wonderful, and I loved him. And by some amazement, when I got away to the one place where I knew my heart could heal from the loss of him, I ran into you. It's almost like my heart picked up where we left off. You're different, I'm different, but we're still so much the same. We both grew and changed, and I feel drawn to you even more than I did then. And it makes me feel like a horrible person. It makes me feel like everything with Gavin was fake, a lie, a placeholder." Looking down at my hands, I shake away the sting returning to my eyes.

Jake moves closer and takes my hands in his, looking down and trying to catch my eyes. "Hey. Look at me." His voice is soft and gentle.

I comply, the tears welling.

"You know that's not true. Feeling how you felt, how you feel, with me. That's not an indication of your relationship with Gavin. You loved him. You loved him enough to marry him. The chances of us seeing each other again were slim, at best. You had put our past in a place in your heart and locked it away. I did too. There was no reason to do otherwise. We moved on, we found other people. You found somebody you loved enough to marry, I didn't. Circumstances changed and brought you here. Us running into each other reopened the parts of ourselves we'd closed off so long ago. That doesn't mean your marriage was fake or a placeholder. You weren't waiting until you could see me again because you didn't think you would." Using the pad of his thumb, he brushes away some of the tears that begin rolling down my cheeks.

"Tell me what else you know about me."

"I know that you still order the same milkshake from John's that you ordered when we were kids, banana chocolate, chocolate chip. You still talk with your hands...a lot. When you're really into a book, you curl a lock of your hair." He twists the spot I know I fiddle with when reading.

"You hate cooking but will offer to do it anyway because you want to be the type of person who likes cooking, and you think if you do it enough, you'll learn to love it. You rock Converse now when you're not barefoot, which is totally sexy."

A mischievous smirk spreads across his lips. "You like it when I do this." Leaning in, he kisses my neck, sucking the little bit and working his way up to my ear. My moan leads to a tiny chuckle from Jake.

"What else do I like?" I try to sound seductive, but I'm sure it doesn't come out that way.

Jake quirks an eyebrow and has me flat on my back, laughing as he grazes his lips over my collarbone. I forgot I'm wearing one of his shirts that's so big on me, it falls off my shoulders. It's easy for him to find exposed skin. Taking the hem of the shirt between his fingers, he pulls it off, reaching behind his head and tugging his off as well.

His eyes and smile widen. Hearing the sound in the kitchen, I hadn't put on a bra, just throwing on one of his shirts and a pair of black panties. Kissing along my collarbone, he glides his lips down before closing them around my nipple.

My back arches, and I can't contain the sigh as my hand tangles into his hair, pulling him closer. He starts moving his tongue with more force, his hand smoothing down my stomach to slide under my panties.

As his fingers graze me, feeling the wetness that has pooled, he groans against my breast. Slowly, he slides in one finger, then another, as he kisses up to my neck. I moan as he starts moving fingers so skillfully.

"Do you like that, baby?" All I can do is nod and whimper as I claw at his back. Responding with a groan, he starts moving his fingers faster.

With the pressure building, I tug at his roots as I writhe beneath him. Knowing I'm mere seconds from coming, he stops, pulling his fingers out, his mouth finding mine.

"Uh, uh, uh, not yet," he says with a gravel in his voice, lips right against mine. Putting my hand around the back of his neck, I pull his mouth to mine, parting his lips as his tongue slips over mine. His hand trails down my side, grabbing my hips and tugging me against him as I skate my hands down his chest to the button of his jeans.

A few quick, hungry kisses down my torso and he stands to kick off his pants and boxers, climbing back over me when they're on the floor. There's a smirk on his face as his lips meet mine. He kisses down along my jaw, my collarbone, grazing over hardened nipples, down my navel. With one quick movement, he has my panties on the floor. He kisses along my hip, down between my thighs. And I gasp as his tongue touches me, wrapping my fingers in his hair, pulling him closer.

I squirm and writhe beneath him as he expertly uses his tongue. He starts slowly, licking up and down. Then he uses the tip on my clit, moving in circles, around and around, alternating speed and pressure, knowing exactly the right time and way to change. With one hand, he starts to gently massage my breast, rubbing my nipple between his fingers.

That's about as much as I can take, and I scream his name as I shudder and buck against him.

Jake kisses the inside of my thighs as he slides himself up the bed, a smile on his face, turning his body to lean over me as he eases himself into me. My head tilts back in ecstasy as a gasp leaves my mouth, and Jake latches on to my neck.

Starting slow, he runs his hand up the side of my body to rest against my cheek, locking his eyes on mine as he moves in and out. His hand stays pressed against my face as he leans in and kisses me hungrily, his tongue pushing its way into my mouth.

When he starts moving faster, the familiar sensation builds up again. As I tighten around him, I pull my mouth from his so my voice can fill the room. His lips find my neck as he moans, teeth resting against my skin, before leaning his head on my shoulder.

Tenderly, he kisses his way from my shoulder to my lips before rolling to his back. Flinging an arm over his head, the other pushes under my neck and pulls me against him. I curl into him, head on his heaving chest, arm reaching up to his far shoulder. As I fling my leg over his waist, he immediately reaches down and runs his fingers along any skin he can reach. His heart hammers under my cheek, just as mine is.

He squeezes me closer, kissing the top of my head. "I love you, Kenz. I'm so sorry I scared you."

Nuzzling into him, I turn my head to kiss his perfect chest, right in the middle of his tattoo. "I know. I love you too. I just, I need you to have more forethought. I know you never had to before. But I need you to now."

I feel him nodding in agreement. "What do you say after this storm, we go find a car charger?"

Somehow, I had almost forgotten about the storm. Now, I can hear the howling of the wind again, the rain pattering against the windows and roof. Jake has this magical ability to make everything else fall away. "I think that's a good idea. Are we going to be okay here?"

"In the storm? Yeah. It won't be that bad. It's supposed to reach a max of category two and it's not hitting us head on. It'll be out to sea a bit." He stops and thinks for a moment as I tense beside him, a new fear setting in. "Oh, that's right, you've never been here through a hurricane. I forgot you guys usually headed out."

In the several years we vacationed here, we only had to leave for storms twice, and both times were when we were young kids, before anything transpired between us. "Yeah. Not really looking forward to it."

When he lifts a shoulder, I shift with the movement. "I've been living here for a few years now, so I've seen my share. Worse than this, for sure." He gives me another squeeze. "I'll keep you safe."

Despite the fear bubbling in my stomach, I feel safe with Jake, so safe that I'm able to drown out the sound of the storm outside and focus on just us in the moment.

SEPTEMBER

Things with Jake have been nothing short of perfection. The day after the hurricane, which was barely more than an intense thunderstorm, we drove to the mainland of North Carolina to do some shopping, the primary focus being a car charger for his phone.

Spending all your time with your significant other seems like it should get old and boring. Maybe even frustrating. But it hasn't happened with us so far. All of my time with Jake is something I treasure. Maybe it's because I know how fleeting life can be, how time can be cut short unexpectedly.

"You were really never married?" Standing pressed against Jake, wrapped in his embrace, is my absolute favorite place to be in the entire world. It doesn't matter if we're in his living room, like right now, or in a store, or on the beach. All that matters is if I'm with him.

Tipping his head slowly from side to side, his eyes look at the ceiling. "Well..."

Immediately, I plant my hands on his chest and push away, backing out of his arms. For weeks, he's been telling me he's single, that he'd never married. Before I can do more than turn to walk off, he grabs my hand and pulls me back against him, wrapping his arms around me so tightly I can't move.

With one hand, he tilts my chin so I can look up into his eyes. "It was a mistake."

Sure, that's what they all say.

"It's not even a divorce; it's an annulment." He brushes some hair off my face. "We had been dating for two years and decided to take a trip. She wanted to go to Vegas. So, we went, were having fun, and then one night we had way too much to drink and ended up at one of those tacky twenty-four-hour chapels and got married."

Anger seering through me, I try to push away from him, but his arm tightens, pulling me closer. I'm pressed up against him so tightly, it feels like his heart is pounding in my chest.

"I woke up the next morning and realized what had happened. I filed for an annulment that day. We broke up before we even got on the plane to come home. She'd planned it all. She wanted to get married. She'd told me about a hundred times, left pictures of rings from magazines on my desk, in my room, even in my wallet. I wasn't sure...I wasn't ready. She thought she could trick me into marrying her in Vegas and that I'd either just accept it and keep it, or that I'd be too lazy to do anything about it."

I glare at him, anger rolling off me. But Jake's soft, looking at me tenderly. "Why didn't you tell me?" It comes out through gritted teeth.

He sighs and looks at the ceiling. "I didn't want you to think less of me? I don't know. I should have. It was a drunken mistake. We were younger, I was twenty-three."

When I got married, I was twenty-two.

He looks down at the ground, shaking his head, his hair brushing against my cheek. "As far as anything is concerned, I was never married. We had it annulled, though it did take a few months." As he looks up at me, I see that his brilliant blue eyes are filled with sorrow and sincerity. "I'm sorry. I should have told you. I think part of me wanted you to think I waited for you. Which is crazy because I never thought I'd see you again."

My lips are pressed into a line while I look into his eyes for a minute. But then the tension oozes out of me, and I melt into him, pressing my cheek to his chest. His grip loosens, knowing that I'm not going anywhere. One arm wraps around my head as he leans down to kiss the top of my head. "I'm sorry."

For a minute, I just let him hold me. Pushing back to look at him, I wrap my arms around his waist, so he knows I'm still staying here with him.

"I just wish you had told me. I don't know why you didn't. It doesn't matter. I would understand if you had been married at one point. Hell, I'd understand if you were when we first saw each other again." I hesitate, not sure I want to say what I'm thinking, but feel like I need to. I bite my lip before I jump off the cliff. "I would probably still be married if...if—"

"If Gavin didn't die." His voice is low but gentle. He looks away from me, scanning the living room from ground to ceiling and around before coming back to lock on my eyes. There are so many different emotions residing in his, I can't figure them all out. How could he possibly feel?

He'd told me he'd never really settled because he compared other women to me. But I did, and it only ended because of a tragedy. We both know that had it not, I wouldn't be here right now.

Pushing up on my toes, I kiss him, taking hold of his face and resting my forehead against his. "I love you."

He nods against my head. "I love you too." There's a sadness in his voice, in his eyes. Wrapping his hand in my hair, he pulls me back against him, kissing the top of my head and resting his chin on it. Every part of my body that's touching his, can feel how tense he is. We stand there for a few minutes before he backs away, sliding his hands up to wrap around my biceps. "I, uh, I have some work to do. I'm going to go down to the office."

Shock steals my breath and twists its cold tendrils through my chest. Most days, he just takes the laptop to the dining room table and works there while I read on the couch. "Oh, okay." There's a waver I can't control in my voice.

"It's just, I'm running behind. I need to focus to get it done. And you know I certainly can't focus around you." He smiles as he says it, tucking some hair behind my ear, but it doesn't touch his eyes. It's forced.

"That's alright. I was thinking maybe I'd run out. I'm running low on books." I give him a grin, also forced.

There's been a shift. And we can both feel it.

While I'm out, I decide to run a few extra errands. I'm able to pick a few new books, get some bagels, groceries, and swing into our favorite coffee shop to grab us some iced coffees.

When I get back, he's gone. There's a note on the coffeepot, knowing that'd likely be the first place I'd go.

Went for a surf. Had to clear my head. I love you Mackenzie. -J

My heart sinks. Not only has he already gone surfing today, but he *never* calls me *Mackenzie*. To busy myself from my wandering and worrying mind, I put away the things I bought, Jake's coffee going in the fridge.

I take my book out to the middle deck, iced coffee in tow. I'm reading on the porch swing when I see Jake coming up the walk from the beach. His surfboard is under his arm, wetsuit still on. He jerks his head to get some hair out of his face. My heart leaps at the sight of him. There's no denying I love him immensely.

I watch as he opens the gate that leads into the pool area of the house, propping his board against the fence. As he undoes his wet suit and pulls it down around his hips, a familiar twinge settles between my thighs at the sight of his toned chest. I'd always found him sexy, but he's really come into his own over the years we were apart.

From the porch, I follow him as he walks toward the outdoor shower to rinse off. If he knows I'm watching him, he doesn't let on. He turns on the shower, giving himself a quick rinse and stripping off his wet suit, then board shorts underneath. Seeing the gentle indent at the top of his board shorts makes me groan, and bite my lip.

Turning off the water, he gives his head a quick shake, water droplets flying from his shaggy hair. I've joked with him more than once about the length. Even though he's always kept it on the shaggier side, hanging a little over his ears and the nape of his neck, I'd thought as he aged, he would have cut it. But it suits him.

I sit back on the swing as he walks into the house. Time is what he needed, asked for without so many words. I don't want to bombard him, so I'll let him find me when he's ready.

About twenty minutes later, I hear the slider closest to me open. Sandwich and iced coffee in hand, he walks out, freshly showered. He sits next to me, picking up my feet and putting them in his lap.

"Thanks for the coffee." He turns to me and smiles. It still doesn't touch his eyes. Whatever clarity he'd been looking for out on the water, he hadn't found it.

Using one hand, he eats and drinks in silence, absentmindedly rubbing my legs with the other. I try to focus on reading, but keep glancing up at him. Every time I do, his gaze is trained on the water. Though I want to keep my composure, I've had enough of this.

"I thought I'd make dinner tonight." Though I've offered a few times, I haven't actually cooked here once. While making this declaration, I glance at him over the top of my book.

"Oh, that sounds nice." Nice? That's all he has to say?

Closing my book, I look at him. "Jake, what's going on?"

He turns to me, face blank of any emotion. "What do you mean?"

"I mean, we had a disagreement this morning and you've been weird ever since."

All he does is shrug. "I'm fine."

Sitting up straight on the swing, I leave my feet in his lap so I can be right next to him. I kiss his shoulder before resting my forehead against it. "Please talk to me." My voice is so low, I'm not sure he hears me.

He's sitting so quiet and still, I'm sure he didn't. Until he speaks. "I'm just...I'm feeling a little confused. A little unsure."

"About what?"

"About us." My heart stutters. When he turns to look at me, I find his eyes swimming in hurt. It matches what I'm beginning to feel in my chest.

The lump in my throat has grown, becoming more cumbersome. "What about us?"

He sighs. "It's just, our relationship feels based on circumstance."

"I'm not sure what you mean." I do know what he means, though. But I want to hear his side, his worries.

"If things had gone differently for you, you'd probably have a family right now. With somebody else. You'd have a baby or a toddler. Maybe a dog. And you'd be living a full life with them. It took one thing, one tragic thing, to change things for you."

"But that tragic thing brought me here, to you."

"I just can't help but think if things had been different. We wouldn't be together. You want me because you don't have another option. There isn't somebody else."

No. That's not the only reason I want him. It can't be.

My stomach drops to the ground and a chill takes over my body as ice crystalizes in my veins.

"But things aren't different. Gavin's gone. I'm here, with you, and I'm happy."

"Baby, I know you are. And I am too. But I guess I just worry that it's for now, while you move past your grief. Then you'll realize this isn't what you want, that I'm not what you want." Dropping his head, his hair grazes my knees, before he turns to look at me. His eyes are glassy.

"I knew in the back of my mind, all those years, that I wanted you. I let it go, I *had* to let it go, because I knew we'd never see each other again. And then you were here, on my beach, and I thought things were finally going my way. But you didn't move here. You came to get clarity, to get your life on track. I'm a detour. Somebody to help you over the hump."

I start shaking my head before he even finishes, my eyes filling with warm, salty water. "No. NO! That's not what you are."

"How do you know? I mean, really. How can you be sure?"

"Because I love you!" The tears erupt and patter against my legs as they roll off my jaw.

Jake brushes the tears with his thumb. "I know you do. But I can't help wondering if it's just because I'm helping you over the hard part."

Everything inside me stills, and I feel like I've been punched in the chest. How can he possibly think that's what's happening here? And how can I make him see it's not?

"You have these residual feelings of your life with Gavin...

you lost your *husband*. You still had all that love inside you. We have a history, so it's easy to transfer those feelings—"

I'm shaking my head emphatically, almost making myself dizzy, the tears coming faster now. "No, that's not what happened. That's not what's happening. It's been two years. Two years, he's been gone."

"And you never moved on. Kenz, you came here to try to find yourself again. You were still grieving, still mourning. I saw that, but I was too excited to see you again to give you the time you needed, the time you deserved, to fully close that part of your life."

Unsuccessfully, I try to hold back the sobs that rise in my chest. I know where this is heading. Jake's unsure, thinking I haven't found myself.

He's going to end things.

I can't believe I'm here again, having to convince the man I'm with that I'm over the man that came before.

With one easy motion, he pulls me into his lap, wrapping his arms around me. Gripping his shirt, I sob into his chest. I can't hear anything but my cries.

"I think...I think we should take some time apart. I think you should go home. This isn't your *home* Kenzie. This is your escape. I think you need to go back to your reality. Your life."

Unable to form a single word, I shake my head as I press my forehead to his chest. This is my life now, doesn't he see that?

"You do. You need to see where you fit. That's your life, in New York. Your family is there, your home is there. You can probably even get your job back."

"No! I don't want any of that. I just want you." Grabbing tighter at his shirt, I pull myself farther into his lap.

His arms tighten around me, and I hear him swallow hard. I know he's holding back tears himself, and Jake's not a crier. "I'd love nothing more. But I don't really think this is what you want. I think it was a nice distraction, something to get you back on track for your life, to help you move on. But not what you want in the long run, not where you're going to end up."

My whole body moves with his deep inhale, and I'm thankful he's holding me, because otherwise I'd fall apart. "I hope I'm wrong. God, I hope I'm so wrong. I hope you go back to New York and realize you can't live without me. But I think you're going to realize it feels good to be back in your old life."

"Are you sending me away?"

"No. But I am telling you that I think you should go. And I'll be here, if you do decide this is what you want." He takes another deep breath. "But I don't think it will be."

How can he think that? After all we've been through, how could he think that I won't want to be with him? Part of me wonders if this is some sort of test. But the look in his eyes tells me he's serious. That he's willing to break his own heart to make sure I know what I want, that I lead the life I'm meant to lead. I want him, I'm happy here, but I know there's no way to convince him.

Sliding my legs off his lap, I stand to go inside. "Well, I guess if that's how it is, I should get my stuff packed, so I can leave." I start to walk away, when his hands wrap around my waist, pulling me back. He'd stood after I did, and I fall flush against him.

His hands cradle my face as he draws me in for a deep kiss before he kisses my temple. "Don't go yet. Stay tonight, just one more night. Please." His voice is pleading. While he wants me to find myself, to know I'll be happy here, he doesn't want me to go.

Not trusting my voice, I simply nod, even though I don't want one more night. I want all the nights.

Taking my hand, he leads me inside. "Listen, I want to just be with you, but I really do have work to do. I'll do it in the dining room, though. I'd rather have the distraction." There's more to the sentence than he says. He wants to say before I leave, but he doesn't. Still not trusting my voice, I nod again.

We busy ourselves for a few hours; he works, I read, then clean a bit. Jake comes into the kitchen with me when I start dinner around five. He pours us both a glass of a wine and stands nearby while I cook, leaning against the counter next to the stove, close enough that I choose to use the burner closest to him so that I can brush up against him every so often.

While I still hate cooking, and am still bad at it, I want to make something for him. My mind is distracted while I cook, which isn't a good thing, seeing as how much I struggle. I'm wishing this wasn't the first time I was doing it, leaving him on this note, but I'm also happy it will be one of his last memories of me.

We sit and eat at the counter, our knees touching the whole time. He frequently puts his hand on my thigh, leaves it for a few minutes, then takes it back. Only to do it again a few minutes later. It's like he's having an internal battle with himself. Very few words are spoken.

We clean up in silence, standing side by side at the sink, me washing while he dries. When he's dried the last dish, he puts his arms around my waist and pulls me to him. "Let's go watch a movie."

Sitting on the couch, he leans against the arm, pulling me down to sit in between his legs, my back against his chest. I lean back, my head resting against his collarbone as he wraps his arms around me, hands on my hips. Instantly I'm thrown back to our last summer together and how safe and loved I've always felt in Jake's arms.

My mind is so full of ways to convince him this is what I want, that I barely pay attention to the movie.

Partway through, Jake brushes some hair off my neck,

dipping his head to the side and kissing the spot he's just cleared. His other hand moves under my shirt, gliding up my stomach to cup one of my breasts. Tilting my head to the side, I give him a better angle, my eyes closing as a small moan eases from my lips. I feel a pulsation in Jake's pants.

Before I know what's happening, he scoops me into his arms and carries me to the bedroom. Putting me down, my feet on the floor, he quickly pulls the gauzy curtains closed over the windows and slider. We prefer them because they help a little with the sun in the morning, but allow us to still see the moon and stars. I wonder if he'll go back to pulling the thicker ones closed when I leave. *Leave.* It makes my entire being ache.

Crossing the room in three strides, his lips crash on mine, hand tangling in my hair, tipping my head back as he parts my lips with his tongue, sliding it over mine. I press my body into his, feeling every inch of him from chest to knees. I know what he's doing, I feel the urgency behind his kisses, the feverishness of his hands. But I want it too; it's all I want. *He's* all I want.

My shaky fingers make me fumble with the hem of his shirt, causing him to take a step back and reaching behind his head to rip it off, pulling mine over my head in the next second. With the flick of his wrist and a seamless motion, he unhooks my bra. His hands are immediately at the band of my shorts, tearing at the button and sliding them down, along with my panties, before flying to his own.

Wrapping his arms around my waist, he grabs my ass as he steps forward, connecting our bodies and pushing me backwards until I fall onto the bed. Immediately, he's on top of me, his lips on mine, as his fingers graze over a hardened nipple, twiddling as my back arches.

He kisses his way from my mouth, down my chest, tongue wrapping around my nipple, hand sliding between my legs. I gasp as he pushes two fingers into me, mine tangling in his hair, tugging slightly. His fingers and tongue work in tandem as I rock against his hand, pressure building. Tightening my grip in his hair, my other hand scraping against his shoulder, I cry out.

Licking his way over to the other breast, he gives a tiny flick of his tongue against the nipple, before kissing across my collarbone to my neck, giving my earlobe a tiny nibble and sighing into my hair as he eases into me. With a kiss against my temple, he rests his forehead against mine, our breath mingling in the space between us as he slowly moves in and out. I know he's taking his time, savoring it, expecting it to be the last time.

His lips meet mine with an urgency as he starts moving faster. I claw at his back as the pressure builds. Some part of me is hoping to leave marks, scratches, a testament that I was here, that I was with him.

Arching towards him, a moan leaves my throat as pleasure takes over, the hardened peak of my nipples graze against his solid abs. His hands tighten into fists against the pillows by my head, a tiny grunt releasing.

Chest heaving, he rests his head against my shoulder, as I trace my fingers up and down his back, across the tattoo that spans from shoulder to shoulder, down his arms, trying to imprint the feeling of his skin. He places a tiny kiss on the tip of my nose and bottom lip before rolling onto his back.

Before he's even settled, I'm already moving to lay on his chest. As he pulls me tightly against him, his hand locks around his other wrist at my waist.

I adjust so that I can hear his heartbeat and trace his tattoo at the same time. The one he got for me. Closing my eyes, I trace over the design with my finger, knowing the outline by memory. I listen to his heartbeat, trying to burn it into my mind.

At some point, I lost myself to sleep. When I wake up, the full moon is high in the sky as Jake shifts to wrap around me again. After falling asleep, we must have moved apart. He pulls the blankets up to cover me before settling in behind me, his chest pressed up so tightly against my back, there isn't an inch of space. As he kisses my shoulder and wraps his arms tightly around me, I feel a tiny drop on my neck and know he's crying.

I settle into feeling his heart beating against my back, trying so hard to memorize the warmth and pressure of him next to me.

There's not a single particle in me that wants to leave. But I also know I won't be able to convince Jake that I want to be here. I'm completely stuck.

If I stay, he'll never believe I really want to be here; he'll think I'm just avoiding my life. If I leave, then I'm leaving him.

My plan is to go to New York for no more than a few days. That I'll be able to convince him that this life, with him, is what I want more than anything.

At six in the morning, when Jake normally wakes up to go surfing, I pack. It takes me three drawn-out hours to pack everything I've brought, anything I've purchased, and one shirt I've stolen from Jake. From the edge of the bed, he watches me with sad eyes before helping me carry everything down to my car. He's thrown on a pair of shorts, and I know the second my car is out of sight, he's going to spend hours out on the water.

When the very last thing is in the car, I turn and fall against him. He pulls me close, wrapping his hand in my hair while the other snakes around my waist. Tears silently fall from my eyes as he kisses the top of my head and lets out a pained sigh. Twisting his fingers into my curls and pulling gently, he tilts my head back and closes his mouth over mine. It's tender and passionate, but filled with sadness. He leans his forehead against mine.

"I love you. I love you so much. But you need to get back to your life." There's so much anguish flowing with his words that it sends an icicle straight through my heart, freezing water trickling through my veins with every half-assed pump of the aching organ.

"I love you too." There's no point in arguing with him. No point in telling him that this is what I want to be my life, that there's nothing left in New York for me. I'd tried all that the day before. If he doesn't know by now from the words I've said and the ways I've shown him over the past few months, the only thing I can do is leave for a few days. And I do plan to make it only a few days.

Walking me to my door, he gives me one last, lingering kiss before ushering me into the driver's seat. One hand on the frame, the other on the top of the door, he leans down, giving me another quick peck. "Let me know that you get home safely. Please? It doesn't matter what time. Or if you stop overnight. Please, I just need to know you're safe."

Not trusting my shaky voice, I nod. My eyes have erupted, and Jake brushes the tears away with his thumbs as he cradles my face. I lean into his touch, my heart begging him to change his mind, my mind reeling for something, anything, to say to convince him that I don't need to go home to know that this is what I want. But he takes a step back, and my mind comes up blank.

My eyes flick to his tattoo, the one he got for me all those years ago. "I love you, Jake." I have to say it one more time. He needs to know; he needs to have zero doubt that I am irrevocably in love with him.

"I love you too, Mackenzie. Please, drive carefully." It sounds so strange, the words pouring out of his mouth. Maybe it's the tone with which he says it, the sadness behind them. It isn't a loved one telling another loved one to drive carefully while they go to the store. It's saying goodbye.

I nod as he shuts the door, backing away from the car. Sliding his hands into his pockets, he stares after the car as I force myself to put the car in gear and push my foot to the pedal. His eyes are full of pain, almost as much as my soul is.

It's at least ten hours back to my parents, house. I know I should stay overnight, but I just want to get back. My head hurts, my heart hurts. My body is already longing for Jake's touch, and I haven't even gotten back to the mainland.

The drive takes an eternity. Everything I do brings back thoughts and memories. Turning the radio up reminds me of our argument of when he said he knew me, that I like to listen loudly. I grab lunch to eat in the car and it reminds me of the trip we took to the mainland and the fun we had throwing French fries at each other.

Right now, merely existing is so painful, I'm not sure how to continue.

The few breaks I take to use the bathroom and stretch my legs, I also check my phone, hoping for a text from him telling me he was foolish and to please come back. There are none.

I make it back to my parents' around seven-thirty at night. When I walk in, I find two stunned faces as I make my way into the kitchen. The exhaustion from the drive and trying to keep myself together for so long finally takes hold, and I break down before Mom can even ask me what happened. Within seconds, she's by my side, wrapping me in her arms.

She helps me up to bed, patting my hair, telling me it will all be alright and that we can talk in the morning, to just rest. Repeatedly, she refers to me as My Fire, telling me I'll get it back. But I know it's extinguished. Whatever flickering of a flame I had left inside me, the one Jake tended and stoked to bring back to force, has been doused with my own salty tears.

As soon as she leaves, closing the door behind her, I pull out my phone, sending Jake a text.

Me: *I got to my parents about ten minutes ago. I'm going to bed, tired from the drive. I miss you.*

The response comes almost immediately.

Jake: *Glad you're home safe. I miss you too.*

The bed shakes beneath me as I cry myself to sleep, alone again.

A FEW DAYS LATER

The morning after I arrive, I explode like a volcano, all over my poor mother, giving her all the details and my utter confusion. At the end, her only thoughts are that she can tell I truly love him and that she understands where his uncertainty comes from.

With a strong need to be in contact with Jake, I text him constantly. I try calling him too, but he never answers. Any waits between my message and his usually occur in the morning, and I know it's because he's out surfing.

But by the fifth day, the texts start coming with longer intervals between my message and his response, while at the same time becoming shorter. Then they stop altogether.

Everything aches, and I feel like history is repeating itself.

By noon, I've had enough and ask him what's up.

Me: *Jake is something wrong? Why aren't you answering me?*

When I get no answer after another hour, I send another message with shaky fingers.

Me: *Jake. It's been hours. Please let me know you're ok. I'm worried about you.*

Just before climbing into bed that night, I get a response.

Jake: *I'm ok. I'm safe. I just think it would be best if we don't talk for now. You can't process if we're still talking every day. That's not the point of this. I won't be responding again. Take care Mackenzie. I love you.*

My heart shatters as I burst into tears and cry myself to sleep again.

The next morning, I have to ask Mom to take my phone away, because all I want to do is text Jake. As I tossed and turned all night, I kept picking it up, hoping for there to be a message that he'd had a bad night, changed his mind. When that doesn't come by eleven, I hand over the phone, proceeding to sulk around the house for the rest of the day, too broken to do anything else.

On my seventh day back home, Mom takes me over to the storage unit they'd gotten for all of my stuff. With a deep breath, clench of my teeth, and straightening of my spine, I brace myself as she opens it. It isn't just my stuff; it was also Gavin's. Clothes, papers, pictures.

"Do you want me to stay?"

"No. I need to do this myself. I need to be able to process." Expanding my chest with a deep breath, I glance around the small space. My whole former life is in here.

With what I'm sure is understanding, she nods. "I'm going to give you your phone so you can call me when you're done."

A weight settles in my stomach, the same heaviness I know the phone will be sitting in my pocket. But I know I need to be able to keep in touch with her. With one more deep breath, I step into the unit, having to find a path through all the piles of boxes. They'd kept my big sitting chair. It had been my favorite place to sit, with quotes from books written all along the fabric. I run my fingers along the back before I sit in it, opening the top to the closest box.

Hours pass, as I file through papers and books and clothes. I've made a huge pile in one corner of things that are garbage. So many old bills and papers that aren't needed anymore. Clothes of Gavin's, some of which are harder to part with than others. Clothes of mine that I just don't feel fit my life anymore. Though right now, I'm wondering what that is.

But this current box, this one is a little tougher. The first thing I see when I lift the cover, is a picture of me and Gavin on our wedding day. Our smiles are huge. I remember this picture. It was taken just after we'd said *I do* and walked back down the aisle as our friends blew bubbles at us.

Ever so gently, I touch the glass over Gavin's face. For the first time in two years, I'm not overcome with grief. I don't fall apart into a pile of blubbering mess. I'm finally able to think back and appreciate our time together. Our life, our marriage.

Carefully, I put the picture to the side, continuing through the box. I can see my mom's handiwork in packing this one. It's all organized as wedding things. Our marriage license is in this box. Our wedding photo album that I flip through and am able to laugh at for the first time since Gavin died. There are some great candid shots, including one of Anna almost licking my face. There are papers from the planning process, including our contract with the venue. I dig all the way to the bottom, where I see two ring boxes.

My breath catches, knowing what they contain. I open Gavin's first, a simple black ring. He'd wanted something dark and liked how light this one felt. He hadn't been a jewelry guy, didn't even wear a watch. He said the lightness made it easier to forget it was there.

With a snap, I shut the ring box and put it back in the larger one, taking a deep breath before I pull out the other and open it. My engagement ring and wedding band sit there, snuggly together. Gavin had spent so much time picking out the ring. It wasn't my style, not something I would have chosen for myself, but I loved it because of the care he put into it. It had a very simple, matching platinum band.

Putting my rings back into darkness, I set them beside Gavin's. I'd taken my rings off a year after Gavin died. Too many people kept asking me if I was married, where my husband was, when we were having kids. It got to be too hard to answer their questions, especially when they asked why I still wore my rings if he was gone.

All the things from the box end up back inside, and I push it over to the keep pile. But through it all, I had retained my composure, not shedding a tear. Two months ago, I'm sure if you had told me I'd be sitting here, going through what was basically our marriage without shedding a tear, I would have told you that you were crazy. And yet, here I am. I realize I've closed the box on that part of my life, once and for all, literally and figuratively.

Though I hadn't cried, it was still an emotional roller coaster. My mind is reeling a bit. This had been my *marriage*. But he's gone. He's *been* gone. And I have moved on. The guilt I'd felt about moving on had passed weeks ago, because Jake truly makes me happy.

Glancing around and pleased with the progress I made today, I call Mom, trying and failing not to double check my text messages. "Hey, mom. I'm ready to go. I'll meet you out front." Deciding to use every second I have, I use the fifteen minutes until she gets here to throw away some trash.

"Wow, you got a lot done today," she says as she appears, meeting me inside instead.

I dust off my hands. "Yeah, I just kind of powered through."

She juts her chin to the top box. "I see you found the wedding box." Just now I notice that the sides are different from the others.

"I did."

"And? How are you?"

"I'm okay, actually. I was able to reflect on that time fondly. It was a happy time in my life, and I'm lucky to have had it. But it's over. It's really and truly over. Gavin's been gone almost two years now. I went to North Carolina to let him go, to find who I am without him. And I did. I found more than that." Thinking about what more I found, and apparently have lost, for a second time, makes my heart plummet.

For the next five days, I go back to finish clearing things out, taking my time sorting through what I want to keep and what can be let go. On the fifth day, I fill up my car with what I want to keep, minus my chair, which Dad will come back for. A whole life, stacked neatly in boxes in the back of my car.

When I get to my parents' house that evening, I search for something I'd tucked in the back of my closet long ago. It's still there, dusty, but no worse for the wear. The container holds all the things from my relationship with Jake: pictures, emails I'd printed, shells we'd found on the beach, the necklace he gave me, broken chain and all. Anything and everything that had reminded me of Jake ended up in there. I sort through it carefully, like I'm afraid it might all turn to dust if not handled with extreme gentleness.

Sitting on my bed, I look through the contents, turning some things over in my hand. At the bottom is an envelope filled with all the pictures I had. After Jake ended things, I went through all my mom's loose photos and albums and stole all the ones of me and Jake, adding to my collection.

I swallow around the lump building in my throat and take a deep breath, gingerly lifting the flap. The picture on top is of us the first summer we met. It's all four of us; Scott, Shannon, Jake, and me.

Flipping through the stack, I watch the gradual progression of not just us growing up, but growing closer. Halfway through and the pictures go from standing awkwardly together, to being against one another. We have giant smiles spread across our faces, arms around each other.

The tears spring free when I come to one where Jake has his arm over my shoulders and we're looking into each other's eyes. I keep flipping to get to the last one. We're sitting on the porch swing together. I'm leaning into his chest, his arm around me resting on my hip, the widest smiles I've seen so far on our faces.

My hand flies to my mouth as I make a sound I don't recognize, and I try to blink away the onslaught of tears. This picture, this last one, says so much. It's an image of a happy and in love couple, comfortable in each other's presence. I can't help but think of all the heartache that came just a few days after this was taken.

It's not so different from what I feel now. A deep hollowness resides in my chest, like something that used to exist is now missing, ripped from me without anesthesia and something no pain medicine in existence can take the edge off of.

Before I can stop them, my hands are on my phone, dialing. Quickly, I swipe at the tears and my nose, taking a deep breath to steady my voice shaky. I don't want him to know I'm crying. It goes to voicemail. Disappointment fills my chest, but I'm not surprised.

"Hi, Jake. I know you said you didn't want to talk but I—I had to call you. I'm not even sure if you'll listen to this, but I needed to tell you. I spent the last few days clearing out the storage unit that my parents filled with the stuff from my house. The one I had with Gavin. And I didn't cry once. Not even when I went through the box that basically contains my marriage. Not when I saw my dress. Not even when I looked at my rings. Not a single tear.

"But then tonight, I found the box I had put together of things from you. Pictures, notes, letters, a CD you had burned for me. Do you remember that? I also had a shirt I stole from you. And you know what I did? I cried. Big fat tears. Because I *miss* you. So damn much. I love you, Jake. I truly love you. I closed the box on my marriage. It's in the past. But you're my future. I want you in my future. I want you in my now and for the days to come."

A wince takes over as a harsh swallow burns my throat. "I want to come back to North Carolina, back to you. That's my home...with you. God, I really hope you hear this." I look at the ceiling, tears welling again. "I'm going to go before I start bawling again. I just...I needed you to know. I love you." Hesitating a moment before pressing end, I hold the phone to my chest, hoping he'll hear the message.

It's been seven days since we last messaged. My heart has ached for every single one. Hearing his voice, even just the tiniest bit for his voicemail message, pulls at the strings and makes it ache more.

I take out the shirt that I stole from Jake before I left. Even though I've pulled it out every day to smell him a little bit, it still holds onto much of his scent. That mix of salty seawater and sweetness. Ripping off my own shirt, I slide his over my head. It's about three sizes too big on me, hanging to the middle of my thighs.

As I climb into bed, I pull the collar up to be close to my nose. I fall asleep with his comforting scent wafting into my nose as my brain pulls up memories of the sound of his heart, and the feel of his body against mine.

The first thing I do the next morning is check my phone. There's nothing from Jake. He probably didn't listen to the message. I haven't heard from him in ten days now. It's over. My heart implodes as I let go of whatever tiny crumb of hope I'd been holding on to.

Now, I have to find a way to get over another love lost; this one having lost for a second time. As horrible as it feels to admit it, this one hurts the worst.

I go through my day robotically. My parents barely get a response from me any time they talk to me. The absolute crushing and searing pain in my heart is all I can focus on. I'd lost my husband and found a way to move on. But I'd lost Jake for the second time. I'm not sure I'll recover as easily as the first time, which hadn't really been that easy at all.

Around five, the sun is starting to hang lower in the sky. "I'm going to take Judge to the park for a while."

My parents look at each other, with they're mouths tight and eyes narrowed. "Are you sure, honey? It's getting late." I know they're worried about me, but I need to go. I need to get out of the house.

"It won't be dark for a little while still. I'd just like to be by the river as the sun sets." It reminds me of being in North Carolina, of being with Jake. But I can't tell them that.

They look at each other again. "Whatever you want. dear. Just be careful."

I nod as I walk toward the front door to get Judge's leash. "Judge! Here, boy!" He comes bounding in from the living room, his yellow tail wagging frantically as he sits so I can put his leash on. "No, buddy, we're going to take a ride. Come on!"

Judge is a good dog; he doesn't run away, always staying close by. He knows his commands and obeys them well.

Following me out to the car, he waits by the back door while his tail goes nuts. Once I open it, he jumps right in. "Good boy."

I drive over to the park I used to frequent with friends. It's big and looks out over the river. There's a playground, a grassy area, even a bike path. On the way out of my parents' house, I had grabbed a tennis ball. I let Judge off his leash and play fetch for a little while until he decides he'd rather chew on the ball than run after it.

Needing a change of scenery, I walk over the edge of the grass, where there's a ledge that overlooks the water, Judge following loyally behind. As I sit, Judge lies next to me, ball between his paws, and I watch the gentle waves, the sun sinking lower and lower over the horizon, shades of orange starting to paint across the sky.

There's a tingle flitting through my body as I sense somebody behind me, and Judge pops up to sitting. He isn't a barker, but his body language—ears perked up, head tilted to the side—tells me somebody is definitely there.

The person behind me clears their throat, clearly wanting my attention. They're probably going to yell at me for not having Judge on a leash. I roll my eyes as I stand and turn around. And my jaw drops.

"Jake," I breathe.

Before he can even answer, I run and jump into his arms, wrapping my legs around his waist. Stumbling back a step, he loops his arms around me, holding me under my legs. He kisses from my neck to my jaw before finding my lips in a bruising kiss.

Lowering me to the ground on my shaky legs, but keeping his hands on my waist, he juts his chin over to Judge. "So I guess you do have a dog, after all."

I roll my eyes while my heart thumps against my breastbone. "This is Judge. He's my parents' dog. Come here, Judge, it's okay." Judge, who had been sitting patiently, comes bounding over and jumps at Jake. "Judge! Get down. He's usually well behaved."

Jake laughs deeply. I had missed his laugh. Kneeling down, he rubs Judge's head, scratching behind his floppy yellow ears. "Hi, buddy. You're a handsome boy."

Once he's standing again, he yanks me against his chest, wrapping his arms around my waist as he presses his lips to mine, my mouth parting for his. When he pulls away, I'm breathless.

I look up into his eyes, searching. "What are you doing here?"

"I came for you." Tenderly, he brushes some hair out of my face. "I had already decided I need you back in my life before I got your message last night. I called my mom and got your address. She had it somewhere from an old Christmas card, said as long as your parents hadn't moved, it was the address. I had to try it. I packed a bag and went to bed early. I left first thing this morning. Your mom told me you'd be here."

"You saw my mom?" Shock coats my words and my chest. Especially since she kept the secret and didn't let me know he was here.

Slipping his pinkies into my back pockets, he chuckles. "Oh, yeah. I swear I'm sore after her hug."

"How long did she talk your ear off?" I can't tear my gaze from his face, afraid he might dissipate into thin air.

"Not at all, actually. I didn't even have the chance to ask where you were. She said she knows why I'm here and that you're here, at the park. After giving me detailed directions, she sent me on my way. I wasn't even invited in. She shooed me away to come find you."

Snuggling into his chest, salty seawater and sweetness surround me, and I never want to leave this spot again.

Holding my shoulder, he pushes me back so he can meet my eyes. "Kenz, I'm so sorry I sent you away. I thought it was the right thing. I thought you needed time, that you were unsure and you'd realize that when you came back here. But I decided I don't care. I need you in my life for however long you want to be, even if you decide one day it's not what you want. And then I got your message."

"It's okay. I understand. I didn't then, but I do now. I'm just happy you heard it. I was so scared I was going to have to figure out how to live without you again." My breath catches at the end and a sting starts to settle behind my eyes.

Brushing some hair out of my face, having blown around in the gentle breeze, his hands cup my cheeks. "You have me for as long as you want me."

My smile is so wide that my face hurts, and I can almost feel my heart healing as I push up on my toes to kiss him. "Good. Because you have me too."

He presses his forehead against mine. "Move to North Carolina with me."

"I was hoping you'd say that." I feel so light that I could float away on the next slight burst of wind.

Jake smiles, really smiles. One that touches his eyes, one I've longed to see for two weeks, since our disagreement that sent me away. "Why don't we stay for a few days, figure out what you want to bring. I'd like to see where you and Gavin lived."

"Oh. Okay." Stunned, I'm at a bit of a loss for words.

"First, though, we should go tell your parents that you're leaving. For good this time."

"I agree. But first..." I wrap my arms around his neck and pull him down to connect our lips.

When he straightens, he's beaming, and takes my hand in

his, kissing the back of it. "I promise there will be plenty of time for that, and much more."

Linking my fingers through his, I pull him in the direction of the cars, giving him another kiss before we climb in. To make up for lost time, I plan to kiss him every opportunity I get.

I drive slowly, slower than I need to, which causes Judge to whine. Every so many miles, I look in my review mirror to make sure Jake is really there, that it isn't some sort of dream my aching heart conjured up. As I pull into my parents' drive-way, I quickly let Judge out, who runs right up to the front door, wagging his tail and waiting patiently to be let in.

Before he's even fully out of the car, I'm grabbing at Jake, needing to feel him to know he's really here.

He takes my hands in his, grinning, brushing a thumb across my bottom lip. "I'm right here, baby. I'm not going anywhere. Not without you. And I'm never letting you go anywhere without me again." With a tiny kiss on my lower lip, he ropes his arm around my waist.

As we walk through the front door and into the kitchen, Mom comes running over to give Jake a hug. "Oh, honey, it's just so good to see you." Jake puts an arm around Mom but keeps the other loose around my waist.

Dad comes over and shakes his hand. "It's good to see you, my boy. It's been quite a long time."

"It has, sir. It's good to see you too."

"Oh please, no *sir*. We're Jim and Ashley."

"I bet you're famished, Jake. How does Japanese sound? It's our Little Fire's favorite." Mom touches a hand to her chest as she talks, her eyes dashing between the two of us.

"I know, and that sounds great."

Reaching up, I graze my fingers along the tattoo on his

chest. It has become something I do subconsciously, and I'm happy I get to do it again now.

We follow my parents in Jake's car. He holds my hand, fingers entwined in my lap. Dinner flows smoothly, making casual conversation, talking about the times when we were kids and catching up. My parents ask about Jake's family and he lets Mom know that his mother wants to catch up soon.

We're touching throughout the whole meal; our chairs so close, our knees rest against one another. He uses one hand to eat, the other twirling my curls through his fingers, grazing down my back every so often. After we've eaten, we continue our conversation, with me now leaning into Jake's chest as he has his arm over my shoulder, tracing circles on my arm.

Mom hasn't stopped smiling at me. I know what she's thinking without her needing to say anything. She's happy, because she knows I'm happy.

As we leave, taking a few minutes to walk through the small town, Jake keeping his hand in mine, Mom loops her arm through mine on the my other side.

"I'm happy for you, Little Fire. But I'm going to miss you." Her voice is low so Jake, who's talking business with my dad, won't hear.

"What are you talking about?" Flicking my eyes over to Jake, I speak in the same low voice.

"I'm talking about you going with Jake back to North Carolina." We hadn't told them at dinner, deciding that waiting a day or two may be best.

"How did you know?"

"Oh honey. He came back for you, to take you back with him, not to see you. And if you weren't going to go, I was going to tell you were foolish and send you on my own. It's clear as day that you two love each other. It always has been. Honestly, I was kind of surprised when you told me you were marrying

Gavin. I had always thought you and Jake may try to find your way back to each other."

I have to force my feet to keep moving so I don't draw attention to our conversation. But my mouth hangs open as my eyes grow wide. For a minute, I wonder if I'm still breathing. "Why didn't you ever tell me that?"

"It was hard for you to move on from him. When you met Gavin and said you were happy, it didn't seem appropriate to bring it up. After that, of course, you got married. And then, well, then you were grieving, and I knew it wasn't right. When you told me you ran into Jake again in North Carolina, I knew this was going to be the outcome. It was the only conceivable possibility. And when you came home, well, I just knew you two had to get here on your own."

There may not truly be words to encompass the way my mind has just been blown. "I'm going to miss you too, mom. You'll have to come stay at the house again for a week or two over the summer. And maybe Christmas?"

"I suppose we will."

Jake's hand tightens around mine. I hadn't even realized we'd reached the parking lot, so lost in conversation with Mom. He opens my door for me, holding my hand until I'm situated.

Once we get back to my parents', we go right upstairs where we lie in bed, looking at each other. "You didn't let go of me all night." A smile tugs at the corners of my lips as I say it. Part of me still doesn't believe he's really in front of me, even though I can smell him and feel his warmth radiating off him.

"I told you, I'm never letting you go again." To further his point, he squeezes my ass where his hand has been resting, laughing as he does it.

My focus is on his chest, tracing the tattoo with my fingertips, still in awe that he got it for me all those years ago. "You know...we could probably find a way to be quiet if you wanted to." He doesn't respond. "Jake?"

I shift my gaze to his face. His eyes are closed. Poor guy had a long day. I know, the drive had exhausted me as well. He lasted longer than I had.

Snuggling into his chest, I sink into the mattress. This time, I don't have to use my memory to feel and hear Jake's heartbeat, it's right here under my hand.

The next morning, I wake up to Jake running his hands up my thigh, kissing my shoulder and my neck. At some point in the night, I had turned to face the wall.

"Oh good, you're awake," he murmurs against my ear. "Have I told you that you look hot in my shirts?"

I stretch my back, pushing my ass into his hips. "Do I now?"

"Oh, yeah." Taking my face in his hand, he turns it toward him as his lips close on mine, pushing my mouth open with his tongue. I roll to face him, pressing myself against him, as his hand reaches under the hem of my shirt to run up my side.

I break away. "My parents."

He smiles against my lips. "They left a few hours ago."

It's not until that moment that I realize it's the middle of the week. My parents usually leave for work around seven. That's all I need to hear. I wrap my leg around his waist and my fingers twist into his hair as I press my mouth against his. His hand glides back up under my shirt to cup my breast as he slides his thumb over my nipple. My responding moan has him flipping me onto my back and peeling off my shirt.

Tipping down, he places his lips against my neck, giving a small bite before leaving a trail of hungry kisses along my collarbone, down my chest and across to cover my nipple with his mouth. After he yanks off my panties, his fingers climb back up to glide along my hip and between my legs.

As he slides in two fingers, I sigh, his tongue and fingers working in tandem to make me moan and writhe. With a tiny nip at my nipple, I yelp, and he moves his mouth away, kissing down my stomach.

Settling his face between my legs, his tongue compliments his fingers. I wrap my legs over his shoulders, grasping at his hair as the pressure builds. His tongue moves faster, pressing harder against my clit, knowing I'm getting closer until I arch off the bed, calling out his name.

He traces his tongue in circles along my inner thigh before pushing himself up to hover over me, eyes locked on mine, smoothing back my hair as he eases into me. We keep our staring contest going as he starts to rock against me. Breaking free from my gaze, he kisses my shoulder and my neck.

"I love you," he whispers into my ear.

I turn to face him. "I love you too." His lips find mine again as he starts moving faster. Lacing my fingers behind his neck, my fingertips catch in his hair, and I press my forehead to his as I sigh his name.

With a few more hard thrusts, our breathing becoming ragged and our skin growing dewy, I dig my nails into his shoulders, tightening around him and tipping my head back with a loud moan.

"Oh, Kenz." He groans against my throat as a shudder tears through him and he slows.

Rolling to his side, he looks at me as I do the same. His gaze follows his fingers as he traces them down my arm. "I don't ever want to go that long without feeling you again."

"You won't have to."

With a smile, he places a tiny kiss on my bottom lip. "I want to go see your house today. Will you show me?"

"Are you sure? Are you sure you want to see it?"

He nods decidedly. "I do. I think it's important. It's a big part of you."

"Okay. It's a drive. It's a few hours from here."

Lifting one shoulder, he trails his palm up my side. "We'll make it a day. I'm sure there are places up there you miss."

"Alright, I'm fine with that. I'll go get in the shower."

A devilish smile crosses his face. "Mind if I join you?"

"I was hoping you'd say that."

Taking his hand, I lead him to the bathroom. He hovers behind me, kissing my back as I lean in to turn on the water. "I actually need to wash my hair, though, mister, so you'll have to restrain yourself for at least a few minutes."

He groans. "Fine. I can give you a few minutes. A shampoo, maybe some conditioner. But after that, I make no promises." We climb in and shut the door.

I press myself against him as the water runs between us. "What if I let you wash me after I do my hair?" My voice is low and sultry.

His eyebrow quirks up. "Sure. As long as I get to make you dirty again after."

"Sounds like we have a deal."

Not wanting to waste any time, I set to my hair right away.

"I missed the smell of your hair stuff," he says wistfully as I rinse out the conditioner, his hands roaming up and down my sides.

"I missed the smell of you."

"Me?"

"Yeah. You still have that salty seawater smell. Often mixed with sweetness...your cologne, maybe? That shirt I stole smells like you. I took whiffs every day. I wore it to bed the night I called you. It helped me pretend you were next to me." Though the daily pain of our time apart is gone, there are still remnants left behind, like shrapnel from an explosion.

Wrapping an arm around my waist, he pulls me into his chest. "You'll never have to pretend again."

And then his mouth is on mine, reaching down to my upper thighs to lift me up. I hook my legs around his waist as he lowers me onto him, pushing me back against the wall. One hand supports me while the other plants on the wall by my head, the water running between us as he slides in and out of me.

It's hurried, vigorous, water sloshing around us. His mouth lands on my neck as I scream his name. He thrusts a few more times, hissing into my shoulder before he stops his movement. His teeth press into my neck before he lowers me, so my feet are back on the ground.

"I love making you scream," he murmurs against my ear before letting go.

Reaching behind him, he adjusts the temperature of the water, as it's starting to get cold. As he leans back up, shaking the hair out of his eyes, he grabs the fresh bar of soap I had put out the day before and starts soaping up his hands. "You said something about washing you?" Cocking an eyebrow, he smirks.

Leisurely, he rubs the soap all over me, taking his time at my breasts. When I realize he's enjoying himself a little too much, I step away, playfully shoving him and stealing the bar of soap.

"We're going to run out of hot water." When I finish washing, I toss him the bar. Quickly, he soaps up and rinses, getting out while I rinse. As I climb out, he holds a towel open for me, wrapping me up and pulling me against him.

A firm finger under my chin tilts it up for a quick kiss. I turn to the mirror and give my neck a quick check. He didn't really bite so much as nip, but I tend to bruise easily. During my time in North Carolina, I had a few marks on me. There were even a few when I came home, but thankfully, they were hidden under clothes. I don't need to be explaining things to my parents. Lifting my eyes, I catch his devilish grin in the mirror.

"I don't know how I'd forgotten that you're a biter."

Something flashes through his irises as he chuckles. "Actually, I'm only a biter with you."

I spin around to look at him. "Really?"

A thoughtful look takes over his face for a moment. "Yeah. I mean, as far as I can remember. You're the only one I want to bite." He chomps his teeth in the air in my direction. Playfully, I push his face away.

"You're twenty-eight. Isn't that too old to be a biter?"

"Hell no! It's a sign of affection. It's just so good I want more. I can't *not* bite you." I laugh, shaking my head, and he winks at me in our reflection.

While he gets dressed for the day, I'm left alone to do my hair. I walk out to him sitting on the edge of the bed in shorts and a t-shirt, the gray fabric tight against his muscles, and his tattoos peeking out from under it.

It makes butterflies flutter in my stomach and a tingle settles in my clit. Never had I expected to be a girl who's into guys with tattoos, and I don't really think I am. But I'm definitely into *this* guy with tattoos. Especially the one on his chest.

"You're staring."

His deep baritone pulls me from my thoughts, and I shake my head. "Sorry. That shirt looks good on you."

A smirk flashes on his face. "Well, if you're lucky, I'll let you rip it off me later."

"Oh, if I'm lucky, huh? I wouldn't have to just, I don't know, drop my towel?" I quirk up an eyebrow as I drop it to the floor. His breath catches as he adjusts his shorts. But I've turned it into a game.

"Nope. Sorry, does nothing for me."

Sauntering over to him with an extra sway in my hips, I stand between his legs, running my finger over his shoulder. "Really? Nothing?"

Though his pupils are wide, he clears his throat. "Nope. Nothing."

I straddle his lap and wrap my arms around his neck. "How about now?"

His hands connect around my lower back, fingers grazing the top of my ass. "Maybe a little something," he says in a gravelly voice against my lips.

Quickly, I slide back and stand up. "Well, I guess I don't need to worry too much about getting lucky later, then." I wink at him.

"Oh, so that's how you're going to play it? Okay. I see. Game on, babe. Game on."

I already have panties and a top on as I shrug. "I'm not scared."

"Oh, you should be." A shriek tears through the room as he grabs me by the waist, pulling me onto the bed. Immediately, he starts tickling me as I scream and curl into a ball, but he doesn't stop.

I flip around, screaming and laughing. "Okay, I surrender!" When he stops, I can barely breathe as he hovers over me.

I'm afraid he's going to start again when he leans down and gives me a peck on the lips, sliding his mouth over to my ear. "I told you I like to make you scream," he whispers, kissing next to my ear and giving my earlobe a nibble before sitting up. Taking my hand, he gives a tug and pulls me up to stand, smacking my ass and laughing as I put a skirt on.

"Alright, you goof, are you ready to go?" I run my fingers

through his hair.

"I think so."

"Alright, we have a few stops to make first. Let's go."

I take him to my favorite road trip spots. The ones I'd stopped at before making my trip down to North Carolina a few weeks earlier. We swing into my favorite bagel place for breakfast sandwiches and coffee, then we go to the candy shop to get some mixed bags of candy for the road trip. We argue over the best gummy candy, appalled at each other's choices and sneaking our picks into the other's bag.

We finally hit the road, on our way two hours north to see the house Gavin and I made together. It's not mine anymore, so we won't be able to go in, but I understand his need to see it.

Jake's tall frame looks uncomfortable in the car. Repeatedly, he adjusts between sitting straighter and slouching. He keeps his hand in mine for most of the trip. It's a pretty straight shot up the highway, easy driving.

We've been laughing and joking, reminiscing on some of our first years together when we really were just children. But as we start getting closer to the exit, he grows quieter, adjusting in his seat more often that it makes me think he probably isn't simply uncomfortable driving. It's then that I realize he hadn't fumbled around that much when we drove to the mainland a few weeks ago.

"What's wrong?" I venture.

"Huh? Nothing."

With a tilt of my head, I look at him.

Briefly, he glances in my direction. "I'm just a little, I don't know, nervous?"

"Why?"

Keeping his eyes on the road, he shrugs, a tick in his jaw. "I don't know. What if seeing your house makes you change your mind?"

With a slight adjustment, I put my free hand against his cheek, squeezing his fingers with the other. "It won't. I went through an entire life, an entire history, and I was just fine. Yeah, it's going to be really weird to be back there, especially not being able to go in, but it won't change anything."

There's a tight smile firmly on his face as he glances my way again before bringing my knuckles to his lips.

We drive the last twenty minutes in silence, aside from me giving him directions. When we pull into my old neighborhood, a flutter starts in my chest. Sensing the change in me, he gives my hand a squeeze.

"This one, right here." He pulls over in front of a small single story white house. I look out my window at it. "Doesn't look like anybody's home," I mumble as I open my door to get out.

Jake walks around to meet me on my side of the car as we lean against it, looking at the house. It takes one quick turn in either direction to see there are no neighbors to be found. Most of the residents in the neighborhood are professional young couples, many without kids. Which is what Gavin and I had been. "I know it's small. It was supposed to be a starter."

"I think it's nice. Looks like it has a decent yard."

Feeling a little self-conscious, I shrug. "It's okay. It's definitely not like the beach house. Or my parents' house. Or what I'm sure is your family's house. Actually, I just realized I've never been there."

Crossing his arms, he lifts one shoulder. "I can take you sometime. But my parents don't live there anymore."

"They don't?"

"Nah. They moved after I took over the beach house. They didn't need anything so big for just them. And Scott's been out for years."

"Oh my God, how had I forgotten about Scott? I didn't

even ask about him in the past several weeks. How is he?"

Jake climbs up on the hood of his car. "Come here." Taking his outstretched hand, he pulls me up to sit between his legs, my back against his chest, as we look at my old house. He brushes some hair behind my shoulder and kisses my neck, pushing my shirt sleeve down and kissing the spot he's exposed.

With a heavy sigh that shifts my hair, he rests his chin there, roping his arms around my waist. "Scott's fine, I guess. I don't know, we don't talk much. You know how strained that relationship is."

While I'd had firsthand experience of what that relationship was like, I had thought that maybe, after all this time, they'd be able to mend things a little like Shannon and I had. "So no change? Not in ten years."

"Not really. I barely see him. He's out in California now with his wife and four kids. They don't come this way much, and my relationship with him isn't so great that I'm interested in flying out there."

"I mean, they are your nieces and nephews." I can't help but frown.

"I know. And that part is tough. But our relationship got worse. Besides the issues we had, the little communication we had disappeared. I haven't spoken to him in years." When he clears his throat and looks away, I know there's more to the story than he's sharing, but I won't press, knowing he'll tell me when he's ready.

"Wow, I'm sorry to hear that." I run my hand down his cheek, trying to soothe him and the ache that this is bringing to the surface.

"I'm used to it. It is what it is. How are things with you and Shannon?" There's resignation in his voice.

"I mean, not as bad as you and Scott, but not great. We chat every so often. She's also married with kids, down in Maryland.

I video chat with the kids more than I talk to Shannon. I actually like her husband, Frank, but it's still strained. She'd been a big help after Gavin died; she came and stayed with me for two weeks and helped take away the sadness the tiniest bit. But it was the smallest glimmer in a sea of darkness that is our relationship. Once she left, things didn't progress much."

"You know having terrible older siblings was something we bonded over." There's a smile on his face, and I don't have to turn around to know.

"I remember. We said it must be something about older siblings whose names begin with an *S*."

His hair brushes my shoulder as he shakes his head, and I vibrate with laughter. "I forgot about that. Well, we were clearly very good at coming up with reasons for things." Turning his head left to right, he looks up and down the block. "So, does anybody else live here? Or was it just the two of you?"

"It's mostly professional young couples. I'd guess everybody's at work."

"Ah, yes, that thing we call work. That's why I love my job. I get to make my own hours."

"I'm still amazed that you're such a sexy nerd."

His mouth grazes my ear. "You think I'm sexy?"

"Mmm, very."

He nuzzles against my neck before sighing. "So, were you friends with anybody in the neighborhood? Anybody you'd want to say hi to?"

"Honestly? Not really. We hadn't lived here for very long when Gavin—before the accident. And then, after that, I was basically a hermit. We weren't really the most social anyway."

"Oh, really? Why's that? Stuck in bed all the time?"

"Ha, hardly. He just wasn't really interested in meeting other people. And I never had the same problem of not being able to leave the bed with him like I do with you."

"Is that so?" He tilts his head to get a better look at me, because I didn't mean to say all that. And he can tell.

"It is." Moving out of his hold, I spin around to face him. "When I say things are different with you, I really mean that they're different. In so many ways. It's not just that the sex is amazing, and I'd gladly spend the entire day in bed with you. It's everything. It's easy, it's fun, and there's just so much history and such a strong foundation to it."

As nerves creep up my spine, I look down for a minute before meeting his eyes, which are focused on me. "It took me a little while to get it at first, to understand. Loving you is not replacing him. Loving you again does not take away from what Gavin and I had. It will always be special. But this?" I wave my finger between us. "This is undeniable. This is my past *and* my future. Gavin was a chapter in a very long book. But the chapters around it, those are yours."

Leaning forward, he closes his lips over mine, tangling his hand in my hair, and lingering as he breaks the connection. He bites his lip, wanting to say something. "God, I can't wait to get you home. We're not leaving bed for two days."

My head falls forward, and I close my fingers around his biceps as I giggle. "I'm okay with that."

"I love you."

"I love you too." Turning around, I slide off the car and hold my hand out. "Come on, let me show you my old school."

We spend the next few hours going to some of my old favorite places, including the school I worked at and a small bookstore where Jake buys me three new books. He takes me to lunch at a local café, and we walk hand-in-hand through the tiny town.

"Oh, I love this store! It's a small little tchotchke shop, but they have a tiny section of Irish things. I mean, you know we're not *really* that Irish, but it's kind of fun and I can actually find my name on all those silly trinkets. It's just fun to look around."

With a pull, he starts toward the entrance. "Well, come on." I duck under his arm as he holds the door for me and then follows me around as I look at everything.

"These were always my favorite types of stores in the banks too. I know down there they're more for tourists, but I just can't get enough of them."

I feel his chuckle against my back more than I hear it. "Are we going to have a whole bunch of Outer Banks items on our mantel?"

Spinning around, I lock eyes with him. *Our* mantel. I'd almost forgotten that we're going to officially be living together. Not that I'm just going to be staying over for a few weeks.

"Maybe." It's all I can say around the lump that has formed in my throat.

As I work on getting rid of the pain in my throat and the sting behind my eyes, I turn back to the shelves. Jake's suddenly right behind, so close I can feel his breath on my neck.

"Hey, no tears," he murmurs against my ear as he slides a hand to my waist, giving a tiny squeeze.

I tilt my head back against his shoulder to look at him. "Happy tears. I promise."

"It was because I said 'our' isn't it?"

My lip trembles, and I nod as the tears threaten again. Holding my waist, he spins me around and pulls me against him, kissing the top of my head. I sniffle a bit, swallowing tightly, working hard to fight back the tears. "I'm okay. It's just a lot."

Loosening his grip, he looks down at me. "You sure? We can leave."

I shake my head. "No, no. I'm good. I promise."

"Okay, good, 'cause there's something I want to show you." Threading our fingers together, he pulls me over toward the section with some of the Irish merchandise. There are key chains and charms, books about Irish culture, books about the different Celtic symbols and their meanings. I already know the meaning of Jake's. When he stops, he's standing in front of a few trays of rings and looks down at me, eyebrow quirked up.

"A Claddagh ring? Aren't they supposed to be engagement rings?" My pulse has ticked up in speed and the blood races through my veins.

A clerk suddenly appears in front of us. "They don't have to be. Many people wear them just to symbolize relationship status." When she starts talking, Jake takes my hand in his, kissing my fingers and then holding it against his chest where the tattoo sits. He wants me to know why he wants to get this for me. "For an engagement, you'd wear it on your left hand, otherwise you wear it on your right hand. In a relationship, the heart points up your arm, single it points out. We have more underneath if you don't see one you like here, so let me know if you need anything." With a smile, she disappears as quickly as she had appeared.

Jake's eyes are still on me. Without acknowledging him, I take to looking, noticing the smile on his face out of the corner of my eye before he starts looking as well. There are three trays on the table in front of us. Narrowing his eyes, he pulls one out and looks at it intently.

"How about this one?" He holds it out to me. It has a red jewel for the heart.

"Oh, it's pretty."

"Red, like fire." I nod, tears threatening again. "Now, I'm not proposing. So let's put this on your right hand." Since he's been holding my left hand, he lets go and gently takes my right, holding it in his with the back of my hand facing up. With the heart pointing up my arm, he slides the ring onto my finger and a big smile spreads across his face. "Perfect fit."

I'm warm and tingling all over, a smile stretching my lips, as he uses his thumbs to brush away a few tears that have broken loose. It takes this action for me to realize I'm even crying. He kisses the back of my hand, keeping his eyes on me. Worry swirls through his pinched blue eyes.

"I'm good. I promise."

"Anything else you want?"

Lips pursed, I shake my head. No. Nothing. Just him.

Jake insists on buying the ring. It's a cheap little fun ring, but I love it.

We head back to the car, too many emotions running through me to keep going. He opens my door for me, but before I can get in, he tugs me against him, leaning down and kissing the tears that are still silently streaming down my face.

"I love you," he says against my lips before kissing me. Roping my hands around his neck, I pull him closer.

As though worried I'm going to crumble to pieces, he helps me into the car, and jogs around to his side, taking my hand in his the second he's seated. The sky is starting to hue in pinks and oranges, as we've spent the whole day in town. It'll be dark within the hour.

We drive in silence the first stretch of the drive, Jake following signs for the highway. There's a gentle squeeze against my hand after about forty-five minutes. I had forgotten my hand was even in Jake's. He feels like such an extension of me that I almost don't recognize where I end and he begins. When I look over at him, I find nothing but worried glances every few seconds.

"Talk to me," he pleads quietly.

My curls flip over my shoulder as I shake my head. "It's just...a lot of emotions for one day. I was fine when we were looking at the house, and looking at school. But then after lunch, we were walking through the town hand-in-hand and it just made me realize that the last time I was there, I left devastated. A shell of myself. I thought I'd be like that forever."

His eyes never leave the road as he kisses my fingers.

"And then we were in the shop, and you said 'our.'" My lip starts to tremble and my vision goes blurry.

Jake notices, quickly moving toward the upcoming exit and pulling into the first dark parking lot he can find. Putting the car in park, he undoes his seatbelt and turns his whole body to look at me.

"Hey, hey. No tears again." As he cups my cheek with his hand, I lean into it as the tears start to flow. His brows knit together and the corners of his lips turn down as concern overtakes his features.

Turning my face, I kiss his palm, hoping to reassure him that I'm not sad or second-guessing anything. "I'm just so happy. Being back in that town, I never thought I could feel any sort of joy. I left in such a dark place I never thought I'd come out of it, sure I was destined to live sad and miserable. I went to the beach for a new perspective, some peace, hoping that at most I'd be able to live without the pain of grief every day and I'd have been fine to just be content. Not happy, but content, not crying daily. But instead, I found you."

A glimmer flashes across his eyes.

"And it was so nice walking around town, actually happy. Not just happy, but in love. Real, true love. Even after the two weeks we were apart." He drops his eyes then. "No, it's okay. I understand why you felt I needed it. I think maybe you were right. No part of me was feeling unsure; I wasn't feeling indecisive on what I wanted. But I think it made me feel more confident in my choice to be able to go through the boxes and not cry.

"I was hurting, my heart was breaking. But not because of my life with Gavin. It was because of what I was afraid I was going to be losing and missing out on with you. I wanted to call you every day, but I was trying to respect your wishes that we not talk. My heart broke for you once, and I had lost you then. By some weird and strange forces in the universe, we ended up back in each other's lives. And I was sure I was losing you all over again."

My cheeks are wet, the tears plunking against my thighs as Jake looks at me with sad eyes. There's so much hurt in them, but I know it's because he's hearing how broken I'd been by him sending me away. "And then you showed up here in New York. To take me back with you. It was all so surreal. I kept looking back at you on the way to my parents' from the park, sure it was just a dream."

I pause, gathering myself, knowing the emotions are strong for this next part. "In that shop, when you said 'our', my heart just couldn't take it. It's what I'd hoped for when we were kids. What I cried about losing ten years ago, and then again three days ago. But it's here. It's really here.

"You want me to move back to North Carolina with you. To move into your home with you. And I'm just so excited and so happy at the thought of that." I look down at the ring on my finger. The first ring I've worn since Gavin died. "And this?" I hold up my hand. "This means so much to me. I know it's a silly little cheapy ring. But it means a lot."

Jake pushes up the armrests and leans across the center to kiss me, reaching his hand behind my head to pull me closer as his lips part mine, his tongue sliding in. His other hand wraps around my hip and pulls me closer. There's not a second of hesitation as I close the space between us, climbing into his lap, legs on either side of his.

Breaking the kiss, Jake holds me against him with one

hand, the other reaching around to mess with the seat adjustments, pushing it the last notch from the steering wheel and lowering the back before pulling me down on him.

His hands slide slowly up my thighs to grab my ass under my skirt, then one hand slides forward and moves my panties to the side.

"Holy shit, Kenz," he murmurs against my lips as he feels how wet I am for him. As his fingers slide in and start moving, I arch up, bumping my head on the top of the car.

I start to move away, to adjust, but Jake's free hand wraps around the back of my neck, keeping me against him.

"No, no, no, don't you dare go anywhere." With pressure against my neck, my lips cover his as I start to rock against his hand, moaning with each movement. With one amazing fluid motion for the tiny car, he adjusts his pants and replaces his fingers with his erection, both of us sighing as I lower myself onto him.

There's so little room in the car, I'm not sure what to do, but Jake doesn't skip a beat, with one hand cupped at the back of my neck, the other on my hip, pushing me forward and backward. His lips are on mine again, hungry for more. Anytime I feel the urge to move my lips to sigh or moan, his hold on my neck tightens, keeping my lips against his as he swallows each sound I make.

When he feels me start to shudder, he lets the hold on my neck go as my head tilts back and the cabin fills with the sound of my voice as I scream out his name. My head falls against the headrest, still riding him as his head tips back and he groans. We lay panting for a moment, as I regain my ability to think and realize we're in a car in a deserted parking lot somewhere off the highway.

Climbing off him and back into my seat, I start laughing.

He smiles as he readjusts his pants and puts his seat back in position. "What's so funny?"

"We just had sex in the car."

"Yeah. And?"

"And we're adults, and I've never done that before. I'm twenty-six and I've never had sex in a car, yet here I am, as a twenty-six year-old, having sex, in a car, like a horny teenager." I know I repeated myself several times, but I'm too stunned to worry about it.

"You've never had sex in a car?" That's his takeaway?

I shake my head. "Nope."

"Really? Never? We never?"

"Nope. I mean, we didn't exactly bring our own cars to the beach."

Running a finger along his lips, he looks up at the roof. "Huh. Yeah, I guess you're right."

"I mean, have you?"

The look that flashes across his face tells me he doesn't really think he should answer. "Uh."

"It's okay. I'm just curious. I know you had a life. You didn't sit there and pine and never touch another girl. I mean, shit, I got married. Though, wait, you did too." I have yet to truly begin to tease him about that.

His chin drops to his chest, and he runs his hand across the back of his neck, still trying to decide if he should tell me. "Uh, yeah, I have.' His eyes flash up to mine to make sure I'm truly as alright with it as I say I am.

"What? I told you it's fine. Listen, as much as I'd love to imagine and pretend you never ever had sex with anybody else and spent your time longing and waiting for me, it was ten years. And we never thought we'd see each other again."

He relaxes. "But really? Never? You and Gavin were in college. Can't always be easy with roommates and stuff."

I shake my head. "Nope. Gavin was a very, bed only, type of person."

"Well, that sounds boring." Jake's entire body freezes for a second, eyes growing wide in horror at what he let slip out. "I'm sorry, I shouldn't have said anything. Not my place."

Not wanting him to feel bad, I wave him off. "It's fine. It *was* boring. I told him that. I told him I wanted to be more adventurous, try more places. We'd even fought about it. I had to convince him to give the shower a try, years after that argument."

"Ah, so your first shower was with Gavin. I guess it's alright, my pride can take it. I'll just take a whole bunch of first places from you to make up for it." There's a devilish grin on his face as he leans in and kisses me quickly.

"Um, excuse me, but if you recall my first shower sex was with you. That summer? Our last summer together?"

His eyes widen. "Oh shit! I forgot all about that."

A laugh bubbles in my chest. "Yeah. Remember we were sure we'd gotten caught. We were going to be in so much trouble. Thank God it was only Scott."

Lacing his fingers together, he stares down at them in his lap as he shakes his head. "Yeah, I'm pretty sure I just blocked all that out."

"Well, we should have been thankful it was just him. We would have been in much more trouble if your parents caught us."

"Yeah, I was real thankful for that black eye," Jake murmurs under his breath.

My hand flies to my mouth, eyes wide, and I rest my hand on his cheek. "Oh, baby, I'm so sorry. I...I forgot all about that. I guess I blocked it out too." My voice trails off at the end, not quite sure how to make up for my forgetfulness of what was a very upsetting situation.

Though he chuckles, it's low and deep, not a happy laugh. "Yeah, great old big brother Scott. Always quick with the fists, not with the words." He runs a hand through his hair, making it stand up at odd angles. "Ya know, I was fit, even then."

"Trust me, I remember."

A smile spreads across his face, but quickly fades. "That day, I could tolerate the yelling, I was used to it. I knew no matter how mad he was, he wouldn't do anything but yell in front of you. Or I guess, I hoped. I honestly wasn't one hundred percent sure, which was why I put you behind me. But when he called you easy..." His hands tighten into fists and his jaw ticks as rage flashes through his eyes.

"I had never wanted to hit him so badly. But I didn't feel like I could actually *hit* my brother, ya know? I was sure my parents would be mad. And I knew that even though I was in good shape, he was in better shape and bigger and could beat the crap out of me if he wanted to. So, I let him hit me now and then. But that summer. Man, that summer sucked."

"Yeah, you spent a lot of it over at my house. Especially at night. Thankfully, my parents knew what was going on. I was still surprised my dad was okay with you sleeping in my bed, though."

His true laughter catches me off-guard. "Oh, trust me, it wasn't without warning."

My brows furrow. "What do you mean?"

"Oh, I had a threat of death from both your dad *and* Shannon." My mouth drops open for a second before I catch myself and regain my composure.

"What? Why didn't you tell me that?"

"I was afraid you'd change your mind. Your dad basically said that he didn't need or want to know what we did in our spare time, but as long as I was under his roof while he was in the house, I was to respect "the rules". That I was welcome to stay the night because he understood that Scott could get rough when he drank and I could stay with you as long as I was respectful. And that if I was caught doing otherwise, I would no longer be welcome in the house. He didn't exactly specify what these rules were, but it was pretty clear that if we were found naked, I'd be gone."

Utterly mortified, I hide my face in my hand. I had some inclination that my parents knew then that we were having sex, how could they not? But this really confirms it and in a truly embarrassing way.

He laughs again. "Oh, Shannon was worse. She basically said, and I'm cleaning up the language here a bit, that she knew we were having sex and if she caught me so much as doing anything but kissing you or sleeping, while fully clothed of course, while your parents were around, she'd, uh, cut it all off."

"She did *not* say that."

"Oh, yeah. She definitely did. It didn't matter, though. I wasn't there for that. I mean, it definitely would have been nice. There were certainly times I considered trying it, but I was just thankful to not have to sleep with an eye open. I felt safe with you. Those were the best nights of my life. Until recently of course."

"I don't understand why Scott still came those summers. He was in college...he was twenty-one. Why was he still there?" It was one thing that had bothered me all this time. The one thing I couldn't understand. Was it just to torment Jake?

"You really don't know?"

I tilt my head to the side as my eyebrows pinch together. "Know what?"

"He had it bad for you."

My jaw hits the floor as my eyes widen. He has to be teasing. "He did not."

"Oh, yeah. Real bad. More than once, he said he didn't understand what you saw in me. Even saying things like he was older, stronger, taller...Which, now I'm taller than he is, just so you're aware." He laughs humorlessly.

"Well, I gladly would have told him. I mean, aside from the facts that he was *way* older and basically abusive."

Jake looks down at his fingers, which are twisting together in his lap. I give him the minute he clearly needs to tell me whatever is on his mind.

"That's the real reason I had to end things, Kenz. Scott...his infatuation with you was only growing. After he put his hands on me that summer, my mind went crazy with thoughts about what he would do if he ever actually approached you and you turned him down. I didn't know what the future held for me with school, with summers and the amount of time I could commit to us."

I shift in my seat and let Jake take the time he needs to continue. Anger and fear twist in my stomach. What would Scott have done?

"He made some comment, just before I left for school. You were here for another few days after I had to leave. He said something about enjoying the time you two would have together. How at some point he'd *make* you see that he was the better choice. Those words haunted me for weeks. At first, I thought maybe something happened and you were scared to tell me. Then, I realized nothing had, but I'd always worry about your safety where Scott was involved. I'd taken a thousand hits for you, but I wouldn't always be able to be there, Kenz." His tone is sad and defeated. I reach over and run my hand through his hair to get him to look at me, but he doesn't, and I know there's a blame game going on in his head.

"Two days before I broke up with you, I talked to my mom. She said that Scott had the 'great idea' to meet your family for

Christmas again. That was the last straw for me. I had to *do* something, so I did the only thing I could think of. And I'm sorry it came to that, Kenz." Now he does look at me, nothing but years of torment in his eyes.

"Jake. First of all, I had *no idea* that any of this was going on, and I wish you would have told me then. What difference it would have made, I don't know, but at least I would have been aware and not just blindsided. Second of all, it's in the past. There's nothing we can do about it now, except move forward. We're together, we're starting our life, our future. It's time to let it go." While this is new information for me, and I want to toil over it and all the possibilities of what could have been, the way things have gone is exactly how they were supposed to.

Despite my love for Jake, and my heartache at our time apart, Gavin was an extremely important part of my life, one that I don't regret and wouldn't trade.

Looking at the ceiling, he chuckles lightly. "You know, now that I think about it, his wife does look a little bit like you." Turning toward me with adoration filling his irises, he brushes his knuckles down my cheek. "But nowhere near as beautiful."

A horrible thought strikes me. "What about his wife? Does he...does he hurt her?"

"No, God no. He worships the ground she walks on. Actually, after he met her, and some sort of thing happened at a bar where he got aggressive with some guy who talked to her, he went to AA and anger management. My mom swears he's a different person, and he even called and apologized at one point. But it's why I won't see him. I just can't. Apologizing doesn't change things."

"I still don't understand why you didn't say anything. And why you didn't tell your parents. Why didn't your parents do anything about it?" Anger starts to boil in my chest as I remember his parents being seemingly unaware of the hell Jake went through.

"They tried when he was little. They sent him to doctors who said he was just an angry kid and needed to get his frustrations out. He wouldn't hurt me when we were younger; he was just a little "extra rough" as my dad liked to say. They put him on medicine once, but he didn't take it. He didn't hit me for the first time until I was sixteen."

He takes a deep breath before continuing. "Mister big powered-attorney dad didn't think that his clients would like it if they found out that he had problems, so that night they begged me not to get the police involved. And he was fine, most of the time. We avoided each other as much as we could."

"You didn't tell me why you didn't tell them."

A smirk dances across his face. "Caught that, did ya?" It's gone as quickly as it appeared. "He just, started holding something over my head."

My brows furrow. "What could he possibly hold over your head? You had leverage. You could have called the cops, he was hitting you."

His eyes lock on mine, his mouth set in a hard line.

Shock weaves through my mind as icy whisps tangle up my spine. "Me?"

He nods, eyes cast down again. "The first time, he told me not to tell my parents. I remember his words exactly. *It'd be a real shame if something should happen to Mackenzie because you opened your big mouth.'* That was two years before you saw the bruises."

His Adam's apple bobs in his throat with an audible swallow. "I wasn't sure if he meant it, because he liked you, so why would he lay a finger on you. But there was absolutely no way I'd even risk it."

Lifting his eyes, they lock onto mine as he cups my cheek.

"Trust me when I tell you there was not a chance in Hell I would have let him even close enough. I would have knocked him flat on his back before the thought even crossed his mind. But I wasn't with you every single second of every single day, and Scott knew that."

A chill races down my spine and tears spring to my eyes. He'd taken those hits for me.

"Part of me is still surprised your parents let me stay more than one night."

A memory invades my mind. I had woken up the morning after Jake came over, alone in bed. A quick glance at the clock told me Jake was out on the water. Heading upstairs, I heard voices and stopped on the staircase, straining to listen. It was my mom and Jake's. They were talking about what happened. My mom wasn't happy. She asked about the previous bruises from that summer. We went swimming together, so she saw Jake without a shirt on a lot. His mom confirmed they were from Scott, saying she thought I would have said something. I remember feeling nervous when I heard my mom say that I had told her they were from surfing, Jake having begged me not to say anything to my parents.

My mom had assured her Jake was welcome to stay, that maybe it was best for him. I remember thinking how thankful his mom had been, but that she should have been dealing with the situation herself. I waited until they changed the subject before going up the rest of the stairs, my mom's eyes fixed on me. She never brought up that I had lied to her.

With a quick shake of my head, I chase away the memory. "Why did you decide to move back to the beach house? Wouldn't it be filled with bad memories?"

"My best memories are at the beach house, because that's where you were. That outweighs any bad memories I could have from him. And now, I have things to remember about that shower."

I roll my eyes. "Well, as awful as Scott was, you have to admit that Shannon was pretty good. Aside from threatening you with bodily harm."

"She was?"

"Mhmm. You don't remember the hickey incident?" Despite that first time, Jake proceeded to leave bites and marks. One afternoon I had on a bikini, the redness or a mark slightly visible on the crest of my breast.

He laughs. "Oh, yeah. She was so mad. I thought *she* was going to beat the crap out of me."

"Well, thank God for her because she helped me cover it up, so my parents didn't see, which also meant that Scott didn't see. She was always better at it than I was. Though, she gave me a hard time that I didn't remember from the first time she showed me." With a smile, I run my hand along his cheek, his stubble scratching along my palm. "Always a biter."

"I told you, I can't help it. Okay, so let's get back to these firsts. Shower, check. Car, check. Let's see. We were never bold enough to try the beach, so I say we try that when we get home." *Home.* My heart flutters thinking about being back in North Carolina with Jake. Permanently.

"I'm not sure I'm bold enough now. We're adults. We shouldn't be doing these things."

"Why not? Who says the fun has to stop because we're adults."

"Because we're running around like horny teenagers, having sex in showers and cars and on the beach."

"And?"

"And shouldn't we be done with that?"

"Why? We're two consenting adults. We're entitled to have some fun with our *fun*."

I giggle. "Okay. I guess I can go along with that. As long as we don't do anything illegal."

"Wellll...."

My eyebrows shoot to my hairline. "What?"

"I mean, technically, what we just did is illegal. If somebody saw us, they could have called the cops, since this is considered public indecency." He laughs at what's surely fear sprawled across my face. "Same would be true of the beach. And some of the other places I have planned."

Adamantly, I shake my head. "Nope, not doing it, then."

"Oh, come on. I'll make sure we don't get caught."

"I think you'd be a little distracted."

He laughs. "Well, yeah. But we didn't get caught here, did we?"

"In a deserted parking lot after dark? No, we didn't. But—"

"But nothing. Now, there is one place I think we need to talk about, since we live on the beach and all." I look at him with an arched brow, not sure I trust his choices. "The ocean."

My heart plummets, my skin chills, and breaths become shallow as I shake my head frantically. "Nope. No way. No. Not going to happen."

"Oh, come on. We have to!"

"Nope. No way."

With a gentleness in his features and movements, he runs his thumb along the apple of my cheek. "Come on. I know you're scared. But I'll be right there. I'll keep you safe."

"You can't keep me safe from sharks."

"I'm out on that water almost every single day."

"And you've never seen a shark?"

He moves his head from side to side. "Well, I wouldn't say *that*. But I've never had a run-in with one."

"Nope. Sorry, no."

"We wouldn't even have to go in that far."

"It doesn't take far for some sharks. Not worth it, sorry."

His hands fly to his chest. "Ouch. Not worth it?" A smirk pulls at his lips.

I push against his shoulder. "You know what I mean."

"Well, I think you should reconsider. Maybe we'll work on just getting you *in* the water first." Turning away, he looks distantly out the windshield, fingers rubbing against his lip.

I shake my head, looking at him, mouth agape. "You're working on a list in your head, aren't you?"

A mischievous look spreads across his face as he shrugs. "Maybe." I smack his chest, causing him to flinch. "What? Can you blame me? You said before we're like horny teenagers. I *do* feel like a horny teenager around you. It's like when everything was so new. I still can't keep my hands off you. I don't want to." To prove his point, he runs his hand up my leg again, dipping under the hem of my skirt.

I push his hand away, smirking. "Okay there, mister, let's get going."

"Why?"

"Because I am *not* having sex with you in this car again."

Starting the engine, he chuckles and winks at me. "Okay, I guess we'll try your car next time. Or maybe we'll buy a new one; this one's not really roomy enough."

I roll my eyes as he pulls out onto the road. Once we reach the highway, he laces his fingers through mine again.

We spend the rest of the ride laughing and joking, reminiscing about our last summer together where we were basically inseparable for the few weeks we had together. We laugh about how sneaky we thought we were being when we disappeared to have sex somewhere, now realizing we were not at all sneaky and we were sure everybody knew what was actually going on and we're just thankful our parents let it happen.

When we pull into my parents' driveway, the house is fully

lit. I'm sure they're expecting us for dinner, since I'd left a note anticipating we'd be home in time. A quick glance at the clock tells me we are only a little later than their usual dinner time. "Think we should tell them you're leaving?"

"Oh, they already know."

"They do? Did you tell them?"

"No. My mom knew. She said there was no way you came all the way up here just to see me. That you came to get me. And she said I should go; she wants me to, expects me to. I think they let us be together as much as we were that summer because they knew we really loved each other. It wasn't puppy, summer love. It was real then, and it's even more real now."

He kisses the back of my hand. "Well, if they know, when do you want to leave? I'm ready when you are, but I don't want to rush you."

"Let's leave tomorrow."

His eyes widen. "Are you sure?"

"I'm positive. I'm ready. I'm ready to move forward. I'll pack tonight and we can leave early in the morning."

"Okay. Whatever you want."

We get out to go inside, Jake throwing an arm over my shoulders and pulling me close, kissing the top of my head. As soon as we walk in the door, my nose is overrun with the aromas of my favorite meal. Mom must have anticipated that we would be leaving soon, that I went up to see my old house to say goodbye.

After dinner, Jake helps me pack. Around nine, I tell him to go to bed, as it'll be a long next day. An hour later, I finish up and spend some time alone with my parents. They promise to wake us up before they leave for work to say goodbye. It's after midnight when I climb into bed and curl into Jake. He wakes just enough to wrap his arm around me and pull me close. I fall asleep feeling happy and at peace.

THE NEXT MORNING

Awake at his usual early hour, his internal clock set for morning surfing, Jake gently shakes me until I groan in acknowledgment.

"Hey, babe, I hear your parents getting ready. We should get up to say goodbye and pack up the car." Sliding his hand down my side, he kisses my shoulder.

With a whine, I push him away. I'm not a morning person. With a laugh, he swoops some hair behind my ear and off my neck, which he then starts kissing gently as he runs his hand down my side, slipping it under the hem of my shirt. I start to stir more, turning to face him.

As my eyes pop open to look at him, I find a smirk planted firmly on his face. "Well, good morning," he murmurs against my mouth.

"MMM...it can be." I throw my arm over his shoulders, pressing my body and lips against his.

Wrapping his arm around my waist, his hand slides to my lower back, and his tongue slips into my mouth. His body responds to mine immediately, his lips becoming more hurried.

Just as I'm about to throw my leg over his, he pulls back, rolling out of bed with a groan.

"What are you doing? Where are you going?"

"For one, your parents are *right there*. Two, we need to say goodbye."

I reach my arm across the bed. "No, come back. We have a few more minutes. I promise I can be quiet."

With a raised eyebrow, he climbs over to lean on the bed, lips grazing mine. "No, you can't. And I don't like you to be." He runs his tongue along my lower lip before backing away, leaving me sighing and frustrated on the bed. "But I promise you, as soon as we get home you're not getting dressed for two days."

"Well, I suppose I can wait a day for that."

"Two."

"Two what?"

"Two days. I figured we'd make a stop tonight. There's no reason to rush back and I have something planned for you." A playful smile pulls at the corners of his mouth as mischievousness flashes through his eyes.

"What is it?"

"I'm not telling. It's a surprise. Now, get dressed so we can say goodbye, pack up the car, and start our life together." I have to bite my lip to fight away the tears as he mentions starting our life together.

Quickly, I jump out of bed and throw on clothes, catching Jake watching me with a pained look as I undress. We say goodbye to my parents, Jake promising he'll drive safely and that I'll let them know that we get there.

It takes no more than three hours. Three hours to pack Jake's car with the things I'm bringing. Mostly clothes, a few boxes of books. I decide to leave the box of my marriage to Gavin and the few things of his in my bedroom closet here.

Jake stands behind me and wraps his arms around my waist, kissing my neck at my collar, and resting his chin on my head. "Are you sure? You don't have to leave it here."

With tight lips, I nod and turn around to face him, roping my arms around his neck. "I'm sure. That life belongs here. That life *was* here. There is a box I want to get, though. It's the box from when we were kids. That's *our* life, and it belongs with us." I pull it out from under my bed where I'd hidden it the night I called Jake.

Sitting side by side on my bed, heads together, we take some time to go through it, laughing at old pictures, making several comments on our age and how we looked then. When we get to the one where we're sitting on the porch swing, all sounds cease and our smiles both fade. Taking it from my hands, he holds it close.

"Man, I loved you so much back then. Leaving you every summer sucked. Scott called it my pouty phase, because for weeks I'd be miserable. Leaving that last summer was the hardest thing I'd ever had to do. Until two weeks ago when I asked you to leave." He hesitates and looks at me. "I never should have done either."

"What do you mean? You shouldn't have gone to school?"

"Well, no. I mean, obviously, I had to go. But I shouldn't have stopped talking to you. I shouldn't have listened when people said it wasn't real, that it was just young love, there'd be more out there. I should have come back those last two summers before you went to school, and figured out a way to deal with Scott."

My chin drops to my chest and my hair creates a curtain of curls between us. "We couldn't have known. Neither one of us. We were young. So young. How many people actually end up happily married to somebody they dated in high school? And we didn't even really date. We were basically friends who fell in love. But we weren't really boyfriend and girlfriend." My body stills for a moment as I realize I just mentioned being happily married to him, though no actual discussion has happened.

"We were Jake and Mackenzie. That's all there was to it. There didn't need to be more." My body releases the tension as he doesn't bring up the mention of marriage.

"We both had lives outside of us, though. My friends called you my imaginary boyfriend until I showed them some of these pictures. Then they were jealous."

"Jealous, huh?"

"Oh, yeah. I mean, look at you. Then and now."

He laughs. "My friends were pretty jealous too."

"You told them about me? And you showed them pictures?"

"Are you kidding? Of course I did! I talked about you all the time, even after those first weeks back home. You were all I thought about, Kenz. The times I didn't talk to you weren't because I didn't want to, it was because it was too hard to. I asked my parents if we could bring you down for my senior prom. They said no, which in hindsight was probably a good thought. Come college, I *had* to let go. I couldn't see a way out from under Scott, too young and naïve to know what else to do, when really, I should have just said "fuck it" and gone to the cops."

My eyes flood. "You wanted to bring me to your prom?"

With a tilt of his head and scrunch of his eyebrows, he nods. "Listen, I'm not saying that I didn't...make the most...of my college and young adult life experience, but I would have happily had you and only you." I lean into him, his salty sweetness mixing in my nose. Taking my hand, he rests it over his tattoo, his fingers closing over mine. "I knew, all those years ago, I knew."

I tilt my head up and kiss him. "Let's go home."

We swing by the same few spots I'd taken him to the day before to get some road supplies, breakfast, coffee, and more candy to snack on.

About four hours into the drive, I fall asleep.

When I wake up, I stretch, looking around. "Where are we?" We aren't on the highway anymore.

Lacing his fingers in mine, he kisses my knuckles. "I thought maybe we could go try to see some wild horses in Chincoteague." His gaze dashes in my direction as he smiles.

My heart swells. "You remembered."

"Of course I did. I've remembered everything from our time together. Okay, well, maybe not *everything* as I clearly forgot that one time in the shower. But most things."

I have always wanted to see the wild horses in Chincoteague. In middle school, I read a book about them. For years, I asked my parents if we could stop on our way down to the Outer Banks, but they never wanted to take the extra time and I wasn't willing to miss a single day with Jake.

"But how? How did you know how to get here? Where are we going to stay?"

He shrugs nonchalantly, one hand on the steering wheel while the other runs along his mouth. "The internet is a wonderful thing."

"Wait. You booked us a hotel room?"

Eyebrows raised, he looks over at me with a giant smile on his face. "I told you, I had a surprise for you."

"When did you do this? We were together all day yesterday."

"I do wake up earlier than you. By a few hours most days. And you sent me to bed at nine last night."

"You are incredible."

"I also booked us a boat tour, so we can go over to Assateague Island to look for the horses."

"Pull over." I say it with urgency, so he slows down to do so immediately.

"What?"

"Right now. Pull over."

Quickly, he pulls the car to the shoulder. "What? What's wrong?" Fear drips off his words.

"Nothing. I just need to do this." Unhooking my seatbelt, I lean over to his side, taking his face in my hands and closing my mouth over his in a breathless kiss before pressing our foreheads together. "Thank you."

He kisses the tip of my nose. "You're welcome. I just want to make you happy."

I shift back to my seat, buckling my seatbelt. "You don't need to plan a trip to make me happy. Though, I must say, it is an excellent surprise."

"Well, I'm glad you're excited. Hey, do me a favor. I think I have a map in the pocket of your door. Can you grab it for me?"

"Why not use the GPS on your phone?" Despite my question, I lean forward to look.

"I like to use real maps."

I pull out a Virginia map. "You knew how to get here from New York?"

"You forget, I'm from Virginia, baby."

"Not this part of Virginia."

He shrugs. "It was a pretty straight shot from New York. And I think I know where to go from here. I just want to be sure."

With help from the map, we make our way into town, finding our hotel right on the water. We walk to dinner and around the town a little, finding a book shop and a t-shirt store. Jake buys us both shirts with horses on them, assuring me I can wear his after he's worn it a few times. He insists on buying me a few new books from the bookstore too.

We're back in our room by seven-thirty. Though he'll deny it, I can tell he's tired. Driving is exhausting.

Lying in bed facing each other, my hand lazily traces over the tattoo that spans his shoulders, as his eyes drift closed.

"You're going to have to stop if you want me to stay awake," he says sleepily.

"You don't have to stay awake."

"We can't have fun if I'm asleep."

"You know, we don't have to have sex every single day."

His eyes fly open. "Of course we do. We have ten years plus two weeks to make up for."

Delicately, I run my fingers across his back and to his chest, over to the tattoo he has over his heart. I start tracing over the Celtic symbol lazily. "Well, I seem to remember you had pretty lofty plans of not leaving bed for two days. Why don't we just add to that?"

His eyes are already closed again. "Hm, that's some pretty tough math there. Two years, plus two weeks, plus a day? How do we work that into two days?"

I giggle breathily and keep trailing my fingers along his warm skin. "How about we just see how far we get in those two days?"

"Mmm...okay." His words are coming out slower, his breathing becoming steadier. As I keep tracing the symbol, slowly and gently, his breathing becomes even, and the arm wrapped around my waist has loosened and grown heavy. I slow my fingers to make sure he doesn't wake up before pulling my hand away. With a tiny kiss to his jaw, I carefully roll to my back, keeping his arm over my waist.

Thanks to my nap on the way down, I'm not tired at all, but I don't want to move away from Jake. I had placed some of the new books on the nightstand and stretch to reach, able to grab one. Jake's truly exhausted because the lights are still on, and he typically can't sleep with light. Right now, I'm not quite sure how I'm going to turn them off without waking him up, but I'll worry about that later.

I read through four chapters before putting the book down, and then turn to look at Jake, my handsome man. It's still so hard to believe I'm really here, with him, after a whole decade apart. In that time, we'd lived such different lives, seemingly taking us farther from each other. And then one accident, one two-hour span, changed *everything*.

At the time, I was confident I'd never be happy again, but now I'm happier and more in love than I ever could have imagined. While I loved Gavin, enough to spend my life with him, I love Jake more and in such a different way. He is my past and my future. Even though at one point I had to move on, he's back in my life and I'm never going to let him go again.

With a start, I realize I'm playing with my Claddagh ring. In the last two days, it's become a nervous habit. Back when I wore my engagement ring, I had done the same thing, twirling it when nervous or thinking. I look down at it, then peek back at Jake. He seems sound asleep.

Carefully, I slide the ring off my right hand and onto my left, holding it out and admiring it. Of course, I've worn an engagement ring and wedding band before, but now I'm trying to imagine a different one. One given to me by Jake.

His arm tightens around my waist, then there's a kiss on my shoulder, and I can feel the smile on his face. When I turn to look at him, his eyes are slits, but open.

"I thought you were sleeping," I say sheepishly, heat sprawling through my body and creeping up my neck.

He shrugs. "I woke up." Probably because of the lights.

"Did I wake you? I'm sorry. I'm not that tired, but I've tried to not move too much," I say quickly.

"It's okay." He juts his chin toward my hand. "Whatcha doing there?"

My face burns at a new intensity. Quickly, I move the ring back to my right hand. "Nothing."

"No, no, no, you've been caught." Moving his arm from around my waist, he laces his fingers through mine, kissing my ear and nuzzling his nose against my jaw. "Know this, Mackenzie Rose Allen. I have every intention of marrying you." His voice is low and deep, an indicator of how much he means them.

Rolling to face him, I take the hand that's linked with mine and place it on my lower back as I rest my hand on his cheek and press my lips against his. His hand glides under the hem of my shirt where his palm scorches my skin as he pulls me flush against him and my lips part, his tongue sliding over mine.

I don't know how long we lie here, kissing like we need the oxygen in the other's lungs, but when we stop, my lips are bee-stung and I can hardly breathe.

He smiles, eyes closed. "Does that mean you like that plan?"

With a tender kiss on his lips, I murmur, "I do," against them, before snuggling down for sleep. Curling into him, his arm around my waist as I rest my head against his chest, all feels right with the world and his heartbeat is the last thing I hear before I fall asleep.

Jake traces his finger gently down the side of my cheek to wake me up. He trails it over my collarbone before starting back at my cheek and repeating the path until my eyes flutter open.

"Mmm...that feels nice."

His fingers rest under my chin and tilt it up as his lips press down against mine.

"Good morning." Peppermint mixes with his salty sweetness as his scent wafts over me. He's already been up for a while. My fingers twist into his shirt and the faintest bitterness of coffee hangs in the air.

Sitting up and tangling my hand in the mess that sits on my head, I take a look around, finding two paper cups and a white food bag on the table. "You went out?"

Dipping his hands in his pockets, he lifts one shoulder. "I've been up for a while, but I wanted to let you sleep. I thought it'd be good to get some caffeine in you before we have to go, though. I got coffee and pastries from the shop down the block."

"The coffee smells good. Thank you for getting it, and for letting me sleep."

"You're cute when you sleep. I hate to rush you, but we don't have a *ton* of time. Our tour is at ten-thirty, and the lady at the desk says it takes about twenty minutes to get there from here."

"It's okay, I'm up."

Breakfast is pretty tasty, and the coffee is quite good. We pack up our stuff and check out before heading to the boat tour. I'm so excited I can hardly stand still, bouncing on my toes and shaking my knees. Jake's being a good sport of acting excited too.

Once we're on the boat, we're able to stand at the railing, or sit on one of the rows of benches. I choose a spot against the railing, Jake standing behind me, arms on either side of me. As we get closer to the Wildlife Rescue, I lean on him.

When the boat starts to slow, I rest my stomach against the smooth metal, eager to see the horses and other wildlife. There are many different kinds of birds to be seen in addition to the horses. Jake rests against me, situating his chin on my shoulder as I excitedly point out horses, ponies, bald eagles, even dolphins. Every so often, he'll tilt his face towards me and smile.

As we turn to head back, he dips down and kisses my neck. "Did you have fun?"

"I really did. I feel kind of silly being so excited to see a horse at twenty-six, but—"

"But you've always wanted to come here."

Shifting in his hold, I meet his eyes. "Yeah."

"I'm glad I could make you happy." Cupping my jaw, he brushes his lips against mine.

"I already told you, I don't need you to buy me anything to make me happy."

"I'll do anything I can to put a smile on your face." His blue eyes sparkle in the midday sun.

"Just being close to you does that."

"Well, that's good because you have a lot of that coming up. Four hours to home and then you're mine." Bending down, he nips at my neck, causing me to yelp and have people look over at us. I hide my head in his shoulder as he laughs.

Somewhere into the four-hour drive, I fall asleep again, waking up just as we're pulling into the neighborhood. "Sorry I fell asleep again, car rides tend to do that to me."

"It's okay. I told you, you're cute when you sleep." Sliding his hand down my thigh, he turns and smiles at me as he pulls into the driveway. Before we even close our doors, we both stretch wide as soon as we're out of the car. Jake walks around to my side and bends down to whisper in my ear. "Welcome home, Mackenzie."

A burn settles behind my eyes and my heart races.

We're barely through the door before Jake has his mouth against mine, one hand cupping my face as the other presses into my lower back, bringing us pelvis to pelvis. He swoops me up into his arms and runs up the stairs, taking them two at a time, while I giggle in his hold.

When we get into the bedroom, he gently sets me down, lips immediately finding mine. As though it's a choreographed dance, he strips both of our clothes off as we take the few steps to the bed. His strong hands grab me around the waist and toss me onto the bed, quickly jumping on and climbing over me.

With parted lips, he runs his mouth over my body, breathing lightly. Starting at my hipbone, he works slowly across to the other side, then up, exhaling an extra breath over each nipple, before stopping at my mouth, brushing his lips against mine.

"I hope you're ready for two days in this bed. It starts right now."

Before I can even answer, he slips his tongue into my mouth, wrapping an arm around my waist and lifting me, moving me farther up the bed where his mouth breaks free from mine. Bringing a thumb up to rub across my bottom lip, he licks down my chest, giving each nipple a quick flick on his way to settle between my legs.

The moment his tongue touches me and immediately sets to work, I suck in a sharp breath. One of his hands is at my breast, nipple between his fingers, while the other is wrapped around my thigh. With one strong tug, he pulls me closer. My fingers tangle in his hair, yanking at it and pushing him closer at the same time.

Every loop and swirl of his tongue, combined with the pinching of my nipple, sends a zing through me, increasing the pressure in my hips. When it starts to heighten and my skin starts to tingle, I buck against him as he tightens his grip until I scream his name.

Freeing my leg from his hold, he gives my thighs each a nip

and moves to hover over me, chest to chest, his nose grazing mine, as he eases into me. His eyes lock on mine as I sigh. The tiniest smirk appears on his mouth as he starts gliding in and out.

The feeling of Jake inside me is something that makes my breath catch every time. It's like he's finally giving my body what it craves, filling a need, yet it feels almost surprised as he slides in.

Putting an arm under my hips, he lifts them slightly, and I claw at his back with a loud moan as the new angle brings on increased pleasure.

There's no controlling the noises that erupt from me, but every one causes a change in Jake. He moves faster, tangles his fingers in my hair, puts his mouth on my neck, pumps harder as my sounds grow louder. I'm thoroughly convinced I'm going to leave marks on his back from the intensity of how I grab at him.

Breaths are hard to come by and my body is almost vibrating, my skin tingling from my hair follicles down to my toes.

My head tips back and I scream his name, my brain going blank. It only takes three more thrusts until he grips the pillow behind my head and groans as he sinks his teeth into my neck.

Playfully, I push him off of me and sit up, pointing a finger at him. "That was three times."

He smirks, leaning on his elbow. "I told you, I can't help it."

"You're going to draw blood one of these days."

Lacing his fingers in front of him, he shrugs. "Worth it."

"To you maybe."

"Oh, come on, you don't like my love bites?"

"Well, I didn't say *that*."

"Ha! See, you *do* like that I bite you." Before I can respond, he grabs my wrist and yanks me toward him. He settles onto his back, and I lay my head against his chest, tracing the edge of the tattoo while he draws small circles on my ribs.

"So, there are rules for the next two days. We're allowed to get up to go to the bathroom alone. Otherwise, we can go get something to eat or drink or take a shower, but we have to do that together. And you're not allowed to get dressed for any of it."

"None of it?"

"Nope." He pops the *P* as he shakes his head.

"Are you allowed to get dressed?"

"Well, I do plan on ordering some food, and I figured it may be a little weird if I answer the door completely naked. But I will make this room a no clothes room. We're going to eat in here too."

"What? No. You know I don't like that."

"I promise I will let you clean all the bedding afterwards. You're going to want to, it's going to get messy. Before...before two weeks ago happened, I went out and bought some whipped cream and chocolate syrup."

I can't help but laugh. "And what do you plan to use that for? Ice cream?"

"I plan to lick it off your sexy body." The heat of his palm as it runs down my side and over my ass, causes a chill to race up my spine.

"None for me?"

"Oh, you are more than welcome to lick it off my body too. I have the perfect place to put it too." I shake as he chuckles beneath me.

Pushing up on my elbow, I quirk up an eyebrow and splay my hand across his chest. "Is that so? And what makes you think I would want to lick you?"

"Oh, please. I've seen you drool."

Trying to appear nonchalant, I casually lift one shoulder,

biting my cheek to prevent a smile from breaking out. "Meh. Not as exciting anymore."

"Is that so?"

"Yeah. As a matter of fact, none of this"—I point up and down his body—"does anything for me anymore."

Pushing up to meet me, his breath caresses my neck, and he nibbles my ear before murmuring against it. "Really? Is that why you're so wet every time I touch you?"

As if to further his point, he slides his hand between my legs.

I turn my head, so my mouth meets his as I glide my hands over his shoulders and push him down on his back, climbing on top of him. Leaning forward, I brush my lips against his, straightening as he tries to close his mouth around mine. I lean in again, running my tongue over his bottom lip, backing away again as his tongue reaches out to meet mine.

At the clear tease, he chuckles underneath me.

Keeping my eyes on his, I lower my head and run my tongue along his collarbone, moving over and tracing his tattoo, then lick my way down his perfect abs, stopping to place a kiss at his naval.

Need pulsates through me as I run my parted lips down his torso, swirling my tongue around the swollen head of his cock before taking him in my mouth. Slowly, I slide my way down his length, eyes locked on his as he tips his head back and fists my hair.

Too eager to feel him to continue, I pull away with a loud pop as the suction breaks, and lace my fingers through his, holding them over his head as I lean down to slip my tongue into his mouth.

When he tries to pull his hands from mine, I push back against him. Cleary he's much stronger than me, and if he really wants to, he can have me on my back in half a second flat, but I also know he's enjoying what's happening by how he kisses me back and tightens his grip on my fingers.

Sitting up straight, I guide him to palm my breasts before sliding them down my body to hold my hips. His mouth parts as I ease down on him, but his eyes stay locked on mine, hunger burning in them. Thumbs press into my hipbones in the front while the rest of his fingers graze my ass. When he starts pushing me with his hands, I lean forward again.

"No, no. It's my turn," I murmur against his ear.

Before moving from his ear, I start rocking against him, my hips sliding forward and back. Flatting my hands on his chest, I push up straight, my head tipping back as my hair cascades down my back.

His nails dig into my skin as I glide on top of him, rubbing against his hard stomach as he fills me, but needing more. Reading my thoughts, he adjusts his hold, his thumb circling around my clit in heavy swoops. With a long moan and large sigh, I increase my momentum, adding a lift to my forward motion.

Every time I sink back down on him, a whine pulls from my chest. Both of us start to have a layer of moisture on our bodies. When my hands slip against his dewy skin, and I lose my traction, Jake grabs my hips, supporting me just above him as he tips his hips up to thrust into me at a hard, fast pace.

"Fuck, Jake."

My head tips back as I start to shudder, and Jake tenses beneath me. Curling my fingers, my voice mingles with the sound of skin slapping skin as I scream. Slipping his hand up my back, Jake tangles his hand in my hair and pulls my mouth crashing down to his as he keeps plowing into me in steady strokes until he groans against my lips, slowly stopping and bringing my forehead to his.

He eases me to my side, shifting away to give a few inches

of space between us, but keeps his hand behind my head. "God, I love fucking you."

"Really? I wasn't sure until you said that." The urge to tease him is just too strong, and I stick my tongue out too.

With a laugh, he pulls me against him as he rolls to his back, tucking an arm around me, his hand resting at my hip. His other hand takes mine and brings it to his mouth so he can brush his lips along my knuckles, my palm, and my wrist. "I could kiss every square inch of you every second of every day, and it wouldn't be enough."

I roll my head to kiss his chest. "So, what are the rules on sleeping?"

"Sleeping?"

"Yeah. We have eating rules, and showering rules. But what about sleeping?"

"Well, the naked rule stands for the whole two days. You are not allowed to put clothes on at any point. But yes, we can sleep. I make absolutely zero promises that I won't wake you up several times a night, though. Or at six."

"I'm okay with that." Something occurs to me as I mull over his plan for a minute. "Don't you have work you need to be doing?"

"Not really. Not anything that can't wait two days." His fingers move erratically at my hip, and he heaves a heavy sigh. "I got a lot of projects finished before I came to get you back. I basically did nothing but work for two weeks."

"And surf."

"Eh."

Shock coils through me, and I'm stunned for a moment before I lean on my elbow to look at him. "You didn't surf?"

"Not really. It wasn't bringing me the clarity it had. I was out there for hours after you left, thinking it'd make me feel better, even if just a little bit. It didn't. And it didn't the next morning, or the morning after that. By the fourth morning, I stopped going."

"I'm just, I'm shocked. The whole two months I was here, I don't think you skipped a single morning."

"That's how big of an effect you have on me. I was that lost without you."

An audible swallow fills my ears. "There's a certain way the light hits the water that reminds me of your eyes. It's the same shade of blue, almost exact. When we were younger, I used to love it. It was my favorite time out there because it was like you were with me in a way. When I first came back here, well, it was mixed. But when you were gone? The pain of it was too much. So I stopped."

I lie back down, resting my head on his chest and reaching my arm around his neck to pull myself closer. "I'm never leaving again."

Squeezing me tightly, he brushes some hair out of my face as he starts tracing circles with his fingertips anywhere he can reach. I fall asleep warm in his arms, hearing his heartbeat, and feeling his hands on me, finally home.

TWO DAYS LATER

I'm aching in places I haven't been in years and in places I didn't know I could be. Jake presses up against my back, kissing my neck. "How sore are you?"

"Mmm...a bit."

"A good sore or a bad sore?"

"I mean, I'm hurting a bit, but it's for a good reason, so I guess a good sore?"

Reaching an arm around me, he leans up on his elbow as he kisses along the track between my neck and shoulder. "I'm glad to hear it. We did some good work here these past two days."

I roll to face him, tracing his chest with my fingertips. "Before I came back two months ago, I had forgotten about it all. Not the time together but how it felt to be together."

"It is pretty damn amazing."

The stubble on his jawline prickles against my skin as I run my hand along his cheek. "This is kind of sexy. Maybe you should leave a little."

With a light chuckle, he turns to kiss my palm. "If that's

what you want. Just know, it gets scratchy." Leaning forward, he scrapes his jaw against my cheek, making me giggle, before lying back on his side and sighing. "I guess our two days are over."

"You're finishing this morning? I figured we'd go until tonight, since we started at night."

A tender look overtakes his features, and he brushes some hair from my face. "No. You're sore. I don't want to hurt you."

"I said I was a *bit* sore."

"And I'm sure that a bit is really more like *quite* a bit. You do that, you make things seem less than they are, especially if you're afraid it will upset me or hurt my feelings. You did it the first time too."

And just like that, memories from our first time filter through my mind. I was laying in his arms, and he asked me how I was. I told him I was fine, because emotionally, I was. Physically, I was hurting a little, but I didn't want to tell him that. I didn't want him to think he had hurt me. When I finally told him the next day, he was mad I hadn't said so when he asked.

"Okay. You're right. It's probably better if we stop, for now." Disappointment weighs like a lead balloon in my chest. As much as I may be a touch achy, I love every second of time in bed with Jake.

"Come on, I'll make breakfast. You are officially allowed to get dressed, though I do encourage that you take to the nudist lifestyle." With a quick kiss, he climbs out of bed and pulls on a pair of shorts.

My muscles scream and my stomach rumbles as I stretch largely across the bed before crawling out. Taking a look out the slider, I have to squint at the assault on my eyes, and my heart leaps when I realize that this is my home now. I take one of Jake's t-shirts from his drawer and slip it over my head, pulling the collar up to smell it. Smells like Jake, like home. I don't need to wear his clothes now to be close to him; I have the real thing in the other room, but it's still nice. It feels like I'm wrapped in him all the time.

I walk into the kitchen to coffee already brewing and Jake at the stove, his back to me, muscles taut. "That smells good."

As he turns to face me with a smile on his face, he's popping a piece of green pepper into his mouth. When he takes in the t-shirt, his mouth pops open and stays agape for a moment before he clears his throat. "That looks good on you."

"I hope you don't mind."

"Not at all. What's mine is yours, babe. I'm making omelets. Any requests?"

"Nope, you know what I like."

"Alright, well, relax, these won't be too long."

Taking a seat on a barstool, I watch him cook. It's become one of my favorite things to do. It's incredibly sexy, as he's confident in the kitchen, with smooth movements and precision. As he turns around to get plates out of the cabinet, he smiles again. "Are you just watching me?"

"I am. I like watching you in the kitchen. It's sexy as hell."

"Well, that's good because I like cooking for you."

He pours two cups of coffee and places one in front of me, leaning across the counter. After plating the omelets, complete with an assortment of fresh berries, he comes to sit next to me. Once he's safely set the plates down, I take his face in my hands and kiss him.

"How did I get so lucky to have you?" Awe and wonder course through me, and I take in every line of his face, every nuance in the shade of his irises and hair.

"I'm pretty sure I'm the lucky one."

A smile pulls at my lips and my face heats as I turn back to my food. It's delicious, as always. When I finish eating, I turn to rest my feet on one of the rungs of his barstool, coffee in hand. Jake tilts his head toward me, a smile on his face, as he runs a hand down my leg.

"I'm surprised one omelet is enough for you after all that," I tease as I pull the mug to my mouth.

The sound of his chuckle ignites tiny fires throughout my body. "Well, I gave myself an extra egg or two. But, I'm sure I'll be eating a bit more through the day to regain my strength." He gives my thigh a squeeze. "I'm going to clean up, and then, unfortunately, I do have to get some work done. But I can do it up here."

"No, let me clean up." Before I even finish, he's shaking his head in protest. "Yes, come on. This is my house too now, right?" With a quick tip of his head before meeting my eyes again, he smiles when I say it. "I should be sharing the responsibilities. You cooked, let me clean. I practically lived here for six weeks, and I *did* help clean up in that time."

Though he hesitates for a moment, he sighs before acquiescing. "Okay, I suppose you're right." As he stands, he leans down to kiss the top of my head. "I'm going to take a quick shower and grab my laptop."

Cleaning our plates is pretty easy since we both ate every bite, and the pan scrubs out quickly. After pouring myself a fresh cup of coffee, I walk out onto the deck, leaning against the railing, and looking out over the ocean. It's quieter now, beachgoers having stopped coming as school resumed. Aside from that one Christmas, I've never really been here later than the first few days of September. The crashing waves are louder now, like they are on summer nights when the rest of the world is asleep. A pod of dolphins swim by not too far out and I smile.

Jake's arms appear on either side of me, holding the railing as he dips in and kisses my neck.

"I could get used to this view." Wistfulness coats my words.

"So could I," he murmurs in my ear. I tilt my head back against his shoulder and find that he's looking at me and my heart soars. Resting his chin on my shoulder, he joins me in looking out at the water spanning in front of us.

"Actually, I was thinking we should buy a house somewhere on the mainland. In North Carolina, or somewhere else." There's no hint of question to his tone, so I know he's put real thought into this.

Spinning in his arms, I turn around to look at him. "Why? What about surfing?"

"I don't need surfing. I have you."

"But surfing makes you happy." I don't want him to give up something he loves because he thinks it's what I want. I'm perfectly happy to make a life here.

"*You* make me happy."

"But what about when I'm driving you insane and you need to do something to get away from me?"

"Impossible." I cock my head to the side and lift an eyebrow, knowing this isn't true and that he knows it's not true either. In the few weeks we'd spent together, I made him batty a handful of times.

Instead of agreeing, he shrugs. "I'll figure it out. Besides, I don't surf as much come mid-October. And we won't sell this place, so we'll have it for summers and Christmases." He leans in and places a tiny kiss on my lower lip. This house will always be special for us at Christmas time. With one hand, he swoops some curls behind my shoulder. "Besides, I think you need to get back into teaching, and the school here is really small."

"Oh, we need money that badly, huh?" While I'm teasing, I'm also a little curious. We've never really talked about finances.

He smirks and hangs his head, laughing as he raises it back to my level. "No, we don't, actually. But I can tell you miss it."

"Oh, really, and how is that?"

"The way you talked about it when you showed me your old school the other day. You were so excited, so electric. Your passion for teaching and your students was oozing out of you. We could even go back to New York, if you wanted. You said your boss had said he'd have a spot for you when you came back."

"That was over two years ago. I'm sure that's long gone." I shake my head. "I don't want to go back to New York. I had a life there. Two, in fact. *If* we do decide to move somewhere else, I want it to be somewhere new, for both of us."

"I can agree to that."

"But I don't want to start looking yet. I want to enjoy beach living a little." Taking a step closer, I slide my hands up his chest.

"It's pretty different without all the visitors."

"That's what I'm counting on. It seems peaceful, quiet."

Solemnly, he nods. "Yeah, it is."

Something flashes across his eyes, so fast I can't detect what it is. "What? What is it?"

"It's going to be nice this year. Not quite so lonely."

I loop my arms around his waist and press myself against him, his arms wrapping around me as he kisses the top of my head. "It won't ever be again," I murmur into his chest, causing him to give me a squeeze.

"Oh! I have to tell you though, the first weekend in October, Lou and I do a big cookout."

Keeping my hold on him, I lean back to look at him. "Lou? Like Loose-lipped Lou?"

His deep laugh makes desire and need twist and turn

through me. "Yeah, he and I got pretty friendly in the last few years. He still lives here. We surf together every so often."

"Why didn't I see him when I was here for two months?" If they're such good friends, I feel like we should have gotten together. Was Jake ashamed to tell him?

"He's super busy over the summer. That's his prime season."

"What does he do?"

His eyes glint as he looks down at me and laughs. "Oh, you're going to love it. He owns one of those t-shirt shops. Down in Duck."

My eyes widen and my jaw drops. "No, he does not!"

He nods, smile huge. "Oh, yeah. And guess who he married?"

The furrowed brow does nothing to clue him in. How could I know who he married? "I have no idea."

His eyebrows reach his hairline. "Stone-cold Susan."

My brows shoot just as high, and I practically have to pick my jaw up off the floor. "No way! She's the one who gave him the nickname!"

While we hung out with Lou and Susan from time to time, they always seemed to hate each other. Or at least, Susan seemed to hate Lou. It was pretty evident that Lou always shot his best shot, and every time was denied.

"But wait, I thought Susan was a visitor?" Visitors were those who didn't own a house but rented instead.

Adjusting his stance, he leans on his hands against the railing, boxing me in even more, and making desire rip through me like wildfire. "She was. I guess she came back a few more summers after we stopped coming and ran into Lou. They fell in love, and she decided to stay. I gotta tell ya, he's not as scrawny as he was when you knew him."

"I mean, okay, we all grew up. You definitely filled out

more. You were always lean and toned, but your shoulders broadened, and you've gotten more toned. You're taller too."

"He's bigger than me."

"No way. No way! He can't be. You had at least a few inches on him. And he had like no muscle tone whatsoever."

As though it's just completely normal, he shrugs. "I know. He was a late bloomer, I guess."

Brushing some locks of hair out of Jake's eyes, I press myself against him. "Well, there's no way he could be as devastatingly handsome as you are."

"I won't argue with you there." Immediately his lips are on mine, hands reaching up under my thighs to lift me and I wrap my legs around his waist. After a few minutes, he unwinds my legs from his torso and untangles his hand from my hair, putting me flat on my feet before taking two steps back. "Okay, woman, you stay back."

"What, you don't want me close to you?" Giggling, I take a step toward him.

In response, he takes a step back. "I'm trying to behave because you're sore. I can't do that if we keep doing *that*."

"What if I don't want you to behave?" I use my best sultry voice, pulling my lip between my teeth.

Tipping his head to the sky, he groans and reaches his long arms across the space between us to hold my hips. "Ugh, you're killing me. Come on, be nice. You know what you're doing to me. I'm doing this for you."

"Alright. I'll stop. But come back over here, I like when you're in my bubble." Uncertainty clouds his eyes. I hold my hand up, palm out. "I promise, I will behave myself and not do anything that may be construed as teasing."

Closing the space between us, he plants his hands back on the railing, putting me back inside the Jake cage that I love so much. "You know, it's hard for you to say that when you're wearing one of my shirts and *only* my shirt." I shrug, not sure what to say that wouldn't seem like I'm playing with fire. "I meant to ask you before we left, it was probably selfish not to. Weren't there any friends you wanted to say goodbye to before you moved?"

I sigh, looking down at the ground. It's a bit of a loaded question. "Honestly? Not really. I mostly had college friends, and after we graduated, we all went our different ways. We check in every so often. You know my friend, Anna? The one who said you were imaginary?" I glance up at him in time to catch his nod. "She's in Texas now, been there for years. We chat somewhat often, but even that's not regular. My closest friend from college, Jess, ended up in Maine."

"You didn't have any friends in New York? No work friends?"

"I had some at work, but that was it, at work. I had a few people I thought I was friends with." I take a deep breath. "A lot changed after Gavin died. In times of tragedy and hardship, you really learn who's a real friend and who's not. As it turned out, the friends I'd made in New York, were, well, not. Most of them were gone before the funeral was even over." Taking a deep breath, I turn around to face the beach.

"There was one that stuck around for a while. I thought maybe she was in it for the long haul. But six months later, she didn't understand why I didn't want to go out to the bars with her, why I wasn't over it. She said I was young, I was twenty-four, that I should be out living life, not stuck inside. That it had been six months and it was time to move on." I shake my head, leaning back into Jake's chest. He's pressed right up against me, so close his warmth heats straight to my core.

"She just didn't understand. And I knew that with the loss of Gavin, I'd changed. I'd grown. And I'd outgrown them. I realize now that I should have left that house much sooner. I kept thinking if I just pushed forward, tried to rebuild my life there, I could eventually be happy. At a certain point, I think I just grew content with the loneliness and empty days." Silence closes in around us and I know Jake's giving me time to mull things over. "So long story short, no, no friends I needed to say goodbye to."

Apparently, Jake has been holding the railing tightly, which I somehow missed until he loosens his grip to wrap his arms around me, and I notice that his knuckles are white. Though he's still behind me so I can't see his face, I can feel his clenched jaw as he squeezes me tightly.

"I'm so sorry you've had to go through all that. What horrible people. You'd just lost your husband and then they disappeared too? Why, because you weren't in the mood to go party? How awful."

I try to spin around to face him, but his hold on me is too tight. I push against him slightly and he loosens his arms the littlest bit so I can make a tight turn. "It's all behind me. It's all in the past. I'm here, with you, and I'm only looking forward."

"Does Anna know you're here?"

A lightness fills my chest as he asks about her, knowing her input is important to me. "Yeah. I told her when we reunited. She joked that I'd really gone off the deep end if I was reuniting with imaginary boyfriends. Until I sent her a picture I'd snapped of you one day when you'd undone the top of your wetsuit. Then she threatened to fly out here to make sure your intentions are pure."

With a low growl, he leans in to bite my earlobe. "They're not."

Choosing to ignore his comment and the throb that settles in my clit, I clear my throat. "She recognized you immediately from the pictures I'd shown her years ago. We had a long talk about how I was doing with it all. I've kept her up to date in messages since then. She was really happy you came to get me. Actually, I was a little scared for you. I was afraid she was going to show up and destroy you. She has a way with words that will make you cower in the corner. When I told her I was moving down here with you, she told me I was finally where I belonged."

Jake swoops my hair behind my shoulders, gathering it in his hand as he brings it behind my head and pulls on the tail, so my head tips back, and he closes his mouth over mine, tongue sweeping in. As he ends the kiss, he wraps his arms around my head and pulls me into his chest.

There's nothing but the waves behind us and Jake's scent infiltrating my nose as we stand here.

"I hate to have to do this, but I really need to get to work."

I lean back, his hand still wrapped in my hair. "Oh, of course. Go ahead. I'm fine. I promise."

Each of my knuckles receives a kiss before he walks inside. Leaning my forearms on the railing, I look out over the ocean again. It hasn't changed much in the years since I first started coming here. Yet I'm a different person entirely. If you had told sixteen-year-old me, that one day I'd be back here, living with Jake, making plans for the future, I would have said it was all I could dream about and everything I'd ever want. If you would have told seventeen-year-old me, I never would have believed it, nor would I have wanted to hear about this beach again.

Despite the ups and downs, the gains and losses, the unimaginable pain, I wouldn't do anything differently. I was able to experience a pure, young love. I was able to marry an incredible man, and while I lost him, I'm changed because of him. And most importantly, I've been given the chance to be with my first love again.

Twenty-Five

Jake and I decide to wait a year until we look for a new house. I want one year of life on the beach, one year of settling into our new relationship and life together. While he's right, I do love teaching, I'm not entirely sure it's what I want to do with myself anymore.

After the tragedy I've been through, I consider going into counseling. Always supportive, he told me to take the time to look at my options, and that we can move near whatever school I want because he can work from anywhere. The one thing we definitely agree on is that we want to stay on the east coast, to be driving distance from the beach house. Even though I haven't decided what I want to do, or where I want to study yet, I'm excited about the prospect of starting something new.

Before making any official decision, I ensure we're okay money wise, telling Jake I can find a job somewhere to make extra money. While I have some funds from selling my old house, I'm not sure it's enough. But Jake assures me we're just fine, that he makes good money with his job as it's his business, so he doesn't have overhead costs. Out of a bit of boredom, I end up taking a job at the local bookstore anyway, needing to spend my time doing something, and I'm excited to surround myself with books every day.

Life quiets down on the Banks during the fall and winter months. It's nice, peaceful. We can go out to dinner and not have a long wait or have it be jam-packed. We see Lou and Susan often, and Susan and I become good friends. It's nice to have a real friend again. Somebody I can go shopping with, grab a coffee, have a girls' night with.

Everything is still easy and comfortable with Jake. It feels like we've been living together for years, not weeks to months. There are, of course, still things we catch each other up on, things that happened over the past ten years, but there's such comfort between us it makes things easy, with no fear to say what's on our minds.

For Thanksgiving, we decide to drive up to my parents' house and spend a nice long weekend there. My parents loved Jake when we were kids and they love him even more now, accepting him into the family without a second of hesitation.

While we're visiting, Mom pulls me to another room for one of the brief moments I'm not right by Jake's side.

"I know you loved Gavin, I really do. But *this* is how your life is supposed to be. Jake is meant to be your life partner. I'm sorry I didn't recognize that when you were younger." While the sentiment is sweet, and greatly appreciated, I've already come to this conclusion.

"It's okay, Mom. It all worked out the way it's supposed to. I did love Gavin, and I'm happy for that time I had with him. Losing him taught me some real life lessons, including grief and mourning." I look over at Jake as he catches my eye and smiles. "But it also taught me to truly appreciate every single day and what you have."

I try every day to show Jake my appreciation for him, for

his role in my life, for our life together. One of the biggest life lessons I learned is that time is fleeting; everything can be gone in the blink of an eye. I want to make sure I'm making the most of my second chance with my first love.

Jake insists that our parents all come down for Christmas, and that I invite Shannon too, though I'm sure she won't come. To my surprise, she agrees when I invite her. My family stays at their house, and Jake's parents stay at a hotel. When I ask why they don't stay with us, he just shrugs and explains that they don't stay with him much because it's his home now and they tend to nitpick at what he's changed, so it's easier for them to stay at the hotel instead.

Seeing our parents reunite after so many years apart is great. They fall back into easy conversation, just like Jake and I had.

On Christmas Eve, Jake and I are sitting out on our porch swing, listening to waves crash on the beach and looking at the decks with decorations. Since a lot of people rent their houses out, there's not many. But what we can see helps bring the feeling of Christmas for me. This is my first year not celebrating any of the holiday season in New York.

The sky is bright with stars and the moon. I'm leaning back against Jake's chest as we rock slowly. It's a cool night, but comfortable. I take a deep breath and sigh.

"What is it?" His voice is low and gentle in my ear as he takes a curl and loops it behind my shoulder.

"It's just...I'm happy. I'm really, really happy."

"Oh, yeah?"

"Yeah."

"Do I have anything to do with that happiness?"

I tilt my head back to look at him. "You have *everything* to do with that happiness."

Adjusting his position and leaning forward, he slides me off his lap.

"Well, I'm glad you say that," he says as he gets down on one knee. My hands fly to my chest. "Mackenzie, I knew I loved you when I was just fifteen years old. My love for you never went away. I was stupid not to hold on to you, and I will spend every day for the rest of our lives making up for lost time, treasuring every moment with you. I never want to be away from you again. I'm so thankful that we found our way back to each other; you are my everything, Kenz. I love you so much. Will you marry me?"

Falling to my knees, I take his face between my hands, kissing him over and over and over before I press my forehead against his. "Of course I will." He smiles as he takes my left hand and slides the ring on. It's exactly the sort of ring I've always envisioned for myself. It's just another sign that Jake knows me, really, truly knows me.

As he presses his lips to mine, he loses a hand in my mess of curls and slowly lowers me to the ground. Our lips are moving hungrily against each other's when he slides his hand under the hem of my shirt, up to cup my breast and rub his fingertip against my hardened nipple. A deep moan pulls me from his mouth, and he removes his hand from my shirt, wrapping my arms around his neck and roping one of his under my waist. Holding me against his chest, he grabs the blanket off the swing, spreading it on the floor before laying me down on it.

In one fluid motion, he reaches behind his head and pulls his shirt off. Almost subconsciously, I extend my hand to trace the heart and the fire of his tattoo. Closing his fingers around mine, he presses my palm to his warm chest.

"You've always been my fire," he whispers as his gaze penetrates me, down to the very depths of my soul, to the very fibers of my being that he's wrapped so tightly around and interwoven with.

Tilting up, I collide my mouth with his. Sliding his hands

down my chest, he tugs off my shirt, giving one flick of his wrist to undo my bra. Just as quickly, he pops open the button on my jeans. His mouth finds mine again as he gently lays me back, his fingers slipping under the waist band of my pants and panties.

"Holy shit, Kenz," he murmurs against my chest as he finds how ready I am for him.

As he slides in two fingers, my back arches and I grab onto his shoulder, his mouth grazing my neck. My fingertips dig into his skin, scratching at the tattoo that spreads across his upper back as the pressure builds. Jake's mouth closes on mine, his fingers moving faster as he knows how close I'm getting to crying out his name.

Hooking his fingers and kissing his way down my neck, my head tips back and I moan loudly as I come. Every time Jake touches me, my body is electrified and even the tiniest breath of air is enough to send me reeling.

With two hands, he rips off my pants, sliding his down, before easing into me. My breath catches in my throat. As he thrusts in and out, the volume of my noises starts to get higher. Jake reaches a hand up to cover my mouth, leaning down to whisper in my ear but never stopping his movements.

"Shhh. You know how much I love to make you scream for me, but I'm worried we may scare the neighbors. If I move my hand, can you be quiet?" His voice is deep and gravelly against my ear, his breath coming out in spurts that ruffle my hair, and every molecule in me ignites and tries to get to him.

Looking at him with wide eyes, I shake my head, because no, I can't be quiet, which brings a smile to his face as he starts moving faster. His hand stays against my mouth even as my head tips backwards and moans rise in my throat, barely muffled by his palm. I feel him pulsate inside me as he leans into my neck, teeth on my shoulder as he groans.

Slowly, he stops moving and lays on me, panting for a moment, his teeth still connected to my skin. Before he rolls to his side, he digs them in a little bit. Immediately, I shiver from the cool air and being exposed without his heat over me. Pulling me close, he kisses my ear.

"Let's get you inside." Scooping me up in his arms, he carries me through the slider.

"What about our clothes?" I gesture toward them.

Shifting in his hold as he shrugs, I lean my head into the curve of his neck. "I'll get 'em later."

He carries me all the way up the stairs to the bedroom, climbing on the bed with me still in his arms as he leans back, propped against the pillows and hugs me against him. Once we're settled, he pulls the blankets up to rest over my chest.

I put my hand out to admire my ring as he plays with my hair.

"Did I do a good job?"

"Absolutely! I love it. It's exactly the sort of ring I've always envisioned for myself. But I would have loved anything from you. You should have just moved the Claddagh ring over."

"No way. This is a right of passage for me." He sounds absolutely horrified I would even suggest such a thing.

"How'd you know this was the right one?"

"I know you, Mackenzie Allen. I know you so well." There's a wistfulness to his words as he swoops some curls behind my shoulder and runs his fingers along my collarbone. "I walked into that jewelry shop, the really fancy one down in Kitty Hawk, and looked around for a bit and then saw this one. It just screamed Mackenzie. I knew nothing else would come close to the perfection of this one."

Resting my palm on his cheek, I tilt his face down to mine. "It's perfect."

"There could be no less for you."

"This is why you insisted our parents come down, and my sister."

"Guilty. I knew you'd want to celebrate with somebody."

"I thought we did just celebrate."

Sputtering a bit, he chuckles. "You know what I mean."

With a sigh, I wiggle my body as I adjust against him and nod. "You know, I may start expecting every Christmas to be like this. Our first Christmas, you gave me that necklace and then we had sex for the first time. This year, I get an engagement ring and sex."

"Well, I'm pretty sure the sex part is going to be mandatory. But I'll gladly buy you jewelry every Christmas."

"I know you would. But I don't need that. I have everything I need right here." Snuggling against him, I close my eyes, breathing in his sweet and salty seawater scent, which he still has even though he hasn't surfed in several weeks. I like to joke with him that he spends so much time in the water it's seeped into him, that it's part of his blood now.

He's still playing with my hair as I fall asleep, wrapped warmly in his arms, happier than I've ever been.

Epilogue

Jake had insisted that we do Christmas at our house. When all arrived, we shared the happy news. Everybody was elated, giving us giant hugs. My dad clapped Jake on the shoulder and told him that he'd considered Jake a son since we were kids. Even Shannon was happy for me, smiling and squeezing me tight. As she pulled away, she whispered she could help me cover the bite mark on my shoulder if I wanted.

Heat flooded my face as I adjusted my shirt to cover it. I thought I'd worn a top that would keep it covered well, but all the hugging must have shifted the collar.

"There's only one thing. We want to get married here, this summer," I said, biting my lip, knowing it was soon.

They all looked at each other. "I'm sure we can make that happen. But we'll have to start planning now. Most things are probably already booked up." My mom, ever the planner, looked nervous as she said it. I knew she was concerned about it all coming together and not about the speed of things between us. She knew I'd marry Jake the next day if I could.

Jake's okay with not having a big wedding. He understands

I've done that, that I don't really want to do it again, and that our home, this house, means so much more to me, to us, than any big wedding in some other place ever could.

The plans go smoothly, and in early June, before the summer rush, we're married on the beach in front of our home, surrounded by family and a few close friends. Anna flies out from Texas, excited to finally meet who she's always considered to be my imaginary boyfriend.

Our parents have set planks out on the sand, creating a dance floor. Lou is friends with a DJ who frequently plays on the beach and one of Susan's friends is a caterer. It all works out well for us to have our wedding fully outside, leaving our house free of people milling in and out.

Jake's holding me against him as we sway to the music. It's not even a slow song. He brushes some hair out of my face, wild from dancing.

"How are you, Mrs. Henshaw?"

Smiling, I bury my face in his chest for a moment before leaning back and looking at him. "Say it again."

His returned smile is wide and reaches his eyes. "Mrs. Henshaw."

"Happy. So, so happy."

Leaning in, he grazes his teeth along my neck. "May I suggest something to make you even happier?"

"We can't! It's our wedding." With a quick glance around, I can see that nobody knows what we're talking about and can't pick up on the sexual tension building between us.

"Exactly. It's *our* wedding. So we can do whatever we want."

"There's like ten people here. They'll notice if we're gone."

All he does is shrug in response. "So?"

"So, they'll know what we're doing."

"We're two sexy people madly in love. And they've known

what we do together for years." He raises a brow and squeezes my hips, making me giggle.

"That doesn't mean they have to be acutely aware of it at the very moment it's happening."

He breathes gently into my ear, running his lips down my neck and across my collarbone.

"Okay, maybe real quick." It's impossible to resist him.

Smiling against my neck, he laces his fingers through mine, leading me away. With a quick glance behind me, I find that nobody seems to be aware of us leaving, or if they are, they're dutifully ignoring it.

We walk in on the downstairs floor and Jake's lips are on mine before we've even closed the door. He walks me backwards into the bathroom, putting his hands on my waist and lifting me onto the granite vanity. His kisses are hurried and hungry, down my collarbone and over the neckline of my dress.

Speedily, he undoes his pants as he slides the skirt of my dress to gather around my hips, easing into me. One of my hands wraps around the back of his head, fingers tangled in his hair, while the other grips the counter for support as my head falls backward.

Twenty minutes later, we're back on the beach. Nobody asks us where we went, but by the look my sister shoots me, she's well aware of what just happened.

I look around at our small group of friends and family. Everybody is laughing, having fun, dancing. Anna seems to be hitting it off with one of Jake's surfing buddies. As Jake stands behind me, his chest pressed to my back and arms tight around my waist, I'm filled with nothing but happiness and love.

Two months later, we're getting ready to pack up and move to the house we bought on the mainland of North Carolina.

As we're packing boxes and pulling down sentimental things that we don't want to leave at the house while people rent it out, I burst into tears. The look on Jake's face—eyes wide, mouth open—is a perfect combination of concern and fear. Up to this point, I've been holding myself together pretty well.

"Hey, baby, what's going on? We don't have to move if you really don't want to." His tone is calm and soothing, and he approaches like he's getting close to a wild animal.

"It's not that, it's just, this lighthouse." When I start wailing while holding up a figurine lighthouse, I know he's really confused, but he pulls me against him nonetheless. I'm confused myself. These emotions are a bit extreme, but I chalk it up to lack of sleep and the big changes coming.

With a kiss to my temple, he stands and walks into the kitchen, coming back a few minutes later with a fresh cup of coffee.

Before I even take it, I'm pushing it back toward him as my stomach rolls. "Ew, no. What kind of coffee is that? It smells awful."

"It's our regular, everyday coffee. The same thing we drank this morning."

"There's no way that's the same. Did you open a new bag?"

"Nope, exactly the same one that I used this—"

When he stops short, I turn to look at him as something skitters through his eyes before they widen and a giant smile pulls at his lips. Taking my hand, he tugs me up. "Come on, we have an errand to run."

"Okay..." Utterly confused, I slip my shoes on and follow him to the car, where he holds the door open for me.

When he pulls up in front of the pharmacy and turns to

me with raised brows and an expectant face, I know he wants something from me, but I have no clue what. Sighing, he rolls his eyes and undoes his seatbelt, walking around to my side to help me out.

Lacing our fingers together, he pulls me through the aisles until we find the right one, where he spins me around to face the pregnancy tests and loops his arms around my waist, his palms resting against my lower stomach, chin on my shoulder.

Shock slithers through my body. Pregnancy tests?

"You...you think I...we could be pregnant?"

"Think about it, Kenz. You've been exhausted, a little overly emotional, and you just pushed away *coffee*. I don't think I've ever seen you do that. Even when you had the stomach bug last winter."

And as though he flicked a switch in my head, it suddenly all makes sense. With shaky hands, I grab a pregnancy test. We rush home, and I take the test, calling him in to wait with me, setting a timer so we know when to check it.

Holding me against him, I barely feel his hand running up and down my arm, barely hear his heart. All my eyes can focus on is the plastic stick sitting on the sink and picking at my lip.

The sounding of the alarm is a distant shrill that I only register when Jake shakes me. After a sharp swallow, I reach forward and pull the stick in front of us, to find two very defined pink lines.

A stunned silence overwhelms me, but not Jake, who scoops me into his arms, spins me around, and peppers kisses all over my face, neck, and chest.

"I love you, Kenz. I love you so much."

"I love you too, Jake." I'm completely breathless as joy and shock twist and work through me.

What may seem sudden to some, has been a long time coming for us. It's the natural flow of things. We didn't need to be together long before we got engaged, just like we don't need to be married long before having children.

Jake sits with me and holds me as I cry on the anniversary of Gavin's death just a month later. He kisses away my tears, holds me against him when I'm okay with it, and leaves me alone if I need a few minutes.

His understanding that my love for Gavin doesn't detract for my love of him is something I'll never be able to truly show my gratitude for. While I had loved Jake first, and love him last, my love for Gavin stands in between. Jake knows I love him, beyond measure, but that tragic loss of Gavin is what gives me a need to grieve and process. I think he also gives me a little extra leeway because I'm hormonal.

In every way, Jake is my equal, my partner, my support. He knows me better than anybody ever has or ever could, because he knows me on the most basic level. There's something inside me, inside both of us, that knows and recognizes the other, that pulls us toward one another. It's something that's raw, real, and undeniable.

Three years later, we have two children, a boy and a girl, born a little over two years apart. We spend most of our summers in the Outer Banks, wanting our kids to love it here as much as we always have. Jake still surfs and plans to teach our kids if they want to learn. He hopes they won't have as much of a fear of the ocean as I always have, though he has helped with that a little.

Jake's an amazing father, not that I'm surprised at all. Connor, our son, thinks he has the coolest daddy because he can surf and has tattoos. He's sure no other dad in the world has tattoos. Because of that, Jake still walks around shirtless frequently, which does horrible things to my hormones because having children makes it very difficult to be intimate whenever the mood strikes.

I ended up going back to school to become a school guidance counselor. I wasn't there for very long though, as the babies came, and I want to be home with them. With Jake still working from home, we're able to have a lot of family time together.

I hear the slider open as Jake walks out behind me.

"Connor gave me a run for my money tonight!" I laugh as he walks up behind me and kisses my neck. "How'd it go with Kayleigh?" Holding up the monitor, he can see Kayleigh's tiny form, sleeping peacefully. In her four months of life, she's been an easier baby than Connor had been.

"So what you're saying is we have some time to ourselves?"

Giggling but not taking my eyes from the dark ocean, I lean into him. "What do you have in mind?"

Hands on my hips, he spins me around to face him. "Well... I'm wondering if you're interested in any more of these little rugrats?" Adjusting to hold the railing behind me, he leans in, mouth against mine as he speaks.

I rope my arms around his neck. "I don't know. While I do love them, and you, I think I'm pretty happy with two."

He smiles. "I had a feeling you'd say that. You're not opposed to more practice though, are you?"

"Oh, definitely not," I reply as I pull him down to kiss me.

Sometimes I find it hard to believe that so much time has passed since Jake and I first met on the beach sprawled out in front of us. I'm frequently thankful for the way the universe works at times.

I was lost, beyond measure. Then, somehow, I made my way to a place I felt at peace, and Jake found me. Not just on the beach that morning, not just in a location. He found me in the darkness and pulled me out. He took the shattered pieces of my heart, of my life, and put them back together. It may not be reassembled the way it was, but it's absolutely magnificent the way it is now.

The End

Bonus

Want a bonus scene from Jake's perspective? Join my newsletter to download it for free!

https://bookhip.com/jhgwtaa

COMING SOON

The following is an unedited preview and subject to change.

The preview contains the following content warnings: mature language, sexual situations, mental struggles including depression, self harm, rage issues, and attempted suicide.

The full length novel contains the content warnings above, in addition to: anxiety, attending therapy, explicit sexual scenes, abandonment, drug and alcohol abuse, promiscuous behavior, and nonconsensual intercourse.

INTRODUCTION

The light flicks on, chasing away the all encompassing darkness. I raise my head from my hands to see Zane standing with his fingers still on the switch, taking in the scene. Me, sitting on the cool tile of the kitchen, knees to my chest, heels of my hands to my eyes. Knife on the floor.

He's kneeling in front of me in half a second, grabbing my wrists and pulling them out straight, looking them up and down, turning them over.

"What happened? Are you okay? Did you cut?" His voice is low, trying to be calm, but I hear the slightest hint of panic seeping through.

"No. But I want to," I whisper.

Crossing my arms against my chest, he curls around me, pulling me into his lap and wrapping his arms tightly around my waist. I let myself feel his strength. I wish I could steal it, or at least borrow some. I'm weak. So much weaker than he is.

We have similar problems, similar demons. But he's learned to control his urges better than I have. He doesn't end up awake at two in the morning fighting himself like I do. At least not anymore. This isn't the first time this month. It's not even the first time this week.

"It's okay. I've got you." His deep voice is low against my ear.

Breathe. Close your eyes. Take in the moment. Go to where you feel comfortable, safe. The only problem with the directions my psychologist gave me when we practiced the exercise, is that I don't know where that place is. Zane makes me feel safe, but I refuse to use him as my grounding visual.

Instead, I keep my eyes open, looking around to find five things I can see. *Toaster, magnet, coffee pot, moon, knife.* My stomach roils at the thought.

Deep breath, keep going. Four things I can hear. *Zane's heart, the tick of the clock, the hum of the fridge, the wind.*

Three things I can touch. *Zane's warm skin, the cool tiled floor, water from the faucet.*

Two things I can smell. *Soap, fresh coffee.*

One thing I can taste. *Tangy iron.* A shudder wracks my body.

"Are you doing your grounding exercise?"

"It's not working." It comes out through gritted teeth.

"Focus on me. See, hear, touch, smell...and taste." With a firm finger under my chin, he tilts my head up as his mouth meets mine, forcing it open as his tongue slips in. Mint crosses my taste buds as my hand splays open over his chest. It's a dual touch sensation, his warmth and the steady beating of his heart beneath my palm.

Zane understands me in a way no boyfriend before him ever had or ever could. I hate that he does because I don't want him having the same struggles I do. But it's what makes us work as a couple. It also makes us toxic together. Kind of like how they say addicts shouldn't date each other. Sometimes if one of us falls off the bandwagon the other does too.

When we moved in together we had strict rules. No breakables of any kind, including glasses and dishes. We eat off paper or plastic dishes and only have plastic cups. No vases of any kind. We learned the hard way that mirrors aren't safe either when Zane connected his fist with one.

At the beginning, he locked up the knives, keeping the key with him at all times. My therapist had recently recommended he remove the locks so I learn self control. It isn't working.

When Zane urgently says "Jules" and shakes me I snap to. Great, I'm dissociating too. When had he stopped kissing me?

"Huh?"

Pain, I feel pain in my shoulders. Zane's hands are gripping me so firmly it hurts. I try to shrug him off but it only makes his grip tighten until I wince, making him realize how strong of a grip he has on me. It's like he's trying to hold onto my sanity for me.

"Feel the pain Jules. Focus on it. Let it be enough."

Closing my eyes, I take more deep breaths. *Nails digging into my skin, warmth rolling off his body, mint lingering in my mouth, clean linen tingling my nose, a heartbeat.* At the moment I don't know whose heart I'm hearing, mine or his, but I try to focus on the steadiness of it. In the blackness behind my eyelids, I pull up visions of flower fields, the beach, a snowy mountain. Any place that may hold calm. Instead, my mind wants to come back to this apartment.

It seems to be working, as my shoulders start to slump against Zane's hands. He starts rubbing small circles wherever he can. I keep my eyes closed, trying to focus on his fingers, even willing myself to think about all the things they can do to my body. But that just brings up other impulses.

Shivers tingle through me as Zane slides his hand up my neck and into my hair, massaging my scalp. It's two fold. It feels incredible and helps ease the tension from my taut muscles. But it's also a move he uses when he's trying to get me to take my pants off. I'm not really sure what his motive is at the moment.

When he tangles his fingers in my hair and pulls my head back as he closes his mouth over mine, it becomes clear.

His lips are hungry on mine, tongue forceful in my mouth. Without words he's begging me to relinquish my body to him, to give him everything so he can clear the darkness. It's worked before, more than once.

But tonight feels different, darker, harder. Even as his hand slips up my shirt, all I can think of is shiny metal gliding across my arm. The pinch, the sting. The *feeling*. It was a hard day with my psychologist. Sometimes those make for the hardest nights. They bring up all sorts of feelings you've tried to bury for years.

Then at one thirty in the morning you realize they're not so dead and buried anymore and find yourself standing in the kitchen holding a knife to your arm fighting yourself not to do it while the tiny voice in your head eggs you on. *Do it. You'll feel better. This pain will take away that pain, the hatred, the numbness.* But it never does. It's temporary, fleeting. And then you're left with the reminder of how stupid you were, how weak.

I have to tell Dr. Ptansky if I cut. I don't have to tell her if I have sex, at least not if it's with Zane. Sex with your boyfriend is not self-destructive. Sex in the bathroom at a bar with a man you just met, especially while in a relationship, is. But in the two years Zane and I have been together I've never once even come close to cheating on him. Dr. Ptansky calls it progress. I call it finally being satisfied in bed.

It helps when that person understands you and doesn't

belittle you. Even that they know when to add a little pain to the pleasure. In more ways than one, Zane just gets me.

A whimper rising from my own chest brings me back to what my body is doing. At some point I straddled Zane's lap and his mouth is against my throat, both hands cupping my breasts. He'd pushed away from the counter, his back now resting against the fridge. Great, I dissociated again.

Focus, focus, focus. Has Zane not had a shirt on this whole time? I'm usually much more aware of his naked physique.

"If I get up will you follow me to the bedroom?" His voice is low and gravelly.

Will I? I don't know. I want to. Oh, I so want to. But I'm also acutely aware of exactly where the knife is and how it would be to grab it. His hands on me feels so good, but I don't want pleasure. I want pain. I need it. It gives me a reason to hate myself, it reminds me I'm not numb, that I can feel something.

"Yes."

"You hesitated." Grabbing my wrists from behind his head he pulls them forward, his grip tight. He leans away as I try to kiss him again. "It's not worth it Jules. Whatever you're thinking, it's not worth it."

"You don't know that."

"I *do* know that. Don't do it. Come to bed with me, let me distract you. Feel me, not the pain."

I nod. "Okay."

Sliding me off his lap, he goes to stand, but he's not careful enough. He doesn't keep control of my hands and before he can stop me, I throw myself across the kitchen and grab the knife, dragging it across my forearm and watching the dark liquid blossom.

I barely hear the knife clank to the floor or Zane

screaming behind me, suddenly at my side pressing something to my skin, blackness invading my vision. As I fall into darkness, I have one last thought.

Pain.

Jules and Zane's story will be coming to you May 25, 2022.
Pre-order *Own Me* today
Link: https://www.amazon.com/Own-Me-Shayna-Astor-ebook/dp/B09MRPB3BD

Acknowledgments

What an amazing journey it's been to get here. With that, comes many thanks.

To my amazing husband and children:

Thank you again for everything you do, all the slack you pick up, and everything you sacrifice to allow me to achieve my dream. I could not do this without your love, support, and help.

With each new book, some things move smoother, but the time devoted never changes, and I appreciate what's given for me to focus on working.

I love you!

To my amazing trio; GC, AK, RL:

I seriously could not do this without ANY of you. All three of you are so integral to my writing and my process. I cannot begin to thank you enough for your hours of time, reading everything, commenting regularly, and being there for discussions on both writing and life. You ladies are so important to me and so very loved!

To my one-woman street team, Jennifer Webb:

I cannot begin to thank you for all of the work you are doing to help me. You are truly amazing, and I'm so honored that you not only enjoy my books, but want to share them with other people and help them get into the hands of readers. You are amazing!

Linnea March and Heather Stewart:

I cannot begin to thank you for coming in at the last moment and doing a beta read for me. It means so much to me! I hope our connection, friendship, and partnership will continue to grow!

To my amazing editor Mackenzie:

This book would not be what it is without you and your input. Thank you for helping me learn how to be a better writer, adjusting my words, and most importantly, keeping my voice my own. And especially for your beautiful words as you read through it.

Thank you to the amazing **Coffin Print Designs** for my stunning cover!

To my ARC team:

Your time and effort does not go unnoticed. Thank you for reading my novel before it hit the public and for your gracious reviews. I know it's not always easy to find the words, but it's all so appreciated.

And most importantly, to the readers:

Thank you for taking a chance on a new author. I know it can be difficult to see a new name and say "hey let me try that" but it is so beyond appreciated, I cannot begin to find the words. I write because it's my passion, but I publish because I want to share my words with all of you. I hope you enjoyed reading it, as much as I enjoyed writing it.

About the Author

Shayna Astor is a romance author who loves writing sweet love stories, with a lot of spice. When she's not writing, she's probably watching The Office with a cup of coffee, spending time with her kids, or playing video games with her husband.

Stalk me for all the latest updates, teasers for upcoming novels, giveaways, and all the goods on what's coming next!
Instagram @shayna.astor.author
TikTok @shayna.astor.author
Facebook Group Shayna's Coffee Corner
Website www.shaynaastor.com